Beautiful Beginner

Claire looked down at the rifle which Fortune O'Brien had knocked from her hands. "I wish I could shoot you," she told him, feeling tears spill over her cheeks.

They stared at each other, both breathing hard. His gaze lowered to her mouth and the moment changed. Their fierce struggle became another kind of clash. Heat blossomed in her cheeks, and she could barely get her breath.

He bent his head toward hers. She tried to turn away, but his arms tightened, and his mouth covered hers, while her pulse drummed wildly. His tongue played over hers, and she moaned, barely aware she had made the sound.

Finally he raised his head, looking down at her, his crystal blue eyes unfathomable. "You've never been kissed, have you?" he asked softly.

"No," she answered, "Not like that."

He bent his head again, and this time kissed her more slowly, his tongue moving over hers. She should make him stop, yet she didn't want him to to stop . . . no more than he wanted to . . . as he led her into a realm of sensation where he had so much to teach and she so much to learn. . . .

by

Sara Orwig

AN ONYX BOOK

ONYX
Published by the Penguin Group
Penguin Books USA Inc., 375 Hudson Street,
New York, New York 10014, U.S.A.
Penguin Books Ltd, 27 Wrights Lane,
London W8 5TZ, England,
Penguin Books Australia Ltd, Ringwood,
Victoria, Australia
Penguin Books Canada Ltd, 10 Alcorn Avenue,
Toronto, Ontario, Canada M4V 3B2
Penguin Books (N.Z.) Ltd, 182-190 Wairau Road,
Auckland 10, New Zealand

Penguin Books Ltd, Registered Offices:
Harmondsworth, Middlesex, England

First published by Onyx, an imprint of Dutton Signet,
a division of Penguin Books USA Inc.

First Printing, April, 1995
10 9 8 7 6 5 4 3 2 1

Printed in the United States of America

To Jeanmarie LeMense

Chapter 1

Savannah, 1861

"There she be. Look at her, a sleek filly," McCudgeon said, running his fingers through his oily black hair.

"You're sure that's her? We don't want to bring back the wrong one. You know what he'd do," Bruno said.

"As long as he gets the babe," McCudgeon said. Spittle collected at the corner of his mouth as he stared at the lighted shop across the wide street. Bay Street was lined with brick warehouses that held offices of cotton factors.

Standing in the shadows of the Customs House the two men waited. The glow of several lanterns spilled from the windows of a millinery shop, where a woman moved back and forth. McCudgeon shifted his weight restlessly.

"He gets the babe he wants, and we get her," he said, running his tongue across his lips, thinking of the money they had been offered. The woman moved to the window to stand on her toes and place a hat on a high rack. The blue dress clung to her narrow waist, flaring slightly over her hips, pulling tautly over full breasts. The evil man in the shadows let out a low whistle.

"I thought he said to bring them both back to him—the woman and the child."

"I asked. All he wants is the babe. We can have the filly."

"If you harm her, we won't know how to take care of a baby."

"Don't be a stone-brained jackass. If she cares about the tot, she'll take care of 'im whether we have our fun with her or not. Look at her. Another ten minutes and she ought to lock up and start for home with the tot." He opened a bottle.

"Careful there. You remember New Orleans."

"Shuddap. She was a weak one. If the fumes hadn't killed her, something else would have. Just a whiff of this, and we can cart her away peaceful."

"Just be careful. He's offering the most we've ever earned." Bruno looked at his burly companion. "What would happen if we brought back another babe and told him it was his?"

"This one has a birthmark on his side—the man knows what this babe looks like. It has to be the right one. Damn, here comes a carriage," he said, glancing up as a carriage approached from the head of the street. Moss-draped oaks stretched their limbs overhead, and down cobbled steps was River Street. The waterfront city was an important port, and below ships came in all hours of the day and night. Bay Street, however, was usually quiet late at night. Shops had closed hours ago. Yet after nights of watching, he knew the woman always worked late.

Bruno gripped McCudgeon's arm. "Look!"

The carriage stopped in front of the shop, and a woman emerged. Dressed in an elegant green moiré dress with a wide-brimmed straw hat trimmed in ostrich feathers, the woman crossed the iron walkway to the shop and unlocked the door to enter.

"Dammit! The owner's back. Why would she come back?" McCudgeon snorted impatiently. He wanted the babe, the woman, and the money, and he had planned to grab her tonight.

Inside the shop the two women talked, and the owner waved her hands. They both moved around the room until the lamps were extinguished. The women hurried out, one of them carrying a small bundle worth a tidy fortune. Why would anyone pay so much for an infant? McCudgeon didn't know or care, he just wanted to get his hands on the babe. The women climbed into the carriage, and it rolled away, turning on Bull to go right past them.

"Dammit to friggin' hell!" McCudgeon exclaimed, tossing down the rag in his hand.

"There's always tomorrow night," Bruno said, staring down the empty street. "We can wait another night. She'll be ours."

McCudgeon stood with his hand on his hips. "Right-o. The filly will be ours for a long time. As long as she pleases us."

When the following night came, the owner again appeared at the shop.

"Are you certain you don't want a ride home again tonight?" Estelle Adams asked.

Claire Dryden shook her head and smiled. "Thank you, but I want to finish some sewing here. It's not a bad night."

"I'm not sure this is the safest area for a woman to walk alone," Estelle said. "We're close to the river and all the traffic from it."

For a moment Claire paused. For the past three nights she had had an uneasy feeling. Was it from working late? She could take Michael and ride home in the carriage, but she needed another hour to finish the bonnet she was making. Adams Millinery had been a godsend, and she wanted to please her employer. And there was no logical reason to feel afraid, just a chill that made her wary of the night. Perhaps the darkness and the riverside mists were causing her feelings of unease.

"I'll be fine," Claire answered, winding a bright red grosgrain ribbon around the straw. Tying a bow, she let the streamers hang down over the brim. She picked up scissors and cut the ends of the ribbon. "I'll be all right. It's only a few blocks."

Estelle extended a sheaf of bills. "Here's your pay."

"Thank you," Claire said.

"Don't work too late, Claire. Good night."

"Good night, Mrs. Adams," she said, watching her employer leave. She sat down and counted the money, drawing a deep breath of satisfaction. She had paid the rent for this month, so some of this could go into her savings. Being independent, even under the circumstances, was heady. She thought of her father and his imperious manner. She never wanted to be dependent on a man again. Never. She glanced at the long cardboard box padded with blankets where a baby lay sleeping, his dark lashes curling above his rosy cheeks.

"This is for you, Michael. And for me," she added. Picking up a pale straw hat, she turned it in her hands. On impulse she pulled pins out of her hair and walked to the mirror. Her thick brown hair spilled over her shoulders, a cascade of deep locks with russet highlights. She placed the hat at an angle on her head and turned to look at it. The hat was becoming, she thought. But perhaps it needed a small spray of silk flowers at the crown. . . . She had learned a trade she could use in any city—all women wore hats. She sat back down to work, losing consciousness of the passage of time until she heard Michael cry.

She put away her things and hurried to pick him up from the makeshift cradle. He gazed up at her as his lower lip quivered. "Ah, my little love. Hungry now? We'll go home, and I'll feed you, Michael." Would she ever look at him without thinking he was the most beautiful baby on earth? Dark brown eyes stared back at her, and tight black ringlets covered his head. He pursed a rosebud mouth and made sucking noises. His lashes were thick and curly, and as she looked at him, she felt a surge of maternal love. "You are a beautiful one." He waved a chubby fist at her, and she caught his tiny hand in hers, kissing his fingers. "Michael, my little love," she whispered. "Just a minute now and I'll take you home." She placed him in the cradle again and smiled down at him while she put on her cape and wrapped him in a blanket.

Stepping to a back window, she looked out at the ships unloading at the docks below along the wide Savannah River. Burning gaslights glowed yellow in the fog, lighting decks and planks. Shrouded by mist, a wagon moved along River Street. When she looked below, she felt safer, seeing people busy, knowing she wasn't alone.

"Now, love, we'll be home soon," she said, picking up the infant and holding him close as she extinguished lamps. She opened the door and stepped out to lock it behind her. Rolling in from the waterfront, mist swirled along the cobblestones. Billows of it drifted in the street, blurring shapes, and the reassurance she had gained from gazing at the bustling riverfront vanished. Bay Street was deserted; in the next block light spilled from a tavern. As she hurried along, she glanced over her shoulder. Two dark shadows were moving behind her across the street. Her heart lurched with fear, and the skin on the nape of her neck prickled.

Stop being foolish. It's only two men headed for the tavern. Still she quickened her steps, aware of how deserted this section of town became once the shops closed. As she squeezed Michael to her and held her skirts, half running and feeling foolish, she wanted to be where there were people and lights.

She heard running steps and looked back in alarm. The two men were coming after her.

Her heart thudded with fear. She broke into a run, turning a corner to race down Abercorn. Noticing a carriage, she dashed into the street to try to stop it. The driver flicked the reins, and it rolled past her. She rushed on, glancing behind constantly. Fog obliterated everything now except the bulky shapes of elegant houses, the soft glow of light showing from windows.

"Get her, man!" Feet pounded behind her.

Panic-stricken, Claire raced into dark Reynolds Square and darted behind an oak. Flattening herself against the thick trunk, she became stock still, her heart pounding. She prayed Michael wouldn't cry.

"Where the hell is she?" a gruff voice said. It was so close, she jumped.

"You go that way—I'll go this. She can't be far."

She pressed against the rough bark, hearing a man walk past, his breath coming in raspy grunts. She looked at his broad back and floppy hat. He carried something in his hand, but she couldn't see what. And then he disappeared into the mist. Wait, wait. Give him time to go away, she thought, fighting the urge to run.

A few minutes later, she edged out softly from the tree. She had to head back the way she had come. It might be the only way to lose her pursuers. As she clutched Michael close, she shivered violently. Leaving the graceful square, she rushed along the street. She took a roundabout route home. Soon she reached plain wooden houses built close together, set back only a few feet from the street. She turned in to enter a narrow two-story roominghouse.

The moment she climbed the creaking stairs to the tiny room she rented, she placed Michael on the sagging iron bed. The room was musty, and Claire hastily lighted a lamp. "We have to go, love. Tonight." She built a fire in the small grate, and within minutes she was spooning porridge into the child, who cooed and smacked his lips. The soft glow of the lamp and the crackling fire couldn't hide the threadbare rag rug or the large cracks in the wall. Another room in another city—would she spend her life running? She looked down at Michael, though, and felt her worries melting away. She would do whatever was needed to keep him safe.

"That's a good boy. You'll travel better on a full stomach. We both will," she said. She proceeded to eat a biscuit spread with jam, her mind racing over what she should do. If the men were after her, they might know where she lived.

She hurried to pull a box from beneath the bed. She removed the lid, looking down at her growing savings. Sixty-eight dollars now. She thrust the money into a reticule and packed a portmanteau while Michael lay propped against the pillows, his dark eyes solemnly following her.

"I'll be right back, Michael," she whispered. She stepped into the hall and hurried into an empty room that was temporarily vacant. It gave a view of the street in front, and she peered through the mist. A carriage went past, and then a tipsy man staggered by. She stood waiting, her skin prickling, feeling certain that the men were still after her.

Suddenly a movement caught her attention. A shadow shifted in the doorway of the house across the street. Then one of the men stepped into view. As another shifted, she saw a thick shoulder. She rubbed her arms, fright chilling her. Two men waited in the recessed doorway across the street.

She returned to her room. Michael was asleep, his tiny chest rising and falling, his lips pursed and fists thrown up beside his head. She lifted him, placing him gently on a small blanket and wrapped it around him.

"Love, I'm sorry we have to move again. I promise I'll protect you. I'll take care of you." Claire bent to kiss him lightly on the cheek. She smoothed the silky curls on his head, overwhelmed with love for him, determined to keep him at all costs.

She extinguished the lamps and pulled the cloak around her shoulders. Picking up the portmanteau, her reticule, and the sleeping baby, she moved toward the door, her skin feeling cold and clammy. The creak of steps came, and she paused.

The scrape outside the door was faint, but she noticed it and stared at the door in the darkness. The handle turned, and her heart missed a beat, then pounded violently.

She ran to the back door leading to the outside stairs,

opened it a crack, and looked over the yard. A man stood beneath a black hickory tree. She closed the door quietly, her heart drumming. One man was below in the back, and the other was in the hall at her door. *There has to be a way to escape. They mustn't harm Michael.* Terrified, she tried to think what to do. Another scrape came from the other side of the door.

Placing Michael on the floor, she hurried to the bed to mound the pillows as if someone were beneath the covers. She moved behind the door and yanked up a small wooden footstool. Holding it by the legs, she raised it high overhead.

The door handle jiggled again. Suddenly someone hit the door, and it burst open. A man entered and moved toward the bed. She brought the stool down with all her might. It slammed against his head. With a grunt he pitched forward and fell.

"Oh, my word!" She dropped the footstool and picked up the sleeping infant. Praying she hadn't killed the man, she dashed down the stairs and outside. She paused only a moment to look around before she hurried onward. Her heart pounded loudly as she ran, staying in shadows, heading toward the train station.

An hour later, she was on a train bound for Louisville, Kentucky. Across the aisle was a snoring couple; the woman was ample, her voluminous black skirts falling over the seat. Six more men were scattered throughout the car. She had watched them continually, but no one seemed to pay any attention to her.

Claire's thoughts returned to the men after her. Maybe if she went west, she would be safe. Abraham Lincoln had just been elected president of the United States, and South Carolina had called a secession convention. Talk was rife about secession in Savannah. If the nation went to war, men wouldn't have the time to follow her because they would have to fight.

Claire held Michael close as they rocked along. Listening to the rhythmic clack of the wheels on the rails, the noise seemed to pound out the words "We're safe. We're safe."

There has to be a way to earn more money, she thought, to find a haven where we won't have to run. She gazed into the darkness outside, wondering about their future. Had the men been sent by her father to force her into a marriage she didn't want? Yet she couldn't imagine her tightwad father spending money to hire men to find her.

How long would it be until the men picked up her trail and found her again?

Chapter 2

Georgia
November 18, 1864

A brisk wind caught the tails of the major's dark blue frock coat and flicked them against his legs. The clomp of horse hooves, the creak of saddles, and the jingle of harness were the only sounds. United States Army Major Fortune O'Brien turned his sorrel and tugged on the reins. "There it is, Belle Tache," he said, pointing at an elegant Georgian house in the distance.

Lieutenant Alaric Hampton reined in his bay. "After Atlanta, it's a wonder anything is still standing. I guess it's far enough west of Jonesboro to escape the army's destruction. Plus General Sherman gave General Howard a letter that Belle Tache is to be spared. According to the letter, the owner of Belle Tache is French and he's away in Europe now. He's not involved in our war."

"The hell he isn't!" Fortune O'Brien stared at the mansion with its dozen columns along the portico. "He's not only got one of the few foundries in the South, but he's got his own ships. I know he's making a huge profit from both sides. My oldest brother is a blockade runner too, and he's told me all about Trevor Wenger."

Set on a slight rise, the house looked as imperious and commanding as its owner. Burning waves of hatred washed through Fortune. He wanted to torch the mansion, but not before confronting Wenger. His gaze swept across the rolling land, the pigeon house and spreading oaks, the gazebo and spring house, and then he froze. "C'mon," he said, staring an iron fence that squared off a tiny plot of land. Lieutenant Hampton rode quietly beside him to the gate of the family cemetery, where Fortune dismounted. Pulling his broad-brimmed felt hat squarely on his head, he strode to the gate.

"Fortune—" When he glanced around, Alaric waved his hand. "Don't do something you shouldn't. Promise me." His blue eyes were clouded with worry.

Feeling a stabbing mixture of pain and anger, Fortune drew a deep breath. "Trevor Wenger killed my wife and baby as surely as I have breath in my lungs. And I intend to kill him for it."

"Don't do it today, Major," Alaric said softly, cocking his blond eyebrows. "You have a war to fight. I'll start back slowly. You can catch up with me. Besides, you said Trevor Wenger is in Europe, and that's what the letter to General Howard said."

They both turned to look at the house. The windows held an empty, dark look, and no sign of life could be seen. A shutter on an upstairs window banged.

Fortune turned away. The cold, biting wind he barely felt as his boots crunched the dried grass while he searched headstones and spotted the newest one. Grass had grown over her grave. A knot came to his throat. Tears burned his eyes, yet he was unaware of them as they spilled down his cheeks. The wind buffeted him while memories swirled like the dry leaves around his feet: Marilee laughing up at him, her dark brown eyes shining, her blond hair spilled over the pillow, her mouth red from his kisses as she held her slender arms up to reach for him, Marilee holding their infant son close.

"I love you, Fortune, and I always will. . . ."

They had been together not even two years, and both of them had been so young. He reached beneath his cape and pulled out a locket and knelt to place it on the grave.

"You left this behind, my love," he whispered. "Marilee . . ." He bent his head as tears came. The loss still hurt with piercing freshness, and he wondered if he would cry over her the rest of his life. Marilee and Michael.

He stood up and eyed the gray headstone: Marilee Wenger. Trevor Wenger hadn't put O'Brien on her tombstone, yet she was an O'Brien. Mrs. Fortune O'Brien. Married in a church—*until death do us part.*

Fortune wiped his eyes and turned, expecting to find the tiny grave of his infant son beside hers. The next stone read Charles Radley Wenger. On the opposite side was John Terrence Wenger. Fortune's gaze swept over the weathered headstones; some were canted at angles with grass high around them.

Reading the names, he frowned and wandered around the family cemetery: Mary Louise Wenger Graydon. He paused beside her grave, running his hand over the tombstone. Mary Louise, Marilee's aunt, who had introduced them and sanctioned their marriage. And later lost her life for doing so. "Mary Louise," he said softly, "I miss her so." He turned to read the other tombstones.

Louise Pearl Wenger, Charlsie Mae Wenger, Mary Wenger Payne, Winston Elmo Payne, Theodore Wenger, Hortense Mary Wenger Falkenham. Edwin Falkenham. Fortune walked the cemetery again, reading each tombstone in growing puzzlement. Where was Michael buried? He stared at the graves. "Marilee? Where's our son?"

There was no infant's grave, no tombstone marked Michael Hanlan O'Brien. Where was he buried? Why wasn't he buried beside Marilee?

Standing over her grave, Fortune remembered the devastating letter: "*. . . Marilee and Michael died from pneumonia. They were not at Belle Tache, where they could receive care. . . .*"

If Michael had died with Marilee, where was he buried? Fortune stared at the grave and then turned to stare at the house with its Doric columns and fan transom over the wide door. Why wouldn't Michael be buried in the family plot?

Like a ghostly apparition drifting past, a tiny glimmer of hope came. Michael hadn't died with Marilee? Fortune's breath caught, and he knotted his fists, feeling shaken, frightened even to think about the possibility and let his hope grow. Where was Michael? Why would Trevor have lied about the boy's death? Trevor had booked passage to England alone after Marilee's death. Fortune knew that from trying to find him. And Wenger had sailed alone. From all reports there had been no baby with him. So where was Michael? Fortune looked at the tombstones again. Michael Hanlan O'Brien was not buried in the Wenger family plot.

Michael must not have died with her! "Michael!" Fortune whispered. *Our son is alive.*

"Michael!" Fortune shouted, bursting out of the cemetery and running for the house, his long legs quickly covering the distance. "Michael!" he shouted.

His heart felt as if it would pound out of his chest. Somehow Trevor Wenger must have kept Michael, notifying Fortune that his son was dead to keep Fortune out of the way, out of his life. Michael Hanlan O'Brien, his son, was alive!

Fortune reached the house, barely aware of hoofbeats behind him or Alaric shouting as he returned at a gallop.

"Major!" he called as he reined in his horse. "Fortune, what the devil are you doing? Come away from there."

Fortune bounded up the stairs and pounded on the front door. Twisting the handle, he pushed, shaking it, impatient with the lock. "Michael!"

Alaric caught his arm and spun him around. "Have you lost your mind?"

Fortune stared at him, unable to focus until Alaric gave him a shake. He blinked. "Alaric, my son is alive!"

"You said he died—"

"There's no grave."

Alaric glanced past him at the house. "He was a baby. He could have been buried elsewhere. Let's get out of here."

"No! Dammit, I know Trevor Wenger. He would have buried his grandson here! Instead he brought him home and wrote me Michael had died." He spun around, looking up at the imposing house. "Somehow he must have taken Michael to Europe with him," he said, his amazement and fury gathering strength. He looked at the house and clenched his fists. Trevor Wenger had taken his son. "You bastard!" he yelled and stepped forward, swinging his foot to kick the door. The wood splintered and Fortune rushed it, slamming his shoulder into it to burst it inside.

"Fortune, for God's sake, come back before someone shoots you!" Alaric pleaded.

Fortune glanced through open doorways into rooms. Sheets shrouded furniture and cobwebs draped the walls. "Michael?" He walked across the hall, the clatter of his black leather boots echoing on the dusty floor. A mouse scurried out of his way.

"My God, look what they left behind!" Alaric said, holding up a sheet, stirring dust motes into the air. Fortune glanced around at a marble statue of a winged female figure.

Fortune pushed the parlor doors open wider. The furniture was covered in dust, the draperies were drawn, and a musty odor assailed him. He turned, looking up the wide, curving stairs. This is where Marilee had been born and raised. And been brought home to be buried.

"Trevor Wenger!" he yelled, and Alaric jumped.

"Lord, don't do that." Alaric pushed his hat to the back of his head, his blond hair springing forward, locks curling on his forehead as he placed his hands on his hips and stared at Fortune.

"Trevor Wenger!" Fortune yelled again, the cry echoing faintly upstairs. "You bastard!"

"Come on, Fortune. Let's get out of here. We have a hard ride ahead to catch up with our unit. General Howard will be all the way to McDonough if we don't get moving. There's no one here."

Fortune turned to look at him, and Alaric drew his breath and stepped back.

"You ride ahead, Alaric," Fortune said, controlling his rage. "Leave my horse, and I'll catch up with you. I have to do something for Marilee."

"You're sure?" Alaric whispered, licking his lips and backing away another step.

"Go ahead."

Alaric left, and Fortune turned away, forgetting him. He ran into the parlor and whipped sheets off a rose satin camelback sofa. Dust rose in a cloud as he dragged the sofa into the hall and raced back into the room to yank away another sheet and pick up a matching chair. He placed the chair next to the sofa and went back to get another chair, dust smudging his blue uniform. As he entered the hall, he heard a scrape.

A door closed somewhere in the house. He lowered the chair, setting it quietly on the floor. As he listened, his hand slid to his hip, to the holster with his Colt pistol. His hand closed around the grip, and he drew out the Colt and pulled back the hammer. He heard shuffling footsteps approach.

A servant with graying hair, a faded cotton shirt, and coarse cotton pants ambled into the hallway. "Suh?" He looked down at the pistol in Fortune's hand. "Suh, this house belongs to the Wengers. You're trespassing here."

Fortune put away the pistol. "Get out of here."

"Suh, Mr. Wenger said this house is protected from soldiers. You need to go. I'm not s'posed to let a soul inside."

Ignoring him, Fortune strode to the parlor and picked up another chair to place on top of the sofa.

"Suh, you mustn't do that. Please, go," he pleaded in a thick southern accent.

Fortune paused and looked at him, and the man backed up a step. "You get out of here," Fortune said, "and you won't get hurt. You can't stop me."

The servant backed up another step. "Yassuh," he whispered.

"You knew Miss Marilee, didn't you?"

Running his thick hand over his gray curls, the man nodded. "Yassuh. Miss Marilee was a beautiful child. She's buried on the hill now."

"Where's her baby? Has he taken the baby with him?"

The man frowned. "No, suh. He's hunting for that baby."

"He's what?" Fortune said, frowning and wondering if he had heard correctly or if the old man's mind was gone.

"No, suh. He can't find the baby. He'll never stop huntin' until he does find him, that I know."

Fortune stopped short, mulling over what he had just learned. Where was Michael? Why wasn't he with Trevor if he wasn't buried beside Marilee? She wouldn't have given him up to anyone. Where was his son?

He drew a deep breath. "Go on. Get out of here. I have no argument with you."

"Mister Wenger said the gov'ment promised the soldiers wouldn't burn Belle Tache," the old servant persisted, his voice filled with worry.

"I'm not burning it because of the war," Fortune said, pausing again to look into those anxious dark eyes. "I was married to Miss Marilee. I'm Major O'Brien, her husband and Michael O'Brien's father."

"Lordy, me." The servant blinked. "You're the Yankee she married?"

"Go on. Get out of here."

"Suh, I wish—"

Fortune raised his head and scowled. The man blinked

and nodded, turning to shuffle out. At the door he glanced back once and then closed the door behind him.

Fortune strode back to the parlor and swept china figurines off a table. As they fell and broke into pieces, he picked up the chair to pile it on the settee. He went to the dining room, carrying chairs back to stack them in the hall.

He yanked down satin drapes in the dining room and rolled them into a ball, tossing them onto the heap.

Glancing up, he took the stairs two at a time and ran from room to room, finally stopping in what had once been a young girl's room. Inside was a four-poster with a canopy. Two cloth dolls were on the bed, stitched smiles on their faces. Moving closer, he lightly stroked the bed, thinking about Marilee growing up in this bed, sleeping here night after night. Fortune picked up one of the dolls and put it beneath his coat. He roved about the room, opening drawers, taking a bracelet made of links of gold. Finally he took a pillow from the bed and left the room, taking one last lingering look at it.

With the pillow beneath his arm he ran to another room, stopping in the doorway. His heart began to pound as he looked at a cradle and a room filled with toys, a room ready for a tiny child. The counterpane and pillows and chairs were deep blue. It was a boy's room. Where was Michael? Was the old servant lying?

Moving along the hall, Fortune entered a bedroom that ran the length of the house, with a fireplace at one end. Sheets draped the furniture in this room, and heavy forest green drapes were drawn, making the room dark and forbidding. Fortune built a fire from logs piled on the grate. He pulled a burning log from the fire and carried it to the bed. Tossing it on the mattress, he stood and watched as the sheet blackened and then a tongue of orange flame curled up. In a minute a fire burned brightly in the center of the bed. With a sudden puff the canopy over the bed ignited. Sparks rose as flames crackled and built.

Fortune turned back to the fireplace, dragging a chair close and thrusting the back of it into the fire. While the fire grew and crackled behind him, he stomped on the arm of the chair. It snapped and he yanked up a broken piece. Wrapping one end in a sheet, he placed it on the fire to get it burning. Heat warmed his back and the crackle became a roar. When he turned, he shielded his face with his arm; the drapes had caught fire and now the room was an inferno.

He strode downstairs with the burning torch. Placing the pillow inside the pile of the furniture, he ignited it. The feathers smoldered and finally caught. He stood staring at the dancing blaze as it leaped and grew.

"That's for us, Marilee. And I will find our son. I'll get Michael back. I promise you," he said, his words loud in the empty house.

In minutes flames twisted high, and billows of gray smoke stung his eyes as they spread throughout the house. He picked up a burning chair and tossed it into the dining room, where it crashed and sent flames shooting upward.

Acrid smoke curled against the ceiling as the fire spread. He backed out the door and crossed the veranda. Alaric had tethered his horse to a post. Mounting up, Fortune rode away with a painful glance at the cemetery. "Good-bye, my heart," he whispered.

Feeling the heat on his back, he turned in the saddle. As flames flickered in the upper windows, the roof crashed in, sending a rolling ball of fire curling skyward. Flames shot out the door and danced up the outside walls. Windows popped with a tinkling of glass. Darkening the sky, smoke rose in a gray spiral above the house. Feeling a grim satisfaction, Fortune turned to ride east. Not far away, Alaric was waiting for him.

Together they watched Belle Tache burn. Fortune thought of the destruction they were leaving behind, Atlanta shelled and burned, tracks and trains destroyed.

Their orders were to burn their way to Savannah, except he had seen General Howard's letter to spare Belle Tache. General Sherman had left Atlanta only days before, dividing his men. With General Howard, Fortune and Alaric would swing west through Jonesboro and Monticello toward Macon. The others, with General Slocum and Sherman, were headed east through Covington and Milledgeville. The two wings of the army were spread over a forty-mile width, ordered to destroy the South's will to fight. He thought about Atlanta, its buildings in ruins, many only charred cinders, and he knew he would be back someday. As long as Trevor Wenger was alive, Fortune would be back to find him.

Fortune looked over his shoulder once more. The entire house was a raging inferno with clouds of smoke rising, blown south by the wind.

"Michael, I will get you back," he promised quietly.

Chapter 3

Atlanta
April, 1867

Crossing Peachtree Street, Colonel Fortune O'Brien glanced at the ruins of the Georgia Railroad Bank Agency, still shattered, only parts of walls remaining, looking as it had when he left Atlanta in 1864. The rest of the street was being restored. Lampposts were being erected, businesses were thriving, and the Concert Hall looked like new. He passed a new dry-goods store still under construction. Men conducted business in front while workmen hammered on walls in back. Fortune was struck with the notion that he would always associate the sounds of pounding hammers with Atlanta. The smell of freshly cut lumber, from a constant stream of wagons, filled the warm spring air, and other wagons rumbled past hauling stone from Lynch's quarry.

People were pouring into Atlanta: Yankees and Rebels, freed slaves, carpetbaggers and scalawags, Atlanta's former citizens rebuilding from the losses they had sustained during the conflict. Fortune crossed the Western and Atlanta railroad tracks, turning on Elliott to Magazine Street, riding toward the edge of town. He passed some of the remaining palisades, a line of cheval-de-frise built to protect Atlanta from the Union army. His gaze strayed over the rolling hills that still had trees cut in half by cannon balls.

A tall black iron fence surrounded the sprawling rebuilt ironworks, and its gates opened onto a graveled drive. In iron over the wide gate were the black letters WENGER IRONWORKS.

With a surge of grim satisfaction, Fortune entered the new, gleaming granite building and crossed a polished hardwood floor. His spurs gave a faint jingle with his step, and he was aware of the empty holster on his hip. Still, he was a soldier. Georgia had voted against the Fourteenth Amendment, and the state had been placed under military rule. Congress was under the control of northern Radical Republicans, who were going to cram Reconstruction down the South's throat. Getting the assignment he wanted in the Third Military District, Fortune had been in Atlanta a week. He thought about how long he had waited to find Trevor Wenger. He had been headed toward this particular moment since he had lost Marilee.

"I want to see Trevor Wenger," Fortune said politely to a man seated behind the desk.

The man looked up, frowning as he peered over rimless spectacles at the man in the Federal uniform. "I'm sorry, Colonel, but you'll have to make an appointment. Mr. Wenger is busy at the moment."

Fortune marched around the desk, and the clerk jumped in front of him. "Sir, you can't go in there."

Fortune brushed past him and threw open the door marked "Mr. Trevor Wenger, President, Wenger Ironworks."

"Sir, I told—"

"Close the door, Smith." Trevor Wenger leaned back in his chair, his dark eyes studying Fortune as the clerk shut the door quietly. In contrast to the utilitarian outer room, the office was resplendent with leather furniture and a carved rosewood desk.

"I'm not armed," Fortune said, feeling an urge to rush across the room and attack the man with his bare hands. Mixed with the anger was a twisting pain as he stared at Wenger. Marilee had had his straight nose, his dark eyes and thick lashes, his lean face. Only her features had been soft, beautiful where his were handsome. His brown hair was thick and wavy, and Fortune suspected women found him irresistible. Fortune held his hands away from his body so that Wenger could see he wasn't reaching for a pistol.

"You have nerve, coming here. I heard you were in Atlanta again."

"You knew I was here before."

"Indeed. You burned Belle Tache. I don't understand that logic. Your wife develops pneumonia, so you burn down her birthplace."

"You know why I burned it—and it didn't hurt her when I did," Fortune said, fighting for control. He glanced again at the elegant office, filled with ormolu mirrors and potted plants, thinking the room was a reflection of its owner, who flaunted his wealth and surrounded himself in luxury.

"You're here for a reason—I'd guess to challenge me."

Fortune gave a snort of derision. "When I do that, it'll be where there are witnesses, not alone like this."

Wenger arched his brows. "You think I'd be afraid to meet you? You'd need witnesses to coerce me into responding?"

"No, I know you'd welcome meeting me."

"You're right. The sooner you're out of Atlanta, the happier I'll be about it."

Fortune moved a step closer. Trevor Wenger's eyes narrowed and his hand moved slightly. His arms rested against his sides, his hands out of sight beneath the desk, and Fortune suspected he held a weapon.

"Where's my son?"

"So that's what this visit is about. You will never have him. I give you my absolute promise," he said, his voice suddenly tight with anger.

"Where is he?" Fortune said, keeping his voice quiet and level. "Where is Michael?"

"You took my daughter from me—"

"I took her?" Fortune interrupted, clenching his fists and breathing heavily. "She'd be alive if you hadn't taken her away with you, dammit!"

"If she hadn't met you, she would have married a southern gentleman and she would be alive today. You took my Marilee; you have Mary Louise's money. My poor befuddled sister willed you her fortune. You may be able to charm women, but you can't charm me."

"Wenger, where is my son?"

"I don't have my grandchild, and I don't know where he is," he said flatly.

"You're lying," Fortune accused. Yet as he stared into those angry brown eyes, he realized the man was telling the truth. Fortune had stared down enough liars to know when he was dealing with someone telling the truth.

"I could call you out right now for calling me a liar."

"Are you challenging me?"

Wenger shook his head. "No. I want witnesses too. I want men in this town to see us agree to a duel. I want them to turn out to watch what I'll do to you. You're a Yankee, and if you think anyone will shed a tear over you, you're mistaken."

"Not everyone in Atlanta hates us, and you're not exactly loved here. People know you were on both sides. I know about the money you gave the Confederacy, and I know about the money you made from the Union. You traded with Yankee as well as Reb. This nice thriving business is because you played on both sides. If I hadn't burned your house, you could have come home to it."

"A fact I never forget." Suddenly he slammed the chair against the wall with a crash and stood up, a revolver aimed at Fortune's heart. "I don't want to shoot you now. This doesn't suit my purposes, but I want you out of my sight. I don't know where my grandson is."

"Marilee would never have given him away."

"Marilee died when she ran away to go back to you!" he yelled.

Stunned, Fortune stared at him. "She got away from you and was coming home?"

"Damn you for interfering in our lives. I promise you, you damn Yankee, you'll regret it a thousand times over."

"Where's Michael?"

"If I knew, do you think I'd tell you?"

Fortune leaned forward, clenching his fists. "You lost them both, daughter and grandson. Are you a monster, that doesn't know how to feel remorse?"

Fortune turned and strode toward the door, his back tingling, half expecting the gun to blast before he left the room. He turned the handle and swung the door open. Past the open-mouthed clerk he strode out into the bright sunshine, where he stopped and blinked, looking around. His heart pounded as he gulped for breath.

He mounted up and rode toward town. He crossed Five Points to stop at a gunsmith to purchase a Winchester rifle and ammunition, knowing someday he would need it. Trying to calm his stormy emotions, he rode back to the hastily thrown-up encampment of the Third Military District of the United States Army on the grounds of City Hall.

As soon as he was seated behind his desk in his narrow office, one of the few in City Hall, he pulled pen and paper in front of him to write. When a knock came at the open door, he glanced up.

"Did you see Wenger?" Major Alaric Hampton asked, flicking his blond hair away from his face.

"Yes. He doesn't have Michael," Fortune said as Alaric entered and dropped in a wooden chair, stretching out his legs. "And he hasn't had him. He can't find him."

"Why not? Where is he?"

"I don't know. He wouldn't say, but he doesn't have him. He isn't lying. He may know where Michael is, but it's not here," Fortune stated, glancing around the small office at a wooden filing cabinet, a hat rack, and a shiny brass spittoon.

"So what are you going to do now?"

"I did some thinking as I rode back here. I'm resigning from the army."

"You didn't give it much thought. We're all of a mile from the Wenger Ironworks."

"I gave it enough thought." He held out the letter he had just written, and Alaric leaned forward, a lock of blond hair falling over his forehead as he took the letter. He read and looked up.

"Why? What good will this do?"

"I want to find my son. While I wait to be mustered out, I'm going to St. Louis. I'll hire a Pinkerton man to find my son."

"Damn, I hate to lose you. We fought all through the war together."

For the first time that morning, Fortune relaxed and smiled. "You won't lose me if you stay in Atlanta. I intend to stay here—at least for a while. I have unfinished business."

"A duel with Wenger."

Fortune raked his fingers through his black hair, which sprang back in unruly waves. "No. That was my first inclination, because I'd like to put a ball through his heart. On second thought, though, I'd prefer to ruin him financially. That would be the kind of slow death I'd like for him."

"When you get on the subject of Wenger, you frighten even me, and I know I'm safe from your anger," Alaric said solemnly. "Fortune, you were so young when you married and it didn't last very long. Let it go. You won't look at another woman. If you relaxed, tried to enjoy life, you'd meet other women. You don't know this son. There are many beautiful women who can give you other sons."

Feeling a surge of anger, Fortune tried to curb it. Alaric was a friend, and his intentions were good, even if misplaced. "You've never been in love, Alaric, so you can't possibly understand."

"Me? I've been in love dozens of times!"

Relaxing again, Fortune laughed, looking at his friend, who was draped over the chair like an indolent cat. "That's just it—dozens of infatuations. You don't know what real love is. I adored Marilee, and it was forever."

"You went from losing a wife to fighting a war. You don't know what it's like to just enjoy life. Fortune, try my way. Go with me to the party Friday night."

"I've been to parties," he said, his mind drifting back to his letter of resignation from the military. "I don't enjoy balls."

"Small wonder! You scowl and dance two or three dances and leave. I've seen ladies who want to fawn over you. They flirt and try to get your attention, and you don't even see them. It isn't natural to shut women out of your life. You do the work of two men to burn off energy—"

"I see women on occasion."

"Oh, yes," Alaric said with cynicism. "When your body can't take any more, you find a woman who will satisfy you physically and leave you untouched emotionally. Look at this," he said, leaning forward and catching Fortune's bony wrist. There a chain of gold links gleamed dully in the light. "You wear her trinket like a slave bracelet. Let go of her memory, dammit, and try to live again!" He leaned back against the chair, hooking his leg over the arm and swinging his booted foot.

"I'm going to St. Louis," Fortune said, trying to end the conversation. He had no interest in other women. He loved Marilee only.

"And Trevor Wenger? What about him?"

"I'll be back to contend with him. In the meantime, he may learn something about Michael before I do. If my son is in Atlanta, I'll know it."

"So you'll stay in Atlanta when you're mustered out?"

"Yes, until I find Michael, I don't intend to let Wenger get out of my sight."

Alaric stood and placed the letter back on the desk. "I wish you'd change your mind. If you'd just let down once, Fortune, just once—it wouldn't be so difficult after that. You might find life is a lot nicer."

"She's the only woman I'll ever love. And I want my son."

A week later Fortune strode into the unpretentious Pinkerton's Detective Agency office in St. Louis. He paused in front of a desk. "I need to see someone about a missing child."

He was shown into another office, and the man behind a narrow, uncluttered desk stood up and offered his hand. "I'm Irving Eisner."

"Fortune O'Brien."

"Have a seat, Colonel," Eisner said, folding his lanky frame onto the chair and giving his black beard a tug. "I wondered how long it would be before you'd be here."

"You expected me?" Fortune said.

"Our agency was hired a long time ago to look for a Michael Hanlan O'Brien, child of Marilee Wenger O'Brien, deceased, and Lieutenant Fortune O'Brien of the United States Army."

"Did you find him?"

"No. I'm not the agent assigned to the case, but I was the first year."

"Who hired you? Trevor Wenger?"

"Of course. The grandfather is anxious to find his grandson."

"Would it matter to an agency that the mother didn't want the grandfather to have his grandson?"

Eisner shook his head and smiled. "Begging your pardon, Colonel, but we have only your word on that."

"You're still searching for him after all this time?"

"Yes, but not as an assignment from Trevor Wenger.

As you know, Pinkerton's has a reputation for success. We always get our man. Sometimes it has taken longer than other times, and this is one of the difficult cases. Trevor Wenger lost patience with us."

"So why are you still searching for Michael? Who's paying you to look?" Fortune asked, puzzled and impatient to get answers.

"A young woman took your son."

"Why? Who is she?"

Eisner continued as if he hadn't heard Fortune's questions. "William Dryden, the father of this woman, wants us to find his daughter. Jonathan Norby is the agent on the case. This Dryden fellow has taken ill, and I think he wants to see her again before he dies."

"Who is she?"

"At this point, I can't talk about the case."

"I want to hire you to find Michael."

"The only way I can take the case is to inform Dryden that you are also hunting for the boy. Since you don't want the woman and he doesn't want the boy, I see no conflict of interest."

"I want my own agent, not the one working for this Dryden."

Eisner nodded, tugging at his earlobe. "It's rather irregular to have two of us on a case like this. I see no reason against it, though. The only catch is, if I find the boy, the agency will have to report it to William Dryden as well as to you."

"If I hire you, you'll report to me first."

"That's agreeable, but I'll warn you now, the case is difficult and it'll be expensive."

"I can afford to pay. Besides my colonel's salary, I have savings and an inheritance."

"Fine. I want two hundred dollars to start."

Fortune reached beneath his coat and withdrew a bag that jingled.

"Good Lord! You came from the South and you're carrying gold?" Eisner asked.

Fortune glanced at him. "I'm armed and I have greenbacks if you'd prefer—"

"Gold is more than satisfactory," he replied with a faint smile.

Fortune counted out the amount and pushed two hundred dollars across the desk. "Now, your agency is still searching after all this time—why?"

"I said, we always find our man, but in this case it's a woman, and she's extremely elusive."

"I don't believe you," Fortune countered, experiencing a flash of anger at the thought of someone keeping his child hidden away. "You haven't found a woman in all this time? A woman has my son and she's eluded Pinkerton's *for years*?"

"The war, Colonel O'Brien," Eisner answered patiently. "We were given the case at the outbreak of the war. Our men were in military intelligence during the war; we were short of manpower." Eisner tugged at his black beard. "She went out West and vanished for several years. We didn't have the manpower to continually search for her."

Fortune ran his fingers through his hair distractedly, thinking about the woman who had Michael. Had she taken good care of him? How had she gotten him in the first place?

"Michael was born before the war broke out, though. What about that first year?"

"She's very elusive. And we don't know what happened, but in 1862 our agent on the case was found shot. We don't know if she was the responsible party or someone else was after her and our agent got in the way. The moment anyone has been able to get close to the Dryden woman, she moves on immediately."

"How does she support herself?"

"A number of ways."

"There's only one occupation where a footloose woman can be assured of income," Fortune snapped, growing angrier at the thought that his child might be with a whore.

"No. From all indications, she avoids men."

"I find that difficult to believe," he said.

"Remember, she is being followed by men. Whom can she trust?"

"Who the hell is she, and why did Trevor Wenger give up the search?"

"Wenger has given up on Pinkerton's. He has not stopped his search. As to who the woman is—on a winter night in the early winter of 1861, your wife and infant son took shelter in a barn belonging to William Dryden on a plantation in Charlotte, North Carolina. Your wife died that night."

Fortune inhaled a painful gust of breath and looked out the window. His gaze drifted among rooftops and church spires as he thought of Marilee ill with pneumonia and alone with Michael in a barn. He turned his attention to Eisner.

"Sorry, Colonel. I thought perhaps you knew. Before she died, Dryden's seventeen-year-old daughter, Claire, found your wife. She promised to care for the baby. Your wife was unable to tell her much except the baby's name was Michael and her name was Marilee O'Brien. Dryden buried her at his place and put the child in an orphanage."

Fortune closed his eyes, wincing. It stabbed like a knife to think of Marilee dying with a stranger, knowing she was going to die and having to give up Michael. He opened his eyes and drew a deep breath. "Go on."

"We don't know exactly what transpired between Claire Dryden and your wife, but Claire objected strenuously to the baby being placed in the orphanage. Eight nights later, the baby disappeared from the orphanage, and Claire Dryden ran away from home. We know she took the baby."

Fortune felt another wave of anger. "Dammit! She had no right to my child. If she had left him there, I could have found him."

"Yes, and so could have Trevor Wenger."

"So what happened then?" Fortune asked, feeling tension knot his shoulders.

"Claire Dryden is clever and cautious. As I told you, every time we've found her and gotten close, she moves. We were to notify Trevor Wenger of her whereabouts, but every time we got word to the agency and back to him, she had spotted our man and taken off."

"I've resigned from the Army. It'll take a while before I'm actually out, and I'm going to stay in Atlanta. I want to know when you locate her next. I want you to get word to me the quickest way possible. You telegraph me, and I'll pay them at the telegraph office to come notify me. I don't give a damn how you do it, but you inform me at once."

"I understand."

"Where was she the last you knew?"

"I took a moment to get her folder when they told me you were here." Eisner opened the folder and riffled through papers, reading a moment and adjusting his glasses. Fortune studied him, thinking he would be incredibly noticeable trailing after someone. He must be well over six feet tall with a long black beard, a bony frame, and from the looks of the way he was handling the papers, he must be nearsighted. Feeling another twinge of impatience, Fortune shifted in the chair.

"She was in San Antonio, Texas, when last we picked up the trail. At that time she was a dancer in a saloon."

"Ahh," Fortune said, biting back an "I told you so." "So she was a dancer. A whore."

"Not what you think. No male friends. Keeps very much to herself." He lowered the rimless spectacles. "Actually, that makes it easier to find her. How many attractive young women avoid men?"

"I can't believe a dancer in a saloon does."

"She fled San Antonio in February, and we followed her to New Orleans. We lost her there. We think she was heading east, but we don't know. I'll report to you regularly on our progress. As far as we know, she's unaware of your existence, of Wenger's, or that both you and Trevor Wenger live in Atlanta. She could settle there as likely as anywhere else in the country."

"Or she could leave the country."

"Yes, but since she hasn't in all this time, we've ruled that out. Although we have word posted at port cities to watch for her."

"So where will you start?"

"I'll pick up the trail in New Orleans. Colonel O'Brien, there is one more thing."

Fortune felt a prickle across the nape of his neck. Eisner's expression was impassive, but there was a solemnity in his voice that made Fortune brace for bad news. "What's that?"

"Trevor Wenger canceled the contract with our agency. All he wants is the boy. He doesn't care one whit for the woman."

"I can understand that."

"He's hired Seeton Harwood, a man who's been out West. Harwood is wanted in Fort Smith for killing a marshal. He's supposed to have killed anywhere from six to fourteen men in gunfights. Harwood's a fighter and, from what we've learned, a deadly shot who doesn't hesitate to kill. We're trying to locate the woman for her father before Harwood kills her. I don't want to add to your worries, but I don't think you'd want your son in the hands of this man. Of course, he's being paid to bring the boy back unharmed."

"Dammit to hell!" Fortune snapped, slamming his knee with his palm. A hired killer after his son. Michael would be six years old now. A little boy. "Dammit, you let me know the instant you think you've picked up her trail."

"I'll start on the case today," Eisner said, closing the folder. As Fortune stood up, he extended his hand.

"Thanks. Good luck. I hope to hear from you soon. Here's where you can reach me," he said, giving Eisner a folded piece of paper. "As soon as I'm out of the army, I'll give you my new address. It'll be an Atlanta hotel until I can build a home."

"You'll settle in Atlanta as a civilian?"

"Yes, I intend to go into business there."

Eisner nodded his head. "Then you and the grandfather will encounter each other."

"Yes. That's why I'm settling there," Fortune answered grimly. "We have a score to settle. And he'll know when I finally bring Michael home."

The following week, back in his office in Atlanta, Fortune looked up as a tall, powerfully built black officer entered and saluted. Returning the salute, Fortune sat back. "At ease, Tobiah," he said, remembering meeting Tobiah when he had visited his brother Caleb.

"Colonel O'Brien—"

"Close the door."

Tobiah closed it and turned around. Fortune waved his hand. "Sit down, Tobiah. And it's Fortune. I know how close you are to Rafferty and Caleb."

"Yes, sir. I came to you because I want to get out of the army. I want to get home to my wife and baby."

"Where are they?"

"In Chicago. I haven't been home since the war started. My son is going to grow up without knowing me." He placed a paper on the desk in front of Fortune, who picked it up and glanced over the letter requesting a release. "Also, I feel uncomfortable living in the South. There's too many people in this town who've been hurt by the war, and they're angry," Tobiah continued. "I had my own business in Chicago, and I want to get home."

"I'll do all I can to help. I don't blame you."

"Yes, sir," Tobiah said with a broad smile. "Thank you, Colonel. I hear you're getting out."

"Yes. Within the month."

"Give my regards to your brothers." Tobiah stood up and saluted, and Fortune returned the salute. Fortune leaned back and watched Tobiah stride through the door, his broad shoulders almost touching the jambs. His brother Rafferty had told him how Tobiah had saved his life after the ship went down carrying the O'Briens from Ireland. Fortune had vivid memories of that harrowing night, clinging to a wooden spar for hours and getting picked up by a steamer headed north. He had been fifteen when they sailed from Ireland after his father had gambled away everything and then died. Seventeen when he met Marilee. He looked out the window at the people going past. Where was the woman who had his son? He kept feeling an urge to go try to find her himself.

Pushing back his chair, he crossed the room to buckle on his gun belt and grab his hat. He mounted his horse and headed for an area beyond town with scattered oaks and tall sweet gum trees. A jay flew past, and Fortune's horse snorted faintly as it shied. Afternoon sunshine cast long shadows while he dismounted and shed his coat and hat. Withdrawing the revolver, he fired five shots and paused to reload.

Twenty minutes later, he turned at the sound of hoofbeats. Alaric rode up and pushed his hat back on his head. "I thought I'd find you here," he said, resting his hands on his thighs. "You need to relax. Let's go find a poker game."

"Sounds fine to me."

"It should. You always win."

"No, I don't," Fortune said. "It's just when I start losing, I stop gambling. That's the secret of my success."

"The secret of your success," Alaric said while Fortune mounted, "is bluffing the hell out of everyone else."

Fortune laughed. "Race you to the bridge," he said, flicking the reins and pounding away.

By two in the morning, he parted with Alaric, striding along Foster Street to his hotel, his pockets filled with his winnings. That was one legacy his father had left; he had taught his three oldest sons to play cards.

At the next corner, he had stepped off the boardwalk onto the dusty street when he heard a noise behind him. He looked around as men emerged in several directions from the darkness, moving close to surround him. A rope dropped over his head and was yanked tight, pinning his arms to his sides.

A group of men descended on him. Fortune kicked and heard a man grunt as he went down. Something slammed against his skull, and pain exploded inside his head. He staggered and another rope was dropped around his neck and tightened. Ropes went around his ankles, and he was thrown across a horse.

He bounced on the horse, struggling to get free of his bonds. Twisting, he looked at the men, who had their faces covered. All were hooded, but he could guess who was behind the attack. He craned his head out to see the men riding in front of him. Trevor Wenger had to be the leader.

Shortly outside the city, the procession stopped. Fortune was cut free from the horse and he toppled to the ground. He lashed out with his legs and knocked down one of his captors, but another kicked him in the side and Fortune doubled over.

"Tie him up" came the voice he had expected to hear.

"Wenger, you coward!" he yelled. "You couldn't meet me face to face. Afraid?"

"Tie the man! You dirty Irish bastard, you get out of town and don't come back."

They stretched his arms out, tying them around the trunk of a tree. Then his ankles were tied around the trunk. Someone cut his coat and yanked away coat and shirt.

"Wenger, you're a cowardly bastard!"

A lash whistled through the air and cut into Fortune's back, making him gasp. Another blow came and another.

Time blurred into white-hot, consuming agony. His head reeled as he gritted his teeth. The blows kept coming until he groaned with each one, sagging. Pain was making him dizzy, and he prayed he would lose consciousness.

A blow fell that seemed to cut to his spine. He heard a dim cry and then oblivion swallowed him.

When he stirred, he heard sharp groans, finally realizing he was making them. His face was pressed against rough bark. Throbbing with pain, his back felt as if knives had sliced into it. Agony washed over him in waves, and he closed his eyes, welcoming unconsciousness again.

He roused, feeling hands, crying out as a searing pain shot up his arms and he fell. Voices were dim, men moving around him. He wanted to strike out, to defend himself, but he couldn't move.

"Bastard," he tried to cry, the word coming out in a hoarse whisper. Someone jostled him, and he yelled in agony, losing consciousness once more. He floated in and out of awareness, feeling a jolt that sent more pain shooting through his body, realizing he was in a wagon. Next he was aware of a bed beneath him, something pouring on his back that felt like burning oil.

"You're home, Fortune," Alaric said loudly beside him.

He clenched his fists, feeling helpless rage, on fire with the hurt.

The next time he stirred, he blinked and raised his head. Every movement was agony, and he groaned.

"Sir?"

He turned slightly, looking across a small, plainly furnished room that had a hearth in one corner and a table and chairs. He gazed up at his friend. "Tobiah?"

"Yes, sir. We're taking turns watching you. I volunteered."

"How long—?"

"Last night. Major Hampton found you this morning and brought you back here. The place belongs to some friend of his, and he said to keep you here. Sir, if you can sit up, I can feed you. You'll get some strength back that way. You need some water."

"Damn." Fortune gasped with pain as he tried to move. He felt hands on his forearms trying to help. Every tiny movement brought searing agony. "I'll kill him."

"You know who did this?"

"Trevor Wenger."

"I heard about your wife and baby. He's a powerful man. Owns the ironworks and lots of land here."

"I'll kill him," Fortune said, shifting and letting Tobiah lower his legs over the side of the bed. His head swam and he clung to the edge of the bed. "Damn, it hurts."

"Here, let me feed you."

"If you'll hold the bowl, I can manage," Fortune said. As he lifted his arm, though, pain shot across his back. Tobiah took the spoon and began to feed him hot stew.

By the next day, Fortune was more alert, sitting up without aid. It was Alaric's shift at tending him, and he was stirring stew in a pot over the fire. His uniform sleeves were rolled high, his hair clinging damply to his face.

"Alaric?"

"Ahh, you're sitting up. You're doing better. I've got something here that you'll like. More stew. My cooking is limited."

"Thank you. You and Tobiah, and Richard. I don't know who else has been with me."

"Sometimes Edwin, sometimes Noah. This place belongs to Robert Horton. We couldn't care for you as easily in your hotel room, and we didn't feel you'd be as safe there." He ladled steaming stew into a bowl and placed it on a tray along with a biscuit. Hooking a straight-back chair with his toe and scooting it close to the bed, Alaric sat down and placed the tray carefully in Fortune's lap.

As Fortune bit into a thick hunk of beef from the stew, Alaric regarded him solemnly. "Wenger has people who swear he was in a poker game with them when you received the beating."

Fortune looked up. "That's to be expected. I won't give him another chance at me. He should have finished the job."

"I think he thought he had. Edwin was with me, and he's the best tracker the U.S. Cavalry has ever had. He's the one who found you."

"Don't know how the hell he did."

"You weren't far out of town. Your fever's gone and Doc Rosenkrantz looks at you every day."

"I'm exhausted. I'd give a lot for a cup of hot coffee."

"That's a simple order to fill. Fortune, he meant to kill you. If we hadn't found you when we did, and if you weren't as stubborn and strong as you are, you'd be dead. When you get well, get out of town. And until you get your discharge, one of us will stay with you."

Fortune lowered the spoon to give Alaric a level look. "I'm not running from Trevor Wenger. I intend to kill him, if I have to walk into the Wenger Ironworks and shoot him in his office."

"You're fuzzy from what's happened. Think about it. You kill him like that and you'll hang. He's got powerful friends here. If you hang, you'll never see that son of yours."

Fortune scowled but what Alaric said was true. Fortune mulled it over. If he killed Wenger in cold blood as he wanted to, he would hang.

"You'll never catch him alone and unprotected the way he caught you."

"You're probably right."

"I know I'm right. Tobiah and I've been following him, and he's never alone on the street."

"Why have you two—stay out of my fight!" he snapped, feeling a rush of gratitude for his friends, but wanting to keep them out of danger. "Dammit, Tobiah Barr barely knows me and he has a young child. I don't want either of you drawn into something that doesn't involve you."

"The man shouldn't escape without anything for what he did to you."

"You stay out of it, Alaric. I'll talk to Tobiah," Fortune said gruffly. "What you and the others have done for me means a lot." He watched Alaric pour a cup of coffee and place it on the tray.

"It's too damned hot for coffee or stew, but both are good for you."

Fortune nodded and finished the stew and a cup of hot coffee. As soon as Alaric removed the tray, Fortune stood, clinging to furniture as he moved around, feeling stiff and feeble, his back still a constant pain. Once he was back in bed, he thought about all Alaric had told him. He would get revenge. Wenger wasn't going to get away with what he had done.

Fortune wanted to find his son, and he wasn't going to jeopardize that by trying to get revenge. Where was the woman? he wondered. Was she good to Michael? That question tormented him the most. Why had she taken him? She was young and unmarried. Why had she wanted Michael when she could have married and had her own sons? To get the answers, he needed to find her before the hired killer did.

Chapter 4

Natchez, Mississippi
May 1867

Steamboats were docked at the foot of Silver Street at Natchez-Under-the-Hill. Across the road from the dark waters of the Mississippi River was a row of saloons. In one of them was a noisy smoke-filled room in which hard-looking men studied cards or studied the dancer on the narrow stage.

Dressed in green satin and black stockings, holding up her skirt and petticoats, Claire Dryden swung her foot high. As a rule she stared over the heads of the men toward the back of the saloon, trying to ignore taunting calls to her and the lust-filled faces watching her. For a moment, though, she lowered her gaze, searching the crowd near the stage for one particular face.

It didn't take long to find him. He was a tall, lanky man wearing spectacles and sporting a thick black beard. He didn't act like the others and he made her nervous. Was he interested in women? Or in her in particular? He did not act like other men who had followed her. He had caught her attention because he didn't do anything except sip a drink. He didn't applaud or yell or leer at her as the others did. He sat there as if he were listening to a speech and about to fall asleep. Yet behind the spectacles his dark eyes were alert. And for the past four nights, after Claire had finished singing and dancing, he had left the saloon.

Claire felt the same cold certainty she had experienced

before. Time to take Michael and move on. Don't run a risk. Get out right now while you still can.

Tossing her head so her brown hair swirled across her shoulders, she twirled the green skirt higher, letting her black-stockinged legs show to her thighs. The men went wild with cheers and stomping and clapping.

Of all the jobs she'd had, dancing was the easiest, quickest way to make money. She danced to the edge of the stage, glancing down. A tall blond man seated in the front row was more the usual customer. Yet he too had been there every night for the past four. He watched her, but his looks were the same the other customers gave her, speculative and lustful.

With a flounce and flip of her skirts she ran offstage.

"Your turn," she said to Stormy, who was the saloon's bawdy singer.

"You've got them ready, Pansy," the singer said, grinning.

Claire thought of all the names she had used: Pansy, Glory, Lizzie, Dawn, Rose, Emily, Gladys. In Natchez it was Pansy Crawford.

Suddenly anxious to get away from the dark man in the front row, Claire hurried to the dressing room and changed to a pink gingham dress. Looking over her shoulder constantly, she slipped out of the noisy saloon and glanced down the street. Two sternwheelers were at the docks, and lights blazed from saloons along the street. Moonlight glistened on the Mississippi, which looked deceptively still. Only the faint ripples in the center gave a hint of the fast-flowing current. In the street in the next block two men were fighting. Somewhere a bottle crashed. Natchez-Under-the-Hill at night was no place for a woman to wander alone.

She rushed the short distance toward the dark end of the street to the small house she was renting with two other dancers. Situated at the bottom of a high bluff, the house was set apart, the last structure at the end of the street. She unlocked the door and stepped into the cabin's one room, which had a hearth and two beds, three worn chairs, and a table and washstand. A kerosene lamp burned on the table.

"Pansy? Michael's asleep," a woman called Tillie Mae said. Gathering up a black cloak, she threw it around her shoulders, fluffing her blond curls over it.

"Thank you for staying with him."

"Thank you for making the dress for me," Tillie Mae said. "Is anything wrong?"

"No. Have you noticed a man who's been there nearly every night this week? He has a long black beard?"

Tillie Mae's ruby lips curved into a broad smile as she shook her head. "That describes half the men in the saloon."

"I suppose it does."

"Why? Does he worry you?"

"No. He's just not like the others. He doesn't yell or cheer or applaud. He's different."

"Who can explain men?" Tillie Mae asked with a lift of her shoulders. "See you tomorrow."

"Thanks again," Claire said, squeezing Tillie Mae's arm. As soon as she locked the door, she tiptoed to look at Michael, who slept on a cot across from her iron bed. Even though it had only one room, it was the first house she had ever rented. Always before she had stayed in rented rooms or hotels, but Michael was six now and full of energy and needed more room to run and play.

She leaned over him in his bed. In the soft glow of a lamp his dark lashes cast a shadow on his rosy cheeks. His skin was creamy, his nose straight. Thick locks of black hair curled in tangles over his forehead, and she brushed a curl back. He was a beautiful child, and her heart filled with love for him. She wanted to scoop him up and hold him close, but she would wait until she was ready to leave to wake him.

Feeling an increasing urgency, she placed a portmanteau on her bed and packed her other dress, a blue calico trimmed in a tiny band of white lace. She folded the two quilts they owned. Was she being foolish in running? She had moved so many times that she traveled lightly, carrying only necessities and a few clothes for both Michael and herself. For a moment she felt a pang. She had made good friends here in Natchez, and the pay was the best she had ever made. But she had kept Michael safe this long by trusting her instincts and skipping town whenever she felt something wasn't right. She would continue to do the same. The tall man with the black beard made her nervous, and that was sufficient cause to move on.

In minutes she was ready and shook Michael gently. "Michael, wake up. Honey, wake up."

He opened his dark eyes and looked up at her. "Someone's after us, Mama?"

It hurt to have him ask that question, yet what choice did she have? "Yes, I think so. We need to go now. You get dressed."

"Yes, ma'am," he said, and she leaned down to give him a squeeze. He was warm and smelled of soap, and she wanted to pull him close and rock him and sing softly to him instead of packing and running away in the night.

"Get dressed, Michael, while I write Tillie Mae a note and hitch the horse to the wagon."

"Yes, ma'am."

As she stepped outside, she paused to let her eyes adjust to the darkness. She scanned the yard for signs of anything unusual. Behind the house the high bluff was a dark, solid mass, moonlight showing on a jagged edge at the weed-covered top. It was a rough part of town, but she had felt secure in the little house and she hated to leave it. She hurried across the yard to the shed, which was merely a roof on posts. She took down the halter and crossed to hitch the bay to the wagon.

"Whoa, there," she said softly. It was dark and more difficult to see in the shed, and a sudden chill made the back of her neck crawl. Something scraped close behind her, and she stiffened.

The tall black-bearded man from the saloon stepped out of the shadows and raised a revolver, pointing it at her. "Miss Dryden, I've been looking for you."

She gasped, turning to run, but his hands caught her and spun her around. He pressed the muzzle of the pistol painfully against her throat.

"Don't run from me!" he said in a rasp. "I'm taking you back. If you want the boy, you'll cooperate."

"Please, don't take him to Trevor Wenger. I'll pay you more than he has if you'll let us go," she said, feeling cold terror. Her heart thudded. *I'm going to lose Michael! I'll lose Michael. They'll take him away from me.* "Please, listen."

"We don't have time now."

"You have to listen. Trevor Wenger is a cruel man."

"I'm not taking you to Trevor Wenger," he said, "and we have to go now!"

Stunned, she gazed at him as he pushed her forward. "Go on, hitch up the horse. If you want the boy to be safe, you'll do what I say as quickly as possible."

Shocked by learning he hadn't been sent by Wenger, she barely heard him. "What did you say? Where are you taking me?"

"Your father wants to see—"

"My father?" she asked. She remembered fleeing home. She had wanted to keep Michael and to avoid a marriage she didn't want. "After all this time, he can't force me to wed a man I don't love. I'm an adult now. Why—"

"He's ill. We have to go. I'm Irving Eisner with Pinkerton's, and I'm not the only man after you."

She drew her breath and remembered the blond stranger who had been in the front row every night this week.

"Get the boy and let's get out of here. Do what I say. I'll watch you while you hitch the horse to the wagon."

She moved quickly, her hands shaking while her mind raced for some way of escape. As soon as the horse was hitched, Eisner caught her arm.

"Let's get Michael and go quickly. We can talk when we're moving." He prodded her with the revolver. Was he telling the truth or lying to her? Either way, she didn't want Michael in his care.

"Please, I don't want Michael to see your pistol."

"He won't, but don't run. Or I'll grab the boy."

Her heart pounded. If Eisner wanted to take her back to her father, he wouldn't grab Michael. Who was he really and where was he taking her? Who had hired him? She remembered her derringer in her portmanteau as she approached the house.

Dressed in denim pants and his white muslin shirt with a broad-brimmed hat on his head, Michael was standing beside her portmanteau, the quilts, and his small satchel. Her heart ached with the thought that Michael might be hurt or she might lose him. He looked small and vulnerable, and she wished she had fled Natchez sooner. When he saw the man beside her, Michael's eyes grew round.

"Michael, this is Mr. Eisner," she said, speaking quickly and trying to sound calm to keep from alarming the child. "He's going to travel with us. Mr. Eisner, this is Michael."

"How do you do, sir?" Michael said, his dark brown eyes somber as he stared at Eisner. *He knows*. Michael knows this is a bad man. She felt more afraid than ever. She crossed the room, smiling at Michael and taking his hand. "We're ready to go. I've packed food to take," she said, handing Michael his satchel to carry.

She locked the door behind them, and the weeds scraped against their feet and legs as they crossed the short space to the wagon. Acutely aware of Eisner, she put their things in the wagon, and then she turned to help Michael into the bed of the wagon, where she kept an old quilt. To her relief, Eisner didn't touch her as she climbed up. He swung up and watched when she took the reins. His hand was beneath his coat.

She shook, feeling desperate to get away from him. Where was he really taking them? Did he intend to shoot her and take Michael? Who had sent him after them? She didn't believe it was her father.

They turned out of the weedy yard and down the street, riding past the saloons on one side, the steamboats and flatboats on the other. Music began to fade as she wound up Silver Street, climbing to the top of the bluff, seeing the bend of the Mississippi below. Eisner waved his hand.

"Head out of town on the Trace. Don't go fast, now, because it would draw attention to us."

She thought of her savings from the past month, wrapped in a piece of gingham and tucked into the bottom of her portmanteau. When she could, she always sent money to a bank in St. Louis. Someday she planned to take the savings and go to a big city in the Northeast and open a millinery shop. Only now, that day might never come. Again her derringer came to mind. It was in the portmanteau on top of everything else, folded in the blue calico dress. If she got it, could she frighten Eisner into letting her go? Would he really shoot?

As they rode, he turned on the seat often to glance over his shoulder. Was Michael worrying him? Was he frightening Michael with his continual stares? She glanced back and saw Michael was asleep, curled on the bed of the wagon, his head on the mound of quilts, his body jiggling as the wagon ran over the cobblestones. Resting beside the two folded quilts, the portmanteau was almost in reach behind her. Looking up at Eisner, she followed his gaze. He was watching the road behind them. He was concerned about someone following them, and his nervousness added to her fears.

Leaving Natchez, they rode past elegant mansions that had survived the war, finally winding along on an empty road, stirring a faint cloud of dust behind them.

She drew a deep breath. "May I stop and cover Michael?"

"Don't stop, and don't try to get away from me. If you'll tell me where the quilt is—"

"I'll do it," she said quickly, turning and reaching back, tugging a quilt over Michael. "I want his jacket," she said, reaching for the portmanteau. She casually opened it, but her head swiftly pushed clothing for the derringer, her fingers closing on the smooth metal grip.

Eisner's hand clamped around her wrist, and he withdrew the derringer. "May I help you find anything else?"

"Please, don't harm him."

"I won't. We need to keep moving. Miss Dryden, both of you are in danger, but you in particular."

She felt a chill at the urgency in his voice. Quickly she looked back along the empty road. They were headed up the Natchez Trace, closed in by trees on either side, and she knew this was a dangerous trail at night because of thieves. Tales of men disappearing in swamps along the Trace were common. She could hear the croak of frogs and the high chirp of crickets, night sounds that should have been reassuring but weren't on the deserted road that had once been known as the Devil's Backbone.

She heard hoofbeats and saw Eisner turn. Emerging from the trees, a man rode at an angle toward them. Eisner whipped out his pistol as the man's hand moved. The twin reports of guns made her jump so violently, she dropped the reins. Eisner gasped and sagged against her.

She grabbed for his gun, but the mounted man was on her in a flash. He swung from the saddle to the wagon seat, pushing her down. When she tried to grab the derringer, he stomped on her hand.

"Mama!"

Claire cried out in pain as he yanked her up hard against him. "Shut up and don't move." He released her, grabbing the reins and tugging the wagon to a halt.

"Mama!" Michael cried again in alarm, and she turned to pull him close and hug him.

Glancing at Eisner, she drew a deep breath. "He's hurt!" she exclaimed, releasing Michael to try to turn Eisner over. He was stiff and heavy, his long body cumbersome for her to move. She felt for a pulse against his cold throat, but there wasn't any. "You killed him!" she gasped, terrified, wondering who both these men were.

"Just do as you're told," the blond man said in a cold voice, "and you and the boy will be all right." He motioned to her. "Get out of the wagon."

He was going to kill her. Michael would be alone with this man. An evil man. At her foot was Eisner's pistol. But her hand hurt where the man had stepped on her, and he continued to hold his revolver pointed directly at her heart.

"I won't tell you again," he said softly.

Terrified for Michael, she climbed down. The stranger dropped to the ground behind her, spurs jingling as he landed on his feet. Reaching out, he shoved her. She hit the ground, scraping her hands, biting back a cry of fear so she wouldn't alarm Michael.

"Don't hurt my mother!"

She heard a click as Michael pulled back the hammer on the pistol. She looked up at the child, at the pistol wavering in his hands. A spasm of fear made her blood icy. "Michael! No!"

With amazing speed the man knocked the pistol from Michael's hands and slapped him. The moment Michael cried out and fell, she lunged at the stranger. Enraged that he would hurt Michael, she threw herself against the man and knocked him back. The voice screaming at him seemed to come from a distance as she tried to claw him.

He hit her, his palm flat on her cheek. He kicked her feet out from under her, and she went down, knocking the wind out of her. Stunned, she gazed up at him as he stood over her with his pistol aimed.

"Leave Michael alone! You monster!"

Rough hands rolled her over, and a boot pressed into the middle of her back. He caught her wrists behind her, and she felt rope being wound around her wrists. He yanked it tight and knotted it, rolling her onto her back.

"Please don't hurt him," she sobbed, shaking with fear, her face stinging from the slap, her wrists chafing from being tied tightly. Michael was crying, and the sound of his whimpering was the worst of all. "Please, don't hurt him."

"Kid, get in the back and sit on the floor, or I'll hit her again."

She felt a twist of pain at the sound of his sob.

"The kid knows how to mind." The stranger nudged her over with his foot and stood over her.

"Who are you? What do you want with us?"

"I'm Seeton Hardwood. I'm collecting on the kid. And I imagine I can sell you for a good price." He pulled out a knife, and she expected him to slit her throat.

"Please take care of Michael," she said as he leaned toward her, holding out the knife. He caught the collar of her pink gingham and hauled her to her feet.

Moonlight glinted on the blade as the knife swung, and she closed her eyes as cold steel grazed her throat. He slashed open the front of her dress, laying bare her breasts.

She opened her eyes as cool air touched her skin. He studied her. She was bound, exposed. No man had ever viewed her half-naked, and she burned with hatred and embarrassment.

"You'll bring a damned good price. And I'll have my fun on the way." He ran his hand roughly over her breast. Repelled, she gasped and tried to draw back from his touch. He laughed, a cold, harsh sound, before he shoved her down and turned away. She twisted, tears streaking her cheeks as Harwood pulled Eisner's body from the buggy and dropped him on the ground with a dull thump.

Was Michael terrified? Was he watching? How badly was he hurt?

"Kid, get down on that wagon bed and don't get up!"

"Yes, sir." His voice was firm, angry. Pride surged in her over Michael's courage. He had been brave to pick up Eisner's pistol and try to shoot Seeton Harwood. Michael was the one Harwood wanted, so he had to have been hired by Trevor Wenger. But who had hired Eisner? He had said her father was ill, but he had also been too concerned about Michael to have had taking her back to her father his sole purpose.

Harwood led his horse past her, intending to hitch it to the back of the wagon. Michael rose to look over the edge of the wagon as the man walked past.

"Raise your hands" came a deep voice out of the dark night.

Shocked, Claire twisted around. *What in heaven's name was happening?* Stunned, she watched a tall man stride forward, a rifle pointed at her captor. The man's hat was pulled low, and his spurs jingled with each step.

"Mama? Are you all right? Michael cried, standing up in the back of the wagon. Suddenly their captor swung Michael in front of him.

"Get back or I kill the kid!"

Chapter 5

"Go ahead," the stranger said quietly, and she felt as if her heart had stopped. The world spun, and Claire barely heard his voice as he continued. "I've been hired to take the woman to her father, William Dryden. You're after the kid. You won't get paid if he's dead. Free the kid, or I'll shoot off your knees."

"Take the woman. I'll take the kid, and we'll both profit."

"Hell, no. The kid's worth something too. Let him go."

There was a pause that seemed like an eternity to her. She held her breath. Michael had a pistol to his throat. Michael . . .

Suddenly the man shoved Michael aside and rolled beneath the wagon, firing as he hit the ground.

Guns blazed while she screamed. "Michael! Get down!"

Yanking at her bonds, she scrambled to her feet. Helpless, she cried in frustration, running toward the wagon.

"You'll hit the kid!" Harwood yelled.

Heedless of being in the line of fire, she raced to kneel beside Michael, who was in the open. "Stay down, Michael!"

Suddenly a burst of gunfire came from Harwood, and he rolled out from beneath the wagon. Grabbing his horse's reins, he flung himself into the saddle. Into the dense brush and trees, he galloped, keeping the wagon between him and the other man.

The man emerged from behind a tree and ran past her, firing at Harwood. Across the wagon, she saw Harwood lurch in the saddle and then disappear out of sight.

Michael threw his thin arms around her. His frail body pressed against her while he cried and hid his face against her neck.

"Michael," she said, "listen to me." She saw the man race to a tree and fire into the darkness. A shot was returned. "Hurry! Climb into the wagon and open the portmanteau. There's a knife in the bottom. Get the knife and climb down on this side of the wagon. Keep your head down," she ordered, watching the man take cover behind a tree and continue to exchange shots with Harwood.

Michael crouched and moved to the front of the wagon. She looked at the tall, lanky man firing at Harwood. They both were killers. Who was paying this one? She didn't believe that her father would want her back now. Had Trevor Wenger hired men from several agencies?

Michael climbed out of the buggy and dashed to her.

"Cut the ropes tying my hands. Michael, hold the knife carefully so you don't cut yourself or me. Take your time."

"Yes, ma'am," he said obediently, and she could feel the rope grow tauter as he began to saw it with the blade.

While the two men exchanged shots, Michael worked in silence. Her heart pounded with fear, for any moment the stranger could turn and see Michael cutting her free. She wanted to cry out to Michael to hurry, but his hands were so small. He was doing the best he could. Be patient, give him time. He's only a child, she told herself, her palms growing damp with sweat.

A shot struck a pan hanging on the wagon. The clang was loud, but it was drowned out by the next exchange of shots.

Her wrists came free, and she twisted around to take the knife. "Michael, run and hide while I try to find my pistol. See that tree? Don't go too far, and I'll find you."

"Can I stay with you?"

"No. Do as I say. Get behind the tree and stay as quiet as possible."

"Yes'm." He ran, his short legs flying. Hastily she tied the neck of her dress together with the torn halves, giving her some coverage. She ran her hand over the floor of the wagon where the derringer had fallen. She spotted it on the far side and had to climb into the wagon to reach it.

As the shots stopped, she dropped to the ground and ran for the trees.

Spurs jingled and feet thudded on the ground behind her. An arm banded her waist and swept her off her feet. As she struggled to twist around, the derringer was yanked from her hands and tossed away. Terrified, she saw a silvery flash as it arced high in the air.

She bit back the scream that tore at her throat. Don't frighten Michael! Don't scream! She struggled and kicked tugging at the arm around her waist. He spun her around to yank her up hard against his solid body. The man looked down at her, the faint smell of tobacco on his breath.

"We've got to get the boy back," he said in a low, deadly voice. "The killer is out there. Call Michael and tell him to come here."

She shook with rage, still kicking at her captor, trying to bite him. Her feet were knocked out from under her, and she fell, her breath going out. He was on her in an instant, straddling her, pinning her hands over her head.

Enraged and frustrated, she glared at him.

"Call the boy."

She would summon Michael from one danger to another. She couldn't trust any of these men sent to find her. All of them wanted to kill her, and take Michael back to Wenger.

"Get him back, you little fool, he's in terrible danger," the man whispered.

"Then you'll take him."

He thrust the muzzle of his pistol at her throat. She gasped as it jammed against her.

"Call him to come here now or you'll never live to see what happens to him. Do you want him to stand there and watch me shoot you?"

Her heart thudded in terror as she gazed up. The man's face was hidden in the shadows, but there was no mistaking the coldness in his voice. Tears of frustration and fear stung her eyes. "Michael! Michael, come here now," she called reluctantly. "Please don't hurt him."

She heard a rustle and the man's head went up. He glanced back at her, pressing the muzzle tighter, making her gag.

"You do anything you shouldn't and you're dead," he said quietly, his voice filled with conviction. In one lithe movement he released her, stood up, and swept Michael into his arms.

"Tell him not to struggle," he ordered.

"Michael, do as he says," she said, coughing and rubbing her raw throat. She looked up in hatred at the tall man holding Michael. She wanted to leap on him and claw his eyes and try to get his gun and kill him!

The man's face was hidden in shadows by a broad-brimmed black hat. His clothing was black and he wore leather gloves, and she could imagine how easily he had slipped up on them. Michael's eyes were wide, and she hurt to see him frightened.

"Put him down!"

"No. As long as I'm holding him, the man after you won't dare shoot. He's after Michael too. Get in the wagon."

She stood up, clutching the front of her dress as she hurried to climb into the wagon. The man tethered his horse to the wagon swiftly, climbed onto the seat, and yanked up the reins, sliding Michael between them.

He yelled and snapped the whip. With a lurch the bay sprang forward. The man urged the horse to a gallop, and they rocked violently on the rutted trail. Alarmed, she clutched the wagon with one hand and grabbed Michael with the other.

They had been captured by a madman who would kill them all. Her wagon was meant only for light hauling, never built to travel like this. Branches hanging down over the trail scraped the sides of the wagon. The man drove as though crazed, and they went careening along the rough trail, his horse galloping behind.

"Mama?"

"It's all right, honey," she said, leaning close to speak into his ear. "Whatever happens, they won't hurt you. And we'll watch for a chance to get away. If I tell you, you move, just like you did tonight." She glanced at the man hunched over, his broad shoulders silhouetted against the sky, and she remembered the feel of his hard body, the solid muscles, the strength of him as he held her. He was going to take Michael from her.

"Oh, Michael," she said, fighting back tears, and hugging him. "I love you. Whatever happens, don't ever forget, I love you more than anything on earth."

"I love you," he said, holding her tightly. She stroked him, running her hand over his thick curls. She glanced around. They couldn't jump. It was too dangerous. The wagon careened around a turn, swinging wide, and she fell against Michael and the man. As she straightened up at once, a branch swiped at her face.

"Mama! We're going to turn over!"

"You're going to kill us!" she shouted. If the man heard her, though, he didn't heed her words.

His horse still galloped close behind the wagon, lather covering its neck, its dark mane streaming out behind it as it ran. Her horse couldn't keep up this pace much longer. Another turn came and she was thrown in the opposite direction. The wagon rumbled partway off the trail, weeds and branches whipping against it.

Was the other killer after them? she wondered. What

would this man do with her? She stared at the driver's broad shoulders, remembering his harsh voice. A chill went down her spine. He would kill her without a qualm.

Too much of Michael's life had been spent running. The war years had been the only reprieve, yet life in the West was hard and dangerous. If she escaped this time, she would take Michael and head north. The bigger the city, the safer she would feel.

If she escaped . . .

She wondered how she was going to get away from this man. Any minute he was going to wreck the wagon, and if she survived being thrown, she might be able to get Michael and slip away. Pray the driver was killed if the wagon overturned.

He tugged on the reins and slowed a fraction. She raised her head and caught him looking at her for a moment before his gaze shifted to Michael. The stranger gestured with his hand. "Son, you may ride in the back of the wagon now if you want."

Michael looked up at her and she nodded, thinking he might be safer if anyone ambushed them again. Michael climbed back obediently and huddled on a quilt.

She looked at the driver and saw he was watching her. Moonlight revealed the lower part of his face, his mouth set in a grim line, a strong jaw. He glared at her, and she blinked. He looked as if he could close his hands around her throat and squeeze the breath from her lungs without a qualm.

"Stop fighting me. You and Michael are in danger," he whispered.

"Mama? I want you to come back here too."

"It's all right, Michael. Get your quilt and lie down and try to go back to sleep."

"Yes, ma'am."

"Is he always so docile?"

"What do you want? A ferocious beast like you?"

"Dammit." The man frowned at her. "We have to slow

down for the sake of the horses. Don't give me trouble. I can get rid of you in a blink of the eye, but he wants you here, so as long as you cooperate, you stay. But don't give me trouble of any kind."

"You filthy bastard," she whispered.

"You better watch for the killer. I want to get away from him."

"He can catch us easily. A wagon isn't difficult to follow."

"Right, except he's hit in the arm. I saw that."

The man sat tall, his broad shoulders tapering to slim hips. He wore a gun belt, and she saw the grip of his revolver on his hip, only a little over a foot away from her. If she lunged against him, could she get the pistol? If she failed, he might kill her and toss her from the wagon. Should she try or not? The revolver was big, far larger than her tiny derringer. She would have to yank it out of the holster. She glanced up from the gun on his hip to find him watching her.

"Don't try for my gun," he said, so low she was sure Michael couldn't hear. "Michael needs you, and you'll get hurt." The stranger spoke softly, yet that cold voice sounded more threatening than any man she had ever dealt with. She studied the stranger's profile and locked her fingers together. This one seemed deadly and intelligent, a combination that terrified her. The only hope was that he wanted to keep Michael safe, and he was willing to keep her alive for Michael's sake as long as she cooperated. She looked at his masculine jaw, the straight nose that gave him an arrogant air. Perhaps he was just telling her he wouldn't kill her so she would cooperate until he could win Michael's acceptance. Then he wouldn't need to bother with her.

They were going slow enough now that she could jump from the wagon without too much danger, but she couldn't leave Michael. She glanced over her shoulder. Would there be some way to tell him to jump?

He lay curled on the quilt, his head on his arm, his eyes closed, and her hopes sank. He was asleep. She couldn't signal to him at all.

"Don't think of grabbing the kid and running," a gruff voice said in the darkness, startling her.

How could he guess what was in her mind? She looked up at him, thinking about the savings she had banked since she first ran away with Michael.

"Let us go. Please. Whatever Wenger is paying you, I'll pay you more."

"You wouldn't have that much money," the man answered dryly, turning his head to look at her again.

"Name your price."

He studied her. "Five million in gold."

She gasped. "Wenger couldn't be paying you that! That would be a ransom for a king!"

Fortune tried to keep a curb on his rage toward her. All he could think was this woman had taken his child and kept Michael all these years. Because of her, he would never know Michael as a baby. He wanted to lock his fingers around her soft throat and shout in anger what she had taken from him.

He had to get his emotions under control. Harwood was fast and deadly, and he wouldn't be far behind. Fortune didn't think the shot in the arm would slow a dead-eyed killer like that very much. Fortune's back prickled, and he glanced over his shoulder. If Harwood caught up with them, he wouldn't stand any more of a chance than Eisner had.

He glanced down at the sleeping boy, and some of the tension left him. Michael was a beautiful, obedient child. Too docile, but that could change. When he had picked him up, he had wanted to crush him to his heart and just hold him and tell Michael who he was. He turned his attention back to the road and flicked the reins, urging the horse to a trot. They had to keep moving, and he had to keep his wits about him.

He glanced again at the woman, feeling anger burn every time he looked at her. What had all this running done to Michael? From the way he had reacted to her commands, he was accustomed to this, and it had to be hard on him. Did he live in constant fear? Was that why he was such a docile child?

Fortune clamped his jaw closed, his fists knotting as he held the reins. He inhaled deeply, trying to relax. They needed to get off the Trace. They could be so easily ambushed on this road. Plus, he needed to rest. He had ridden hard, only dozing in the saddle the last three nights so he could catch up with Eisner. And it terrified him to think how close he had come to missing them.

Where was Harwood? Was he already galloping after them?

While they rode in silence, Claire anxiously shifted on the seat as she tried to think what to do. When they stopped to camp, she had to watch for a chance to escape. A tide of exhaustion filled her and she fought against it, knowing she had to stay alert.

"I need to stop. I have to relieve myself."

He drew on the reins. "Hurry up. I have the boy. And don't wander far. If Harwood gets you, I'll let him keep you."

She climbed down and hurried behind a bush, her mind racing for some way to get Michael. If she shouted for him, he might not even wake and he would never escape. The man was too quick and too strong. In the end, she climbed back on the front seat, and they drove on.

Several hours before dawn, they rode into Vicksburg. The stranger went straight to a livery stable to leave the wagon. As he unfastened his saddlebags and placed them over his shoulder, she wondered what made the bags bulge. Could he have another revolver in one?

He lifted Michael up carefully and paused to look at her. "Don't try anything while I'm carrying him. When we get inside the hotel lobby, you go stand by the stairs to wait for me. I don't want the clerk to be able to give a good description of us."

She could agree with that, because Harwood was still after them. "Why are we stopping here? Wouldn't we be safer riding on and camping somewhere?"

"No. I need some sleep, and he'll be less likely to attack us in a hotel room than out on the Trace."

They entered the quiet hotel lobby. The clerk was asleep behind the desk, and after giving him a glance, she moved toward the stairs. She blinked in the brightness of the lamp light and turned to look at the man who held them captive.

His tall frame and straight back, the slight thrust of his broad shoulders with each step, gave him an air of command. Dressed in a leather vest, white shirt, and denim trousers, he crossed the lobby of the hotel as if he owned the place. She studied his profile as he stopped at the desk. The masculine jaw and straight nose only added to the air of arrogance and self-assurance. His skin was brown, as if he spent a lot of time in the sun. The gun belt hung low on his slender hips, and her gaze drifted down his long legs to his dusty black boots.

He cleared his throat, and the clerk came to his feet. As soon as he asked what he could do, Michael stirred. The man set him carefully on his feet, holding his hand to keep him steady, and she noticed how gentle he was with Michael. With wide eyes Michael looked around. When he spotted her, she smiled, wanting to reassure him that he was safe.

She stood by the stairs and watched them. The man's deep voice was too low to hear. Nodding, the clerk bustled about, getting a key, motioning to a boy to carry her portmanteau, summoning drowsy help to fetch a tub and hot water. A bath. She drew a deep breath, her fury stirring again at the thought of their captor ordering a bath. She didn't want to share a hotel room with a naked man! He crossed to her, and his fingers closed on her arm. She glanced up to meet his gaze, for the first time looking at him clearly in the light.

His eyes were a startling crystal blue, like spring water in a mountain stream. That blue was intense, filled with such burning anger she drew a deep breath.

"Let's go," he said. When she attempted to yank her arm from his grasp, his fingers tightened painfully. She turned to climb the stairs to the second floor. He held her arm firmly as they followed the clerk, who opened the door to a suite.

She stepped inside and paused, startled by the lavishness of the place. Not since she had run away from home had she been in such elegant surroundings. The extravagance was appalling. For the past six years she had counted every penny, and the stranger was wasting an incredible amount on this suite. For what this one night would cost, she and Michael could live for two months. She faced the man and found he was watching her.

"We don't need all this! Good heavens, it'll cost you a fortune!"

He arched his brow. "A woman who thinks I'm spending too much money?"

"This is frivolous," she said, looking around, crossing the room to run her fingers across a marble-topped table. "For what this costs, you could stay a year in a comfortable room."

They fell silent as two porters appeared with a copper tub. "Place it in the bedroom," the man said, waving his hand. Another brought a tray with glasses and a pitcher of water.

"Mama, this is fancy," Michael said in awe, running his small fingers across the silk settee. He touched a crystal vase and turned to look at the man, who was watching him with a strange, fierce expression that softened the moment Michael glanced up at him.

"You can touch that, Michael," he said in such a gentle

voice, she stared in surprise. And then the porters left, and her thoughts shifted as the man shed his coat.

"Michael, come with me. I'll help you wash."

Michael glanced at her, and she nodded. "It's all right."

The man crossed the room with Michael, and she looked for a weapon. While he was gone, she might find some way to get an advantage. At the door to the bedroom, the man paused.

"Go on, Michael. Undress and get in the tub. I want to say a word to"—there was the slightest pause—"your mother, and then I'll be there."

Michael did as he was told, and the man closed the door, turning to her. He untied a neckerchief from around his neck and approached her. Suddenly she wondered if he was going to strangle her.

"I didn't want to alarm him. I'm tying you up while we bathe."

"Please reconsider. You're taking him to a cruel man."

"How the hell do you know whether he's cruel or not?"

The stranger yanked up a straight-back wooden rocker and set it down beside her. "Sit down," he commanded.

"Who are you?"

He gave her a stony look, clamping his mouth shut, a muscle working in his jaw, and she bit back another question.

She glared at him, her heart racing. She had to try to escape, and now seemed as likely as any time. She lunged at him, grabbing for his gun, hoping to knock him down and get the weapon.

It was liked knocking down a tree. She hit a solid body that didn't yield an inch. Arms closed around her, and she struggled, trying to bite him. As they grappled, the knot at the neck of her dress came untied. He tossed her down in the chair, caught her wrists, and held them high over her head, sidestepping her efforts to kick him.

Stepping behind the chair, be brought her arms down behind the chair and tied them. She gasped in frustration and anger, panting from the exertion, feeling her arms pulled tightly, realizing for the first time that the neck of her dress gaped open and her breasts were exposed.

"This will alarm Michael!"

"I wasn't going to truss you up so tightly, but you've given me little choice." The man's voice was quiet, yet it was laced with unmistakable fury. He stepped in front of her. His hat was still on his head, his hands on his hips. He stood close, his narrow hips at eye level. She looked up to see a fiery expression, his mouth in a firm line, his gaze on her breasts.

She burned with embarrassment, steeling herself for his touch as the other man had. His hand reached out, and he caught the ends of her dress. Swiftly he knotted it again, his knuckles just brushing her flesh.

Startled, she looked at him. "I'll get you a needle and thread tomorrow, and you can sew that up."

"I have a needle and thread, and I'll mend it the first chance I get."

"Don't give me trouble," he commanded in a cold voice.

He frightened her badly, more than any of the others who had tried to get Michael. This man looked as if he were fighting the temptation to close his fingers around her throat. "You filthy ruffian!" she snapped back in a low voice. "Taking a child and his mother."

Giving her another hard look that sent a chill down her spine, he turned on his heel and disappeared into the bedroom. The door was left ajar, but the tub was out of her vision. She could hear his deep voice as he talked to Michael, but she couldn't distinguish what he was saying.

When she heard splashing, she struggled to get free. Frightened that she wouldn't get away from this man, she yanked on her bonds. Her wrists were tied tightly, and she couldn't reach the knot with her fingers. She glanced down at her tightly knotted dress. She had always dressed plainly, trying to avoid attracting attention from men, except when she was on stage dancing. Most of the time she was ignored, and the lack of attention had always suited her. This one looked as if the only emotion he felt toward her was rage.

She waited, hearing them splash and talk, wondering if he was winning over Michael. After a quarter of an hour had passed, she realized the man must be bathing also.

It was another quarter of an hour before she heard Michael make a peculiar noise. The man appeared in the doorway with the boy perched on his shoulders.

As the stranger came into the room, he was bare-chested, barefoot, wearing only his tight denim pants. His shoulders were broad, and his chest and arms bulged with hard muscles. Michael wore only his pants as well. His fingers were locked in the man's hair, his eyes round while he looked halfway uncertain, half enjoying himself.

As she eyed the two of them, her heart missed a beat and her breath caught. She felt as if all the blood drained from her body. If she hadn't been sitting, she would have fallen.

Before her were two heads of wet, curly black hair, two straight noses, and prominent cheekbones. Michael was tiny, but his jawline was a miniature copy of the man's firm jaw.

"Who are you?" she whispered, understanding his rage now and knowing what his answer would be.

Chapter 6

"My name is Fortune O'Brien," he said, looking at her white face. Something had shaken her badly at the sight of them. From the looks of her, he wondered if she had guessed the truth about his identity. "I told Michael to call me by my given name—Fortune."

He glanced up at the boy. "Now, my little friend, you go to bed in here on the settee. Let's get that hair dry before you bed down and soak the silk." He swung Michael down carefully. The child was too solemn, too scared. Claire Dryden had mothered him to the point of smothering him. "Run and get the towel, Michael, and dry your hair more."

Michael walked back to the bedroom, and Fortune crossed the room to stand in front of her, his long, slender fingers splayed on his hips. "I'll untie you. He won't be alarmed if you don't make a fuss." He knelt behind her to unfasten the knots, and in seconds she was free. He stood to see Michael rubbing his head with the towel.

"There are covers. Make Michael a bed on the sofa while he dries his hair," he ordered. Watch her all the time, he warned himself. She'll try to get away again, but as long as she can't get the revolver or the boy, she's no problem. *If she had the revolver, I'd be dead.* She must be the one who killed Pinkerton's agent, because she looks as if she could do so without a qualm. She was attractive enough—why had she taken Michael in the first place?

Why hadn't she given him up and married and had her own sons?

Out of nowhere came the vision of her tied to the rocker, the neck of her dress gaping to her waist, her breasts revealed, lush, pink-tipped. He felt a stir in his groin, and he glanced at her as she worked. She shook out the quilts and smoothed them on the sofa. As she leaned down, the skirt was tight around her tiny waist, falling over her rounded bottom.

She would fight him. He was exhausted and he had to have a decent night's sleep. So what was he going to do with her?

"Michael," he said, catching a frown from her. She made it obvious she didn't want him to talk to Michael or touch him or have anything to do with him. "This is your bed."

She studied the windows. "He'll be safe," Fortune said. "We're on the second floor with no balconies. The door is locked, and I'll put furniture in front of it. I'm a light sleeper. You can have the tub of water now, or you can sit here while I tell Michael good night."

He met her defiant gaze. He didn't want to use force, but he would if he had to and he hoped she realized it. Hatred, anger, defiance, clearly smoldered in her eyes. He drew a breath. If she started something, he hoped he could maintain control, because each time he had fought with her, he had checked his rage only with great difficulty.

They stared at each other, tension and anger swirling between them. She blinked and turned to walk to the bedroom and close the door.

He knelt beside the settee and brushed Michael's curls from his face. As he looked into the boy's wide brown eyes, Marilee's eyes, a knot formed in his chest and he wanted to crush Michael in his arms and tell the child that he was his father. But it was too soon and would be too startling. And he didn't know what Claire Dryden had told Michael about his father. Michael's dark eyes focused on him with trust.

"You sleep, Michael," he said gently, his heart beating wildly with joy at finding his son and finally being with him. For this moment everything was almost right in the world—the only thing lacking was that he couldn't tell Michael he was his father. But the time would come.

"No one will bother us tonight. I promise you," Fortune said. "I'll protect you."

"Will you protect Mama?" Michael asked softly, his wide, dark eyes studying Fortune.

Fortune felt another lurch of his heart. When he gazed into Michael's dark eyes, he could see Marilee so clearly. "Yes, I'll protect her too," he said gently.

"I love Mama."

"I know you do," he said, pained that Marilee couldn't have known her child and Michael hadn't known his real mother.

"You're not going to hurt us?"

"Never. I promised you that before. You can always trust me," he said gruffly, tears burning his eyes as he stroked Michael's soft cheek. He wanted to tell Michael how much he loved him, how long he had searched for him. He took Michael's hand in his and ran his thumb across the small knuckles. "I'll protect both of you."

Michael studied him and blinked. "You're crying!"

"Something in my eye," Fortune said, wiping his eyes, aching so badly to hold Michael close. This beautiful child was his and Marilee's. "You're a good boy, Michael," he whispered.

"Yes, sir."

Fortune leaned forward and brushed Michael's forehead with a light kiss and stood up, tucking covers around him and trying to get his emotions under control. Michael turned his head to look up at him. "You're staying with us?"

"Yes, I am."

"So that bad man won't get us again?"

"Yes. He probably won't find us here, but if he does, I won't let him get near you."

With a smile Michael rolled over, and Fortune tucked the covers around him.

He glanced at the door. She could be bathing—or she could be fashioning some kind of weapon to use against him. He crossed the room and opened the door slightly, bracing for her to lunge at him.

She was in the tub, her head bent over, washing her hair. Her skin was ivory and sleek with water, her brown hair dark and wet. She moved her head and he could see her bare breasts. His breath caught and his pulse thudded as he stared again at her full, upthrusting breasts tipped with pink nipples. He backed out and closed the door without a sound.

He extinguished the last lamp and moved to the window, shifting the curtain to watch the street. Moonlight splashed over the center of the street, but doorways were dark shadows. Even though no one was in sight, Fortune rested his shoulder against the wall and stared down, waiting, watching.

Remembering their awe when they had first entered the suite, he wondered where Claire Dryden and Michael had lived all these years. Had it been a constant change of cheap rented rooms?

He heard a slight sound and turned, watching a sliver of light show as the bedroom door opened. Claire appeared, her hair spilling over her shoulders. She wore a wrinkled blue calico dress, and her hair was still damp.

"Michael's asleep?"

"Yes, he is," Fortune said, moving toward her. He took her arm to guide her back into the bedroom and closed the door. A brass bed was across the large room. Marble-topped tables flanked it. A china washbowl and pitcher were set on a commode with a gilt mirror above it. Mirrors decorated the walls and potted palms were in the corners while a hanging lamp glowed softly. Fortune crossed to the saddlebags to remove a bottle of brandy and uncork it. Standing with his back to her, he poured the brandy into two glasses. His muscular back was laced with horrible scars. When he turned to bring a glass of brandy to her, she stood frowning at him.

"Your back—?"

"The scars are from a recent beating," he said. He held out a glass of brandy.

"No!" she said, shaking her head and backing up. "I don't touch spirits."

"One glass isn't going to hurt you. I'm exhausted and I want a few hours sleep. I don't want any trouble out of you. Drink it or I'll hold you and pour it down your throat."

Fortune stared at her, feeling the clash of wills. Anger radiated from her gaze, and he could see her refusal.

"If you cause a disturbance you'll frighten Michael. Think about him," he said grimly.

"I do think about him!" she snapped, taking the brandy so swiftly, a little sloshed out. She gulped it down and coughed, and he wondered if she was accustomed to drinking. He drank his.

She lowered the glass to study him. "You're his father, aren't you?"

"Yes. And you're not his mother."

A stricken look crossed her features, and she bit her lip, all her anger vanished. "Are you going to tell him tomorrow?"

"No," he answered, hurting, wishing suddenly that this was Marilee with him, wishing that he had them both back, something that would never be.

"Why haven't you told Michael?" Claire asked in surprise.

"Because I love him," Fortune said hoarsely, his anger at her returning. He gained control of himself. "Michael needs to get accustomed to me before he learns I'm his father. I don't know what you've told him."

"I told him his father died very early in the war, that his father was very brave and fought for the Confederacy."

"That's going to make it damned hard. I'm a colonel in the United States Army. Or was. I was discharged last week."

"When are you going to tell him I'm not his mother?"

"I don't know. I won't rush."

"But you will tell him," Claire said bitterly. "Why did you have to find him now after all this time? I love him and he's like my child. I've protected him and taken care of him." Knowing she was losing Michael, she fought back tears. She had never expected to have the father confront her. Now he would tell Michael the truth, and Michael would know that she had lied to him all these years about being his mother.

It hurt and terrified her. This dark, powerful man wanted to take Michael from her. And when he did, he might as well put a knife in her heart.

She remembered that night in the stable when she had found Marilee O'Brien, who had taken shelter from the storm. Marilee had begged Claire to take care of her tiny baby. She could barely murmur the words, gasping a plea to Claire to protect him. And when Claire asked whom to protect him from, all she heard was one syllable, a whispered part of a name that sounded like the first syllable of *father*. Claire had guessed father, and one of the men pursuing her had talked to her employer, telling that Trevor Wenger, the father of the dead mother, was after the child, so she had assumed that Marilee had said father. Yet with her mumbling, it could have been the first syllable of *Fortune*.

Colonel O'Brien reached out to turn her face toward his, staring at her as tears brimmed over and ran down her cheeks. She jerked her chin away from his fingers. As she glared at him, she felt a chill down her spine. He could be the man Marilee had been fleeing from. He was a formidable man and overpowering. She was acutely conscious of his bare chest and arms. A chain of gold hung on one wrist, and she wondered why he wore it. She had never been alone with a man in an intimate situation like this and never with one who was enraged with her.

"Will you let me stay with him for a while longer?"

"Yes, for now. I'm a stranger to him. I want him to like me and trust me before I change his world. But I want my son back. I've waited six long years."

"I didn't take him from you! And I love him! And he loves me! He doesn't even know you," she cried, trying to keep control of her emotions, hating to let him see how badly she hurt.

"One more glass of brandy," Fortune said, pouring another glass. "You won't be intoxicated on two glasses," he said as amber liquid splashed in the goblet.

"Where are you taking us?"

"Back to Atlanta and unfinished business."

"Atlanta, Georgia?"

"Yes. Drink the brandy."

She wanted to throw the brandy in his face, but it was important to avoid frightening Michael unnecessarily, to wait and cooperate until she had the right opportunity to escape. And she knew it was not going to be easy with this man.

She gulped down the second glass and set it on a table with a loud clink. "Now, I've done what you asked. I'll sleep in a chair by Michael."

She started to flounce past him, but he caught her arm and spun her around. She pushed against him, beating on his chest. He yanked her up, holding her upper arms tightly, almost lifting her off her toes.

Claire's heart thudded as she was pressed against his bare chest. His blue eyes blazed with anger, but she lifted her chin and gazed back at him defiantly.

"No, you're not sleeping in there, where you can take him and go." His strong arms picked her up with ease, and he tossed her down on the bed.

Claire tried to lunge at him, to get off the bed, but he caught her wrists, yanking them high. He wrapped his handkerchief around one wrist and tied her to a brass rail at the head of the bed. Her heart pounded. He was going to rape her. If she screamed, it would only bring Michael.

"You bastard," she whispered.

He tied her other wrist with a piece of rope from his pocket, and then he stood over her. Her heart thudded as he reached out. He caught the covers and lifted her slightly to turn them down and then pulled the sheet up over her to cover her.

Shocked, she stared up at him.

"I told you, I intend to sleep," he said flatly. "And I'm sleeping in the bed with you. I've been traveling for days to find you. I don't want your body. I want my son."

She blinked and drew a breath, and his gaze ran down over her breasts as if contradicting his words. "What will Michael think if we're here together?"

"He's too young and innocent to give it a thought," he answered dryly.

"And what if Michael comes in and finds me tied?"

"I can't trust you. Does he often roam at night?"

Michael slept like a hibernating bear, but she didn't want to tell Fortune O'Brien. "Sometimes."

"You're a damned poor liar," he said, moving away from the bed. He extinguished the lamps and opened the door, going to look at Michael. She heard a steady scrape and guessed he was pushing a chest in front of the door to the suite in case Harwood tracked them down.

When Colonel O'Brien returned to the bedroom he hung his gun belt over the head of the bed, letting it slip down where he could get it instantly. Silver moonlight played over the ripples of his muscles, and she lay still, her heart beating wildly in uncertainty about what he would do next.

She was aware of the shift of the mattress as his weight came down upon it. Every nerve felt raw. She was tied to the bed, only inches from a man who despised her. She knew nothing about men, and she was acutely aware of him. She turned her head. Fortune O'Brien's chest was rising and falling, covered in a mat of black curls that made her pulse jump in a strange way. She had never known a man, never become friends with one, never been kissed by one.

Her gaze went back over him slowly. Hard muscles bulged in his chest and shoulders and arms. The mat of thick black hair again arrested her, making a warmth start in her body, creating strange feelings she hadn't experienced before. His stomach was flat, his long legs stretched out. She felt perspiration dot her brow; the room was hot, the bed a small space. Only inches separated her from him. He shifted, his face turning toward her, and she looked at thick black lashes over his cheeks, a mouth that was well defined with a full lower lip. What would it be like to be kissed by him?

Blushing furiously, she turned her head to stare at a window, seeing stars twinkling in the dark sky. In moments, though, she looked at him again. Had Marilee O'Brien been warning her against a father or had she been trying to say Fortune? After watching him tonight with Michael, she thought it had to be the father, not this man.

Colonel Fortune O'Brien, Michael's father! She would lose Michael unless she could get him away from the man beside her. But would it be right to take Michael from his father?

He shifted and she turned, feeling a stab of fear. He moved restlessly on his side, his arm sliding over her, and she drew a deep breath, her skin prickling. Frightened, she looked at him to see his chest rising and falling evenly and realized he was still asleep and unaware he was holding her. His skin was smooth and cooper-colored except his jaw, which had a dark stubble. Thick black hair curled in a tangle over his forehead, and she was aware of his arm across her, his leg over hers. Her body was growing hot, her skin tingly, conscious of every point of contact with him. What kind of man was this Colonel Fortune O'Brien? How soon would he take Michael from her?

Chapter 7

Claire stirred, her arms feeling stiff. Groggy, she shifted and opened her eyes. For a moment disjointed thoughts swirled in mind while she tried to think, remember what town she was in. She started to stretch and felt her wrist jerked back.

Her memory returned instantly. She raised her head, yanking at her wrists, recalling the wild night, Michael and his father. Twisting, she looked at her hands tied to the brass rails of the bed. She turned her head, her gaze sweeping the room, stopping at the image in the mirror as she looked into Fortune O'Brien's eyes. He was bare-chested still, his jaw lathered, a razor in his hand as he shaved. He seemed intensely masculine and overwhelming.

"I'll be out of here in a few minutes and you can dress. I'll take Michael downstairs and we'll have lunch. He's still asleep."

"What are you going to do with us?"

"Take you with me. We have to lose Harwood first."

The razor slid down his jaw, and she felt her cheeks heat with embarrassment. She had never been around men, and it seemed incredibly personal to be tied to a bed and watch him shave. If it disturbed him to have an audience, he gave no indication. Calmly he performed the ritual of running the razor over his jaw, then dipping the razor into the washbowl. She looked away, but in seconds was curious enough to watch again. He wiped his jaw clean and dropped the cloth. For a second time she noticed the gold-link bracelet circling his wrist and wondered about it.

He dried his hands and crossed the room to her. As his gaze swept over the length of her, for the first time she became aware of her disheveled state. Her hair was down, her dress hem up over one bare knee. She eased her leg back beneath the covers and looked up modestly at him.

She saw the smoldering anger in him while sparks crackled between them. She wanted to scream at him that she didn't want him to take Michael from her. Instead she clamped her lips closed and watching him, wondering what he intended. He continued to watch her carefully as he reached out to untie her right hand. She was conscious of his warm fingers brushing her wrist, of his nearness, his bare chest and slim hips so close to her. His physical presence made her acutely aware of him and of herself. As he leaned across her, she looked up at the curly black hair spread across his chest. Intrigued with him in spite of her fear, she drew a deep breath.

"Why did you take him from the orphanage?" he asked in a low, tight voice as he straightened and looked down at her.

"Your wife asked me to take care of him," she replied and saw a flash of pain cross his features. In spite of everything else, she felt a moment of compassion for him, because he must have loved Marilee.

"Why had she run away from you?"

"She didn't," he said, his hands resting on his hips. "Her father didn't want us to be married, and he took her and Michael from me. He was on his way back to Atlanta and their plantation when she got away from him." Colonel O'Brien looked out the window, and a muscle worked in his jaw. He looked as if he hurt badly, and Claire felt a strange mixture of emotions. She didn't want to feel sorry for the man who would take Michael from her. Suddenly she wished they weren't discussing what had happened so long ago, because she had a feeling that with every word she was losing Michael. She couldn't take him from a father who loved him deeply. She tried to stop thinking about it, to hold back her tears. They would mean nothing to this man who was so angry with her for taking his child.

He turned back around and stiffened. "Why are you crying?"

"Why do you think?" she exclaimed. "You'll take Michael from me."

"He's my son. He's not your child and he never was," Colonel O'Brien said with the hardness of steel. "Marilee didn't ask you to keep him from me."

"She asked me to keep him from someone. I don't know if she was trying to say 'Fortune' or 'father.' "

His chest expanded as he inhaled deeply, and she was conscious of how close he stood, of her helplessness, and his anger.

"She was trying to say father. We loved each other," O'Brien snapped. Irritated, he reached down to untie her other wrist.

As soon as she was freed of her bonds, the colonel moved away. While she sat up in bed and rubbed her wrists, he picked up his shirt and yanked it over his head, buttoning the neck. Sucking in his breath, he tucked the tail into his trousers. She felt a blush creep up as she watched him dress and knew she should look away. She turned her head to stare out the window, listening to him move around the room.

"I'll take Michael downstairs to eat. At any sign of trouble, meet us at the livery stable," he said, crossing the room to her as she sat on the side of the bed. He tilted her face up, his fingers lightly touching her jaw as his blue eyes seemed to bore into her. "Just remember, Harwood wants Michael. He'll take you and use you if he can, but he doesn't really care what happens to you. And he wants me dead."

Fortune leaned closer to her, his fingers still under her chin. "Harwood is a hired killer. He was hired by Marilee's father. I don't want my son with a man like Harwood, and Michael is not going back to that bastard Wenger."

She nodded, relieved they were on the same side at least on this issue.

"Don't let him take you hostage. I'll sacrifice you for Michael."

She drew a deep breath, looking into eyes as cold as a frozen lake in winter. "I believe you," she snapped, jerking her chin away.

"You better join us in eating, because we'll have a hard ride ahead of us."

He picked up his gun belt and buckled it around his waist. The leather was cracked in several places, as if it had seen hard use, and she wondered about his years in the war. She could imagine him on a battleground and suspected he had been a courageous leader. "I'll have Michael. Don't try anything because it won't do you any good and it'll only hurt Michael."

"You wouldn't hurt him—"

"Of course not, but I don't think it will help him to see me hurt you," he said bluntly.

The strain of the past hours suddenly came to a head. Without stopping to think, she lunged at him, her fingers curled, hitting him in the temple. Catching him by surprise, she sent him staggering back.

She came at him, but the moment she grabbed the revolver from his holster, he shoved her back, throwing his weight against her. He pushed her onto the bed, his weight holding her down while he pinned her arms over her head.

"Don't fire it! You'll only frighten him, and you're not going to hurt me."

She wriggled, struggling to get away, enraged with him. "Damn you!"

He scooted up, straddling her with his knees. In a flash he released her left hand and yanked the revolver from her.

As he climbed off the bed, she came up, wanting to rush past him, refusing to give in to tears in front of him. He caught her arm and spun her around. "Tears?"

"You'll take Michael from me!"

"You took him from me a long time ago," he said harshly, both of them breathing raggedly.

He released her and jammed his revolver back in the holster. Striding across the room, he didn't glance back as he opened the door and closed it behind him. She could hear his deep voice as he talked to Michael. She covered her face with her hands and cried quietly, feeling desolate, knowing that all too soon she would lose Michael forever.

Finally she moved to the pitcher, tossing out the water he left and pouring some fresh water into the washbowl. She dampened a cloth and washed her face to clean and get ready for the day.

At the entrance to the hotel dining room, she gazed about the dark wooden tables set on a white tile floor until she found the colonel and Michael near the window. The two sat facing each other, and Michael was laughing at something his father was telling him. Fortune was a strange name, and as she studied him, he smiled at Michael. When he did, his features softened and he looked handsome and appealing. And she could imagine that someday when he was grown, Michael would look very much like him.

Her heart seemed to lurch against her ribs at the realization that now she wouldn't see Michael grow up. How permanently would Fortune O'Brien separate her from Michael? Would she ever be allowed to see him? When Michael learned the truth about what she had done, would he forgive her?

Shoving aside the questions and worries, she forced a

smile for Michael's sake. She was aware of her rumpled appearance in the wrinkled blue calico she had slept in, but the pink gingham was torn, so she had little choice. As soon as Michael looked up at her, Fortune O'Brien turned and pushed back his chair and stood up.

"Good morning," he said, motioning to a waiter and holding a chair for her.

"We've ordered and I was telling Michael about army life." She sat down as a waiter appeared and handed her a menu.

"Order a hearty lunch because we'll be traveling a long time today, and the fare may not be as good," the colonel said pleasantly. He was courteous and polite, and she recognized that he was being careful in front of Michael.

"Mama, Mr. O'Brien is Colonel O'Brien in the United States Army."

"I know, Michael."

"He's a Yankee."

"I've tried to explain to him that Yankees aren't always bad," Fortune said lightly.

"We're from southern families, so Michael has been raised to favor a southern view."

"Now he's expanding his understanding of the conflict—if anyone can understand it."

"Mama, Colonel O'Brien had a mule he had to ride in one battle, and he said the mule didn't like to hear the guns fire, so he kept running away. Colonel O'Brien said he finally gave up and fought on foot."

She smiled at Michael, whose eyes sparkled, and glanced at O'Brien, who was watching his son with an expression of warmth that would melt ice. The pang she experienced was quick and stabbing. When a waiter came to take her order, she suddenly had no appetite.

Her meal had hardly been served when Colonel O'Brien said quietly, "Let's go. Michael, we need to leave now." He was looking outside and she followed his gaze. She drew a sharp breath. Across the street, with his arm in a sling, Harwood stood outside a saloon. Gazing up and down the street, he looked at the hotel. He stepped off the boardwalk and started across the street.

Colonel O'Brien and Michael were already hurrying toward the counter, where he paid for lunch. Frightened all over again, she joined them at the door, and they hurried across the lobby and climbed the stairs. At the top she glanced down at the empty lobby, feeling the old familiar panic at having to run. Just then, though, her gaze swung around to the colonel. This man, this battle-hardened colonel, was going to protect them this time.

Hurrying to their suite, they gathered their few belongings swiftly.

"There are back stairs. Let's go that way." O'Brien took her arm and Michael walked beside them, carrying his small satchel.

They rushed outside into the dusty alley. Turning a corner, they paused outside a general store while the colonel went inside to send a telegram to Pinkerton's to inform them about Eisner's death. As soon as he finished, they hurried to the livery stable where they had left the bay and the wagon. Colonel O'Brien talked to the owner, and shortly she realized he was buying two horses.

"Take what you need from the wagon. We're leaving it here."

"You can't leave my wagon!" she snapped. "Do you know what that cost me?"

"We can travel faster on horseback, and we'll be able to avoid Harwood more easily if we're mounted. The wagon stays."

"You can't do that!"

"I'm doing it," he said, his blue eyes implacable.

"That wagon cost me months of work."

He eyed her severely before turning abruptly to find the owner again. In minutes he was back. "Mount up. Take just what you need. I paid a deposit and told him you'd be back for your damned wagon."

She lifted her chin, refusing to thank him for something she didn't want to do in the first place. In a few minutes they had the satchels attached and their bedrolls fastened, all the gear they could easily take secured, and they mounted. She longed for a riding outfit and hooked her knee over the saddle horn, knowing as soon as they got out of town she would ride astride, because she didn't care how unladylike she looked.

"You're heading south?" she said as the horses turned onto the street.

"I want to try to throw Harwood off the trail. We'll ride south and then turn east. I may not be able to lose him permanently, but I can shake him off for a while."

She rubbed her upper arms and looked at Michael, who was looking up eagerly at the sky, his eyes sparkling and eager for adventure.

All that afternoon they rode hard, and she was proud of Michael for keeping up. At times she forgot all the terrible things hanging over her and enjoyed the beautiful day. Michael was brimming with enthusiasm about the sights they passed. Together they spotted two foxes, a deer, and two small brown bears when they stopped once to drink from a stream. When they slowed, sometimes Colonel O'Brien rode beside Michael and spun another tale. Michael's laughter sounded marvelous in the stillness of the countryside. As she watched man and boy together, she knew that even if she had the chance, she shouldn't take Michael from his father. Fortune O'Brien was good with the child, patiently answering his questions, taking time to point things out to him, laughing in tune with him. It hurt to watch them together because she knew Michael belonged with him, and she wouldn't be able to change or stop what was happening.

When they camped for the night, they built a fire, and Fortune took Michael to hunt something for dinner. She heard two blasts of his gun and they returned with rabbits. She watched as he carefully showed Michael how to skin them and get them ready to cook on a spit. At first Michael's brow furrowed, and she expected him to refuse to watch, but he glanced up at Colonel O'Brien's intent face and then down. In another moment he was nodding and paying attention to what he was told.

The man's regard did not extend to her. As she cooked the rabbits, she looked up to catch Colonel O'Brien staring at her. The hardness in his glacial blue eyes sent a chill down her spine. It occurred to her that out here in the wilds, he could easily kill her when Michael was asleep and he would solve his problems. The boy would grieve, but time would heal the loss.

Dinner was as delicious as the repast at the hotel, yet she couldn't eat a bite. While the fire burned low, O'Brien showed Michael his pistol, holding it in his strong hands, telling the child how to load and fire, finally handing it over. As Michael's small hands turned the big revolver, her dislike for guns filled her with disgust. Yet at the same time, she knew he might be better off knowing how to kill and skin animals. She watched their two heads bent together, father and son who looked so much alike that only a small boy like Michael didn't notice it.

By the light of the fire she sewed a patch on Michael's shirtsleeve. The night became misty and cool, and she was aware of the darkness surrounding them. If Colonel O'Brien was worried, he gave no indication. He talked easily to Michael. He hobbled the horses while they each got their bedrolls. When Michael had to relieve himself, though, Colonel O'Brien did go into the woods with him. He was not taking any chances, no matter how slight.

Finally Michael was curled in his bedroll, sleeping across the dying fire from her. Her uneasiness increased because the more time that passed, the more likely that Colonel O'Brien would get rid of her. Anxious, she sat on her bedroll with her knees drawn up, a blanket around her shoulders. She watched the colonel kneel by the fire, poking it with a stick. When he moved back, he sat down beside her, leaning back against a tree, one leg bent at the knee. She studied him, thinking he looked relaxed.

"Don't you worry about Harwood slipping up on us?"

"No. We've ridden hard all day. We're well off the road, and he can't track us tonight. I think we're safe."

She glanced into the darkness and rubbed her arms. "I don't feel safe."

He stared into the fire, and they fell silent. A small log broke and fell, sending a shower of orange sparks drifting skyward. The faint smell of woodsmoke tinged the air. She glanced at the dark pines and hackberry trees surrounding them. The blackness beyond the small ring of light from the fire would hide anyone or anything.

"Tell me about that night and Marilee," he said quietly, and she turned her head to look at him.

"I found her in a stall in the barn. I had gone out to check on my horse and heard her—" She broke off, remembering she had heard Marilee moaning. She took a deep breath. "I looked in the empty stall—"

He leaned forward, his blue eyes compelling. "What did you hear? You started to say something and you stopped."

She bit her lip, knowing if he had really loved Marilee, a description of that night would hurt him. Yet why should she care? He was a hard, tough man who was going to hurt her more than anyone ever had or ever would.

"She was moaning," Claire answered quietly. He stood abruptly and turned away, striding to the edge of the circle of light. As he stood with his back to her, she realized he couldn't control his emotions about his wife.

Once again, in spite of all else she felt a wave of sympathy for him. He must have loved his wife and baby terribly to agonize like this after all this time. Yet her gaze came to rest on the revolver on his hip. What would he do once he had pumped her for what she knew about his dead wife? Would he then proceed to kill her?

Without thinking it out, Claire rose to her feet. She rushed across the distance to grab his revolver. Her fingers had just touched the grip when he spun around.

Her fingers closed around the revolver, yanking it from the holster. He pushed her, his hand closed like iron around her wrist and shaking the revolver free as he rushed her back into the trunk of a tree. He pushed up against her, his one hand holding her wrist, his other pinning her arm to her side.

She gazed into his stormy eyes and felt her heard thud. "Don't kill me where Michael will know," she whispered.

He frowned, his scowl like a lash. "I don't intend to kill you."

"What are your plans? I know you won't let him go with me."

"No," he answered, studying her. She became aware of his hard length pressed against her. Only inches separated her face from his.

"What are you going to do?" she insisted.

"You're going to tell Michael the truth. He has to know that Marilee was his mother and I'm his father. You can stay with us while he gets accustomed to the truth, but at some point you'll have to go." He paused, and his grip eased slightly. "But I don't intend to kill you. If I were going to do that, I would have long before now."

"It would be easier out here," she whispered, barely able to talk. She looked away, suddenly not caring because she hurt so badly. When he forced her to tell Michael the truth, she might lose Michael's love. Whether she lost it or not, Fortune O'Brien would take Michael from her and she couldn't stop him.

Colonel O'Brien abruptly released her and moved away. Picking up his revolver, he strode back to the fire. As he knelt to poke it, she saw his pants pull tightly over his muscular legs, remembering the power in his body as he had grabbed and held her.

Feeling helpless, she returned to sit on her bedroll. After a moment he stood up and moved around the fire to stand over her. "Finish what you were telling me about Marilee. You found her in the barn."

"She had a baby, and she said she had to get home," Claire said, seeing his jaw tighten. "I told her I would get a doctor, and she tried to stop me. She said to take care of Michael. She told me his name was Michael O'Brien. She didn't want me to leave her."

"Was she hurt?"

"She was ill. She was coughing, her voice was raspy." The scene came back more clearly as she remembered. "She shook with cold, but she was burning to touch." Colonel O'Brien ran his hand across his eyes, and groaned. "I ran to get Papa, and when we returned to the barn, he said she was dead. He gave me Michael and we went to the house while he sent a servant to fetch Dr. Aikens."

She paused, staring at the fire and remembering that eventful night, with all the house servants up and Dr. Aikens and Papa and her brother, Roarke, talking about the baby while she made him a bed in her room and sat rocking him all night, holding him in her arms.

"Papa posted flyers about Marilee in the city, and they called Mr. Hopkins with the newspaper and he ran an article about her, but no one showed up. Papa buried her in the cemetery where my mother is buried. He and Dr. Aikens felt she might be from a well-fixed family because of her clothes." Claire's gaze shifted to him.

"I wanted to keep Michael and argued with Papa. He had an older friend, a widower, Franklin Hosford, who wanted to marry me. I didn't want to marry Mr. Hosford," she said in a tight voice, remembering that time in her life. "He had had five sons by his first wife before she died. Papa insisted he wouldn't want a stranger's baby. Papa didn't want the baby and wouldn't listen. He took Michael from me and placed him in the orphanage."

She met Fortune's steady gaze, but his features were

impassive, and she couldn't guess what he was thinking. "I didn't want to marry Mr. Hosford, and Papa was on the verge of announcing our betrothal. I couldn't bear to think of Michael in that orphanage. It came to me to run away. I knew Papa kept gold in his office in the bottom drawer of his desk. I packed a bag, got things for a baby. One night when Papa had gone to play faro, I took part of the gold and went to the orphanage. I told them we had found the parents and Papa had sent me to fetch the babe."

"They didn't question you?"

"Why would they? They had too many children to feed as it was. Papa was an upstanding member of the community. There was no reason to doubt what I said." Claire's voice was vibrant now. "I had all night to get a head start on Papa. I went south to Columbia, and then I turned and left the main roads. I had taken one of Papa's buggies. I made it to Wilmington on the coast and caught a boat headed for New Orleans."

"It didn't matter to you that your father would have been sick with worry?"

Annoyed, she looked at Fortune. He had no right to pry into her business like this. Yet she wanted to talk about her father, wanted someone to know how she had felt. "If I had stayed, I would have had to marry Mr. Hosford. Besides my father and I were not that close. I have an older brother, and he always favored my brother."

"Evidently he's had a change of heart, because Pinkerton's was hired by your father to find you. I hired Eisner to find Michael."

"Mr. Eisner told me my father hired him."

"No, he didn't. There was another Pinkerton's agent hired to find you."

"Well, in any case, I didn't believe him. I can't imagine, after all this time, my father trying to find me. I'm sure Mr. Hosford married years ago."

"I talked to Eisner in St. Louis, and he told me your father is in ill health and wants to find you to make amends."

She drew a deep breath, looking into the dark night. How many times as a child had she wanted her father's love and he had brushed her off? She turned her head. "What about the grandfather who wants Michael?"

"He's a powerful, wealthy man. He was cold and harsh with Marilee, determined to destroy our marriage. He wants Michael badly, but he isn't taking my child from me. And I have an old score to settle with him."

His features were harsh, his voice quiet and deadly. She felt a cold spasm of fear for Michael, who would be caught between these two men.

"How did you manage to marry if he was so opposed to it?"

"She had gone to Baltimore to visit his sister, Mary Louise, her widowed aunt. That's where we met, and I had Mary Louise's approval. She thought her brother was cold and uncaring where Marilee was concerned. And like your father, Trevor Wenger intended Marilee to marry someone he had selected, a wealthy older man."

Fortune seemed to be looking through her, as if gazing into his past. "Marilee and I were both so young. We were seventeen," he said, his voice becoming mellow with a tone she had heard him use with Michael. "We loved each other very much," he added.

"You were fortunate," she said, looking at the dying fire, embers glowing orange. "I've never known that kind of love and never will."

"Never will? You don't know."

"I'm a spinster now. I'm twenty-three, too old for marriage." She face him again.

"I'm twenty-five," he stated, and she paused to stare at him. He acted and looked so much older, yet she supposed the war made many men seem older.

"Besides," she continued, "I've been dependent only on myself for all these years now. I don't ever want to be dependent on a man as I was with my father. He ruled my life completely."

"What had you planned to do?" Colonel O'Brien asked, anger returning to his voice. "Were you going to keep shuttling Michael around all his life?"

"No. I've been saving money in a northern bank. With just a little more, another year's savings, I planned to take the money and go back to a city in the northeast, Philadelphia, New York, Boston. I intended to open a bonnet shop and take a new identity."

"Why did you keep Michael's name? You could have easily given him another."

She met Fortune's gaze. "I liked your wife. She seemed brave and so alone."

He looked away, his chest expanding, and she stopped talking, knowing she had said enough for him to realize why she had kept Michael's name.

"His name is Michael Hanlan O'Brien. My father was Hanlan O'Brien."

"That's a nice name. Michael Hanlan," she said, glancing at the sleeping child, knowing she would always think of him as her own son.

As the fire burned down to gray ash and smoldering embers, Fortune studied her, mulling over what to do with her. He couldn't get rid of her yet because Michael wasn't accustomed to him. What's more, his opinion of her had changed. She was brave and intelligent, and she had kept Michael from Trevor Wenger and out of an orphanage all these years. He had to admit to a grudging respect. If Trevor Wenger had traced Marilee's trail and brought her body home to bury in the family cemetery, he would have found out that Michael was in the orphanage.

Even knowing all Claire Dryden had done for Michael, Fortune couldn't shake the rage at her taking his son all these years. Had he been with Wenger, Fortune would have discovered it that first year and he would have gotten Michael back when he was a baby.

Feeling torn between the anger she stirred and the knowledge that she had been good for Michael, he stared at her. She met his gaze, her dark brown eyes wary. She expected him to kill her, and he could understand why she would think he might.

"I'll give you the amount you would have made in a year," he said finally. "That way when we part, you can take the money and go east and open your bonnet shop."

She came to her feet, her eyes flashing. She advanced on him and stopped, her fists clenched and her feet apart. "You keep your money! I don't need to go east and open a shop if I'm not trying to hide Michael. You mean to take him from me when he has been my whole life for all these years. I've been with him every single day. Now you're going to make him hate me and send me away. I don't want one cent of your money!"

She turned away, striding into the darkness. He let her go, knowing she would be back. He hadn't meant to offend her. She had fought like an angry cat to keep her wagon, so he knew money was important to her.

When she returned, her eyes and nose were red. She sank down on her bedroll and finally glanced at him. "How long do I have?"

"A while yet," he said, knowing it was no real answer.

Fortune watched her as she smoothed out her bedroll. Her brown hair was down, tied behind her head. She had led a strange, lonely life if it was true what she said and what Eisner had reported. Fortune found it difficult to believe she had sung in saloons and hadn't taken any men to bed. Every saloon singer he had ever known was willing and eager to spread her legs. Yet he knew Pinkerton's did a thorough job, and they had said there were no men. His gaze wandered down the length of her, remembering her lush breasts, her tiny waist.

She turned and sat down, facing him again. "How can you sleep? Harwood could slip up on us in the night."

"I'm not going to sleep for a while yet, and as I told you, I don't think he has picked up our trail yet."

"Why are you going back to Atlanta if the grandfather is there?"

"I have things to settle with him. And he'll keep hunting Michael. He'll find out through Pinkerton's and Harwood what happened. He won't give up searching for Michael."

"No, he won't. How do you intend to fight Wenger if he's as powerful as you say?"

"I want to ruin him, to run him out of business, because that's the most important thing of all to him. Sooner or later we'll face each other across pistols. I could have challenged him already, but that seems too easy for him after all he's done."

She rubbed her arms, frightened at this sort of talk. She reached behind her head to untie her hair, letting it swing free across her shoulders. He felt his breath catch. It was a rich brown, tumbling over her shoulders and back in a silken cascade that framed her face. Claire Dryden was a beautiful woman, and he found it impossible to think she had led the solitary life she claimed.

Feeling exhaustion overtake him, his muscles aching from long days in the saddle, he stood up and unfastened his neckerchief as he crossed to Claire Dryden. She looked up, instantly wary and coming to her feet. He caught her wrist, so slender that her bones seemed fragile.

"Lie down," he ordered quietly. "I'm tying you up so I can sleep. You're the most likely one to slit my throat. Lord knows, you look as if you'd like to."

She glared at him, staring up, her dark eyes filled with anger. "Michael will see."

"You'll think of some explanation. Or you can tell him the truth now and get it over and done," he said harshly.

Suddenly she grabbed his shirtfront and yanked him close. "Why do you have to take him from me?" she asked, her luminous eyes brimming with tears that caught on her long lashes. "Let me be a nanny or something. Let me stay close to him."

"No," Fortune answered flatly. "You took him from me. I would have had him back long ago if it hadn't been for you. Do you know how much I've missed getting to do with him? I've missed watching him grow all those early years."

"Whether you like it or not, he loves me and you're going to hurt him."

"You're going to hurt him when you tell him the truth." He wound his hand in her hair and jerked her face up closer to his. "But you'll tell him the truth. He's my son and he's going to know it." Fortune released her head abruptly. "Now lie down."

Looking as if she might spring at him again she eyed him a moment before she released his shirt. When he dropped her wrist, she stretched out on the blanket. He came down to lash her arm to the tree, knotting the handkerchief quickly, too aware of her full breasts so close he could easily brush them with his palm.

Turning away, he yanked off his shirt and wiped his brow with it. When he turned back, he found her looking at his bare chest, and her gaze flew up guiltily to meet his. Her cheeks became pink, and he wondered what she had been thinking.

He sank down on his bedroll and stretched out, his revolver in his hand. "You can sleep. When I get tired, I'll wake you and you can watch."

"Suppose I won't? Suppose I make a deal with him?"

"He's a cold-blooded killer. Don't forget that."

She watched him settle and in minutes she stretched out, sleep coming quickly.

When she stirred, it was the first gray light of day and Fortune was stripped to the waist, standing by a tree with a mirror propped on a branch while he shaved. Her gaze roamed over him, and she felt a flush of heat at being so bold.

Crossing to her with lather still on his jaw, Fortune knelt down and untied her. He smelled clean and soapy; his chest was inches above as he leaned over her. She looked at his thick chest curls and felt heat rise in her.

"Get dressed," he ordered, straightening up. "I'll cook something, and we'll get Michael up and go. If you hear any strange noises, let me know at once."

"We'd be safer if I could carry a gun."

He gave her a cynical look and turned away, leaving her alone while he finished shaving.

A half hour later, strips of beef fried in a pan. She shook Michael and he came awake, rubbing his eyes. He stood up, his denim pants rumpled, his chest and feet bare. He turned to walk into the woods away from their camp. "Mama, I need to—"

Just then Claire saw the snake coiled in front of her child.

Chapter 8

"Mama!" Michael's cry was high and shrill.

Without hesitation Claire ran between Michael and the snake. As she looked wildly for a stick, the snake lashed out, striking her skirt swirling in front of her legs.

The blast from a gun sent birds flapping from the trees. She looked at Fortune, who had his revolver poised as the snake fell limply, shot through the head.

She spun around to hug Michael, who threw his arms around her waist. Trembling, he clung to her tightly, his head buried against her.

"Are you all right?" Fortune asked her.

"Yes," she answered, feeling breathless, her knees quaking with fright.

"It was a rattler," Fortune said, crossing to kick the snake into the brush. He stood looking at her hugging Michael while he placed his revolver back in his holster. She had been willing to risk her life to protect Michael. She had acted without thought, on pure instinct, and Fortune realized the strong bond between them that might hurt Michael irreparably if damaged.

"As soon as he calms down, we need to eat and go. The sounds of that gunshot will carry a long way."

She met his gaze solemnly and nodded her head. "Michael," she said, gently extricating herself from him. "Are you all right?"

"Yes, ma'am."

"We should hurry and leave here."

Within a quarter of an hour, they were mounted and moving through the trees, still headed south. At noon they stopped near a river to water the horses and eat. Michael helped the colonel unsaddle the animals and see to their feed, following his father around the campsite. O'Brien was patient with him, teaching him calmly, talking to him as he would another adult. Claire felt a pang as she watched them together; Fortune O'Brien was good for Michael.

As they sat down to eat, she asked, "When are we turning east?"

"I want to go to New Orleans," he said quietly, but she could hear the firmness in his voice.

"New Orleans will take days!"

"Yes, but I want Harwood off my trail for a while. In New Orleans I'll book passage for us on a boat heading west to Galveston. I want Harwood to think we've gone out West. I'll also book passage on a boat to Mobile or Apalachicola, and we'll head back toward Atlanta."

"My wagon is waiting. If we don't go back the way we came, I can't get it."

"I'll write him to sell it, and I'll buy you another damned wagon."

"Fine," she said, frustrated. She couldn't work. While they traveled, she couldn't get a job and earn money. Yet at the same time, she suspected that as long as they were traveling, the colonel would allow her to stay with them. And earning more money for savings suddenly seemed so empty without Michael as part of her plans.

"What's wrong?"

His question startled her, for she didn't realize she had given any indication of her feelings. "I was thinking about my savings. It doesn't seem important any longer."

Michael wolfed down his lunch, and soon was up and wandering along the river, examining different rocks.

"Do you know how to swim?" the colonel called out to him.

"No, sir."

"How about I show you a little about swimming?"

Claire looked nervously at the wide river nearby. It was swift and muddy, and the sight of it gave her chills. She had never learned how to swim, and her brother had almost drowned once.

She stood up swiftly. "Michael, you go on, I want to ask Colonel O'Brien about our plans this afternoon."

"Yes, ma'am," he said.

"Does he have to learn to swim?" she asked, suspecting she couldn't change the colonel's mind once it was made up.

"He'll be safer if he knows how. As it is, he can drown. Do you know how?"

"No! and I don't intend to learn."

O'Brien shrugged. "Whatever you want, but I want Michael to know how. I won't let him drown."

"I know you won't, but you might frighten him."

"I won't frighten him as much as he'll be frightened if he falls in someday and doesn't know what to do," he answered firmly.

Here was another clash she could tell she would lose. And in a way, she knew that he was right. "Just remember he's a little boy. He isn't big and tough and fearless like you!" she snapped.

A hint of amusement flared in his eyes. "I'll try to remember," he said dryly, and she felt foolish.

He pulled off his shirt and hung it on a branch. Muscles rippled in his back as he untied his neckerchief, and she felt a strange, unaccustomed fluttering as she watched. He was fit and healthy, his copper-colored skin taut over sleek muscles. She looked at the crisscrossing of white scars across his back and wondered who had given him the whipping. He strode away, the gun belt riding low on his slender hips.

"Colonel O'Brien?"

He turned to look at her, and her eyes widened at the

bare chest covered with dark hair, his flat stomach, the pants riding low on his hips. She jerked her gaze up, her face flushing. "Suppose Harwood rides up. I have no defense, no way to warn you."

"Scream. I'll be close enough to hear you."

And you don't care if he takes me prisoner, she thought angrily.

Colonel O'Brien walked away leisurely, as if they had no one after them. He had fought all through the war and was a high-ranking officer, so she suspected he was aware of the risks of stopping. She tensed as he led Michael out of sight. But then it dawned on her that they would be swimming in the nude.

She glanced at the river, wishing they would get back soon. Hot and alone, she sat down to pull off her black cotton stockings and her shoes, wiggling her toes and pushing a stray tendril of hair back in place in the braid wound around her head.

It was an hour later when she heard noises of someone coming. She stood up swiftly, her pulse speeding up.

"Mama!" Michael's high voice carried clearly and she relaxed.

"Yes, Michael?"

He ran into sight. He was shirtless, his hair a tangle of wet curls, his eyes dancing with delight. "Mama, you should see me! I can swim!"

"No!"

"Yes, I really can. Next time come with us and watch me. Next time we'll wear pants, and you can come watch. All right, Colonel O'Brien?"

"Yes, it's all right," he said lightly, striding up, watching her to see her reaction.

Flustered, she turned away and busied herself with packing up the last of her things. She wanted to avoid letting him see her blush as she thought about him swimming nude with Michael.

"We're refreshed now. If you'd like to go down to the

river, I can show you where it's shallow and you can wash and cool off."

She looked again at the wide, muddy channel and felt the old fears rise. At the same time, it was blazing hot.

His hand closed on her arm. "Come on," Fortune said, lightly tugging on her arm. "You'll feel better and it's perfectly safe."

"C'mon, Mama!" Michael said, tugging her other hand.

She nodded and walked between the two of them until Michael dropped her hand to run ahead. "You're very good with him."

"I love him," he said quietly.

She glanced again at the river. "I'm afraid of water. Is this shallow?"

"Yes. There's a place where it's little more than ankle deep."

"That's what I want. I don't like muddy water."

"Yet you stepped in front of that snake without hesitation."

"That was to protect Michael."

He nodded solemnly as he studied her, his eyes full of speculation. Soon they stepped out of the trees. Sunlight sparkled on the water, and Michael danced on the bank. "Can I wade?"

"Yes," Fortune answered easily before she could.

"Do you want privacy or will you feel better if we're here?"

She looked at the water and shook her head. "I'd rather you'd stay for a few minutes. You're certain it's shallow?" she asked and watched as Michael pulled off his shoes, rolled up his pants, and waded into the river.

A familiar rush of fear engulfed her as she gazed at the brown surface. Michael waded with water over his ankles, splashing and running out into the middle.

"C'mon," a deep voice came at her elbow. Colonel O'Brien took her arm, and she was instantly conscious of his gentle touch. He had pulled off his boots and rolled up his pants. He paused. "Take off your shoes."

"They're off," she said, holding up her skirts. He glanced down at her bare feet and led her into the water. For a moment she panicked and clutched his arm, seeing the muddy water swirling around her. Still, the water felt blessedly cool and she relaxed. That's when she realized how tightly she was holding him, and she released his arm at once. She blushed as she looked up at him. "Sorry."

He looked at her seriously. "Will you be all right? We'll leave you alone and you can wash."

"I'm all right," she said, still uncertain, as if with any step she would sink out of sight. "You're certain all this is shallow?"

"Yes, as long as you stay right here. Michael, let's leave her alone."

When they were out of sight, she waded back and forth, relishing the cool water. Finally she slipped her dress off, wading out to pull off her underclothes and get back in the water to wash, wondering if she would be as muddy as the water. It was cool on her skin, and as she sat down in it, she tried to curb her imagination about what was below the opaque surface.

When she returned to camp, they mounted up and rode until long after dark. After eating roasted rabbit and settling Michael in for the night, she set about getting her own bedding ready. Finally she sat down on her blankets with her mending. Michael lay asleep between them, all of them near the dying fire with the horses picketed within yards.

As she sewed a tear in Michael's denim pants, one of the horses whinnied sharply. All of them began snorting and pawing the ground. Dropping the sewing, she edged toward Michael while her pulse raced.

Colonel O'Brien yanked his revolver from the holster and started toward the horses. A black shadow shifted and she saw a raccoon. The colonel waved his hand, scaring it away, and it went lumbering into the darkness.

Her gaze shifted and she saw his rifle, the stock protruding slightly from beneath his bedroll. Claire yanked it up, swinging it up and cocking it as she aimed at him.

He spun around, the revolver still in his hand.

"Drop your gun," she said softly.

He let it fall to the ground immediately. "You and Michael can't get away from Harwood without me," he said softly. "And I'm not going to let you take my son from me again." He took a step toward her.

She raised the rifle higher to aim at his heart. "You stop. Stay where you are."

"No, I won't," he said grimly. "You know I love him. If you pull the trigger and gun me down here, you won't be able to live with it. And he'll see what you've done." All the time O'Brien talked, he steadily advanced toward her.

Her heart pounded and her palms became damp. Now, when she had a gun, was the time to take Michael. This was her only chance. He continued toward her and she stood stiffly watching him, her finger on the trigger.

"Stop or I'll shoot. It'll be your doing. I'll tell him you threatened me."

Without hesitation, his blue gaze cold, Colonel O'Brien took another step toward her and another. Her pulse roared in her ears, but she could not fire.

With a sweep of his arm he hit the rifle, sending the barrel pointing skyward. His arms wrapped around her as he jerked the weapon from her. His face was inches away. "You can't kill me. You know how much I love him, and you know he's beginning to like me," he said, grinding out the words.

"I wish I could shoot you," she said, feeling tears spill over her cheeks. They stared at each other, both breathing hard. His gaze lowered to her mouth and the moment changed. The fierce struggle became another kind of clash, and she could feel it. His hard body was pressed against hers. His arms were around her. His eyes were filled with male curiosity. Heat blossomed on her cheeks, and she could barely get her breath.

"They said there haven't been any men in your life," he said in a hoarse whisper, studying her.

"There haven't been!" she answered.

He bent his head. She tried to turn away because she didn't want to be kissed. His arms tightened, and his mouth covered hers, his lips firm on hers.

Startled by the pressure, by the sensations he caused, she stopped struggling as much. His lips moved on hers, brushing hers lightly, rubbing over hers in a warm, sensual friction that vanquished her resistance. Her lips parted, and a drumming of her heart started as she relaxed in his arms. His tongue touched her lips, and she felt as if a flame had licked within her. Startled, she looked up to find him watching her through narrowed eyes.

With a silky wetness his tongue went into her mouth, an invasion that was more than physical, that seemed to shatter the wall of isolation she had kept around herself toward men, and she felt faint from the sensations that swept over her. She protested briefly, a slight moan that died in her throat. Her lashes came down and she closed her eyes, drowning in new sensations. This was what it was like to be kissed! She had been kissed sweetly by James Thornton one time when they rode together and once by Haskell Whitmarsh, and each time it had been chaste, lips barely pressed against lips. Never had it been like this, with his tongue probing deep into her mouth until she felt as if she would faint.

Heat started low in her body, flowing through her while her pulse drummed wildly. His tongue played over hers, sliding slowly over the inside of her lower lip. She moaned, barely aware she had made the sound, when her tongue touched his.

Finally he raised his head, looking down at her, his

crystal blue eyes as unfathomable as ever. "You've never been kissed, have you?" he asked softly.

"No," she answered, "not like that."

He bent his head, his mouth brushing hers again and then settling on hers while he kissed her slowly, his tongue moving over hers. She should make him stop instead of letting him do whatever he wanted, yet she didn't want him to stop.

With a quick movement he placed the rifle on the ground and shoved it away with his toe. He shifted his body, his arm sliding beneath hers, banding her waist to draw her up against him again, and she felt his manhood press against her with a shocking hardness.

She pushed away, stepping back, blushing furiously. "We should stop. I'm not experienced at that sort of thing." She was embarrassed, her heart pounding violently, and underlying her uncertainty was the knowledge that she had liked his kisses, liked them more than she would ever have dreamed possible.

"You'll take him from me and I can't stop you," she said, pushing past him and walking into the darkness, finally stopping to place her hands over her face and cry quietly. She was crying because she would lose Michael, because it no longer mattered whether she could get a gun or not because she would never shoot Colonel O'Brien and he knew it. And she was upset because she had liked his kisses. She wanted him to kiss her again.

She wiped her eyes and turned around to go back. He was seated with his back against a tree trunk, his rifle nearby, the revolver still buckled on his hip.

Flustered, more conscious than ever of him as a handsome man and aware of her disheveled appearance, she sat down cross-legged, the skirt of the calico billowing around her. She began to take down her hair.

"I've been thinking about Harwood," O'Brien said. "If he comes in the night, you take Michael and run. He's after Michael, and he won't shoot you if you keep Michael right with you."

"What about you?"

"I'll stay and fight him."

"What if I take Michael and get away from you?"

"I'll find you," he said, looking at her, and she knew he would.

She nodded. She felt more intensely aware of him since he had kissed her, wondering what he thought about her. She glanced at him, surprised to find him studying her. "Do you have relatives or parents in Baltimore?" she asked. "Does Michael have grandparents there?"

"No. My parents are dead," he said flatly. "I have three brothers. My two older brothers, Rafferty and Caleb, are married. Rafferty lives in New Orleans and Cal lives in Memphis. Rafe is a cotton factor and Cal is a railroader. My younger brother, Darcy, divides his time between them. He hasn't been with me much because of the war."

"Were all of you born in Baltimore?"

"No, Ireland. My father gambled away everything we owned and my mother's health was terrible, so we came to the United States, hoping it would be better for her. Off the coast the ship went down, and she drowned."

"That's dreadful," Claire said, frowning as she studied him. Her fingers unwound the long braid pinned around her head. "My mother died of pneumonia when I was seven years old, so I know the loss hurts terribly. Were the rest of you picked up by another ship?"

"Yes, but different ships. We were separated in the storm when the ship sank. It was years before we got back together. I ended up in Baltimore and intended to go south to look for my brothers, but then I met Marilee and I had a good job in shipbuilding. Shortly after we married, we knew Marilee would have a baby, so I didn't get to the South until after the war had started and I was fighting."

While he talked, answering her questions about his

family, he was assessing her. She had told the truth about never being kissed. She was an innocent. Knowing it shouldn't really matter, but he was relieved all the same because he hated to think of Michael waking up to find different men in his mother's bed all these years.

Fortune watched her comb out her hair with her fingers. Finally she shook her head, and the dark hair swirled across her shoulders. He drew a deep breath, remembering her lush curves against him, her soft mouth beneath his, the quick response to his kiss.

"Do your brothers have children?"

"Only Rafferty, who has a girl and a boy. Darcy isn't married, and he works for Cal."

"My brother and I aren't very close. He's twelve years older than I am. By now I'm certain he's married. He probably helps Papa run our place. We raise cotton. Although the war may have changed everything at home."

"Eisner didn't say anything about your family being ruined by war and your father was able to hire Pinkerton's, so he must have come through all right."

"That seems so long ago. I don't think about home often, and I've never missed it."

A twig snapped somewhere nearby and Fortune stopped listening. He felt a prickle across the nape of his neck. He slid his hand to his revolver, his gaze searching the dark.

"I'd think you would have missed your home terribly when you first left it," he said, listening for any other strange sounds. The snap had been to her right, to the east. He kicked dirt on the last of the fire, and she looked up at him with a questioning gaze.

She leaned forward, watching him intently. He made a motion with his hand indicating he wanted her closer. She looked down at Michael, feeling O'Brien must think they were in danger.

"Michael may need a cover," she said, moving close to him.

"Your childhood must have been happy," O'Brien said casually, continuing their conversation.

"It was in some ways, in others, I was lonely. Roarke was older and we weren't close," she answered, trying to keep up the conversation. He slid his rifle to her and she looked up at him, surprised that he would trust her with his gun.

As his gaze drifted about, she felt a prickle on her spine. "My brother was always busy trying to learn how to run the place. We raised cotton," she said, trying to continue to talk in the same tone. She glanced down at Michael, ready to throw herself over him to protect him. Remembering Harwood, she shivered with loathing.

When she glanced back around, she was startled to find Colonel O'Brien was gone.

Chapter 9

Trembling, she looked around. A harness jingled and she heard a horse snort. Someone was moving through the trees toward her. She yanked up the rifle and took aim.

Leading their horses, now saddled, the colonel came into view. His hat was pulled low and she couldn't see his eyes. The horses swished against the brush, and their hooves made small thumps as he approached her. Letting out her breath with relief to see him, Claire lowered the rifle.

"Mount up. I'll get Michael up with me," O'Brien whispered, leaning close, his warm breath fanning on her ear.

She held out the rifle, and he placed it in the scabbard fastened at the rear of his saddle. He lifted Michael with ease and swung up into the saddle, placing the sleeping child in front of him and holding him upright against him. With her back prickling, she mounted, knowing how vulnerable they were. Every sound seemed magnified, yet the steady deep bass of frogs and chirp of crickets were reassuring sounds that made her feel no one was close.

They moved away at a walk, going through the trees, and she wondered how the colonel knew where he was going. He seemed as at home out in the wilds as he was in a hotel room. Claire looked around at the tall trees and vines. The creak of their saddles and their horses moving through the thick underbrush were noisy in the quiet night. How did Fortune O'Brien know so unerringly that he was headed in the right direction?

He moved slightly ahead of her, his wide shoulders a dark silhouette in the night as he sat straight in the saddle. She rode up closer beside him, feeling as if Harwood could emerge out of the darkness at any moment.

At the edge of a stand of pines, while they were still in the shadows, the colonel reined in his horse and shook the boy. "Michael, wake up." He stirred and looked up at the colonel.

"We need to escape in a hurry," O'Brien said in a calm voice that sounded as if they were going for a sprint for the sheer pleasure of it. "I'll put you on your horse, and we're going to gallop across that field."

"Yes, sir," Michael answered sleepily, and she regretted that he had to be put in danger. And she knew that Colonel O'Brien hated it as much as she did.

Ahead a grassy expanse was bathed in moonlight, and it would be easy for anyone to see them. The next line of trees was over half a mile away.

As soon as Michael was seated, O'Brien looked at her and raised his arm. "We're headed south. We'll be in the open, and I want you to go as fast as you can. Stay low over your horse, and if there are shots, don't stop."

"If something happens to you, I'm supposed to ride away and leave you? Don't be ridiculous—"

"You'd try to save me?" His brows arched, in his expression a fleeting look of curiosity.

As she gave it thought, she knew she would. In the dark she was uncertain whether she glimpsed a mocking amusement in his expression or not. And then the moment was gone.

"You get Michael to safety," he said under his breath. "I'll take care of myself. Are you ready to ride?"

"Yes, I'm ready." Wondering how far behind Harwood was, she glanced back over her shoulder at the darkness.

Colonel O'Brien moved closer to Michael, touching his shoulder lightly. "Ready to ride fast?"

"Yes, sir."

"Don't stop for anything and stay close to your mother."

"Yes, sir," Michael whispered, nodding his head.

O'Brien looked at her a moment, and then he slapped his horse, urging it forward. They surged into the open, racing across the rolling ground at breakneck speed. She leaned low, holding her horse back to let Michael ride between them. Wind whipped her skirts and her hair, tangling it and blowing locks of hair around her face.

The horses were lathered when they finally reined in close to a stand of oaks. O'Brien twisted in the saddle to look back. "You two ride ahead." He dismounted to place the rifle in her hands. "Try to keep going in the same direction. I'll wait here for a while."

Her pulse jumped. She would have Michael to herself. She looked past O'Brien over the open terrain they had just covered. By waiting, the colonel could see if Harwood was coming after them. Her gaze ran across the field to the tall pines beyond it. Was Harwood in the trees, gazing back at her, determined to get Michael?

"How will you find us?"

"I'll find you," the colonel answered. He sat facing the field, watching for Harwood. With a tug of the reins, she turned her horse and they moved beneath tall trees. In moments she knew they had to be out of Colonel O'Brien's sight. Yet now that she was away from him, it was as impossible to ride away from him as it had been to pull the trigger of the rifle.

"Michael, I love you," she said suddenly, reaching over to squeeze his hand.

"I love you, Mama," he answered, as he always had. His voice was filled with trust, and she longed to pull him close and hug him.

"Michael, whatever happens, I want you to always remember that I love you more than anything else and I have since the first moment I held you in my arms when you were a tiny baby."

"Yes, ma'am. Is someone after us now?"

"Yes, there might be."

"We're safer with Colonel O'Brien, aren't we?"

"Yes, we are," she answered, trying to keep her voice light so Michael wouldn't realize she was crying.

"Mama, he's nice. I hope he stays with us."

"He will, Michael."

"Does he have any family?"

"His wife died a long time ago, and he loved her very much. His mother and father have both died. He has some brothers."

"That's too bad about his wife." Michael looked at her. "Maybe he'll marry you," he said, sounding hopeful.

"No, Michael. He said he won't ever marry again." Fortune had said no such thing, but she had to get the notion out of Michael's head that Fortune might marry her. The colonel was just biding his time to get rid of her. He wouldn't even allow her to be his nanny. He couldn't keep her from living in the same town, though, where she would get a glimpse of Michael. In that moment she decided she would open her millinery shop in Atlanta.

"I hope he stays with us a long, long time."

She rode in silence, wondering if they were going straight, if Colonel O'Brien really would be able to find them. She looked overhead, not familiar enough with cross-country travel to know the stars or how to tell in which direction they were going.

Dawn finally came, the sky growing lighter. Tiny drops of dew caught the sunlight and sparkled on green oak leaves. They had ridden through the night and she was exhausted. She was also worried about Michael, who was slumped slightly in his saddle. She hadn't heard gunshots, but there could be a long distance separating her from

O'Brien, perhaps too much now for her to hear if he did fire at someone.

Finally at mid-morning, she stopped beside a meandering, muddy trickle in a wide stream bed. "Michael, let's wait. We may be hopelessly lost. The horses need to water and be fed. We need to eat."

"Yes, ma'am," he said, climbing down from the saddle.

She unsaddled the horses and let them drink from the stream while she carried their things beneath the shade of a tall hackberry. She spread a brown blanket and placed a cold repast of biscuits, slices of pink ham, and a jar of thick purple damson jam. She peeled an apple and cut it into thin slices.

As they ate, Michael looked at her. "Do you think Colonel O'Brien is all right?"

"Yes, I do. He fought in some terrible battles during the war. He's fine," she said, not only to reassure Michael but also because she truly did feel that Fortune O'Brien was a match for Harwood.

In the coolness beneath the spreading branches, Michael stretched on the blanket and in minutes was asleep. She watched a yellow butterfly swoop over wildflowers, waiting, wondering what they would do if they had lost Fortune O'Brien. Yet soon fatigue overcame her as well. She stretched out on the blanket, gazing at blue sky and green leaves overhead until her eyes started to close.

She snapped upright at the sound of hoof beats. Quickly she reached for the rifle. She saw a shadowy figure moving through the trees, and then she recognized the familiar wide shoulders. Relieved, she replaced the rifle on the blanket as Fortune O'Brien rode out of the trees and dismounted, leading his horse to water. He glanced at Michael, who was stretched out asleep, his black lashes a dark shadow on his rosy cheeks.

"Nothing wakes him short of shaking him, does it?"

"Not easily. What happened?"

"It's Harwood. I never did see him, but he's after us. I

thought maybe we could stay far enough ahead of him to lose him, but we haven't. We'll get into Pineville tonight if we ride hard."

"Do you want to eat?"

"Yes. You've ridden all night," he said. "Go ahead and sleep for a few minutes."

She nodded, feeling safer now that he had joined them. She stretched out, glancing at him to find him watching her. "What about you?" she asked.

"I'll sleep tonight."

She closed her eyes, sleep coming at once.

Fortune stretched out, closing his eyes, wanting just a few minutes' sleep. He knew Harwood had to be more than an hour behind them, but he couldn't risk staying in the open during daylight too long. He would have to face Harwood and fight it out. Otherwise they could be slipped up on. His gaze wandered down the length of Claire, and he felt a stirring of desire as he looked at her curves and tiny waist. The blue dress draped over her, outlining her long legs.

Wiping perspiration off his brow, he settled back, feeling the scratchy wool blanket beneath him as he closed his eyes, going to sleep almost instantly.

Within the hour they were mounted and heading south again. They rode into Pineville that night, and he checked them into the hotel, taking two rooms that were comfortable with chipped mahogany furniture and a rag rug on the floor.

They gave Michael a bed in one room, and the colonel left her alone while she bathed in a tin tub of warm water. Relishing the chance to wash, she sank back, her long hair swirling in the water around her. With reluctance she finally stepped out to dry and put on the blue calico dress. As she brushed out her hair, she heard a light rap on the door.

"Michael's asleep," Fortune said, entering the room. "We won't have to worry about Harwood tonight, and we can get some sleep. I won't touch you, but I want to sleep on a bed."

She stared at him as he yanked his shirt over his head. She left, going to Michael's room to give the colonel privacy.

In ten minutes the door opened, and he motioned to her. She crossed the room, and as soon as she stepped through the door, he closed it behind her. "I'm finished bathing," he said, facing her. His wet hair clung to his head, ringlets curling around his face. Water still glistened on his shoulders, and she couldn't keep her gaze from lowering to look at his broad chest.

"You could put Michael in here and take the sofa or give me the sofa."

"No. This way I'll know where you are and what you're doing."

"If I had wanted to run away with Michael, I would have today."

The colonel studied her, his head tilted to one side. "Why didn't you? I expected you to."

She walked away, running her fingers along the edge of a table, feeling a small chip in the dark wood. "I know Michael needs you."

"I hope you're telling the truth."

She glanced around, feeling a flash of annoyance at his reply. "If I hadn't felt that way, I would have run with him today."

"Not if you didn't know where to go," he answered with a cynical note. "You were in the wilds. You couldn't have gotten far without getting lost. You had already started heading west instead of south."

She clamped her lips closed and looked at the four-poster bed. She walked around to the far side of it, turning her back to him. Feeling self-conscious, worrying because in minutes he would be only inches away, she lay down.

The lamp went out, and the bed jiggled and sagged

with his weight. She lay as far on her side of the bed as possible, her fingers touching the cool sheet beneath her. It was miserably hot in the room in her dress and underclothing. She inched her skirt higher until it rested just below her knees, certain he was unaware of what she was doing.

He shifted, jiggling the bed, and she was acutely conscious of him, feeling the warmth radiate from him.

"Lord, it's a hot night," he said in a husky voice.

"Yes, it is," she answered stiffly without turning to look at him.

"Miss Dryden." Hearing her name spoken in his deep voice stirred a tingle in her. "Tell me about Michael. Anything you remember when he was a baby. I missed all of that. I didn't see him get his first tooth or take his first step or say his first word."

She turned her head, emotions warring in her, feeling anger that he wanted her to share all those moments with him when he was going to take Michael from her forever.

"He cut his first tooth when he was eight months old, and he began to crawl before that. By the time he was nine months, he could move around by holding onto things. I remember that time. I worked for a milliner in San Antonio, and I would take him to the shop with me. He was into so many things. We made a little corner and placed a desk and a cabinet so it blocked him into a small space. She had five grown children, and she brought some wooden toys for Michael to play with. It was a couple of months after that when he could toddle around without holding on."

"Do you remember his first word?" he said. She felt the bed creak again and glanced at him. He leaned off the bed, stretching his long arm out to reach a table to pick up a paper fan. Moonlight played over the muscles in his back and arm, and she drew a deep breath. The gold link bracelet on his wrist held a dull sheen in the moonlight.

He lay back and she turned to look up at the ceiling

while he waved the fan and stirred a welcome breeze over her.

"That feels better." She felt him shift again and glanced at him. He lay on his side facing her, his head propped on his elbow while he fanned them.

"Do you remember any first words?"

"Yes," she said, looking at the ceiling, more conscious than ever of the colonel lying next to her. Yet he didn't seem aware of her. All his curiosity concerned Michael.

"He said mama before he started to crawl. I remember when he first started saying it," she said, recalling the moments when he was so tiny and his first smiles would give her thrills of joy. "I know he was just babbling and making sounds, but it was marvelous." She turned on her side to face Fortune, suddenly forgetting her self-consciousness, momentarily lost in memories. "Michael was beautiful. Everywhere I went, ladies would come up to me and tell me what a beautiful baby I had. And he was always so happy. He hardly ever fussed. When he started saying mama, he began to make other noises within days."

"How'd you provide for him?"

"I took some of my father's gold when I ran away—"

"I wondered what you did."

"And I worked and we lived in small rooms," she said defensively. "He didn't know the difference when he was a baby. And he's always seemed happy wherever we were. The owner of a house where we rented a room in San Francisco had a shaggy mongrel dog. Michael loved that dog, but one afternoon he got my shears and cut its hair. There's no way to describe the haircut Michael gave him, but the dog didn't seem to mind and it grew back out." She laughed, remembering, and then saw Colonel O'Brien smiling as well.

Suddenly she forgot what she had been saying. His broad shoulders, his strong body, lay only inches from hers, and the awareness disturbed her.

She rolled over and scooted away from him. "I'm sorry you missed all that."

There was a long moment of silence and she lay still, her heart racing while he still fanned her. "Michael reads well for such a young child. You must have taught him."

"Yes, but he took to it easily. I wanted him to be educated, and there was no chance to stay in one place long enough to send him to a school," she said quietly, turning to face the colonel, seeing a faint frown.

"That will all change, and he's quick and intelligent. I think you did a fine job teaching him," Fortune said.

"Thank you," she answered, feeling pleased and surprised.

He rolled onto his back, tossing away the fan. She glanced at him. "Colonel, why do you always wear that bracelet?"

"Call me Fortune." He lifted his arm, turning his wrist, dark hairs curling over the bracelet. He didn't answer, yet he was studying the bracelet, so she knew he had heard her question.

"It was Marilee's. I had it made for her and it was something she left behind. I had some more links put in it so it would fit me because until now it was all that I had of her except memories."

Feeling another surge of sympathy for all he had lost, she turned her head and stared at the ceiling. He didn't move, and in minutes she glanced at him again to see his chest rising and falling evenly.

She couldn't sleep. She had enjoyed talking to him in the intimacy of the darkened room, talking about Michael. With a pang she longed for all she had missed, for a husband and family and for things she would never know—a man's loving, kisses, her own children, the companionship of long, quiet talks with someone she loved. She heard Fortune's deep breathing, and she turned to look at him again.

He was bare-chested, the denim pants low on his hips

as he slept. His body looked powerful, male, overwhelming.

Perspiration beaded her forehead as she remembered all too clearly being held against him while he had kissed her. Just the thought of his kisses started a fire in her. She licked her lips and wondered what he had been like with Marilee. Had this hardened man ever been charming and carefree and loving?

Trying to stop the unbidden memories and images, Claire turned her back to him. She slept only fitfully, though and woke at dawn.

They ate early in a nearby roominghouse. Over steaming cups of black coffee and plates of sausage and eggs, Claire looked out through a window at the wide street as it filled with people and wagons and horses. Sunshine and a blue sky made danger seem less threatening, and the presence of so many people was reassuring. She thought about traveling again, the dark shadows in woods hiding attackers. "Wouldn't it be better to face him in town?"

"He'd just wait for the right opportunity to strike. We're better off getting supplies here and moving on."

This made sense, and she nodded. She also realized that if they stayed, she'd be sharing the same small hotel room with him night after night.

"Mama said you don't want to marry again ever," Michael said suddenly as he studied Fortune. O'Brien's gaze swung from Michael to her. His blue eyes bored into her a second and then shifted back to Michael.

"No, I don't," the colonel answered.

"She said your wife died."

"Yes, she did."

"My daddy died too."

Claire held her breath, waiting for Fortune's reply.

"That's what I was told," he finally said, giving her another hard look. "We should go. I want to go to the store for supplies. If there's anything you or Michael need, let me know. We'll go there on our way to the livery stable.

Michael, the man who is following us is the man who tried to take you that night out of Natchez. Would you recognize him if you saw him again?"

"Yes, sir."

"If you see him at any time, let me know at once."

"Yes, sir."

"I told Michael a long time ago that it's his grandfather who sent those men to get him. He knows that his grandfather wants to take him away from me," Claire said in a tight voice.

"Just watch for Harwood. Both of you."

Fortune paid the bill, and they went upstairs to get their things. As soon as he paid the clerk to have their baggage carried to the livery stable, he took Claire's arm and Michael's hand to steer them toward the front door of the hotel.

"Isn't that incredibly extravagant?" she asked in a low voice. "We can carry our own things."

Fortune glanced down at her, wondering how difficult her life had been in trying to provide by herself for Michael. "We'll have flour and rope and supplies to carry."

As they stepped outside, he glanced up and down the street. As he did, he noticed Michael searching each face as well. Fortune swore under his breath, wanting to be rid of Harwood, to get Michael home to Atlanta so he could live a normal life.

They walked across the wide, dusty street to a general store. After buying staples, Fortune purchased hard candy for all of them. Michael smiled as he accepted it. "Thank you, sir."

He held out a piece to Claire, who studied it and finally took it. "Thank you." She placed it in a pocket. "I'll save it for Michael."

Again Fortune wondered about her. From what she had said, he guessed she had grown up well fixed, and he knew her manner of living must have changed drastically for the worse when she ran away with Michael.

When they mounted up with their meager supplies and possessions packed on their horses, he told her, "Both of you ride out ahead. I'll trail behind."

She nodded, and as soon as they were out of town, he let them get half a mile ahead, where he could keep them in sight yet could see if anyone was following them. All day he pushed them, and by late afternoon they rode through a low-lying area filled with cypress. Claire Dryden kept her head held high, and he realized that she was frightened by the swamp. To Fortune's satisfaction, Michael showed no fear, but an engrossing interest in everything around him.

That night they camped on a slight rise. Only yards away, the land disappeared beneath still water, and when he had the horses unsaddled, watered, and fed, he cut a long branch from a tree to use as a fishing pole.

"Michael, we'll catch something for supper."

"Should you do that?" Claire asked, staring at the murky water.

"That swamp is filled with things we can eat."

She shivered, rubbing her arms. "It looks as if it might be filled with snakes and gators."

"I've got my Colt and my knife. I'll be right beside Michael. You can see gators coming, and we're not wading into the swamp. Let's go, kid."

By the time they returned, Claire had a fire going. Fortune sat with Michael, showing him carefully how to handle a knife and clean the fish, finally placing them over the fire. As he watched his son with his head bent over the cooking fish, the urge came more strongly than ever to pull Michael into his arms and hug him and tell him he was his father. He glanced up to find Claire Dryden watching him. She looked away quickly, and he knew she was worried about how soon she would lose the child. Michael moved away from the fire, sitting down to pull off his shoes and stockings, wiggling his toes and taking a bite of apple from a bowl.

When the fish were cooked, as Fortune was eating, Claire glanced at him. "Are you still getting a boat to Mobile?"

"We can catch a boat to Mobile or to Apalachicola and then go straight north to Atlanta."

Michael sat with his bare feet toward the fire. He finished eating and stood up to carry his plate to place it in the bucket to wash. Suddenly he screamed and jumped, hopping on one foot.

Fortune came to his feet instantly, tossing his plate of food to the ground as he ran to Michael. He stomped on a long centipede, yanking Michael up.

"My foot stings! Mama!"

Fortune set him on a log and tried to get his foot still to look at it. "Michael, let me look."

"No! Mama! Mama!"

Kneeling beside him, Claire hugged him. "What was it?"

"A centipede bit him," Fortune answered while he tried to pat Michael and quiet him. "Michael, let me look at your foot."

"No!" he sobbed, clinging to Claire.

"Michael, let us see," Claire said quietly, stroking his face and wiping away his tears. He quieted, and Fortune turned his foot, looking at the ugly red welt on the bottom.

"If I draw out some blood and cauterize that, he'll stand less chance of infection, but it'll hurt."

"Michael, you heard what he said. Let him take care of your foot."

He buried his face against her, crying while she nodded at Fortune.

Hating to hurt Michael for any reason, yet knowing it was the best way to get the wound to heal quickly, Fortune moved to the fire to heat his knife. While the blade lay in the burning sticks, Fortune removed a bottle of brandy from his saddlebags. "Michael, take a big drink of this so it won't hurt so badly."

Michael burrowed closer against Claire, holding her tightly. She patted him. "Michael," she said in a patient voice, "drink some of this and it will help your hurt."

He raised a tear-streaked face and drank from the bottle, coughing and sputtering. "I don't like it."

She looked at Fortune, who nodded, and she turned back to Michael. "It'll keep you from hurting so much. Take another big drink."

"Mama—"

"Please, Michael."

He drank and coughed and drank again, handing the bottle back to Fortune, who replaced the cork.

Fortune got his knife, looking at her. "Michael, this is to help you heal. It's going to hurt."

"Yes, sir" came a muffled reply.

Gritting his teeth, Fortune sliced into the cut and clamped his jaw shut as Michael cried out. Fortune uncorked the brandy and poured it over the wound. Bending down to suck out the blood, he spat it onto the ground. Finally he poured brandy on it again.

"I'm done, Michael," he said while the boy clung to Claire and whimpered. "It's all over except wrapping your foot." Hunkering down, he worked quickly, wanting to take Michael in his arms and soothe him. Finally he reached out to turn Michael to face him. "You'll be better now."

Michael nodded and flung himself back to hug Claire. She picked him up and sat with him on her lap. Crooning softly to him, she held him in her arms like a baby, his long legs dangling off her lap. In minutes he was asleep.

Fortune cleaned the dishes and put things away, getting out the bedrolls and getting ready for the night. As he worked, he studied them obliquely. Michael needed Claire, depended on her. Within days they would reach New Orleans, where he had intended to buy passage for

Claire to any eastern city of her choice and give her enough money to get started in her own business. He paused, studying her holding Michael, singing softly to him as she stroked his hair back from his face. She had asked if she could remain a nanny and he had refused, wanting to break all ties in his rage, wanting her out of their lives. Yet Michael loved her and needed her.

Fortune hated to acknowledge it, but it was obvious how close they were. Michael obeyed her without question, and he turned to her when he was hurt.

Fortune crossed the campsite to them. "He's asleep. I'll take him," he said, leaning down to lift Michael into his arms easily. He knelt and placed the child on his blanket gently, smoothing his hair from his face. "I hope he forgives me for hurting him."

"He will. He'll be reasonable tomorrow. I shouldn't have let him take his shoes off."

He stroked Michael's hair and finally stood up. Fortune kicked out the dying fire and replaced his knife in his boot. Claire had pulled out sewing and had her head bent over it.

"Night's coming."

"I know. I can barely see what I'm doing," she said without looking up.

He looked at the swamp, the dry area opposite where they had just traveled, and he moved to his belongings. He gathered clothing from his saddlebags, carrying it to a tree where he knelt to stuff his coat with the other clothing. He glanced at Claire and found her watching him.

He pushed clothing into a sleeve, filling out the coat. He propped it against a tree trunk, balling up a shirt on top of it and then placing his hat on top of the shirt.

"That won't fool anyone," she said quietly.

"In the dark it'll resemble me."

"What good will that do if we're being watched?"

"I don't think we're being watched now. But he may catch up with us before the night is over. When it is good and dark, I'm going to move Michael to your blanket and stuff some clothing on his blanket to look like someone sleeping."

Fortune retrieved his rifle and crossed to squat beside her, handing her the weapon and talking softly. "You keep the rifle, and you stay close to Michael. You'll be safe that way. I'm going to circle around. I'll be out there in the dark."

He moved away, picking up Michael and placing him gently beside her. He went back to bundle more clothing on Michael's blanket, and she tossed him her sewing, letting him roll it into a mound. When he removed his spurs and drifted into the darkness, she felt goosebumps rise up and down her arms.

Fireflies flickered, tiny bright spots in the night, and the deep croaks of a chorus of frogs were loud. She felt alone and she placed her hand on Michael's shoulder as her gaze roved constantly over the area. The water of the swamp was complete blackness now, impossible to see, and she wondered if there were gators close at hand.

She cocked the rifle, wanting it ready to protect Michael. She sat down, looking at the stuffed coat and hat. It would fool no one if they came close, but perhaps in the distance in the dark it would look like Fortune sitting against the tree.

"I'm tired. I think I'll go to sleep early tonight. This makes me think of times at home long before the war when I was just a girl," she said brightly, wondering if Harwood was near, if her steady patter would convince him Fortune was her audience. She rambled about her childhood, talking in the silence, her finger on the trigger of the rifle.

Amid the deep bass of frogs sounded a jingle. It was faint, but she had heard it. She remembered Fortune removing his spurs. She inhaled deeply, her ears straining to hear, her eyes sweeping the area. It was impossible to see anything more than a few yards away. Tense, she waited, and then she heard another jingle. Hairs prickled on her neck and arms.

Suddenly there was a whispering sound and a solid thunk. She looked at the stuffed coat: a knife was embedded through it into the trunk of the tree.

She jerked up the rifle, coming to her feet as two shots rang out and pieces of the coat flew into the air.

"Lay down the rifle, missy, or you're dead" came a cold voice out of the darkness, and she recognized Harwood as he stepped into view. He held a revolver pointed at her.

Chapter 10

"Don't hurt us," she said, placing the rifle on the ground and raising her hands.

"Get the kid awake. You're going with me now."

"Harwood." Fortune's voice came from somewhere to her left.

Harwood spun around, his revolver blasting into the night while she saw a flash from Fortune's gun. She raised the rifle as Harwood fell.

"Mama?"

"It's all right, Michael," she said, keeping the rifle pointed at the inert figure on the ground. With a rustle Fortune emerged from the trees with his revolver in his hand.

The moment he knelt beside Harwood, Michael stood up and she pulled him close against her side.

Fortune glanced at her. "Harwood's dead. We don't have to worry about him ever again. Let's saddle up and take the body to the next town. Michael can ride with me, and I'll put the body across his horse."

She nodded, patting Michael's shoulder. "Are you all right?" she asked Fortune.

"My hat has a new crease," he answered lightly as he thrust his revolver into his holster.

In a quarter hour they were packed up and moving. She was relieved to know that Harwood was no longer a threat, and she was dazed from the confrontation. It had happened so swiftly. Within minutes she saw Michael had slumped against Fortune, and she realized he had fallen asleep again.

"Thank goodness he wasn't wide awake, and it was dark through all that. He's never seen a man shot in front of him before."

"When we get to Atlanta, he won't have to see anything like that again."

"You don't expect any violence from Trevor Wenger?"

"I expect him to try. I don't expect him to succeed."

Fortune's voice sounded hard and cold, and she wondered how much of a struggle lay ahead and how it would affect Michael.

"Are you positive you can't work out something agreeable with the grandfather? There's no reason he should object to your keeping Michael."

Fortune's head swung around. "He objects to me to the point of wanting me dead. He's the one who gave me this lashing. He hoped it would kill me. He hates me for marrying his daughter and taking her away from the wealthy man he had planned for her to wed."

Shocked, she stared at him. She understood that a father could be so determined and callous to his daughter's feelings, because hers had been that way. Yet she was unable to fathom a person who would want to kill the man who was the father of his grandchild. She flinched as she remembered the scars that crisscrossed Fortune's back.

"I'm a Yankee, I married Marilee when in Wenger's opinion I had little to give her in the way of money. He despises me. And his reasons for wanting Michael are selfish. Anyone who cared for a child would never hire a killer to go get him."

Agreeing with this last, she rode in silence. What kind of monster was Trevor Wenger? How could such a man have blood ties to Michael?

They rode into a small Louisiana town in the early hours of the morning. The street was empty except for light from a saloon. When they reached the sheriff's office and jail, the place was locked. Fortune reined in and dismounted carefully, lifting Michael down from the saddle. "If you'll wait here, I'll find the law."

She dismounted and sat on the boardwalk while Fortune knelt down to place Michael by her with his head in her lap. She looked at Fortune, whose face was close to her own. "Tired?" he asked.

"Yes."

"You should have been in the Confederacy. You'd have learned to sleep in the saddle."

She smiled, wondering if some of his worry had eased now that he was free of Harwood.

"I'll walk down to the saloon and see if I can find a lawman to take the body. And I'll get us a place to stay."

"That would be very nice, Colonel, because I don't feel like getting back on my horse."

He got the rifle out of the scabbard and placed it beside her. "Just in case someone comes along and bothers you. Fire it, and I'll come on the run." She watched him go, his long legs covering the distance easily on the hard-packed dirt street.

The street became quiet. She leaned her head against a post, fighting sleep. In minutes she looked up and saw him leave the saloon with a stocky man at his side. The two walked down the street and out of sight in the darkness. They returned with a third man. Struggling to stay awake, she watched them approach.

"Sheriff Laville and Edwin Pogue. This is my wife, Mrs. O'Brien, and her son, Michael, who is asleep."

"Pleased to meet you, ma'am, but sorry it's under these circumstances. Let's get this done."

The men went to haul Harwood's body inside the office, and she closed her eyes.

"Claire."

She opened her eyes. With his hat pushed to the back of his head, Fortune O'Brien knelt in front of her.

"There's a roominghouse down the street that belongs to the sheriff's sister, and we can stay there."

She nodded and took the reins of their horses while Fortune picked up Michael. "When we get there, I'll carry him upstairs and get him settled. Then I'll come back to tend to the horses."

"I can take care of the horses."

"No. You stay with Michael."

She wasn't going to offer again, feeling as if she might fall asleep on her feet. A light burned in a two-story Victorian house, and a woman stood in an open doorway. "You must be the O'Briens," she said when they climbed the steps to the porch. "Look at the little one. Bring him inside. I'm Ingrid Royer. You poor things. My brother told me that terrible renegade tried to rob you. I hope your little boy wasn't too frightened by him."

"It happened so fast," Fortune said, following her. She pulled her blue cotton wrapper close about her, a long brown braid hanging down her back to her waist.

"It's a hot night again. I'm sorry we don't have two rooms, but we have four boys, so our house is crowded."

"It's so nice of you to take us in," Claire said.

"One room is a blessing," Fortune added.

Claire knew besides it being scandalous, she wouldn't ever become accustomed to sharing a room with him no matter how tired she was. But it was that or camping out again.

Ingrid Royer opened the door and motioned them inside to a long, narrow room with a plain iron bed. There were two mahogany tables, a rocking chair, and a washstand and chest. A lamp burned and the windows were opened. "I tried to get it ready for you. I have blankets there on the floor if you want to put your son on them to sleep. That's what we do for our boys when we have relatives and the beds are filled."

Fortune placed Michael on the blankets. "He'll sleep

through most anything. I'll tend to the horses and then lock up when I come back inside."

She laughed and waved her hand. "I know you had a dreadful experience, but you don't need to lock the door in this town. My brother hasn't had anyone in the jail except for drinking too much. Well, I guess Henry LaPorte let his goat eat his neighbor's garden twice. Tomorrow the whole town will be talking about the renegade. I imagine they'll want to display the body for a time before they bury him."

"They can do what they want," Fortune said as he left.

"If you need anything, you can knock on my door. Our bedroom is the first one at the end of the hall."

"Thank you so much for taking us in," Claire said again.

"I'll close the door, Mrs. O'Brien." The name made Claire intensely aware of her deception and the impropriety of sharing a room with him, yet Michael hadn't questioned it, and no one else would care.

Claire knelt to look at Michael's injured foot, which was not discolored or swollen. She moved to the pitcher and bowl to wash and in minutes took off her shoes and stockings, knowing Fortune would return at any time. She stretched in bed and was asleep at once.

As Fortune entered the room, only one small lamp burned. As he pulled off his shirt he crossed the room to look down at Claire. She was stretched on the bed on her back, one arm flung above her head, her hair spread over the pillow. Perspiration dotted her forehead, and her skirts were up over her knees. Her bodice was unbuttoned more than he had ever seen before. The deep V revealed the full curve of her breasts, and he remembered that first night he had seen her bathing. His gaze roamed over her, watching the rise and fall of her breasts, looking at her narrow waist. Her legs were long and shapely, pale in the soft glow of the lamp. One leg was bent at the knee, and as his gaze traveled back up, he mentally stripped away the blue calico.

His body responded, his manhood throbbing as desire rose in him. He reached out to smooth locks of hair away from her cheek. Her skin was hot and damp in the sweltering heat of the room. He let her hair slide slowly through his fingers, feeling its silkiness. He found a fan on a chest and came back to fan her a while as he looked down at her.

Finally he moved away and knelt to look at Michael and check his foot. The bite was healing, and Michael was as sound a sleeper as Claire. Fortune smoothed his wet hair, which he had washed downstairs beneath the pump, and sat on the side of the bed to pull off his boots. As he did, he studied Claire, remembering her raising the rifle to shoot Harwood, remembering Michael clinging to her after the insect bite.

They were at an impasse with Michael. She could have tried to run away and she hadn't, and he believed the answer she had given him. She had seen that it was right for him to have Michael.

With a sigh he stood up, longing to strip down to get some relief from the heat. Putting out the lamp, he lay down in bed, looking at Clair. A trickle of desire warmed him again. With his hands behind his head he turned onto his back and stared at the ceiling until sleep finally came.

In the morning when Claire stirred, the room was empty. Both Michael and Fortune had gone downstairs. She washed from the basin of water as best she could, longing for a tub. As she brushed her hair, she heard children's laughter. She went to the open window. In the yard below, Michael was running with three other boys. Starting to lean out and call to him, she frowned, wondering about his foot, but he was running as carefree as the others. Horses grazed behind a shed and the morning was cool; her spirits lifted now that the danger of Harwood was gone.

After braiding her hair and pinning it around her head, she went downstairs. Mrs. Royer and Fortune were drinking coffee at the dining room table.

"Come in, Claire," he said, rising to his feet and holding a chair for her.

"Good morning." Mrs. Royer greeted her with a wide grin that showed a large gap between he front teeth. "Everyone in town is talking about you folks and the robber. Four neighbors have already dropped by to meet your husband and son."

Smiling, Claire sat down, far more aware of her name being said by Fortune than she was of Ingrid Royer. It was the second time he had called her by her first name, and each time it had sounded special in his deep voice. And it was one of the few times that anyone besides Michael had known her real name.

"You sit right there and I'll get your breakfast," Ingrid said, leaving the room and returning with a cup of black coffee. Fortune passed a pitcher of cream to her, his hands brushing hers lightly. He looked fresh in his chambray shirt while she felt the blue calico was dreadful, torn, wrinkled, and mud-spattered.

"Here's your breakfast," Ingrid said, placing a plate of ham, hot biscuits, hominy, and eggs in front of her.

After eating, they told the Royers good-bye and mounted to ride out of town. She sensed an easiness to him that he hadn't shown before and wondered whether his anger was cooling or if Harwood's death had removed some of the strain.

Fortune pushed his hat to the back of his head and turned his horse, riding close to Claire. "Today we'll still head south to New Orleans. As long as I'm this close, I want my family to meet Michael, and I want Michael to meet them."

They rode quietly all morning, passing stands of tall pines. In late afternoon they entered Baton Rouge along

Plank Road and wound into the heart of town, passing an imposing building that looked like a medieval castle.

"There's the Louisiana state capitol, Michael," Fortune said, and she glanced at the large structure. Her thoughts shifted from the sights around her to her appearance. As thankful as she was to reach a city, she felt too disheveled to go into a hotel. "They won't let me in a hotel in this state," she said, motioning to her wrinkled dress.

"Of course they will. I'll tell them we've been traveling."

"I've sewed up the front of the dress that Harwood tore, but it needs to be washed. We haven't stopped long enough for me to wash anything and then let it dry."

"We'll try to remedy that," he said, turning on the wide street. In minutes they stood in a hotel lobby, and she looked at the tall potted plants, the elegant leather-covered furniture and oil painting on the wall.

"Mama, this is another fancy place," Michael said.

"Yes, it is. After so many nights traveling across country, this is going to be very nice."

Fortune approached them, taking her arm. "I have a suite for us, and I've ordered a bath. Michael and I will go out for a while to buy a few things, and we'll leave you alone. Then we'll clean up. The hotel has someone who will wash and iron your dress."

"Thank you," she said, thinking it sounded wonderful after all the hard riding they had done. They climbed a wide, curving staircase with a thick blue carpet that was soft beneath her feet. On the third floor, they entered a suite, and once again she was awed by the elegance of it. She stood in the center of the sitting room, looking at dark walnut furniture, thick patterned rugs, gilded mirrors on the walls, and plants in the corners. French doors opened onto small balconies with black wrought iron chairs and tables. The hotel was elegant, yet it still seemed a terrible extravagance to her.

"Mama, isn't this fine!" Michael said, touching a marble-topped table. "It's fancier than that other hotel."

"Yes, it is," she said, wondering how Fortune could afford such luxury. The last time it had seemed an unnecessary expense, but this time she was thankful to be able to spend a night in such a place. And she knew when they parted, she would never be in rooms like this again.

She ran her hands over a wingback chair upholstered in rose damask. Glancing around, she found Fortune watching her, a curious look of speculation in his eyes, and she wondered what was going through his mind. More and more she caught him studying her intently, and she wondered what he was thinking.

"Michael, you and I will go out for a while to make some purchases," Fortune said.

"Yes, sir. Look, I can see the rooftops and the treetops," Michael said, leaning out a window.

Colonel O'Brien glanced at her. "When we return, you'll have to let us have one room while we clean up. Give me the dress you want laundered, and I'll leave it to get washed."

"If you'll wait a moment, I'll change and give you this one to have washed. It's the most acceptable to meet your family because the other dress is patched." She went into the bedroom, pulling off the worn blue calico and wrapping herself in a blanket, leaving her shoulders and arms bare.

She stepped to the door. "Fortune," she said, conscious of the familiarity of calling him by his given name.

He turned from the window and crossed the room to her, his gaze going over her shoulders, making her suddenly feel more bare than she was. He took the dress from her. "Michael, let's go now."

She watched him leave, his spurs jingling with his steps, his hand resting casually on Michael's shoulder. Claire lounged in the tub until the water cooled, relishing it on her skin, and washed her hair thoroughly. Refreshed, she climbed out to dry, wishing she had something clean to wear. When she was dressed in the patched pink gingham, she walked out onto the narrow balcony. Brushing her hair until it was almost dry, she braided it and wound it around her head.

When she stepped inside, she glanced at the carved bed and her pulse quickened. She would sleep there tonight with Fortune O'Brien on the other side of the bed.

She wondered where he had taken Michael and what they were doing. As time passed, she went back to sit on the balcony and look at the courtyard below. It was filled with wrought-iron benches and beds of flowers and exotic tall green plants. If Colonel O'Brien had noticed the lavishness of these surroundings, he had not been as awed as she and Michael. He had seemed to pay little attention to any of it, accepting it as readily as he did the hard ground when he camped.

Shadows lengthened as dusk came.

"Mama!" Michael's voice was excited, and she hurried into the front room of the suite to see the boy place an armful of assorted items on a chair. Fortune was carrying parcels under his arm as he closed the door.

"Mama, look what Colonel O'Brien bought!" Fortune held up a book. Knowing how much Michael loved the few books he owned, she crossed the room to take the book in her hands and look at the spine. *Mississippi Jim* by John St. Claire.

"How nice. Michael loves books."

"Look at this," Michael said, holding a wooden soldier. "And this," he said, holding up a stick of candy. "And he bought a new pair of pants for me!"

"That's wonderful, Michael!" she exclaimed, realizing how much more Fortune O'Brien could do for Michael than she ever could. She turned to look at him. Dusty from traveling, his shirt wrinkled and vest pockets bulging, he stood watching the child, a look of joy on his face that erased all his harshness. As Fortune tossed his hat on a desk, his gaze shifted to her. He held a bundle in his hands.

"This is the best I could do under the circumstances. They sell ribbons and material and shawls, so I brought this for you. With your sewing, I thought you could make a dress."

She took the folded material from his hand. It was a deep rose silk, and she drew a swift breath, running her hand over the soft material. "It's lovely!" she exclaimed. "It'll make a beautiful dress! Thank you." She looked up to meet an impassive gaze. A knock came, and when Fortune answered, two hotel employees were waiting with another tub and more water. He motioned them inside.

"Thank you," she said, surprised he had brought her a gift. Hugging the silk to her middle, she envisioned a dress. It was her first gift in years except simple things made out of paper by Michael. Until now she had always turned down the gifts offered by men, but she knew there would be no obligations with Fortune. "It's beautiful," she repeated, feeling the silk. "I'll go downstairs and leave you and Michael alone. I'll be in the courtyard."

"We'll join you soon and eat dinner."

She nodded, placing the silk on a chair and leaving the room. She went downstairs, sitting in the shade on one of the wrought-iron benches.

When they came striding up, her pulse jumped. Both of them had damp black curls. Other than his dark eyes, Michael looked like a miniature of Fortune O'Brien. Even though the black coat he wore was wrinkled from packing, Fortune looked handsome. He took her arm and they went to the hotel dining room, entering a spacious room with a high ceiling and cool interior, mirrors along one wall behind a mahogany bar and only a few patrons seated around the room. Tables were covered in white cloths and they sat at one beside a large window. She sat across from Fortune and Michael sat beside him.

When she opened the menu, she stared at the prices

and was aghast. She leaned over the table toward Fortune. "This is too expensive," she whispered. "We can find somewhere in town that won't be this costly."

"Claire, I'll pay for our supper," Fortune replied dryly. "It isn't a problem. After eating catfish and rabbit, we can have a hotel dinner." He turned to Michael. "What would you like, Michael? A steak sounds good to me."

"My word! Michael doesn't eat steaks, and look what it costs!" she exclaimed in a low voice, thankful no one sat at tables close to them to overhear her comments.

"I'll wager that Michael can eat a steak, and if that's what he wants, that's what he'll have. How about a steak for each of us?"

"I couldn't possibly eat something that cost that much!" She looked at the menu: the least expensive thing was a bowl of stew. "I'll have the stew."

"Not tonight. It the steak was free, would you eat one?"

"Yes, but it isn't."

The waiter appeared and Fortune ordered three steaks and two glasses of wine. She stared at him, wondering about how well fixed he was. Or was he doing this just because of the rugged traveling they had done?

When the juicy steak and a fluffy potato were placed before her, she stared at her plate, thinking it looked like the most delicious dinner she had ever seen. Picking up her fork and knife, she cut into it, chewing with her eyes closed, opening them to find Fortune watching her.

"Mmm, this is marvelous."

Sipping his wine, Fortune studied her, almost forgetting to eat. She was chewing the steak as if she were in ecstasy. She was as easy to please in some ways as Michael, and Fortune realized she must have made sacrifice after sacrifice for him. He glanced at the child beside him and back at her, realizing what kind of life they had led through the years. If he yelled to duck, they both would react immediately. They were as accustomed to danger as the most seasoned soldier. But neither of them were accustomed to luxury. He was willing to wager that the rose silk was her first gift since running away from home. When he thought about Rafe and Cal and their generosity, the Christmases he'd had as a child and with Marilee, he had been blessed with presents.

"Aren't you going to eat that steak you wanted so badly?" she asked, closing her eyes to chew without waiting for his answer.

"Mama, this is good!"

"It's heavenly," she said with a sigh. The tip of her pink tongue ran across her lips, and she dabbed her mouth with a napkin. Her table manners were excellent, and he knew she had to have come from a good home. He took a bite of steak, discovered it was tender. Even while he ate, though, he watched her with fascination. He had never seen anyone relish a dinner the way she was.

They had a special treat of ice cream, and he was too intrigued watching both Michael and Claire eating their ice cream to eat his. "You've never eaten ice cream before?" he asked.

"No! This is wonderful!" she said, running her tongue over the spoon and licking it off. He watched her pink tongue flick out again and back, her full red lips closing. He shifted, remembering kisses that he tried to avoid thinking about.

Finally dinner was over and they walked through the cool, sweet-smelling courtyard before they went upstairs. The freshly laundered clothing had been returned by the hotel and placed on the settee. Claire carried her blue calico dress to the bedroom, thankful to know she would be able to wear something clean tomorrow.

When she returned to the sitting room, Fortune and Michael were stretched out side by side on the settee. Fortune read to him from *Mississippi Jim,* and she listened for a long time before finally getting up and going to sit in the dark on the balcony, where the air was cooler.

A lamp burned in the bedroom, imparting a faint glow onto the balcony. She glanced overhead at twinkling stars. Fortune came out on the balcony and sat down near her. He lit a cheroot, inhaling and blowing out smoke, the tobacco smell strong. He stretched out his legs and propped his feet on the balcony rail. He had shed his coat and cravat and now had his shirt unbuttoned at the throat. As they sat in the cool night in silence, she was more aware of him than ever. Nervously she thought about going to bed. She glanced at him to find him watching her with a disconcerting stare.

"Claire, I want to talk to you."

Her heart dropped, and she wondered if he was going to ask her to leave them here in Baton Rouge. She waited in silence while he leaned forward, placing his feet on the floor, putting his elbows on his knees and lacing his hands together. A dark lock of hair curled over his forehead. Finally he looked up at her.

"Tomorrow we'll ride into New Orleans," he said in a deep, quiet voice. "I've told you that my brother and his family live there, and I want them to meet Michael. In the morning I want to tell Michael the truth."

She drew a deep breath and stood up, brushing past him to go inside. A pain twisted deep inside her, and she couldn't control her tears because now she would lose Michael. It had come far sooner than she had expected. She strode to the wash basin, reaching for a cloth to wipe her face, trying to get control of her emotions.

"Claire, Michael has to know sometime," Fortune said close behind her, having followed her into the room. "Trevor Wenger will talk about Marilee. I know I can't keep Wenger from ever seeing Michael. And I want Michael to know his uncles. I want him to know I'm his father," Fortune stated flatly, and she heard the unyielding note in his voice.

"I know," she said, trying to get control. Her knees shook and she couldn't stop the tears. "I just love him so much!" She spun around to face Fortune. "I've given him everything—all my love and attention and dreams for all these years. He's like my own child!"

"But he isn't your child," he stated, looking at her with his cold blue eyes. She could feel the anger returning to his tone. "He's my son."

Nodding, she placed the cloth against her eyes. "I'll get control. Just leave me alone."

He waited in silence. She knew he hadn't moved away, but she kept the cold cloth against her eyes. All her muscles were tense as she tried to keep from breaking into sobs. She hurt more than she had ever hurt in her life.

"Claire, do you want to sit down?"

She shook her head.

"Claire?"

She lowered the cloth from her eyes and turned her back to him.

"I've been thinking," he said with quiet deliberation. "I've watched you with Michael, and I know that Michael loves you and needs you."

She whirled back around feeling a glimmer of hope. Would he let her be a nanny for Michael?

He fidgeted restlessly, running his fingers through his dark hair, rubbing a hand over his jaw. "I loved Marilee with all my heart, and I'll never love another woman again." He placed his hands on his hips. "She was the love of my life." He stared at Claire and she waited, not following his drift.

"Michael needs you and you're good for him," Fortune said reluctantly.

Her heart began to drum. He was going to relent and let her be Michael's nanny. Locking her hands together, she held her breath.

"While we've been traveling, I've seen how much Michael loves you." Fortune paused, and she waited, not daring to breathe. "There won't be any love involved, but I'm willing to marry you so you can stay with Michael."

Chapter 11

Stunned, Claire felt her mouth drop open. *Marriage!*

Her knees began to shake and she felt light-headed. She moved to a chair to perch on it.

When she looked up, he was frowning slightly. "I can provide for both of you. I don't expect to ever love again, so I won't be giving up something in my future." He rubbed the back of his neck as if he were wrestling with a knotty problem. "This way you could be a mother to Michael and get to stay with him." He paused, studying her. "If you want a physical relationship, I'm willing, but I love only Marilee. If you don't want me to touch you, I'll honor your wishes."

She barely heard any of the last because her heart thudded wildly. She felt as if she might faint. She could stay with Michael always! She wasn't going to have to part with him. She could remain his mother. She realized Fortune was watching for her reaction and suddenly the relief was overwhelming. She burst into tears, trying to stop her shaking and crying, but overcome with joy that she could stay with Michael.

"Claire?"

She tried to get control, sobbing and waving the wet cloth at him. Wiping her eyes furiously, she looked up. "I can't keep from crying. I thought I was going to lose him. I love him so very much."

"I know you do. That's why I'm offering this proposition. It's the only solution I can see if you want to stay with him."

"You were so angry with me—"

"That will pass with time. It angers me, but that's all in the past and we might as well stop looking back. Do you want to marry me?"

"Yes! Oh, sweet heavens, yes!"

"There's no love between us, and that won't change," he said, his blue eyes intent on her. "With time perhaps we can become close. You haven't ever loved a man. I don't know if you can understand, but I loved Marilee with all my heart."

She wiped tears that spilled down her cheeks. "I understand, and I can accept that. I never expected to have a man in my life or love or marriage," she said, still astounded that he had asked her to be his wife.

"You're young. You may be throwing away your own future."

"Oh, never!" she gasped, wanting to leap into the air and dance around the room with joy. "I love Michael with all my heart, and to think I can see him grow up and still be a mother to him is all I want."

Fortune moved closer to her, and his warm fingers tilted her chin up. "I intend to be part of Atlanta society for Michael's sake. We'll mingle with lots of people. You've never been in love, and you may meet a man you'll fall in love with," Fortune said, his voice getting that quiet, deadly tone. "I don't want one breath of scandal to hurt Michael."

"I would never do that to him!"

"You don't understand what it's like to love someone. But I'm warning you now, if you fall in love with some man, I'll let you go, but you can't take Michael."

"I understand."

"You're trembling," he said, frowning at her.

"I thought I was going to lose him!" She pulled from his grasp and wiped her eyes.

"Claire," he said, his voice changing to an impersonal tone, "I told you, we can have the physical side of marriage if you want, or I'll refrain from touching you."

She looked into his crystal eyes, barely able to think beyond Michael. "I don't know anything about men. For now, since you don't love me"—she felt the heat rise in her cheeks—"I would rather we didn't have anything physical."

"I have needs and I'll satisfy them, but I swear to you I'll be discreet. I wouldn't hurt Michael with scandal either. You'll never know, and neither will any of our friends."

She nodded, unable to consider anything except that she could be Michael's mother and watch him grow up.

"As much as possible I want us to be friends," he said solemnly, and she nodded.

"I think that's possible if you become less angry with me."

"I told you, the anger will pass. We've managed to travel together well enough. Michael will be happier if he thinks we're happy."

"I agree."

"I want to share a bedroom."

She looked up at him sharply, drawing in her breath.

"It'll look better to servants, it'll give us a better chance to become close, and you may change your mind about the physical part." He dropped his hands from his hips. "I promise you, I will never force myself on you."

She nodded, not caring at the moment what requirements he placed on her if it meant keeping Michael.

He held out his hand. "Then we have a bargain."

She reached out to give him her hand, a peculiar sensation racing across her nerves as she pledged herself to him. His fingers closed around hers, his grasp strong and firm, and she shook his hand solemnly. He turned away abruptly and strode outside, and she wondered what he was feeling. Was he grieving for his lost Marilee? Was he already having second thoughts? Was he wishing she was Marilee?

Claire crossed the room and tiptoed in to look at Michael. His curls were damp against his forehead, his chest bare, the sheet pushed down to his waist. He looked young and frail and vulnerable. Feeling love well up, she brushed the damp curls from his face, her heart singing with joy that she wasn't going to have to give him up. When she turned, Fortune was standing in the doorway. He had shed his shirt and was barefoot. With a final glance at Michael, she rose and crossed the room. Fortune stepped aside as she entered their bedroom.

When he closed the door behind her, she turned to face him, drawing in her breath. The soft glow of the lamp highlighted his wide shoulders. Her gaze ran across his broad chest, the mat of thick black curls, his flat stomach, and her pulse jumped. Blushing because she shouldn't have looked him over in such a bold manner, she glanced up to meet his gaze.

"I still want to tell Michael the truth in the morning. He has to know Marilee was his mother."

"I understand," she answered, feeling the first touch of worry tinge her joy.

"We're close enough that we can ride into New Orleans tomorrow and to my brother's house. We can be married there or wait until we get to Atlanta. Since I'm registering us in hotels as husband and wife, I figure we might as well marry in New Orleans. There won't be a wedding trip except to go home to Atlanta."

"New Orleans would be good," she answered solemnly, frightened he would change his mind. "The sooner we wed, the happier I'll be."

"I won't change my mind," he said dryly. "We should notify your father, and if you want to go visit him, you may."

She nodded. "I'll write. After all this time I don't have

any wish to go home unless he's ill and wants me to come."

Fortune crossed the room to a table with a decanter of brandy. He held up the bottle. "Would you like some?"

"No, thank you," she answered.

He poured a glass and took his out to the balcony. She removed her shoes and stocking and climbed into bed, staring into the darkness. She shifted and could see him sitting on the balcony, his long legs propped on the rail, while he sipped the brandy. She wondered what he was thinking. When she thought about a physical union with him, her nerves became raw. She didn't want that when the man didn't love her. Tonight she was just thankful for Fortune O'Brien's generosity.

And suppose Fortune fell in love again?

She pushed aside the worry. All that was important was she would not lose Michael.

She was awake when Fortune came inside and sank onto the bed. When she heard him breathing evenly, she turned carefully to study him, feeling heat rise in her as she looked at his long length. Within days he would be her husband, bound to her by law.

She turned back to stare at the ceiling, wondering how badly Michael would take learning the truth about his mother's death. Would he hate her for what she had done? Worries plagued her, but she loved him deeply, and she felt he knew she did. After the shock wore away, she hoped he would remember how much she loved him.

The next morning when she stirred and opened her eyes, Fortune was shaving. She watched him through lowered lids, thinking he was incredibly handsome, her pulse beating faster when she thought about his proposal and her acceptance. He would be her husband! Her gaze ran over his faded denim pants, down to his dusty boots, and back up to his bare chest.

"Michael isn't up yet, but as soon as he's dressed, I

want to talk to him," Fortune said quietly, his gaze shifting to meet hers in the mirror.

Embarrassed that he had caught her looking at him, she blushed. How had he known she was awake? "Whatever you want."

"That way we'll go eat and then ride south. He'll be too busy tending his horse to brood over what he's been told."

He continued to shave in silence while she climbed out of bed. Hanging her head down, she brushed her hair over her head. When she flipped it behind her to apply some more strokes, she caught him watching her with a solemn, intense look while he buttoned his blue chambray shirt.

"I'll leave you alone. Let's let Michael get dressed and ready to go, and then we'll tell him."

She nodded, dreading the moment. "Can we tell him first that we plan to wed?"

"Yes. I think the idea of our marrying will help him because I know he loves you."

"Thank you. You're very generous."

"And I love Michael very much. That's why I'm doing this." He left the room and she swallowed nervously as he closed the door. As soon as she married, according to law, a husband was master of his wife, so Fortune would control her, and she would become dependent on someone else again. She washed, dressing in the freshly laundered calico. She studied herself in the mirror: the dress was worn, but since it was clean, she felt better wearing it. She turned to join Fortune while Michael had the bedroom to himself to wash and dress.

Fortune stood beside the French doors, and as they waited for Michael, her nervousness grew. When the boy appeared, his black hair was wet and combed down, his worn cotton shirt tucked into his patched denim pants, his dark eyes filled with eagerness. Fortune turned around.

"Michael, we have some things to talk about before we go down to eat breakfast," he said gently.

"Yes, sir."

"First, Claire and I have agreed to get married."

Michael looked from one to the other with such eagerness that her heart seemed to turn over. "Criminy! You're going to marry," he said, his voice filled with wonder, "and you'll be my father!" Breaking into a broad grin, he ran across the room, and Fortune caught him up in his arms to hug him.

"I'm glad you're going to marry!" he exclaimed. "I told Mama you might marry her, and she said you wouldn't marry again."

Fortune looked over Michael's head at her and she blushed. "Michael, come here and sit down," she said, patting the sofa beside her. "I have some things to tell you too."

"Yes, ma'am!" he said as Fortune set him down and turned away. When Michael ran across the room, she noticed his pants were shorter. Was he growing again? she wondered, realizing he was going to be tall like his father. While he perched on the sofa, she reached over to take his hand. His wide eyes gazed up at her while he wiggled slightly, as if he found it difficult to sit still.

"I love you, Michael."

"I love you too," he replied in his high, childlike voice.

"I want to tell you about when you were born. You don't know what really happened, and it's time you do."

His eyes widened as he stared at her. "What happened?"

Noticing that Fortune stood in front of a window, his back to them, she took a deep breath. There was no easy way to tell Michael the truth. Praying that he wasn't hurt too badly, she squeezed his hand and tried to fight back her tears.

"Michael, when I was a girl, I lived in North Carolina. One night I was going to the barn to see about my horse. When I was in the barn, I heard someone moaning. There was a beautiful young woman in one of the horse stalls.

She was ill and she had a tiny baby with her. She gave me the baby and asked me to take care of him. She died that night because she was very sick."

Michael's eyes were huge. She continued, "I held the baby all that night, and the next day I begged my father to let me keep the little baby boy. My father wouldn't, and placed the baby in an orphans' home. My father wanted me to wed a man I didn't want to marry, so one night I ran away from home and went to the orphanage and told them the family had been found for the baby and I was to take him back to them. They gave the little baby boy to me and I ran away with him."

"That was me?" he asked, tilting his head to study her.

"Yes, it was."

"You're not my mother? She was my mother?"

"Yes, Michael. She gave birth to you, and that night in the barn, she asked me to take care of you and I promised her I would."

"You're my mother!" he exclaimed, suddenly throwing himself at her. He wrapped his arms around her neck. "You're my mother, not her!"

"I love you, Michael," she said, ignoring tears that spilled on her cheeks as she hugged his slender body, "even though I'm not the mother who gave birth to you. She loved you very much, and I love you very much."

"You're my mother!" he insisted.

"Michael, listen to me," she said, extricating herself from his arms around her neck. "Michael, I'll always be a mother to you. But you also have a mother who gave birth to you, loved you very much, and died. And you have a father who did not die. I told you that he died to explain the lack of a father to you because I ran away with you. Before she died, your mother didn't tell me her name or your father's name, but she did tell me your name. Your father is alive and loves you. That night she told me your name was Michael O'Brien. Michael, Colonel O'Brien—"

Michael turned to look at Fortune, who was watching them now. His eyes were red. A muscle worked in Fortune's jaw, and she realized he was fighting to control his emotions. "I'm your—" he started to say, taking a deep breath and moving toward Michael, tears filling his eyes. Michael ran to him, and Fortune caught the boy up to hug him.

Michael clung to him, and she could see Fortune's eyes squeezed shut, see his tears.

She retreated to the far end of the room, waiting until finally she heard Michael's high voice. "You're my real father?"

"Yes, I am. Claire told you how she took you from the orphanage. Your grandfather is a stern, harsh man. He didn't want me to marry your mother. One night when I wasn't home, he took both of you from me to go to Georgia. Your mother became ill and ran away from him, trying to get back to me. She died as Claire told you. When you disappeared with Claire, your grandfather wrote me that both of you, you and your mother, had died. I didn't know you were alive until a few years ago, and then I started searching for you. I've had a detective agency searching for you."

"Detectives?" Michael asked, looking back and forth between them.

"Now I've found you, and the best solution seems to be for me to marry Claire because she's the only mother you know."

"Yes, sir." Michael turned to look at her. "Mama?"

She moved toward him, wondering what was running through his mind. He came to take her hand. "I'm glad you took me away from the orphans' home, and I'm glad you and Colonel O'Brien are going to marry," he said fiercely.

She nodded, leaning down to kiss his soft cheek.

"Michael," Fortune said, moving to his side and swinging him up in his arms. "It's going to be different at first, but I'd like you to call me Papa instead of Colonel O'Brien."

"Papa," he said, giving Fortune a hug around the neck.

Fortune looked at her, smiling, his features softening. For a moment all his animosity vanished. She smiled in return, realizing that Michael had accepted the truth and adjusted to it easily. Fortune set the child down.

"How about going down to breakfast and I'll tell you about your uncle and aunt? You're going to see them today. I've written them about you, Michael."

"Yes, sir."

"And you have two cousins: Daniella, who is five, and Jared, who is three." Fortune dropped his hand on Michael's shoulder, and they headed toward the door. He held it open for her, and she went through with Michael.

At the door to the hotel dining room, she paused and placed her hand on Fortune's arm. "It costs dreadfully much to eat in there. I'm certain a town as large as this one will have a less expensive place."

"Claire, I'm paying for things now, so you let me worry about the bills," he said with amusement. He took her arm and steered her into the dining room as a man in a white coat came forward to seat them.

When the waiter placed a menu in front of Claire, Fortune reached across the table to take it from her. "Let me order for you, and you'll enjoy your breakfast more."

Disconcerted, she gazed at him and then shrugged. "Fine. Most anything besides rabbit, apples, or cold biscuits sounds wonderful."

He smiled, and she felt a flare of hope that they would be friends and the anger he had shown toward her would vanish.

During breakfast they answered Michael's questions, and finally they went upstairs to gather their things to go. As they traveled along the river road and approached New Orleans, her trepidation over meeting his family began to rise. She wondered what they would think of her.

Glancing at her dress, she felt rumpled after the days of travel. The blue calico that had started the day freshly laundered and ironed now was wrinkled and damp, clinging to her arms and back. And she wondered if the O'Briens would dislike her, because it would be obvious that there was no love between Fortune and her.

As they rode into the city, she pressed her lips together hoping Michael didn't remember or say anything about the places they had stayed when they had lived in New Orleans. Along the waterfront were big ships with tall masts; she saw the saloon where she had sung, remembering men trying to fondle her, men wanting to take her out. Her gaze slid to Fortune, and she wondered about him. His only touches had been casual, never taking liberties or attempting to, as many men often tried to do. When he kissed her, though, he hadn't been casual. The thought of his kisses still sent heat rushing through her, making her draw in a deep breath.

Riding alongside the muddy Mississippi River, they reached the open market with its long array of stalls. Tempting smells of melons mingled with smells of fish, and she saw the fresh catches of crawfish. Servants in black dresses with white aprons shopped with women in silks with parasols while fisherman moved through the crowd and vendors hawked sweets. Fortune dismounted to make purchases. She and Michael followed along while Fortune asked Michael what he wanted.

When they left the market, the horses were laden with Fortune's purchases. Doubling back the way they had come, they turned to ride down Decatur through the Vieux Carré and crossed Canal to turn on St. Charles in the American section. The homes were breathtakingly elegant, and she glanced again at Fortune, realizing how much he was going to change Michael's life as well as hers.

When they passed mansions set back behind high iron fences, her worries mounted. In minutes Fortune turned up a winding drive, and her breath caught as she caught sight of a grand establishment.

The Greek Revival house was spectacular with eight large Ionic columns across the front. Beds of bright pink and purple crepe myrtles competed with roses in bloom. Fortune barely gave it a glance as he rode up the drive.

Suddenly the door burst open, and a woman with golden hair and large dark eyes came running out. "Fortune!"

He dismounted, hugging her as a small child dashed out behind her.

Looking at the woman's elegant pink moiré dress trimmed in lace and rose ribbons, Claire felt shabbier than ever. She halted as a groomsman came forward to take the horses. Michael dismounted, standing shyly and watching Fortune.

As the woman stepped back, her gaze ran over Claire and Michael and she paused, staring at the boy and smiling. "Fortune?" She looked at him with curiosity.

"I want you to meet the woman I intend to marry," Fortune said, taking Claire's arm. He dropped his other hand onto Michael's shoulder.

"Claire, this is my sister-in-law, Chantal O'Brien. Chantal, I want you to meet Claire Dryden."

"How do you do?" Claire said while Fortune's words *the woman I intend to marry* filled her with warmth.

"I'm glad to have you here," Chantal said.

"And this is my son, Michael."

Claire heard the note of love and pride in Fortune's voice as he gazed at Michael, who smiled up at Chantal. She hugged him lightly. "Michael, we're so happy to get to know you. Here's your cousin Daniella," she said, urging a blond child forward. The girl had large dark eyes, her coloring like her mother's, but Claire could see a resemblance to Fortune in the child's wide forehead, straight nose, and prominent cheekbones. "And here is

Jared O'Brien," she said, motioning to a small blond boy who bore little resemblance to Michael.

"Come inside. I've already sent someone to fetch Rafe."

"We've been traveling a long time, so one thing we'd like, Chantal, is a chance to clean up. I hope that brother of mine has an extra shirt. I want to burn what I've been wearing. And I hope we can get a dress made quickly for Claire. We had to leave Natchez in a rush."

"Of course we can do those things! Come inside." She linked her arm through Claire's and Fortune's to go up the steps. A servant held the door and smiled in greeting.

Claire walked through the most elegant house she had ever seen. She could remember fancy homes of friends of her father's, but nothing like this. Her own home had been comfortable but plain. She looked at oil paintings and Queen Anne furniture as they went through a wide hall and climbed the stairs.

"I'll wait for Rafe," Fortune said from the foot of the stairs. He watched the ladies climb the stairs, Michael and his niece and nephew trailing up behind them. He turned to roam through the house, finally stepping outside on the veranda to wait for his brother. In minutes he saw a carriage coming down the street with a servant and Rafe. As they turned into the drive, Fortune hurried down the steps. Rafe jumped down from the carriage while the servant headed toward the back.

His brother strode toward him, looking slightly thicker through the shoulders, his blue eyes sparkling, his black hair tangled by the breeze. "Fortune!" Rafe hugged his brother who clasped him and pulled away.

"We've ridden hard as hell and need to get home to Atlanta, but I wanted to stop in New Orleans to see you."

"Thank God you did. I hope I can get you to stay for several weeks. And who is *we*? Come in and we'll have a drink."

"I've got my son with me."

Rafe looked at him sharply. "You found him!"

"Yes. And I intend to marry the woman who had him."

Rafe grinned and slapped him on the back. "We can write Cal and have a wedding here! Unless her family—"

"Wait a minute. It's not what you think." They went up the steps and crossed the veranda. Inside the house, Rafe motioned toward the library. He closed the doors behind them, crossing to a table to pour them both glasses of red wine.

"Now tell me."

"She's raised Michael, and he loves her. I saw I couldn't take him away from her, so I told her I would marry her."

The sparkle went out of Rafe's eyes, and his expression became solemn as he stared at his brother. Feeling an argument brewing, Fortune gazed back steadily.

"Fortune, don't marry if you don't love her. You'll make a hell on earth for yourself."

"I think it will be all right," he said, swirling the wine and moving restlessly toward the fireplace to rest his elbow against the mantel. The room was filled with books, and he longed to build a house for Michael and see that he had books available.

"You were in love with Marilee, so you know what a marriage with love is," Rafe argued, shedding his coat. "You won't be happy."

"What can I do with her except marry her? Michael loves her. To him she's his mother."

They stared at each other, Rafe with furrowed brow. He shook his head. "Do anything except marry her. When you wrote me you were going to find her, you didn't sound as if you would ever consider marrying her."

"I hadn't seen her with Michael then. I've traveled day and night with her, so I've seen her under the worst circumstances. I think we can both tolerate this marriage, and it'll be good for Michael."

"If it isn't good, it'll be worse for him later. Children

are sensitive to their parents. If both of you hate each other, he'll know and he'll suffer from it."

"I'm marrying her, Rafe. I'm not going to separate them."

Rafferty studied him and Fortune returned his gaze. Finally Rafe nodded. "Very well. Do you want to have the wedding here?"

"Yes. We've been staying in hotels as man and wife—" He saw Rafe's brows raise. "Not living as man and wife. She knows nothing about men."

"You wrote me she had worked in saloons."

"She's sung in saloons, and I thought the same thing you're thinking, but she's as innocent as a child. Pinkerton's told me there had been no men and I didn't believe them, but I do now. It's not difficult to tell an innocent woman from an experienced one."

"She may want your money."

With a flash of white teeth Fortune laughed and shook his head. "There you couldn't be more wrong. This woman has the first few cents she earned, but she doesn't want me to spend mine on her. She doesn't want me to spend it at all."

"Fortune, where women are concerned, you may be a little inexperienced. I've never known a woman who didn't want to spend money."

"Take her out and try to buy her something and see what a battle you have. I've traveled with her, and she didn't want me to buy myself things. Only where Michael is concerned will she relent. I think she would let me buy him all of Louisiana if I could."

"You're making a hell of a mistake," Rafe said quietly.

"Reserve your judgement until you meet both of them. Their clothes are threadbare. And I asked Chantal for one of your shirts. I've worn the same three for too long now."

"I'll write Cal. Darcy is here and working for me. He

was out of the office on an errand, and I left word for him to come home."

"I'd like to see Cal, but I feel an urgency to get Michael back to Atlanta and get settled. He's had too much upheaval in his life. They've been on the run since the first night she took him from the orphanage. Let's have this wedding tomorrow, and then we'll leave for Atlanta."

"Day after tomorrow. You can't do Chantal out of the pleasure of a party, and I want to get to know my nephew and see my brother."

Fortune smiled. "All right. Day after tomorrow. Then we leave for Atlanta."

"You don't want a wedding night alone with her?"

"No," he answered flatly.

"That's no way to start a marriage."

Fortune shrugged. "It's a marriage in name only. Maybe with time it will change and we can become friends—"

"Listen to you! You're talking about man and wife, not some Sunday picnic with a stranger. Fortune—"

"Enough said. I'm marrying her."

Rafferty studied him. "All right. Want to settle here and go to work with me?"

"Thanks, but I'm going to Atlanta and open a steel mill. Before I left, I'd already started looking into it. If you have any need of steel, then you can send business my way."

"You wrote me of your plans. I'd like to talk you out of returning to Atlanta as well as marrying."

"Wenger will come after Michael. I'd just as soon go back and face him now. Now, tell me about your family and your business.

"Business is booming. And if you need a partner in your venture, I'll go in."

"Good Lord, that's great! Of course I want you in!"

"I trust your business judgement." He grinned. "Besides, I'll check on you. My business is growing. I'm shipping cotton and other goods, grain, corn, and I've bought two more ships. The South is crippled, but I've kept my British and European contacts and markets through the war, so I still can have a good trade. And as for my family—the children are growing too fast."

Fortune crossed to sit down on a straight-back chair and relaxed as they talked about the city and industry.

After half an hour, he leaned forward. "Rafe, I have to have a bath and clean clothes before I see anyone else or go to dinner."

"All right. Let's go find my nephew."

"And then I bathe. We've been sleeping on hard ground most nights."

They stepped into the hall, and Fortune admired all the paintings and furnishings. When they got back to Atlanta, he would build a house, and until now he hadn't given any thought to what he would like. With a deeply carved banister, a curving staircase swept to the second floor. Rafe's house was large, grand, and comfortable.

As they climbed the stairs, Fortune glanced back down at a seascape on the wall. Windows along the wide upstairs hall shed a profusion of light, and the oak floor gleamed with polish. From a room down the hall he heard Chantal's ringing laughter. He had never heard Claire really laugh, but then neither one of them had had anything to laugh about.

He introduced Rafferty to Michael, who sat on the floor of the children's nursery, building wooden logs into two cabins with Daniella while Jared sat a few feet away playing with extra logs.

As soon as Rafe sat on the floor near them, Daniella climbed into her father's lap, winding her arm around his neck and shaking her blond curls from her face. Rafe talked quietly to Michael, and in minutes he was helping both Daniella and Michael build their log cabins while Jared came to lean against him and then climb onto his shoulders.

Fortune watched Rafe, knowing he was good with children. Michael was so eager to build that Fortune wondered how much Michael had been able to play with other children. Finally Rafe set Jared on the floor and stood up.

"I'll take your Uncle Fortune and show him his room now. I'll come back later."

Daniella nodded, already lost in concentration on her wooded logs.

"He's a fine-looking boy," Rafe said when they were in the hall. "But then I can see a strong O'Brien resemblance."

"Yes, there is. He looks more like me than Marilee. We've told him about her, so he knows now that Claire isn't his birth mother."

"And how did he take that?"

"He wants to think of Claire as his mother. That's understandable, but there will come a time when he'll want to know more about Marilee."

"Take this room," Rafe said, motioning to an open door, and Rafe entered a spacious bedroom with the south windows raised high.

"You have a bathroom through that door."

"Right next to my room?"

"Yes. You haven't been to New Orleans since we moved into this house. I'll show you through it after you've cleaned up."

"I'm surprised Chantal would leave the Vieux Carré."

"We have that home too," Rafe said with a smile. "Her cousin lives in it right now. I'll see you downstairs. I'm glad you're here."

"We'll leave by boat for Apalachicola, so I'll need to book passage."

"No, you won't. I have two ships docked now. I'll send the smaller one and you can go to Apalachicola on it."

"Thanks. I'll be down soon." When Rafe had left, he looked around at the elegant bedroom with its satin drapery, lace curtains, thick woollen rug, a carved rosewood bed with a high headboard that reached within feet of the ceiling. Pulling off his shirt, he sat down to remove his boots. As he tugged at them, Rafe's arguments swirled in his mind.

"Don't marry her . . . hell on earth . . ."

All the time he soaked in a bath and smoked a cheroot, he thought about Rafe's arguments, always coming back to the same thing. There was no other way except to marry her.

"Suh" came a voice from the bedroom.

"Come in."

"Mistah O'Brien sent some clothes for you. I'll put them on the bed."

"Thank you, Matthew."

"Yes, suh."

Clamping the cheroot in his teeth, Fortune stood up, water splashing off his body. Drying himself, he went into the bedroom and found a half-dozen shirts and pairs of pants as well as a coat. He grinned, as he fingered a shirt, knowing Rafe's generosity.

When he had dressed in a white linen shirt, black trousers, and a black coat, he joined Rafe on the veranda on the east side of the house, overlooking a yard filled with magnolia trees and beds of flowers. For the first time since he had started after Claire, he felt calm and relaxed as he sank into a chair and crossed his legs.

In minutes a servant held a tray with mint juleps. Fortune accepted the cool drink. "Sitting here, you wouldn't know there had been a terrible war and that the South is in the throes of Reconstruction. God knows how long Atlanta will be under military jurisdiction."

"It was bad here during the war, but not as bad as Atlanta or many other places, and I was out of the country most of the time. New Orleans isn't the port it was before the war."

The sweet scent of honeysuckle wafted from the garden, and Fortune took another sip of his drink. “There’s constant building in Atlanta.”

“I’ve heard it’s Yankee money. Carpetbaggers abound in the South. I know some northern men who’re investing in business in Atlanta.”

“Labor is cheap because convict labor is available, it’s a central area, and the railroads are trying to get established again as quickly as they can.”

“There you are,” Chantal’s lilting voice came. Fortune stood as she stepped outside and Claire followed. Startled, his breath caught as he gazed at his fiancée.

Chapter 12

Claire's lustrous chestnut hair was parted in the center and caught up on either side to fall in curls with red ribbons. She wore a red silk dress that was cut low enough to show her soft curves. The dress had tiny sleeves trimmed in lace, leaving her slender arms bare. She looked beautiful and graceful as she came toward him.

His gaze swept over her, and it wasn't until she glanced at Rafe that Fortune remembered there were others present.

"Claire, I want you to meet my brother," he said, going to her side. "This is Rafferty. Rafe, this is my fiancée, Claire Dryden."

"I'm glad to meet you," Rafe said warmly as Fortune took her arm. He caught a faint scent of lilacs and was aware of her arm in his grasp. He leaned closer to her as Chantal talked to Rafe and sat down.

"Come sit down. You look pretty," he added quietly, realizing he was getting a better bargain than he had expected. He had been so absorbed in thinking about her as a mother to Michael that he had given little thought to her appearance. He had known she was pretty, but tonight she was breathtaking.

"Thank you. Chantal was so kind and thank heavens, I don't have to wear either of my calico dresses tonight!"

"I'll get you lots of dresses when we get to Atlanta."

She glanced up at him, her full lips curving in an inviting smile. "I won't need lots."

She sat on a chair and he pulled one closer to hers, aware of her at his side and wanting this fetching creature to sit where he could look at her long and leisurely.

They talked about New Orleans and Rafe's family and business while Fortune stole glances continually at Claire. His gaze ran over her profile, her straight nose and her small chin that could set in a defiant manner, her full lips that were soft as rose petals. She must have won Chantal's approval; he suspected he would know if she hadn't. He noticed her bare throat, and he wondered if she owned any jewelry, doubting that she did. He forgot about the jewelry as his gaze drifted lower over the soft swell of her bosom. He looked away, taking a sip of his drink and trying to pick up the thread of conversation that he had lost thinking about Claire.

"Here's where everyone is" came a cheerful, deep voice, and Fortune looked up to see Darcy stride onto the veranda. Tall and lanky, dressed in a white shirt and brown pants, Darcy shook hair back from his face as he glanced at Claire and then came toward Fortune.

He stood up to meet Darcy, clasping his outstretched hand and pulling him close to give him a quick hug.

"I've already met my nephew. He's a handsome little devil."

"You say that because he looks like you!" Fortune remarked with a grin. "Lord, you're still growing!"

Claire looked at the two brothers, who bore a close resemblance. Darcy was a fraction taller than Fortune, more lanky and younger-looking, but his eyes were the same startling blue. Meeting the O'Briens had worried her, but after minutes with Chantal, she had relaxed. They were all warm and accepting, and the look Fortune had given her when she stepped onto the veranda had set her pulse racing. She had seen lust in men's eyes too many times when she sang in saloons, but this had been different—surprise, approval, pleasure, all seemed part of his reaction. Perhaps he wouldn't regret terribly this union that he was being forced into for Michael's sake.

And she knew she would never hold a regret. With every new discovery about him, she was more thankful for her coming nuptials. Tonight Fortune looked so handsome that it was difficult to keep from turning to stare at him. Her thoughts shifted as Fortune faced her.

"Claire, this is our youngest brother, Darcy. Darcy, meet Claire Dryden, my fiancée."

Darcy gave her a broad smile as he reached down to brush her cheek with a kiss. "Welcome to the O'Brien family."

"Thank you. You've all been wonderful. Michael is enjoying himself immensely with his new cousins."

"Tonight the children will eat early, and we will have a quiet dinner to ourselves," Chantal said as Darcy sat down and stretched out his legs. "This is Wednesday. Saturday we will have a wedding."

"Friday is when I had planned, Chantal," Fortune said.

Waving her hand, she wrinkled her nose at him, her eyes sparkling. "Tell him," she said, smiling at her husband.

Fortune glanced at his brother, who smiled blandly and shrugged. "You know Chantal. She insisted I send a telegram to Cal. And I've received one back. He and Sophia will take a train tomorrow. You can wait until Saturday now that we all have a chance to be together."

Claire looked at Fortune, who grinned good-naturedly. How different he looked! Seldom had he looked relaxed or happy when she had been traveling with him. His grin kindled a warmth in her, and along with it she felt a stab of caution. What would happen if she fell in love and her husband never returned it?

He glanced at her. "Saturday it'll be. All right, Claire?"

"Of course," she answered, surprised he had consulted her. "Chantal already has two seamstresses sewing a dress for me. I tried to talk her out of it."

"And I'm sure you lost," Fortune said, smiling at Chantal.

"Of course she lost! I love weddings, and to have a wedding party here at our house is wonderful! You should stay a week. Our friends would love to throw some parties for you."

Fortune smiled and shook his head. "I can't stay a week. So Cal gets in tomorrow?"

"Yes, and we can hear all about his railroad," Rafe said. "He was here little over a month ago on business."

"Why don't you live here in New Orleans?" Darcy asked Fortune.

"I have plans for a business in Atlanta. I'm going to open a steel mill. You can come to work for me."

"No, he can't," Rafe said with a smile. "I need him here."

"Fight over me and maybe I'll get a higher salary," Darcy said, giving Claire a wink. Pleasure shot through her because Darcy as well as the others seemed to enclose her in the O'Brien family as much as if Fortune were wildly in love with her. She was conscious of him, aware that his hand had drifted to her upper arm, his fingers trailing back and forth casually as if he were unaware of touching her.

She gazed out over the landscaped lawn, such a haven after their nights in the wild. A hummingbird hovered over tall pink hollyhocks, and Claire could feel the weight of her worries easing with every passing hour.

When dinner was announced by a female servant, Fortune linked her arm in his as he laughed at something Rafe said. They moved through the parlor to the large, high-ceilinged dining room and a table set with gleaming crystal and silver. She was seated at Rafferty's right, across the table from Fortune.

A servant tugged on the rope of a punkah that sent a refreshing breeze across the room. Rafe carved a golden turkey, and as they ate it with dressing, golden yams cooked in brown sugar, and fried okra, Claire was dazzled by the O'Briens, astounded that she was marrying into this warm, close family and that Michael was a part of all this.

For a moment she felt a strange surge of discomfort when she thought about how long she had kept Michael from knowing his family. She glanced uncomfortably at Fortune, who was laughing, his white teeth showing. He looked at her and she blinked, disconcerted that he might be able to guess what she had been thinking.

"And how's your friend Alaric?" Chantal asked. "He'll be disappointed he wasn't here for your wedding."

With another flash of white teeth, Fortune grinned. "My friend Alaric is in for a surprise." His gaze shifted to Claire. "I never expected when I left Atlanta to return with a wife. I'll send him a telegram."

"Nor did I expect to wed within the month I left Natchez. Or to find I'll be part of a family like this," Claire added quietly.

"We'll have to show you New Orleans," Rafe said.

"I am going to try to talk you into staying longer. Our friends would have parties—we could spend a day at Belle Destin, my father's home," Chantal explained to Claire.

"We can't stay that long. The parties will come with our next visit," Fortune said, flashing another smile at Claire.

Warmth filling her, she felt compelled to smile in return. He was relaxed, revealing a charming side that she had seen little of in their travels. Would he be this way when they left his family and returned to Atlanta?

They returned to the veranda, and in the leisurely late hours of evening they sat in the dark. The men's voices were deep, occasionally bursting into laughter as they talked about Ireland.

With a rustle of her skirts Chantal stood up. "I'll leave you now. Do what you want, Claire. When Ireland becomes the subject, these three can talk until the rooster crows."

"I'll join you," Claire said, glancing at Fortune, who was watching her.

As they walked through the house, Claire felt a rush of gratitude toward Chantal. At the top of the stairs, she turned and placed her hand lightly on Chantal's arm. "Thank you for all you've done for me today."

"I'm happy to do it. Michael is precious, and I'm glad you're marrying Fortune."

"He asked me because of Michael," Claire said shyly, feeling as if she were coming into the family on false pretenses.

"Fortune is a fine man. He'll be good to you."

Claire drew a deep breath. "We're caught in this because I love Michael, and he does too and neither of us can give him up."

"You shouldn't have to give him up. You're so pretty. You've never been in love?"

Claire looked into Chantal's dark eyes and shook her head. "I don't know much about men. Or to be more truthful, I haven't wanted anything to do with the men I've known."

"Fortune is different. I will pray love comes to both of you, because it should. You and Fortune should have a good marriage. He suffered terribly over Marilee, and thank heavens, he has found Michael and you." Chantal gave her a quick hug. "Give him time. Love should come."

Startled by Chantal's statement, Claire smiled, but in her heart she was unable to imagine that love would ever come.

"Good night, Chantal." Claire turned to go to her room and closed the door behind her. For the first time since she had run away, she had a room to herself. She walked around it, touching the fine furniture, thinking how lucky she and Michael were that Fortune had found them.

Claire gazed out the window at the bright silvery moon while she wondered about Trevor Wenger. How much trouble would he cause them when they reached Atlanta? With Michael having a mother and father, she didn't see how he could continue to try to get Michael back. She remembered Fortune's back: ". . . he wanted to kill me . . ."

A cold whisper of worry came for a moment. If something happened to Fortune—she brushed away the worry. He was going to be a solid shield for Michael and her, and he would provide for them.

She turned to look at herself in the mirror, touching the red silk dress that was so beautiful. Chantal had taken up the waist and the dress was slightly short, but not enough to detract or look unfashionable. Instead of seeing her image, she saw Fortune's expression, remembering when he had turned to greet her on the veranda. If only she could bring that look to his eyes again! There had been no doubt of his approval. His image danced in her mind, his sparkling blue eyes and rugged, handsome features. Her gaze shifted to look at her reflection.

She leaned forward, staring at herself. "Are you falling in love with this man who will never love anyone except Marilee?"

She shook her head. She didn't think she was, but she was drawn to him, she had to admit. And the more she was with him, the stronger the attraction became. She shook her head again. "Beware, because Fortune O'Brien lost his heart long ago and now he will take yours."

She wrinkled her nose, thinking how Chantal had made a face at him. With a smile she reached up to unfasten the tiny row of buttons on the red silk, taking care in pulling them apart. She thought about his question about the physical part of their marriage, and she felt a rush of excitement, though tinged with uncertainty. The thought of yielding to his lovemaking made her tingle, yet if he wanted only to satisfy his lust she didn't want that.

Maybe the day would come when they were both more

familiar with each other and she would feel differently. She undressed, thoughts returning to the evening, the friendship of the brothers. When she was dressed in a batiste nightgown with its dainty lace and ruffles, she brushed her hair and looked at her image in the mirror again, so pleased with the transformation Chantal had wrought, hoping while she was here she could learn to fix her hair in a more becoming fashion.

She stepped upon a footstool and climbed into a high rosewood feather bed, relishing the comfort of it. She felt a strange pang of loss that Fortune would not be beside her in it, then was startled that she had grown accustomed to their nights together.

The next day, she was busy with Chantal and the seamstress until the afternoon. Then she sat on the back veranda watching Michael run with Daniella, Jared trailing behind on chubby legs.

"He likes it here" came a deep voice, and Fortune appeared, walking up to drape his hand casually on her shoulder.

"He is gloriously happy, and he plays like a six-year-old child should. So much of the time I had to treat him like an adult, and he was only with me or other women I worked with. This is good for him."

"We're going to the train station to meet Cal. Want to come along?"

Surprised that he bothered to ask her, she stood up. "Yes, I'd like to."

He turned to face her, placing his hands on her shoulders, his gaze sweeping over the pink muslin dress she wore. "Thank God, Chantal has lots of dresses."

Claire smiled. "I know you were tired of seeing my poor blue calico, but I'll have to go back to wearing it when we leave here."

"I doubt that. By the way, I didn't have a chance to tell you last night with everyone around, but you looked beautiful, Claire."

She gazed up into his blue eyes, wondering what he felt for her. To her relief, all signs of anger seemed to be gone. "Thank you," she said, feeling a rush of warmth from his compliment.

He moved away. "We're about ready to go."

She went inside, going with him to the buggy where Rafe and Darcy waited. Chantal stood alongside in a bright pink organza dress, looking cool and fresh, as if the steamy afternoon could not affect her. Fortune helped Claire into the backseat and climbed up beside her.

"I'll see you here," Chantal said, waving at them as they started down the drive. While Rafferty drove, Claire was aware of Fortune's shoulder touching hers, of her skirt billowing over his long legs. They drove into the Vieux Carré with its wrought-iron balconies and wide shutters on narrow brick houses set only a few feet from the street.

"Darcy's bringing a wagon from work, and we'll meet him at the station," Rafe said. "I know there will be at least one trunk to haul home. If Sophia travels like Chantal, we'll fill the wagon with baggage," he said good-naturedly.

At the station Darcy joined them, and they stood with others on the platform, the smell of iron and coal in the air. Claire imagined Caleb would be another tall, black-haired, handsome O'Brien. With the engine roaring and a long hiss of steam as the train charged into the station and slowed, the platform shook. Then as the O'Briens moved forward, she waited, watching passengers alight. A man swung down and both brothers headed toward him.

This brother didn't resemble the others at all. Shorter than his brothers, Caleb O'Brien was thicker through the shoulders, his hair a mat of curly brown locks instead of black like theirs. His skin was a deep brown.

He turned to assist a beautiful golden-haired woman, taking her by the waist and swinging her off the train steps to the platform. She laughed and held her hat as

Rafferty and then Fortune hugged her. She turned to Darcy to give him a squeeze.

They all came toward Claire, and Fortune stepped forward, his arm circling her waist. "Claire, meet the last brother, Caleb, and his wife, Sophia. This is Claire Dryden, my fiancée."

"Welcome to the O'Brien family," Caleb said, stepping forward to give her a light hug while Sophia smiled at her.

"Let's go home where we can talk," Rafe said, picking up a satchel.

"We have to get our trunks. You don't think that's all Sophia packed," Caleb said with a smile.

"They should see how you travel," Fortune said lightly under his breath to her.

Before Claire could reply, he linked her arm with his and took Sophia's hand to head toward the buggy. "They'll get the porter to bring the trunk," he said. "Come on, Sophia. Tell us all the Memphis news."

"Memphis is still growing. So many people are coming through there now headed west. Have you ever been to Memphis, Miss Dryden?"

"No, I haven't," Claire answered, suddenly feeling wary, hoping she didn't have to explain her past too much. And what would happen if they ever found out she had sung in saloons?

"Then you'll have to come to visit us soon, Fortune, and let us show Memphis to her."

"That's nice, Sophia. How's your brother's paper?"

"It's steady. It doesn't have a big circulation, but John is changing as time goes by, and the paper reflects his attitudes. I suppose Cal has been an influence because John isn't as adamant against railroads as he once was. He's not even as opposed to whiskey."

"That's the O'Brien influence," Fortune said with a grin, and she laughed. He helped her into the front seat of the buggy, and turned to help Claire in back, where he climbed in to sit beside her again.

As they rode home, Claire sat quietly, listening to talk about Memphis and Caleb's railroad, aware of Fortune's long arm around her.

She spent the rest of the afternoon upstairs with Sophia and Chantal, and she found Sophia just as warm and welcoming, if quieter, than her sister-in-law. That night at the long dinner table, Claire looked at the O'Briens and felt a pang. It was clear that both Rafferty and Caleb were deeply in love with their wives. She looked down at her plate, her appetite suddenly gone because she knew hers was a marriage of convenience. *Don't expect love and you won't be hurt.* But she felt a longing for something more.

The next day passed swiftly, and then Saturday arrived. Chantal and Sophia both hovered over her all morning, getting her ready for the wedding. Finally they rode to the church and went to a small, empty room to dress.

"I should go see about Michael," she said while Sophia brushed her hair.

"Nonsense!" Chantal said from across the room. Sophia looked at Claire in the mirror and laughed. "All his uncles will take care of getting him dressed."

"We didn't expect all this fuss," Claire stated, watching Sophia carefully loop up a lock of hair and pin it with a small pink rosebud.

"You might not have expected this fuss," Sophia said, "but Fortune knew what to expect when he brought you here."

"This is different than your weddings. We're marrying for Michael's sake, not for love."

Sophia's eyes opened in surprise, and she took a few moments to reply. "Still, it's your wedding and it will happen only once. And you both want this."

"Yes, we do. I want it very much because now I can stay with Michael."

"Then it should be a very special wedding. One you

will remember," Chantal said, pulling a thread through a seam on the wedding dress. "This will be finished in just a few minutes."

Claire watched Sophia loop and pin her hair in curls on the sides and top of her head, placing rosebuds in her hair. Locks cascaded down the back of her head. Knowing that her hair had never looked prettier, Claire wondered what Fortune would think.

"Now I'm finished," Sophia said, stepping back, shaking her blond hair away from her face.

"You both have been so kind to me," Claire said.

"I love a wedding!" Chantal exclaimed, handing Claire a crinoline. She wore a corset and thin batiste chemise Chantal had gotten for her. A servant came forward to help her into her dress, lifting the crinoline over her head, careful to avoid touching her hair.

Next came the dress. All of them helped her into it, and the smooth satin shifted down over her. Claire felt fluttery and nervous, curious about Fortune and praying he wasn't having qualms about going through with it.

As the maid pulled the white satin dress up over Claire's shoulders and began to button it, Claire gasped at her image in the mirror. She looked down at the satin dress, which had lace inserts and tiny pearls sewn into the bodice and skirt. "This is so beautiful."

"And you look beautiful in it. We'll leave you to dress now," Chantal said, smiling at her. She wore a pale blue silk, and Sophia was in a pink silk. Both of their skirts rustled as they hurried out of the room.

Finally Claire was ready, taking one last look at herself when she heard a rap on the door and turned. "Come in."

The door opened and Rafferty appeared, his gaze sweeping over her as he smiled. He looked handsome in his white ruffled shirt and black coat and trousers. "Are you ready?"

"Yes," she answered, crossing the room while her nervousness increased. In a short time she would be Mrs.

Fortune O'Brien, part of this family, stepmother to Michael. Rafferty took her arm. "You look beautiful, Claire."

"Thank you."

"Claire," he said, pausing before they left her room, "give Fortune time. He may change."

Feeling a deep stirring of longing, she gazed up into Rafferty's eyes, wondering if he had any idea how angry Fortune had been with her only a short time before. She nodded. "Whether he does or not, I'm so happy that I can be with Michael. That's enough for me."

"Someday Michael will be a grown man, and you and Fortune will still have years ahead of you. Marriage won't end when Michael is grown."

She nodded. "Your brother has made it very clear how he feels." She looked into Rafferty's blue eyes, so like Fortune's. "Shall we go?"

Chapter 13

As they headed down the hall to the narthex, her attention shifted from Rafferty to the buzz of voices within. The church was filled with people, all to see her. Music began, and Claire's nerves fluttered with the strains of the organ. While heads turned to watch, Chantal walked down the aisle, followed by Sophia. Then Rafferty tugged on Claire's arm, and they moved to the doorway.

A sea of bright colors and black coats filled the church. There were far more people than she expected, yet she should have known Chantal and Rafferty would have many friends. To hear Chantal talk, Claire had thought they would have only the family and a few friends, but she realized Chantal loved parties and weddings and wasn't going to let the opportunity escape.

In the next moment she forgot all the faces. Down the length of the aisle, Fortune looked incredibly handsome in a black coat and trousers, a ruffled white shirt and white cravat. She felt a rush of gratitude toward him for taking her as his wife. It was swiftly followed by a sudden longing that he really did want to marry her.

Her gaze moved from him to Caleb and to Darcy, standing nearby. And then she saw Michael seated in the front row. She felt a lump in her throat as he smiled at her. His black curls had been neatly combed, but already were escaping into a tangle, and his dark eyes sparkled with joy. His small hand went up slightly to wave at her and she waved back.

As the music rose, the congregation stood, and with Rafferty she walked down the aisle, unaware of anything except Fortune's eyes steadily on her. Again she saw that look of admiration in his eyes and she felt better.

When they halted before the altar, Rafferty gave her to Fortune to repeat her vows, placing her cold hand in Fortune's warm one.

". . . to love, honor, and obey," she repeated solemnly, feeling with all her heart that she was going to try to please Fortune.

As he said the same words in his baritone voice, she gazed into his eyes and felt a longing that he meant what he said. The ceremony was long while they knelt and prayed and then stood again. Finally the balding minister looked at them both as Fortune's fingers clasped hers firmly.

"I now pronounce you man and wife."

The words made her heart leap. *Michael is my son forever!* She turned to face her new husband, gazing into his blue eyes, for a fleeting instant overwhelmed by gratitude toward him. With a solemn look he leaned forward to kiss her lightly, his lips barely brushing hers. Smiling, he linked her arm in his, and they hurried up the aisle.

Soon they climbed into a carriage to go to Rafferty's house, and Fortune motioned to Michael to climb up with them. As the boy settled between them, the driver started the carriage. Michael's eyes sparkled, and he linked one hand in Claire's and his other in Fortune's. "Now I have a mother and a father!" he said, grinning at her and then at Fortune.

"That's right, Michael," Fortune said, smiling at his son, and if he felt regret or grief, he kept it hidden. His blue eyes went over Michael's head to look into her eyes, and her breath caught. He was so handsome, so good to Michael.

The reception was at Rafferty's. People spilled over the lawn and all through the house, and almost as soon as they arrived, she was separated from Fortune. Only later on, as she passed the library and glanced inside, did she see Fortune. He and Rafferty were talking. Both held glasses of brandy, Fortune standing with his back to her while Rafe frowned at him. She moved on, wondering what they discussed because they seemed to be having an argument.

Inside the library Fortune crossed the room to look out at the bright yellow cannas and a row of purple and white cosmos. He swirled the brandy in his glass.

"Take her down to the hotel," Rafe urged. "Give your marriage some kind of chance instead of starting out for Atlanta tonight."

"I told you, I don't love her and she knows that. And I asked her if she wanted the physical side of marriage. I told her I'll oblige her, but she said no."

"Lord's sakes, Fortune! What did you expect her to answer?"

He turned from the window to face his brother, feeling annoyed. "I'm not about to lie to her. She knows I don't love her."

"She's a beautiful woman and so caring with Michael."

"You should know that's not the same as being the woman you love. If you had to go into a second marriage for your children's sake, you might understand."

Rafferty raked his fingers through his hair. "It's none of my business, but I think you're cheating yourself as well as a fine woman. Marilee is gone and she's not coming back. If you'd stop dwelling on the past, you could make a fine life for yourself. Claire is a wonderful, beautiful woman."

Fortune slanted him a look. "You've known her how long, Rafe?" he asked dryly.

"We've all been together for several days now, and Chantal and Sophia have spent time with her. I've seen her with Michael. And any man here will tell you she's a beautiful woman."

"That she is." Fortune looked at the brandy in his goblet, raised it, and drank it down, feeling it burn inside. He faced Rafe. "I can't fall in love just because it's convenient. Love comes from the heart, and you know it isn't always logical. But it's something that you can't conjure up just because it would make life more orderly."

"Dammit, you could give her more than you are."

"She's more than satisfied. Ask her."

"I don't have to. I can see that. But someday some man will come along and take her from you, and you'll wish you had opened your eyes a lot sooner."

Curbing his annoyance, Fortune set down his goblet with a faint clink. "We're leaving tonight for Atlanta." He strolled toward the door. "Michael is packed and ready. Thank you for everything. I'll talk to Chantal, because this was much more than I expected and it was good to have all the family together again."

"You know what you want to do. Fortune, give her a chance."

Fortune nodded tightly as he reached out to shake Rafferty's hand. "Thanks. I'll get them and go. Come to Atlanta."

"I'll come see about my investment. And you keep in touch."

"Thanks again for all this." Fortune left the room to get Claire and Michael.

After hugs and kisses and promising to come visit, they finally climbed into a buggy driven by one of the servants. As they left, Claire turned to look back at the house. The late afternoon sun splashed over it, and she wondered if she had just spent a brief idyll in her life that might never happen again.

She gazed at her new husband. With each turn of the wheels he seemed to transform into the tough man she had known while traveling. He was quiet, Michael chattering to her as they rode to the ship. When they reached the busy dock, Michael was enthralled with the ships.

"Look how big they are!"

"You'll sail on one, and part of the time I'll see to it that you get to handle the wheel," Fortune promised.

"Criminy!" he exclaimed in awe. "Mama, look how huge it is." Sails were furled, lines tied to the dock and men were scurrying about while casks were still being loaded.

"Let's go," Fortune said, leading the way up the gangway onto the ship, his boots scraping the boards. Halyards clinked in the faint breeze, and the cries of gulls were shrill and constant. The servant carried a trunk on board, and she thought of the dresses Chantal had given her wondering if Fortune would even notice them. Michael was excited over the prospect of riding on a boat, something he couldn't remember because he had been a tiny baby the last time he'd been on board a ship.

They went below and were shown their cabin and one next to them for Michael. She glanced around at the narrow room and the bunk bed, the simple furnishings, realizing they would be in close confines.

"I'll take Michael to talk to the captain, and he can watch them get under way," Fortune said.

She nodded as he left. She glanced at an oval mirror secured to the bulkhead, seeing her image in her bridal dress. She was alone, her husband above decks with his son. She felt another pang of longing, wishing the wedding could have been because of love. She reached back to unfasten the dress, but quickly decided she would have to wait for Fortune because she couldn't reach all the buttons.

She felt the ship shift and wood creak. Hastily buttoning the dress again, she caught up the train and went above decks. Sails were unfurled, sailors scurrying over the deck. Fortune and Michael stood in the bow, wind blowing their hair as they watched the ship sail out of the harbor. She stepped to the rail, looking at the spire of the church where she had married, over the trees and rooftops of New Orleans, a city that would always hold memories of one of the happiest times in her life. Her gaze shifted to swirling water of the muddy Mississippi, and she felt a chill as she stared at it, wondering what lay ahead.

Lifting her chin, she looked for Michael and was reassured. Always when she feared the future with Fortune, she could look at Michael and know how blessed she was by the marriage.

A fine spray blew against her, and she stepped back from the rail, lurching forward again as the ship changed course slightly. Atlanta, Georgia. In all her travels Claire had never been there. She heard it had been burned during the war, and she wondered what kind of home Fortune had, wondering if he even had a home since he had just got out of the army. She watched docks give way to muddy banks covered by tall cypress draped in Spanish moss.

Fortune shifted, looking the length of the ship, seeing Claire standing at the rail, holding the train of her wedding dress, the wind whipping her hair lose from pins. He talked to Michael, gesturing toward the captain.

"You'll get that dress wet."

She turned to face him, her dark eyes wide and compelling. "I can't unfasten the buttons without help."

He glanced back at Michael. "I'll take Michael up to the captain and come below to help you."

He left, taking Michael's hand. She could hear the boy's voice raised in excitement, but they were too far away and the wind was blowing too strongly for her to tell what he was saying.

With a last look at New Orleans as it receded around a bend, she turned from the rail and went back to the cabin. In minutes Fortune stepped inside, seeming to fill the tiny space.

He started to remove his coat. "Let me get out of this," he said, untying the cravat and crossing to a bottle of champagne. "Compliments of my brother."

With a pop of the cork he opened the bottle and she waited, watching him while he poured the champagne. As it bubbled, he picked up the glasses, handing one to her and looking at her solemnly. "Here's to a good marriage."

Touching her glass to his, she wondered if he already had regrets, because he didn't sound happy.

He gulped down the champagne and moved away from her to refill his glass. Watching him with a fluttery nervousness, she drank the bubbly champagne. He came back to her. "Turn around, and I'll unbutton you."

She turned her back to him and felt his fingers tug the buttons. The air was cool as the dress opened, and his fingers were warm, brushing her flesh.

Fortune turned the buttons, desire rising in him in spite of the desolation he felt when he remembered his wedding to Marilee. He'd had brandy at Rafferty's, and he knew it was clouding his thinking. As he freed the row of tiny pearl buttons, Claire's slender back looked satiny smooth. Locks of brown hair fell over her shoulders, parting to reveal the nape of her neck. When he looked at her, he wanted to touch her. She was a beautiful, desirable woman.

His hands shook as longing burned in him. Her waist was tiny, narrow enough he could easily span it with his hands. His gaze ran over the thin chemise, the laces of her corset. He looked at her nape again and leaned forward to brush his lips over it.

She shifted slightly, but she didn't stop him. He moved locks of her hair, feeling their silky softness as he kissed her neck. He turned her around to slide his arm around her waist and pull her up against him.

Claire's hands flew against his chest. Her heart pounded violently as she looked up at Fortune, whose gaze lowered to her mouth. His arm tightened around her, pulling her against his chest. When he did, her hands slid to his arms. He bent his head, brushing her mouth with his, his lips warm and enticing. He placed his lips over hers to open her mouth. His tongue entered her mouth, sliding slowly over her lower lip, and she moaned with pleasure. As she tightened her arms around him, she felt his hard arousal press against her.

Thoughts vanished, her senses reeling. He pushed away the wedding dress, sliding it off one shoulder. She started to protest as his hand slid across her exposed breast, his fingers brushing her nipple. Warmth shot through her, heat starting low in her body. She felt as if she might melt against him. She moaned softly again, the sound muffled by his mouth upon hers.

He pushed away the other sleeve of the dress, and it slid down around her waist. Leaning away from her slightly, he caressed her, his hand cupping her breast, his thumb brushing across her nipple. On fire, she began thrusting her hips against him, desire awakening. She hadn't known what it would be like to be loved by a man, but this was beyond anything she had imagined. She felt faint from his touches, and she wanted him to keep on and never stop. Her arms slid around his neck as she clung to him. Her tongue entered his mouth, touching his tongue, and a dizzying bombardment of sensations rocked her.

He bent his head to take her nipple in his mouth. She gasped with pleasure, her fingers winding in his hair. He hooked his fingers in the satin and slid it down over her hips, letting it fall with a whispery rustle to the floor. Her pulse roared in her ears, drowning out everything else while he stroked her.

She glanced at him to see him looking at her breasts, his gaze filled with unmistakable desire, but then she realized what she was letting him do so easily. There was no love in his heart. He was taking her as he would one of the sporting women.

Claire hurt because she wanted more from him. If she yielded now so easily, she felt she would give up all chance of winning his respect and, maybe someday, his love. "Fortune," she said quietly.

As she paused, she leaned down to catch the dress, pulling it up to her waist. "Fortune—I don't want it like this between us. I have to have more."

His lashes raised as he looked at her, a hungry look that made her wonder if he would take her by force.

"I have to have love," she whispered, stepping back from him. "We talked about this," she said, wanting to see the tender expression he sometimes gave Michael or the happy look shared with his brothers.

Instead Fortune took a deep breath, his broad chest expanding. "All right, Claire. I told you, I'll do what you want." He turned around and she ached as she sensed his retreat. She felt on fire and she wanted his arms around her. She wanted his kisses, his arms holding her, his companionship in the night.

He drank another glass of champagne and moved toward the hatch. "I'll go above."

As soon as he had gone, she felt a loss. She clutched her hand to her middle, wondering what had happened to her independent life. Had she already fallen in love with her new husband, with a man who had told her emphatically that he would never love her?

She closed her eyes, feeling panicky and alone, wondering what kind of marriage they would have. She could call him back, have him make love to her, but it would be so empty. And afterward he might think she was little better than the sporting women.

She took a deep breath. "I love him," she whispered in the empty cabin. "I'm in love with him, and he'll never love me in return."

She removed the crinoline and her underclothing, changing to the white cotton nightgown Chantal had given her. Not wanting to hang the beautiful wedding dress on a hook, Claire carefully folded it, feeling as if she were folding away her heart. As she lay down on the bunk and wondered about Fortune, she felt confined in the tiny space. What was he thinking? Was he overcome with regret? Or had he accepted their bargain and dismissed her from his mind? She stared at the timbered bulkhead, wondering if they could find any happiness except with Michael. She sat up on the bunk and gazed out a porthole at the wide river. The summer evening was still early and she got up to change, rummaging in the trunk, gathering her underthings and pulling on a pink organdy dress that had a skirt covered in ruffles, a low neck trimmed in lace, and tiny sleeves.

Fortune leaned on the rail, letting the wind cool him. He ached for Claire, yet he kept remembering the last vows he had made to Marilee at her grave. He had thought then they would be for a lifetime. Had that been only a year ago?

He watched the sun sinking below the horizon, casting an orange streamer across the surface of the brown water. He gazed down at the water, bubbles frothing as the ship gained speed. Claire was a fine woman and she deserved more, but he couldn't pretend to love her. He wanted her badly. She was beautiful and responsive and innocent. He could have seduced her, but she was the type of woman who wanted love. If he took her tonight, tomorrow, or a month from now, she would want his love and he couldn't give it. And then it would be worse between them than it was now.

Now neither one was in love and she would not be hurt if he stayed out of her bed. He drew a deep breath, wishing his body could follow the logic of his mind. In vain he tried to shut out the images of Claire, of her pale breasts in his dark hands, of the softness of her that made him want to bury himself in her.

He groaned, wishing they were in Atlanta, where he could give all his attention to work and Michael. He would have to find a mistress, someone who would be quiet and not cause rumors. If he didn't have a mistress, some night he would seduce Claire, because she was an enticing woman. And when he did, if it was against her wishes, they would both regret it.

He turned, striding toward the wheel to find someone else to talk to and try to forget Claire, to stop imagining her stretched in the bed below, her hair fanned behind her head, her supple body minus the corset and the crinoline. He could hear Michael's voice and knew he was excited.

"Michael?" Fortune asked, looking at Michael and Captain Smith, who stood at the wheel. The captain turned, his face ruddy, his blond hair showing beneath his cap.

"He let me hold the wheel with him!" Michael exclaimed in a high voice. "And Captain Smith has told me about sailing all around the world."

"That's good. I hoped you thanked him."

"He's a fine lad," Captain Smith said.

"Let's go to the rail, Michael, and leave the captain to steer."

"He's fine, Colonel O'Brien," the captain said with a trace of a Danish accent. "I have a son, and I know they like the sea. Leave him with me."

Fortune nodded reluctantly, going back to the rail. It was almost dark, with the sun below the horizon when he went back to get Michael. "Come on. I'll show you over the ship."

"Yes, sir," he exclaimed eagerly. "Thank you, sir," he said to the captain, and Captain Smith gave him a broad, toothy smile.

"You'll make a fine sailor someday, Michael."

Michael's grin widened as he moved beside Fortune, who walked toward the mast. "I'll help you climb part of the way up if you want," he said.

"Yes, I do!"

Fortune swung the boy up onto the foot ropes and climbed up beside him, letting Michael go ahead and moving beneath him so if Michael lost his footing, he could catch him. Scrambling up with agility, Michael climbed without any seeming fear of heights, which pleased Fortune.

"Now, let's stop," Fortune said because they were high enough for Michael to have a view.

"Criminy! Is this the ocean?"

"We're still on the Mississippi. It's just widening out, and then we sail into the Gulf. In the Gulf is where our ship went down when I came from Ireland with my brothers. Your grandmother O'Brien drowned that night."

"Your mother?" Michael said, becoming solemn, his dark eyes studying Fortune as wind ruffled his hair.

"Yes. I was separated from your uncles and we were all picked up by ships, but different ones, so we landed different places. Finally we got back together."

"Were you with any of them?"

"No. Your Uncle Caleb and Uncle Darcy were together. I was alone and Uncle Rafe was alone. He landed in New Orleans and later the others moved there. I ended up in Baltimore." He glanced down and saw Claire standing on the deck, looking up at them. She wore a pink dress without a crinoline, and the wind whipped the skirt against her slender form. Her hair was tied behind her head with a pink ribbon, and he remembered the moments earlier in the cabin when he had held her close in his arms and caressed her.

She studied them, and he wondered if she was worried about Michael.

"There's Claire. Let's go down now, Michael."

"Yes, sir. Papa, tomorrow can we climb to the top?"

Fortune glanced up and then down at Michael's expectant face. "Yes, we can go as high as the crow's nest, that platform," he answered, pointing overhead.

"I want to tell Mama."

They climbed down, and Fortune swung Michael to the deck.

"Mama, we're going up there tomorrow." As she

looked skyward wind tugged strands of her hair out of their pins, and Fortune detected the enticing smell of honeysuckle on her skin.

"That's fine, Michael, if you wait for Papa and if you're very careful."

"You can come too!"

She laughed and at that moment Fortune realized how solemn she was except with Michael. She shook her head. "Michael, dresses weren't meant for climbing to the top of a ship."

"You could wear some of Papa's trousers."

She smiled and glanced over his head at Fortune. "I'll be willing to oblige," he said lightly.

"Thank you, no. Michael, I'll leave climbing ropes to you and your father."

Fortune was mildly surprised that she had no objection because on the trail she had seem protective toward Michael. Had she grown to trust him so completely? he wondered.

They moved to the rail again, and as darkness fell, they stood watching the moon rise over the water. Finally Michael became quiet, and Clair took his hand to lead him below to bed.

She returned much later, moving to stand at the rail near Fortune. "This is his second boat ride. The first was when we fled from my home. He was a good baby, so quiet and happy."

Fortune turned to lean against the rail and face her. "How long was it before the first man tried to take him back?"

She gazed at the water in silence a moment. "I disembarked in New Orleans and got a job at a dress shop. I could keep Michael with me while I sewed, and I rented a small room. We were there several months, and then I realized one afternoon that a man was watching the shop and that he had been across the street the day before. Without any other reason I felt something was wrong. I took Michael out the back way to our rented room, packed our things, and left on a train to Vicksburg. In Vicksburg I worked in my first bonnet shop, and I liked the work. When I saw the same man outside the shop, I fled again. So the pattern started."

"You must have had to look over your shoulder all the time."

"Yes, but that was the price I had to pay for what I had done. One time we were in St. Louis—"

"Why didn't you go back East to the big cities?"

"I thought I would need more money to live there, and I was young and frightened."

"Go ahead, I interrupted you," he said quietly.

"In St. Louis, I was carrying over three hundred dollars I had saved, so I opened an account in a bank, and after that I've sent money north to go into my account. You know the rest."

They stood in silence and she wondered what he was thinking, if he disapproved of everything she had done. Finally she turned away. "It's much cooler up here."

"There are some chairs," he said, pointing at deck chairs and leading her to them with his fingers lightly touching her arm. She was conscious of his touch; the slightest contact was volatile. She settled on a wooden chair, and Fortune sat on another beside her.

There was a crisp, cool breeze. The only noise was the splash of water against the hull. In only a few minutes she began dozing.

Enjoying the coolness, Fortune studied the stars, thinking about Claire as a seventeen-year-old girl taking Michael and trying to support him and care for him when she was all alone and knew men were after her. Fortune glanced at her and saw her head loll, her lashes dark against her cheeks. He stood and when he picked her up she seemed frail, soft, and warm.

Below, after placing her on the bunk, he removed her shoes, his hands lingering on her slender, delicate feet.

He turned and left the cabin, going back to the deck to sit on one of the chairs, thinking about Atlanta and his new business. He would build a house, and he wanted a fine one. And he wouldn't let Trevor Wenger come close to Michael.

Finally Fortune settled back on the hard wooden slats and closed his eyes, going to sleep.

Two days later, they changed to a smaller boat to go upriver to Chattahoochee, Florida, where Fortune bought a wagon for the rest of the journey to Atlanta. It was late when they stopped for the night in Donalsonville. Fortune rented adjoining rooms for them in the two-story hotel, and after Michael was asleep in bed and Fortune returned to the room he shared with Claire, she faced him.

"By now Trevor Wenger probably knows that Harwood is dead. Do you think Michael is safe in there by himself? His grandfather could send someone else after him."

"By this time Wenger will have figured out we're returning to Atlanta. And I'd guess that he knows by now that I have Michael. I don't think there's any worry, but I locked Michael's door. We can hear him if he calls."

Fortune moved restlessly around the small room, which held a washstand and a rocking chair and a bed. His shirt sleeves were rolled high, and he had unbuttoned the neck of his shirt. He opened a satchel he carried and removed a knife to place it in his boot. He put a derringer in his waistband and pulled on his coat, turning to face her.

"Claire, I'm going out. It's hot and I'm not going to sleep any time soon. I'm going to find a game of faro."

She nodded, watching him leave and wondering if he was seeking a game of chance or a woman. All the time on board ship, he had slept somewhere else besides the small cabin with her.

She ran her fingers across her temple and moved to the window, letting a breeze blow across her. She checked on Michael several times, each time finding him asleep. Finally she left the door open between their rooms.

She changed to her white cotton nightgown, looking at herself in the long mirror. The gown was opaque, yet not quite heavy enough to hide the darker areas where it rested against her nipples. It was too hot for a wrapper and she didn't expect Fortune back for hours.

She stretched in bed, unable to sleep, damp with perspiration in the hot room. She unbuttoned the neck of her gown, pushing it open and wiping her throat. She was staring into space almost dozing when she heard a clink.

Chapter 14

The lamp was out and moonlight spilled into the room. Fortune stopped beside the table, emptying his coat pockets. As coins rolled and clinked, she sat up.

"My word! Did you win all that?"

He raised his head to look at her. "Sorry if I woke you."

"I haven't been able to sleep. It's too hot," she said, climbing out of bed and going to the table to run her hands over the coins. "A gold piece! Great heavens, how much did you win?"

He struck a match, the tip flaring and highlighting his cheekbones, reflecting in pinpoints in his blue eyes as he squinted and lit a cheroot. He glanced at her. "You can count it, Claire." His gaze flicked over her before he shook out the match. She looked at the money, shifting it and sitting down while he turned to light a small lamp.

"The men I've seen gamble usually lose more than they win."

"I quit when I lose. My father gambled away a prosperous farm and everything we had. It killed him and ruined my mother's health and drove us all from Ireland. I won't gamble away our money, so you can rest easy there."

"That's good." Counting, she bent her head over the money, and Fortune studied her. Her brown hair fell forward, shining in the glow of the lamp. Her gown was unbuttoned and pushed open, and he could see pale flesh and the soft curve of her breast.

"Claire, half of that is yours."

She raised her head, her dark eyes meeting his. "Thank you, but as your wife I belong to you, and all that I have belongs to you."

He stood with his hands on his hips, feeling the warmth of too much brandy and the heat of the room. "You can keep your savings."

"Thank you. I'd like that," she answered solemnly.

"In case you want to run again," he said, knowing he sounded cynical. She bent over the coins and he felt desire stirring. He wanted to pull her into his arms and kiss her, to push her down on the bed and possess her.

He moved restlessly, suspecting neither of them would be able to sleep. Turning around, he looked at her.

"Claire, want me to teach you to play poker?"

She raised her head to study him, considering his question. "Yes, it would give us something to do. I can't sleep and you don't look as if you're going to."

"You can use your half of the money."

"Then I imagine you will win it all back easily."

"It's more interesting if there are some stakes."

He sat down and as they divided the money, she looked up at him. "My heavens, you won a lot! Have you ever lost this much?"

"Yes, but I've won it back. I told you, I'm not going to lose everything gambling." As he leaned forward to explain the hands to her, his gaze strayed to the V of her nightgown. She was too busy studying her cards and looking at the stacks of money to notice. The cotton was unbuttoned inches below her collarbone, one side falling open enough to reveal the full curve of her breast. He wanted to reach across the table and shove the gown away completely, to cup her soft breast in his hand.

He brought his attention back to the cards. By the second round, he waited, looking at her bite her lip and frown.

"Claire, the way to win at poker is to bluff. Don't let your emotions reveal what kind of hand you have."

Her dark eyes met his. "I see why you win."

He felt a flicker of amusement as he tossed a gold coin on the center of the table. "I'll raise you."

"Now, you already know that I don't have anything."

"You don't know what I have. It might be better and it might be worse than what you have."

"It couldn't be worse," she said, tossing down the cards. He scooped up the winnings and was amused again at the expression on her face as she watched her money being raked across the table.

"How big are your savings?" he asked.

"Not very big probably by your standards. You're more accustomed to money than I am. I have four thousand dollars."

"That's a great deal of money," he said, surprised. She had either sacrificed a lot to save money, or she had earned more than he would have guessed possible.

"You told me you intend to be part of Atlanta society for Michael's sake. How can you expect them to accept you when you fought with Sherman?"

He raked his wavy hair away from his face. "I don't intend to mention General Sherman. I was under General Howard's command. And you're southern. My brother was an officer in the Confederacy, Rafe was a blockade runner and supplied the South with goods. All three brothers are southerners. Besides, Atlanta is starting over and rebuilding, and people from everywhere are pouring in there. There's plenty of northern money in Atlanta. They'll accept me."

She gazed at him solemnly. "Yes, they will. You may be the one to meet someone and fall in love," she said quietly.

"No, I won't. Marilee's been gone a long time now,

and I've never felt anything beyond a physical need for another woman."

Claire looked down, but he couldn't imagine his words hurt her because there was no love between them. He shuffled and dealt the cards.

The next hand her eyes danced with excitement, and Fortune had to bite back a laugh because she might as well have announced that she thought she had a winning hand. He glanced at her dwindling pile of money and bet a large amount, wanting to let her win back what she had started with, not caring if she had it all.

"I'll call!" she exclaimed triumphantly, and he tossed down his cards, looking at her turn over three aces and two queens.

She looked at him. "You knew I was going to win, didn't you?"

He grinned and shrugged, stretching and leaning back in the chair. "You still haven't learned to hide your feelings."

"Maybe I'll learn soon. This doesn't seem right. You gave this money back to me when you had won it all."

"Take it, Claire. I don't care if you take all of it."

"You don't value money."

"It's necessary. When our ship went down, we lost everything. I had nothing when I arrived in Baltimore, and I don't want that ever to happen again," he said, remembering the first frightening days. "I was fifteen years old, and I had a hell of a time until I got a job building boats. But I'm comfortably fixed now, and I intend to start my own business and I intend to succeed at it. So other things have become more important in my life. Michael is more important. He's more important to you than money. You wouldn't have sold him to me."

"No, I wouldn't have!" She stood up, taking the blue calico from her satchel and wrapping the coins in it.

"What are you doing?"

"I don't want people handling our things to hear this jingling and know this bag is filled with money."

"And I don't suppose you'll get rid of that dress even when you have new ones."

She looked at him with wide eyes. "Why would I? It seems a waste."

He stabbed out the last of the cheroot and crossed the room to get a drink from a bottle of brandy. As he lowered the bottle, he watched her move around the room. Perspiration beaded her forehead, and short tendrils of brown hair clung to her temples. His gaze ran down the length of her gown. She stood between him and the lamp, and he could see the outline of her figure, her full, upthrusting breasts, her slim waist and flat belly, her long legs, the saucy curve of her bottom. She wore only the gown, and as his gaze roamed slowly back up over her, desire burned in him. He set down the brandy bottle, knowing he had to leave the room or he wouldn't be able to keep his hands to himself.

She turned, placing the satchel in a stack with their others, standing only inches from him. His gaze lowered to the open neck of her gown.

"Dammit," he said, reaching for her and pulling her to him. "I know it's hot, but you're unbuttoned—"

Her eyes flew wide, her hands touching his upper arms lightly as he bent his head to cover her mouth with his. The moment he touched her soft lips, desire consumed him. His tongue thrust deep into her mouth, touching the wet softness, feeling her curves against his body, knowing only the cotton gown covered her. He slid his hand down her back and over the full curve of her buttocks, wanting her, too aware it would complicate his life if he took her.

With a racing pulse Claire wound her arms around his neck, yielding to him, returning his kisses as his hand roamed over her back, down to her thighs. Her head reeled with the exquisite sensations he caused. He was hard and strong and she wanted his kisses, yet she knew they were as without love as before.

She pushed against him, leaning away. His hand slid beneath her gown to cup her breast, his thumb rubbing slowly over her nipple, bringing it to a hard peak as she gasped and momentarily forgot that she had intended to stop him. He bent his head, taking her breast in his mouth to tease with his teeth and tongue.

She pushed again and stepped back, yanking together the neck of her gown. "I didn't realize I was unbuttoned. It was so hot . . ."

She trembled with longing as she faced him, because the expression in his eyes made her want to fling herself back into his arms. He looked as if he could devour her. His trousers bulged from his arousal, and she felt weak-kneed, burning with her own yearning.

"I'll go for a walk," he said, and strode from the room, closing the door quietly behind him.

She stared after him, wondering about their marriage, wondering if she should yield to him, to enjoy his kisses and caresses without love. And every time she considered it, she knew she wanted love. If she gave him her body, she would fall in love with him.

She moved to the window, wishing she could have gone outside with him to let her body and emotions cool. What kind of marriage would they have? Would it be filled with torment like this until he took a mistress? At the thought of Fortune taking a mistress, Claire felt a swift surge of anger. She didn't want him turning to another woman, yet she couldn't hold him if she didn't have his love.

He didn't come back until almost dawn, and then he settled in the chair with his long legs propped on the table. As soon as it was daylight and he discovered she was awake, he wanted to go.

Before the sun had risen above the rooftops, they were

heading north with Michael asleep in the bed of the wagon.

During the day Michael was excited about everything around him, and Claire heard Fortune promise to bring him back to the Gulf for another ride on a ship.

When they traveled from dawn to late at night, Claire knew Fortune was pushing hard to get back to Atlanta. He seemed tense and was quiet around her except occasional moments with Michael. Sometimes she would catch his gaze going over her in a hungry appraisal that set her pulse pounding.

That night they stayed in Abbeville along the Chattahoochee River, and as soon as Michael was asleep, Fortune left. The room was even hotter than the night before, and she sat by the window, wondering when he would return. She fell asleep in the chair by the window, and when she stirred in the morning's first light, she was in bed. Fortune stood across the narrow room, wiping his jaw from shaving.

"As soon as you're ready, I'll carry Michael to the wagon and we can get moving."

They rode hard all day again and did not stop until late at night at Columbus. She marveled at Fortune's stamina because she knew he had slept little since leaving the boat.

They stayed nights in Columbus and LaGrange, finally riding through rolling hills into Atlanta late at night, coming in on Peachtree Street. Past city hall the army's tents filled the grounds. The soft glow of gaslights on street corners seemed welcoming in the dark night.

She sat on the wagon seat beside Fortune as they turned onto Whitehall Street. "Do you think about being here in the war and the burning of the city?"

"No. That's over and done, thank God. They're rebuilding. Atlanta was a railroad city before the war. That's how the city came into being. The Georgia General Assembly decided to build a state railroad to carry cotton.

The railroad was to run from Tennessee to the Chattahoochee River, but instead the terminus was located eight miles south of the river, where several roads converged. The town was called Terminus at first and was later changed to Atlanta."

"I've never been to Atlanta."

"You've been to New Orleans more than once, haven't you?"

"Yes. Early this spring I sang in a saloon there."

"You didn't wear that blue calico dress to sing in New Orleans."

"No. Sometimes I could borrow dresses. I had to leave Natchez in a hurry, and I left my one silk dress behind."

"When you worked the saloons, what did Michael do? You couldn't leave him in a room by himself."

"No, I took him with me," she answered, looking up to see Fortune frown. "The women loved him, and he was young enough that he didn't notice too much about his surroundings."

"That's over now." Along Whitehall Street he stopped in front of a new three-story hotel. "This is where I've been staying since I got out of the army. Wait with Michael and I'll get someone to take our things. I'll carry Michael inside."

She watched Fortune stride into the hotel, where lights burned in the lobby. Down the street two men rode past on horseback and a buggy moved briskly along, and she wondered what her life and Michael's would be like in the growing city.

Soon Fortune returned to help her out of the wagon and to lift a sleeping Michael into his arms. "The clerk will take care of everything, including taking the wagon to the livery stable. All we have to do is go to our rooms. I've taken several rooms, and I'll move my things into them tomorrow."

They climbed three flights of stairs with two porters

carrying baggage. One held open the door to a room, and Fortune entered.

"Here are the keys, sir."

While one of the men lit lamps and then opened windows, Claire found a suite that was as elegant as any they had stayed in before. And everything looked new, as if they were the first to stay there. The smell of new wood and fresh paint was in the air. Mahogany furniture and pale yellow damask-covered chairs and settees were in the room. Fortune entered an adjoining room with Michael, and in a few minutes he returned.

"He's sound asleep. I think he could sleep through a siege. We have several rooms here, Claire. We'll live here while I get a house built for us."

She turned to stare at him. "You can afford to stay here that long?"

A smile flitted across his features. "Yes, I can."

"This is so extravagant! I'm sure we can find a room somewhere in this city."

"Yes, we can, but I can afford this, and I want to be comfortable while we're building a house. And it's time Michael had a little more luxury in his life."

She bit her lip and turned away, wondering if Fortune considered her a terrible mother to his son. She moved around the room, feeling the awe she had experienced in the other fancy rooms, but even more so to think they would live here while Fortune had a house built. She turned around to look at him, wondering how wealthy he was.

"Do you have as much money as your brother?" she asked bluntly.

Fortune pulled off his shirt, looking amused as he tossed it over a chair. "It doesn't matter how fancy the damned hotel is, it's still hot! No, I don't have as much as Rafferty. I don't know about Caleb. I have more than Darcy, who has next to nothing at his age. I'll take you to the bank, Claire, and let you look at my account."

"Oh, my heavens, I didn't mean to pry."

He looked even more amused, crossing the room to place his hands on her shoulders. "I have enough for you to stop worrying about it. And I have enough for you to hire a seamstress tomorrow and get dresses made."

All she could think about was his hands touching her, his bare chest only inches from her. She didn't know where to look or where to place her hands.

"And you're not prying. We're married. It isn't a normal marriage, but we're still man and wife, and you're free to ask me whatever you want. We're not going to have secrets between us. Marilee's aunt left me a large inheritance. In addition to that, I have my savings from my army pay. You aren't going to have to worry about an income."

She barely heard him. He was standing too close, and her gaze finally slid down to his mouth. She felt heat start low within her, an unfolding that seemed to run up through her veins and alter her heartbeat. His hand caressed the nape of her neck, and her gaze flew up to meet his. His blue eyes had darkened, his gaze intent as he watched her and then looked at her mouth.

He bent his head, his mouth covering hers, kissing her slowly, his tongue entering her mouth in a sensual touch that made her sigh and close her eyes and move into his arms. She kissed him back, wondering if each time she would be bound more closely to him, wondering if kissing had any effect on him except to stir his physical cravings.

"This is madness," she whispered, leaning away and looking up at him. "When you're close to me, I want you to kiss me. But I don't want to bed without love."

"I'll honor what you want, but it's obvious I like to kiss you," he said in a husky voice that was like another caress.

"Maybe sometime, Fortune, I can let you go on and not care, but I can't yet. I don't mean to try to entice you."

He gave her a sardonic look, one corner of his mouth curling up. "God forbid, Claire, that you should entice your husband."

She blushed, embarrassed, feeling as if he were laughing at her. "I can't help what I feel. I know I want to be loved if a man . . ." Her voice trailed away and her blush deepened as she moved away from him.

He let her go and she heard him go into the next room. When he returned, he was barefoot and still bare-chested, a burning cheroot in his mouth. He placed it on a crystal ashtray and crossed the room to her.

Turning her chin up, he looked into her eyes. Her pulse skipped and she wondered if she would ever get accustomed to the unusual blue of his eyes or ever be able to stand close to him without her heart lurching into a gallop.

"Claire, there's something I want you to understand. You are never to allow Trevor Wenger to see Michael."

She frowned, seeing the firm set to Fortune's jaw and hearing the cold, harsh note back in his voice.

"Do you think he would hurt Michael?"

"No. I think he wants him because he's his own blood; I don't think he would ever hurt him physically. I don't think he would do what's best for Michael."

"They're blood kin. Don't you think that's extremely harsh?"

"Are you forgetting he sent Harwood after you? You don't think that's harsh? I'm sure he didn't care what Harwood did with you," Fortune said, his voice becoming more deadly and anger showing in his eyes. He turned around. "Look at my back. He meant that beating to kill me."

She looked at his broad, muscular back, the fine lines of scars across it, and she drew a deep breath. "I know he's a terrible man in some ways, but never to allow him to see his grandson—"

"He deserves that," Fortune declared, facing her again.

"You can't keep him away when you both live in the same city," she argued, feeling tension grow between them.

"Yes, I damned well can! I'll hire servants who will guard Michael as well as you."

"He won't do anything to me. Trevor Wenger, of all people, will know that you don't love me. He'll know why we married."

"Don't take chances with him. He might want to hurt you himself for keeping Michael through the years." Fortune leaned closer, his hands closing on her upper arms. "Now promise me you won't allow him to see Michael."

"I'll have to think about it," she whispered, knowing that answer would incur his wrath. She saw the blaze in his eyes.

"Claire, so help me, you're going to do what I want on this or I'll lock you both up."

"You'd never lock Michael up. It isn't in you to be cruel. All right, I'll keep him from Trevor Wenger, but you should reconsider. Some part of Marilee was her father, and some part of Michael is his grandfather."

"I prefer to think there's nothing in Michael, and there wasn't anything in Marilee of Trevor Wenger!"

"I told you I would keep Michael from him. The least you can do is to think about letting him see Michael. It's only natural that he would want to. He can't take your child from you now. You're his father and you're married, so you're providing a family for him. There's no way he can take Michael."

"Oh, yes, there is. He could take him and leave the country, and I'd have a hell of a time getting him back."

"Will you just think about it, Fortune? Hatred never helped anyone, and you're filled with it when it comes to Trevor Wenger."

"You've never been whipped like this, Claire. That makes you hate someone. And he killed Marilee when he took her from me." Fortune clamped the cheroot between his teeth. "There's no way in hell I'll let that man near Michael."

Later as she lay in bed, she glanced at Fortune across the darkened room. Since leaving New Orleans, he had slept in a chair, his feet propped on another chair or table. Now he sat in the dark, the red tip of another cheroot glowing.

"You can't sleep?" she asked, sitting up. "You haven't slept more than two hours a night since we left the boat."

"You haven't slept a great deal yourself," he answered dryly. "I'm thinking about business. And maybe we should have separate beds, Claire. It's getting more difficult for me to keep from touching you."

"Whatever you want," she said, lying down again. "Why not separate rooms?"

"No. I want Michael to think we're married and happy. And I think we'll have a better chance if we're together."

"Chance for what, Fortune?" she asked softly and saw him turn to study her.

"For happiness and friendship. That's one thing we can have, although sometime soon it may not be enough for you."

"Fortune, I'm so grateful to be with Michael, I will never regret this marriage. Never!"

"I hope not." He placed the cheroot in an ashtray and crossed the room to take her chin in his hand. "I don't think I'm going to have any regrets either." He leaned down, kissing her lightly, his lips warm and tantalizing on hers. He turned away to stand in front of the window.

Moonlight highlighted the bulge of his shoulders and biceps, and longing swept through her. Quickly she looked away, staring determinedly into the dark.

She was aware hours later when the bed jiggled. She waited a few moments and finally turned over. He was stretched on his back, his arm flung over his head, his chest rising and falling evenly.

She longed to reach out and touch him, but she knew how easily he could be wakened.

She didn't know when she fell asleep, but when she woke in the night, she was pressed against his side. His body was curled around hers, his arm holding her tightly. Her eyes opened wide and she caught her breath: his hard arousal was pressed against her bottom.

He shifted away in his sleep, and she remained frozen, not knowing whether he was awake or not, her body aching for him, her heart filled with even more longing.

The next few days seemed a whirlwind, and she came to see another side to Fortune. He was in and out of the hotel constantly, men coming and going, servants appearing. One morning he came in with a strapping black man at his side.

"Claire, this is Badru Udell. Badru, this is my wife, Mrs. O'Brien."

"How do you do, ma'am?" Badru said in a quiet voice that held an accent that was not southern but sounded Caribbean.

"Badru is going to be our butler and groom. And he's to watch Michael."

She glanced at the man's shoulders, which were wider than Fortune's, his thick chest and huge hands. "Fine," she answered, hoping Fortune knew the man's background.

"Badru was recommended by a family friend, Tobiah Barr, who was stationed here recently. Badru can shoot as well as I can," Fortune added softly, and she felt a chill because she knew he had been hired to protect Michael from Trevor Wenger and he probably had orders to kill Wenger if necessary.

"Anytime you go out," Fortune continued, "Badru can drive you."

She nodded, understanding exactly what Fortune was saying. "Badru will be here with Michael. Want to ride out with me to look at the land I'm buying for my foundry?"

"Yes," she answered, getting her parasol and reticule while Fortune took Badru to meet Michael. She wore a pink muslin dress given to her by Chantal, but within days, she knew, she would have six new dresses. With what Chantal had given her, she could see little reason to get more than one made, but Fortune had insisted.

They stepped outside into warm June sunshine. Whitehall Street was busy, filled with wagons and buggies and people walking. Across the street three different buildings were being constructed. Fortune took her arm, and when they were settled in the buggy, she turned to him. "Fortune, how do you know you can trust Badru?"

"I told you, he was recommended by Tobiah. I sent a telegram to Tobiah and got a telegram back to look for Badru. Tobiah said he would trust him with his life. And I can trust Tobiah. He saved Rafferty's life more than once. And Chantal saved him once. He said a letter would follow."

She nodded, glancing at him. Fortune had shed his coat and vest and had his sleeves rolled high, his hat pushed to the back of his head. Her pulse quickened as she admired him. "Perhaps we should have brought Michael. He gets tired of the hotel."

"I'll take him with me when we get back. On the way home, I have to stop at a hardware store, so if you want to take anything to Michael, you can get something while I'm getting my supplies."

"He's so happy, Fortune. You're a good father to him."

"I imagine Michael is happy most of the time."

"He is and always has been, but he loves you so much already."

Fortune turned to give her a long, measuring look, and her smile faded. She looked away, suddenly afraid he could see how much she was in love with him.

As they turned on Pryor Street, they passed a park that

was filled with blooming flowers. He stopped at a tin shop and then turned to take Whitehall Street again, finally heading west. They passed factories and a mill before reaching the river. He turned onto a lot where a building was under construction. The red Georgia earth was littered with crates of machinery and stacks of lumber. Men worked and wagons pulled by teams of mules hauled loads of equipment back and forth. A cistern held water for animals to drink, and she saw several casks of water for the men. She was amazed at the size of the place.

Fortune drew the reins to halt the team. "There. I've bought this land and I've bought most of my equipment. There's a new process now for steel. William Kelly and another man, Henry Bessemer, have developed it. This is the future, Claire, more than iron. With this new process we can mass-produce steel at a good price. Cal's already given me an order for boiler plates and rails, and Rafe has ordered a boiler."

"That's wonderful, Fortune!"

"I think I may steal Darcy away some of the time to work for me. Do you mind if Darcy comes to stay with us later?"

"Of course not! Your family is charming." And so are you, she thought, glancing up at him. Taking her hand, he stood up to point toward the river. "The ore storage yard and the coal storage will be there, where I can unload from boats." He jumped down and walked a few yards away through the weeds. "I'll put the office here," he said, turning to face her. He seemed so vibrant and full of energy, and suddenly she wished revenge wasn't the underlying motive for his business.

"I'm building the ovens there, the soaking pits over there," he said, waving his hands. "That building is the mill itself," he said, pointing at the construction. He glanced up at her. "While we're here, I want to talk to the men." She nodded, watching him walk away in long strides while she sat in the shade. Her virile, handsome husband was throwing himself wholeheartedly into his business. Would she see him less and less? she wondered.

Fortune returned to climb into the buggy and head back to town. "The steel mill is an O'Brien enterprise, because Cal and Rafe have both put money up with me."

"I know you'll succeed," she said, as certain of that as she was that the sun would rise.

As they reached town again, riding along Whitehall Street, she grasped his arm. "Fortune, there's a confectionery. I want to get Michael some sweets. Then I'll go next door to the general store to get some ribbons."

He pulled the buggy over to the hitching rail. He came around to lift her down, swinging her to the ground easily.

"I'll meet you back here," he said. "The hardware store is across the street."

She nodded and left him, going into the confectionery first to purchase a small bag of sweets for Michael, then getting a few more because Fortune liked sweets as much as Michael. She stepped outside to stroll to the general store, enjoying being outside.

Making her selection in the store, she paid for pink, blue, and scarlet satin ribbons, and she glanced out to see Fortune walk toward the buggy. She took her purchases and stepped out into the sunlight, the bell over the door jingling as she closed it.

"Lizzie!" came a man's deep voice close by. "Lizzie!"

She glanced around and drew a breath, looking at Dagget Horn, who had owned a saloon where she had worked in New Orleans.

"Lizzie, look at you! Aren't you doing fine?" he said in a booming voice, walking up to put his hand on her waist.

Chapter 15

Fortune raised his head to look at the man approaching Claire. He was tall and burly, his coat frayed; his long black hair stuck out from beneath a hat with a tattered brim. After the first shock wore off, Fortune saw that Claire knew him. The man walked up to her without hesitation and placed his hand on her waist, and Fortune drew a deep breath because the man acted as if he were accustomed to handling her. No man would walk up to a well-dressed woman on a busy street and place his hand on her if he didn't know her well.

Stunned, feeling a rising anger, Fortune stared at them while he felt the hot sun beating on his shoulders, and the moment became etched in time.

He had thought Claire was a poor liar, yet there was no mistaking the man's familiarity. Maybe she was a better actress than he had guessed, fooling him about her innocence. And maybe Pinkerton's had been wrong. It would account for the large amount of money she had saved. Watching her cheeks flush a deep pink as she drew herself up, looking lovely and remote in her new pink dress, Fortune was certain she knew the man.

"I'm sorry," she said coldly, looking up at him, "but you have the wrong person. I'm Claire O'Brien."

"Ahh, Lizzie. You look fine and you must have found a man to set you up. I've got a place in Mahogany Hall and you can—"

Fortune felt as if he couldn't breathe. Mahogany Hall

was the booming red-light district. People were pouring into Atlanta, and along with businesses there were saloons and gambling houses and brothels going up.

"Sir, get your hand off me before I scream," Claire snapped.

"Lizzie, don't be so damned unfriendly," he said, sliding his hand farther around her waist. "Claire O'Brien—"

Fortune went around the buggy and in long strides reached the man. "Take your hands off my wife," he said.

The man turned and blinked as Fortune swung, smashing his fist into the man's jaw and sending him reeling back against the hitching rail.

Breathing hard from anger, Fortune took Claire's arm and led her to the carriage, swinging her up inside. He was filled with anger, wondering if she had deceived him, if Michael had spent time with various men or, worse, stayed in a brothel.

The buggy creaked beneath his weight as he climbed up beside her. He could feel Claire's eyes on him, and he looked at her while he flicked the reins. "Who was he?"

"He owned a saloon in New Orleans," she said.

Fortune closed his eyes, despising every word she said. "He seemed to know you damned well."

"He's the kind of man who always puts his hands on women. I worked for him two nights and quit because the second night he caught me in the hallway and tried to—" She looked away and he glanced at her, seeing spots of color high in her cheeks. He wondered whether she was telling the truth.

"I quit that night and left."

They rode in silence the rest of the way to the hotel, and when they entered their suite, Fortune left to go to Michael's room. "I'm taking Michael and Badru with me," he said, thrusting his head back into the parlor and then leaving, banging the door behind him.

She stared at the door, realizing he didn't believe her. She paced the room until she finally calmed down. She couldn't change anything until he returned. Finding the silk material Fortune had given her in Baton Rouge, she sat down to work on a dress she intended to make from it.

Late in the afternoon, she bathed and washed her hair. Looking at the new dresses in the mirrored armoire, she selected a crisp blue and white organdy. She parted her hair in the center and fastened it high on both sides of her head, letting it fall over her shoulders.

When she heard the door bang, she went in to greet them. Fortune's blue eyes still held a glacial coldness as he looked at her. He passed her going to the bedroom to dress and closed the door behind him.

"Papa ordered a bath for me and told me to get dressed for dinner," Michael said, leaving her alone in the parlor.

The boy returned before Fortune, his wet hair plastered against his head. He wore one of his new white linen shirts and black pants, and she smiled at him. "Come here, Michael, and let me comb your hair."

He stood dutifully while she tried to smooth down the unruly ringlets. "There."

"Papa showed me some of his new machines today. He said he would take me with him again tomorrow."

"Good."

The door behind her opened. Fortune had bathed and changed to a fresh white shirt. He wore a black coat and trousers and looked handsome, masculine, and unmistakably angry.

As they went downstairs to the spacious dining room, his anger seemed to ebb and he became more his usual self, talking easily with Michael about the things they had seen during the day. She glance around the room at potted palms, tables draped in white cloths, and she wondered how long they would live in the hotel.

"Sometime you'll have to show Mama the machinery," Michael said in his high voice.

"I'd be glad to," Fortune answered lightly, "but I'm not sure she'd be as interested as you are."

"I'd like to see it, but I won't know what I'm looking at."

"Papa can tell you."

The waiter brought Michael and Fortune plates of fried chicken, golden corn bread, black-eyed peas, and mashed potatoes covered in thick gravy while Claire had fried catfish and rice and peas. After dinner they walked for several blocks, rounding a corner on Marietta, walking down to look at the ruins of a building facing the railroad tracks.

"People are calling these 'Sherman's monuments,' " Claire said.

"That building was the Georgia Railroad Bank Agency," Fortune said.

"Did you fight here?" Michael asked.

"Yes, I did," he said, squatting to talk on Michael's eye level. "My army went through here. Before we did, a man named Lemuel Grant in the Confederate engineers built defenses around Atlanta—"

"Like the ones we saw on the way to the mill?"

"Yes. Do you remember what they're called?"

"Palisades. Those pointed stakes."

"That's right. Lemuel Grant built over ten miles of them around the city, and they were very effective. General Sherman finally had to go around the city, and he destroyed the railroad that brought in supplies. When he did that, the Army of the Tennessee couldn't hold the city any longer."

"What happened when they couldn't? Did General Sherman attack then?"

"No. For days the city was shelled, and as soldiers withdrew, some civilians fled. When the Confederates departed, it left the city open for the Union army to come in. Atlanta was the connecting link between the Confederacy in the West and in the East. See all the tracks?"

Fortune said, turning Michael about. "This was the railroad center of the South, so this city was vital to both sides. You've seen some of the ruined buildings and houses. People won't ever forget, Michael. It changed so many people's lives and they'll remember and their children will remember."

Michael nodded solemnly.

"Sometimes, Michael, boys may taunt you that your father is a Yankee. Just remind them that your mother is from Charlotte, and your uncle was an officer in the Confederacy."

"Yes, sir."

"The war's all over now," Fortune said, standing up. "Atlanta is rebuilding. It's rising out of the ruins and it'll be a fine city someday."

Michael began to walk on one of the rails, waving his arms as he balanced himself.

"Do you think he'll have difficulty making friends?"

"Not at all. Has he ever?"

"No," she said, watching Michael.

"I just wanted to have him prepared for taunts because feeling runs high here. This town suffered terribly, and no one has forgotten. Thank God you took him out west."

"It was difficult there."

"C'mon, Michael. Let's go back. It's getting late," Fortune called. Michael returned, moving ahead of them, picking up and throwing rocks as they went.

"Out west living was rougher," she said as they strolled back down the wide, busy street. "I couldn't find work as easily, and there were long distances between towns."

Fortune remained silent, and she wondered if he was still angry with her. And she wondered how often she would run into men and women from her past. She glanced down the street, thankful she hadn't worked in Atlanta.

As they climbed the hotel's curving staircase, Fortune said he would read to Michael, and the two of them went to Michael's room. She went to the bedroom to sit in the rocker near the window, lighting a lamp while a gentle southern breeze blew through the open window, fanning the lace curtains. Claire concentrated on sewing her silk dress until she heard Fortune's boots and looked up to see him enter the bedroom and close the door. He had shed his coat and cravat, and his shirt was unbuttoned at the throat and the sleeves rolled high. He crossed the room to pour some brandy. As he slugged it down, the gold link bracelet on his wrist caught the light.

"You're still angry about today, aren't you?" she asked.

"I just don't know whether to believe you or not," he said, canting one hip against the table. "If it was what you said, the man had to be incredibly bold to walk up to you like that and put his hands on you."

"He put one hand on me," she answered coolly, standing to fold the material and carry it to the chest of drawers. "I'm telling the truth."

"I'm going out. It'll be late when I get back." He bolted from the room and fairly flew down the stairs and outside, trying to control his temper.

All through the next hours while he played faro, he kept seeing the man walk up to Claire and put his hand on her. Fortune's winnings grew, but his attention was only halfway on the game. The night was hot, the saloon noisy and smoky, and twice Fortune noticed burly men at the bar, thinking he was seeing the man again only to decide it was a stranger each time.

Long after midnight Fortune drank a last glass of whiskey and pushed back his chair. He pocked his meager winnings. As he well knew, gambling when his thoughts weren't on the game was a bad idea.

He reached the hotel and took the stairs two at a time, his jaw set. There was only one way to find out whether Claire had been truthful or not.

He saw Badru seated in the hallway and nodded to him before he entered Michael's room. Fortune paused beside the bed. His son was stretched out, arms flung wide, his curls damp against his forehead. Fortune's anger evaporated as he gazed at Michael, and he bent down to kiss his cheek lightly.

He marveled that he had his son back, thinking Michael was the most wonderful thing that had ever happened in his life. He touched Michael's small hand, feeling a knot in his throat as he fought his emotions.

He turned away to tiptoe from Michael's room into the parlor. The bedroom door, he noticed, was ajar on the darkened room. A small lamp burned in the parlor, and Fortune crossed the room to pour a glass of brandy. He took only a sip and set the glass down. He shed his shirt and sat down to remove his boots. Noiselessly he strode to the bedroom and closed the door, going to the bed to look down at Claire.

She stirred, her eyes coming open to gaze up at him. "Fortune?"

The anger in him tightened, burning hotly. He reached down to slide his arm beneath her back, feeling her delicate bones as he pulled her up. He set her on her feet, winding his hand in her hair. Her brown brows drew together, her fair brow furrowed slightly.

"Fortune?"

"I can't forget that man today walking up to you and putting his hand on you," Fortune said, grinding out the words as her eyes flew wide.

"You're drunk!"

"The hell I am," he answered. He tightened his fingers in her hair and pulled her head back. "If you've lied to me—if you've had Michael in a brothel—"

She pushed against him, infuriated by the accusation. "Leave me alone, Fortune! I've told you the truth."

"We'll see," he snapped, pulling her against him. He placed his lips on hers, kissing her hard. Her resistance was only momentary, and then she sagged against him, her arms winding around him.

His temper flared another notch. She liked to be kissed. Had he been taken in by wide eyes and innocent looks?

He caught her white cotton gown in his fists and yanked it open, listening to the material rip.

"Fortune! You said you wouldn't force yourself—"

"I'm not," he said as he cupped her breasts and ran his thumbs over her taut nipples. "You want this, Claire," he said in a low, harsh voice, watching her gasp as he stroked and rubbed her breasts. Her eyes closed and she clung to his arms. "There's no force here," he said, bending his head to flick his tongue over her nipple, hearing her soft moan.

"I can't resist you," she whispered, clinging to him. His gaze ran down the length of her, the dark curls at the juncture of her thighs, her long, slender legs. He slid his arm around her waist. Her hands ran over his chest and he sighed, wondering if he could maintain his control if she touched him. She was passionate and responsive, and his anger soared another notch. He held her with one hand, stroking her breasts. He turned her around, pulling her up against him to cup her breasts and fondle her while he kissed her nape and trailed his tongue to her ear, his hands moving lightly on her.

"Fortune—" She turned around, her arms circling his neck again. He kissed her hard, his tongue sliding over the silky insides of her mouth while his hand moved down between her legs to her moist warmth. He pushed her legs apart, his hand finding the feminine bud and stroking her.

She gasped, arching her hips against his hand. "You like that, Claire," he whispered in her ear, his tongue flicking her ear. He rubbed her as she gasped and clung to him, her hips moving wildly. He kissed her open mouth. She was lost to passion, his hand firm against her as she moved against him. He slid his finger inside her, feeling her tight, warm flesh. He felt the tight maidenhead against his finger.

Shock poured over him, sobering him. She had told him the truth all along. Suddenly he regretted his anger and how he had hauled her out of bed. She clutched his upper arms, whimpering with passion, her hips moving rhythmically as she reached a brink and gasped, "Oh, Fortune, please—"

Feeling guilty, sorry for his suspicions, he caught her to him, winding his arms around her while he kissed her gently.

"Claire, I'm sorry," he whispered. "I should have believed you." He kissed her throat, showering kisses on her. He ached for more, feeling as if he would burst if he didn't take her, but he wouldn't. He had promised he wouldn't force himself on her, and seduction would be just the same now. She was a virgin, as innocent as she had said, and he had just pulled her from bed and aroused her when she hadn't expected it. Would this be what she wanted if she had a chance to think about it rationally?

He trailed kisses over her, wanting her, knowing he should respect her wishes, calling himself a bastard for doubting her virtue.

She pushed against him, tears bright on her cheeks. "Leave me alone. You don't love me and you don't trust me."

He caught her chin and held her face, leaning forward to kiss her sweetly. "You know why I don't love you, but I respect you and I do trust you. I shouldn't have questioned you and I apologize."

She gazed up at him, tears sparkling on her thick dark lashes. She was beautiful, and he was as hard as granite with a need for her body. It took all his control to stop now.

With a twist she moved away from him and caught up her torn gown. "I can't give myself to you, Fortune."

"I'll get you another gown," he said. "Go to bed, Claire. I'll leave you be."

He turned away and left the room. As he closed the

door, she clutched the gown, standing still in the empty room. "I love you," she whispered. Claire moved to the chest of drawers and pulled out a new batiste gown. Her body ached for him, and she longed for his arms around her. If nothing else, she wished he would just come back and talk to her. She looked at the light shining beneath the door and thought about going to him, but it might just start the same thing over again, and some time soon she wasn't going to be able to tell him to stop.

She crawled into bed to stare into the darkness, wondering if he had decided to stop sharing a bedroom with her.

In the next few days she saw little of him. He left at dawn and came home from work late at night, although sometimes he came by in the afternoon to take Michael with him. He was working constantly, trying to get the mill built, and they had started building a house. If he slept in the same bed with her, she didn't know it because he came home after she was asleep and left before she awoke.

On Sunday evening, as he pored over drawings spread on the floor, they heard a knock. Raking his fingers through his black hair, Fortune went to the door. Suddenly he swung it wide. "Alaric!"

"I heard you were back. You're at that damned mill all the time."

She watched as a blond man entered and Fortune hugged him. He was almost as tall, and his slightly rugged features, large deep blue eyes, and prominent cheekbones made him handsome. He was in a Union uniform, and he looked past Fortune at her.

"Why didn't you come by the mill?" Fortune asked.

"Because I heard you married and found your son," the man answered, moving away from Fortune toward her, a wide smile revealing his even white teeth.

"I want to meet your wife. I have to meet the woman who melted the man with a heart of stone."

"Claire, this is my friend Alaric Hampton. Alaric, meet my wife, Claire."

Alaric smiled at her, taking her hand in his large, warm ones. "Now I can see why the granite melted. You are a beautiful woman, Mrs. O'Brien."

"I may call you out if you don't stop," Fortune said lightly.

"And be widowed and leave her with me? Go ahead," Alaric retorted, taking her hand and raising it to his lips to kiss.

"I've heard about you and I'm glad to meet you," Claire said, amused and flattered. "Unfortunately, Michael's asleep."

"But you can come look at him," Fortune said with a note of pride. "You don't even have to worry about being quiet. He could sleep through a cavalry charge."

Alaric smiled at Claire and turned to go with Fortune to Michael's room. Shortly they returned and Fortune crossed the room to pour glasses of brandy. He glanced at her. "Claire?"

"No, thank you."

Alaric seated himself on the settee near her and reached over to take a bit of material in his hand. "Sewing a dress?"

"Yes."

"I know a very fine dressmaker if you need one."

"Alaric knows everyone in Atlanta," Fortune said dryly.

"Not so. Some of these Georgians aren't about to make my acquaintance. And you're from Charlotte?"

"Yes, but I haven't been back there since the night I left with Michael."

"Do you have family still there?"

"Yes, my father and I suppose my brother. I wrote my father, but I haven't heard from him yet."

He looked at Fortune. "Thanks for sending the telegram that you were getting married. I wish I could have been there. How's your family?"

"Fine. Everyone's fine. Look, I want you to come out to the mill tomorrow."

"I'll do that. So where did he find you?" he asked Claire, giving her his full attention.

"In Natchez." She related the events of that fateful night, ending with Harwood's death.

"Have you seen Trevor Wenger since you got back?"

"No," Fortune said flatly, and she wondered when they would encounter each other, because it was bound to happen soon.

"I see you have someone watching the place."

"I don't want to leave them here alone during the day when I'm at work."

"I would guess you know how to shoot as well as we do," he said to Claire.

"No, not that well, but I know how."

"Has he showed you Atlanta yet?"

"Some of it."

"It changes daily, but there are still a few places that are intact. I have a friend you might enjoy meeting. She's widowed and has a little five-year-old boy, Edwin. Her name is Priscilla Hawkins, and she's lived in Atlanta all her life."

"That would be nice. I don't know anyone here except Fortune."

"Great grief! I'll bring her by to meet you."

"Have dinner with us tomorrow night," Fortune said. "I work late."

"We'll come early and talk to Claire," he said, smiling at her.

"That would be wonderful! Tell her to bring Edwin, and he can meet Michael."

"I'll get dinner sent up here and Penthea, who looks after Michael, can sit with them while we eat downstairs," Fortune said.

"Fine."

"Where's your home, Captain Hampton?"

"Philadelphia, and I don't plan to go back. The winters are too cold. I like the South. It has the most beautiful women on earth."

Fortune gave a cynical laugh. "Until you get up North. I recall hearing you say Philadelphia had the most beautiful women."

"Perhaps I thought so once." He glanced at Fortune. "Word's all over town about the two lots you bought on Peachtree."

"I want a big, comfortable house."

Alaric laughed. "You want a bigger, fancier house than Trevor Wenger. You want one that will awe people and make sure that Michael is accepted."

"That's right."

"I'm sure you'll succeed."

Alaric leaned back, crossing his legs, and talked to them for the next hour, giving Claire his full attention. When he stood, Fortune came to his feet.

"Claire, it's nice to meet you," Alaric said as she stood up, and Fortune moved to her side to drape his arm lightly across her shoulders.

"It's so nice to meet you. I'll look forward to tomorrow night."

"Good." His gaze shifted to Fortune. "I'll ride out to the mill in the morning. How early do you get there?"

"By seven?"

"I won't be there that early," he said dryly and headed toward the door. Fortune stepped into the hall with him, closing the door behind him.

Claire had enjoyed Fortune's friend, and the thought of having a female acquaintance was nice because she had been spending long hours alone when Fortune took Michael with him.

In the quiet hallway Fortune strolled toward the stairs with Alaric. "I wish you'd consider going to work with me."

"Me? At a steel mill? I wouldn't be any good to you. I don't know anything about the business."

"You don't have to know about steel. You need to know how to keep everything running smoothly."

"I'll think about it. Your wife is very beautiful and I'm happy for you. Sometimes when love comes, it comes swiftly—"

Fortune glanced at him. "Alaric, I'm not in love with Claire. I'll never stop loving Marilee," he said quietly.

Frowning, Alaric stopped to face him. He looked down at Fortune's wrist, and Fortune knew he was looking at Marilee's bracelet.

"Good Lord, why did you marry her, then?"

"She's been a mother to Michael all his life. He loves her and he needs her."

"She knows you don't love her?"

"Yes, she does."

"Why the hell—oh, I suppose she wanted you to take care of her."

Fortune grinned and placed his hands on his hips. "Not this one. She is as independent as you and I. She can't bear for me to spend anything on any of us."

"I don't believe you."

"It's true. She married me to stay with Michael."

"Good Lord!"

"There have been worse reasons for marriages."

"I don't know. She could marry and have her own sons."

"Alaric, she has been his mother all these years. She adores him. I saw her risk her life for him time and again."

"Well, I hope you haven't made a prison for yourself. And I think you're blind, Fortune. She's a beautiful woman. And if she's independent and doesn't want you to spend money on her, you've found a dream woman."

"Leave her alone, Alaric. She isn't accustomed to men flirting."

"It would serve you right for someone to come along and take her from you. And someone will do exactly that!"

Fortune laughed. "Why did I think I missed seeing you!"

Alaric grinned and shook his head. "You rotten bastard. I'll see you tomorrow."

Fortune went back to the parlor. Closing the door, he went to get the plans he had been looking at when Alaric arrived. "Well, I think Alaric is half in love with you."

She laughed. "He was very nice."

"He's always nice to beautiful ladies. He saved my life once, and I'd risk mine for him." He crossed the room. "I'm going to try to get some work done."

She sewed quietly, glancing at him occasionally. He sat at the desk, his head bent over papers as he made notations.

The light shone on his black hair. His skin was getting darker from hours in the sun at the mill. The sight of his narrow waist, his long legs, reminded her of the night he had come home from faro so angry with her. She felt her cheeks warm as she recalled his lovemaking. She had an intense yearning to cross the silent room, put her arms around him, and kiss him.

He shifted his arm as he wrote something in a ledger. His shirtsleeves were rolled back, his arm sprinkled with curling dark hair. The gold bracelet that bound him to memories of Marilee clinked faintly as he moved his wrist. Yearning tore at Claire, and she wondered if he would remain unaware of what she felt for much longer. Right now it wouldn't matter to him if he knew. Except he would pity her and she couldn't bear that.

She bent her head over her sewing, trying to concentrate.

"Lord!" He tossed down the pen. "I have the house plans and drawings from the architect to show you, and I forgot."

He pushed back his chair and marched into the bedroom, returning with papers rolled under his arm. He glanced around. "There's no table big enough. Let's sit on the floor."

Setting aside her sewing, she moved down beside him, aware that his shoulder brushed hers as he untied the roll. She helped him hold down the corners, and he smoothed out the projected drawing of the house. Stunned, she stared at an elegant Victorian dwelling.

"I want six bedrooms. We'll have a front and back parlor and a ballroom—"

"Fortune, this is as large as your brother's house!" she exclaimed in surprise.

"I don't think so. Not quite."

"I can't believe I'll be living in something like this!" she said in awe. "Fortune—" She turned to stare at him. "You must be as wealthy as Croesus!"

He grinned and tugged a lock of her hair. "Claire, I can see that you're calculating what this will cost, and you're on the verge of telling me how we can live in something smaller and save all that money."

"Well, heavens, yes! We don't need something this grand!"

"Claire, this is the house. Forget what it costs. I want my son to have a fine home."

"It doesn't have to be this fine. Did you grow up in something like this?"

"No, but I grew up in a nice comfortable home, and I want Michael to have that kind of home."

"This is far more than nice and comfortable!"

He laughed and hugged her neck affectionately. "I

should have known. Claire, stop worrying. I can afford this—"

"Even when you're going into business?"

"I think so."

"Why don't we build something smaller until you see how your business goes?"

"Claire, this is the house I want to build."

She sighed and turned to look at it, unable to imagine herself in it. "There's just three of us. We'll be lost," she said more to herself than him. And then as her gaze ran over it wistfully, she wished she could plan on filling it with children.

She glanced up at him as he turned to the next sheet that showed the downstairs floor plan. He bent over it, telling her about the rooms. "We'll put the ballroom here, all right?"

"Yes." She studied him. She had told him she didn't want the physical part of marriage, but maybe that had been a mistake. Maybe she should reconsider. Fortune could give her another baby.

The thought made her pulse drum, and she didn't hear a word he was saying. She looked at his strong, capable hands on the paper. The golden bracelet lay against his hand. Finally he straightened and studied her, amusement lighting his eyes. "Stop worrying about the cost."

She looked at his thickly lashed eyes, his sensual mouth. He touched the tip of her nose. "Promise me you'll let me worry about the money."

She nodded, thankful he couldn't guess what was really on her mind.

Rolling the plans, he stood and reached down to take her hands, pulling her to her feet. He continued to hold her hands as he looked down at her. "You're a good wife, Claire," he said quietly, leaning down to kiss her. She slid her arms around his neck, standing on tiptoe to kiss him. His arm went around her waist, pulling her close while he kissed her.

He released her, gazing down at her with desire and speculation. "I better get back to work," he said gruffly.

That night she lay awake for hours, but he did not come into the bedroom and she knew he had stopped sharing the bed with her. When they moved into the big house, would she see him much at all? Suppose she asked him to father a child? The thought sent a rush of pleasure through her. Another precious baby like Michael. It would bind Fortune to her more than now. She thought about it, excitement coursing in her. If she had his love-making, the intimacy of a shared bed and nights together, would there be a greater chance of winning his love? She sat up, the sheet rustling around her legs as she moved. Longing and excitement filled her as she thought about what to do.

Chapter 16

Fortune strode from the hotel and mounted his horse. "Thanks, Badru," he said as the man stepped away from holding the animal. He watched Badru stride back into the hotel and glanced upstairs at their windows. He didn't worry about Michael when he knew Badru was with him. Fortune turned the horse, riding through the sleeping city that hadn't started the day.

He passed new houses and more homes under construction at the edge of town and headed into the rolling countryside. He rode along the isolated road conscious of his revolver on his hip, remembering how easily Wenger had taken him before. His gaze swept back and forth over the peaceful scenery, and he listened carefully for strange noises.

He was aware as well that if something happened to him, Wenger would take Michael from Claire within twenty-four hours. More than likely she wouldn't know he was coming after her.

Something shifted in the trees ahead, and a rider emerged. Fortune yanked out his revolver, and Trevor Wenger raised his hands, his brown coat falling open.

Fortune glanced around, but didn't see a sign of anyone else. Hairs on his neck prickled and he tried to listen for any sound. "Stay where you are."

"I'm not armed and I'm alone," Trevor Wenger said.

"That tempts me," Fortune snapped.

"I don't think you'd shoot me down when I'm unarmed." There was a moment of silence. "You managed to outwit Harwood and get my grandson. I'll give you one million dollars for him."

Fortune shook his head. "Ten million wouldn't be enough."

"One million for a little boy you barely know. You're young. You can have a dozen boys."

"Get out of my way, Wenger," Fortune said, his anger rising.

"When can I meet him?"

Fortune gazed into Trevor Wenger's dark eyes. "Never. You will never meet him or talk to him or get near him. Not until he's older and I can't supervise where he is and what he's doing."

"You bastard!" Wenger snapped, his face flushing and his mouth setting in a grim line.

"Get out of the road."

"You can't keep him from me. And the next time I won't stop with a beating. I'll finish the job, and then it will be easy to take him from the woman. I'll get my grandson, O'Brien, and you'll never live to know it."

Fortune pulled back the hammer of the pistol. "Everyone who knows me knows of the hatred between us. And quite a few men know the beating I received from you. I think I can convince them I pulled the trigger in self-defense. Now get out of my way."

Trevor Wenger turned his horse and rode into the trees. Fortune reined around, riding into the opposite woods and backtracking to warn Badru to keep Michael in sight when he wasn't with Claire or Penthea.

After talking to Badru, Fortune took a different route to his mill, deciding he would vary his route every day.

One Sunday evening Fortune was at the hotel by eight to eat dinner with them. As they left the hotel coffee shop, he linked her arm in his. "Michael, this way," he said, motioning toward the door with a shake of his head.

He looked down at Claire. "Let's go look at our new house."

The boy ran outside ahead of them, and she watched him jump in the air. "Michael's changing. He's more lively, not so cautious."

"He's just growing. I stopped by the house today. They're making progress. I want you to tell me what kind of furniture you want in the back parlor and some of the bedrooms, Claire. I've already ordered some furniture."

He helped her into the buggy. As she straightened her blue muslin skirt, Michael scrambled into the backseat and Fortune climbed up beside her. He placed his coat in back and rolled back his sleeves. They rode away from the hotel, and the breeze created by moving down the street was welcome. They reached Five Points and turned north on Peachtree. As they passed elegant mansions, she wondered if she would ever become accustomed to living in such an area or be able to view her neighbors without awe. And she couldn't imagine their own house.

"Our house is going to be big, isn't it?"

"Yes, Michael," Fortune answered. "Very big."

"Will I have my own room?"

"Yes, you will, and you can have bookshelves so you'll have a place for your books."

"I don't have very many books."

"You will as you get older." Fortune glanced at her. "You did a good job of teaching him to read."

"He was interested from an early age. Plus, sometimes we had to stay in our room for long hours at a time."

They stopped in front of a lot that still had three tall live oaks with spreading branches casting cool shade. The framework was up for the house, and Claire stared at all the boards, unable to imagine living in such a palace. "Let's look at it," Fortune said eagerly, jumping down and coming around to lift her to the ground.

Michael climbed down from the buggy. "Soon they'll

have the walls up. Papa, you said I could have a big bedroom."

"That you can. And we'll have water piped into the house like your Uncle Rafferty's house."

"Criminy!" Michael scampered up the slight incline and ran through the structure. Grass grew high and lumber was stacked beside a barrel of water. Fortune draped his arm across her shoulders, and a tingle ran through her as she walked close beside him. He touched her lightly and casually, but it had been weeks now since the night he had stormed in and kissed her passionately.

"Fortune, I had a letter from my father. He said he's better, and in the fall when we're in our house, if he feels well enough, he would like to come visit us."

"That's fine, Claire." Fortune glanced at her. "I'd rather you didn't go to Charlotte and take Michael now."

"You worry about Trevor Wenger. Has he tried to see Michael?"

She saw the grim set to Fortune's jaw and realized the two men must have already clashed.

"He knows Michael is here. He stopped me on the street and said he wanted to see Michael. I told him he never would."

"Fortune, he's bound to see Michael when you're in the same town. And it just doesn't seem right never to let him talk to Michael."

"We've discussed all that. Wenger isn't going to get near my son," Fortune said, a muscle working in his jaw.

She bit her lip, thinking he never said *our son,* yet that was the way she thought of Michael. She had thought of him as her own for too long now to stop.

"Try to reconsider. Trevor Wenger is Michael's blood kin. And I know there has to be some good in him somewhere."

"No." Fortune separated from her, running his hand idly along the brick fireplace in the area that someday would be the front parlor. "If you think of any other furniture you want made for the house, just tell me. Don't worry about the cost. If we can't afford it, I'll tell you. Sometime after my steelworks is running smoothly, I'll take you and Michael to Europe, and we can get more furniture and have it sent over."

Fortune examined the carpentry in one corner before he added, "I've ordered some furniture for this room. I didn't consult you on it because I thought the price would worry you."

"That's fine," she said. "I'm sure I shall think every inch of it is the most beautiful house in the entire world with the most beautiful furniture."

Fortune smiled at her, crossing to her to place his hands on her shoulders. "I don't have to worry about you foolishly spending my money. It's going to be a beautiful house and a happy home. I think we can give Michael a good life."

"That takes more than beautiful things."

"I know that. You've seen my family. The love they have is what's important, but if we can have these trappings, then we will."

He stood close to her, gazing down at her, and she thought how long it had been since he'd kissed her. Her gaze lowered to his mouth, and she seemed to feel a clutch in her middle. "Ready to go, Claire?"

"Yes. Whenever both of you are," she answered breathlessly.

"I'll find Michael."

They rode back to the hotel and soon settled in the parlor. She had her sewing, working on dainty lace and batiste to make a chemise, while Fortune sprawled on the floor with Michael, reading to him. She eyed father and son, both dark heads bent over a book.

And as she stared at him, she wished more than ever that they would have a baby. She thought about it every day now. If they did, it might bring them closer together, and it would give her another precious child to love. She stared at Fortune, remembering his promise to oblige her if she wanted a physical relationship.

And she was already lost in love with him. She knew that as surely as she needed air to breathe. If they had a child, she not only would have another part of him, but she would also have his arms around her, have his kisses. Even without his love, his caresses and kisses were better than this isolation and only casual touches. She didn't know whether he had a mistress or not; he was gone such long hours, he could be seeing a woman easily.

Claire stared at him, feeling another rush of shyness, wondering what he would say if she asked him to father a child. She knew he would willingly do so. It was blatantly obvious to her that he had fought for control the times they kissed, and she had seen desire in his eyes often. Should she wait until they had their own house? Or by waiting, would she lose him to a mistress?

She decided to wait, to give it thought, because once she made the commitment, there would be no turning back. Yet the thought of another baby was wonderful. And the thought of Fortune making love to her sent a thrill surging through her.

Her gaze ran down the long length of him. His boots were dusty, his tight-fitting pants hugged his long legs and slim hips. He had his sleeves rolled back, revealing his muscular forearms covered in dark hair. Her gaze shifted to his hands, looking at the blue veins, the blunt, strong fingers. She looked at the golden links around his wrist that always reminded her that she didn't have his love.

When they moved into their new house, she would ask him about a baby. The thought of asking Fortune to father a child sent her pulse pounding, and her gaze ran over him again while she felt longing, wishing that he might someday learn to love her.

Two months later, on a warm, sunny Saturday in August, they moved into the house. Michael danced around the hotel room with excitement as the last things were packed and carried out.

She put her blue silk bonnet on her head and studied her reflection, her pulse beating with eagerness. She wore a blue silk morning dress with ebony trim and onyx earbobs.

"Ready?"

She turned to see Fortune watching her from the doorway. Her breath caught at the sight of him, wearing his black coat and trousers and one of his fancy white linen shirts. "Yes, I'm ready," she replied.

"Michael is jumping around like a toad in a rainstorm. We need to get him out of the hotel."

She smiled at Fortune as he linked her arm in his, and they left, climbing into the buggy.

"Mama, will I have my new bed?"

"Everything is there, Michael, just waiting for us."

"William lives behind our house, and he told me to come see him when we move in. And Edwin's grandfather lives only three blocks away, so I can see Edwin a lot."

"You unpack your things first," she said, looking at the wide street, the newly planted trees, the elegant, recently built new mansions that looked as if the town had never seen a war.

"Claire, we've been invited to a ball Friday night."

She turned to look at him. "Good heavens, Fortune, I don't know how to dance!"

He glanced at her and smiled. "Then I'll teach you how before Friday night."

She nodded uncertainly. "Fortune, there's so much about society I don't know. I was a schoolgirl and hadn't had a coming-out party when I left home."

"You'll be fine."

She forgot about the party as he turned the buggy up the drive. She gazed at the sprawling three-story Victorian with fish-scale detailing on the upper dormers and turret, fancy corbels and fretwork along the wraparound veranda. Fortune pulled beneath the porte cochere, and beyond it she glimpsed the carriage house. She knew there was a servants' quarters for Badru, a greenhouse and springhouse on the grounds. The yard was rutted and barren from workmen tracking over it, but she could imagine that it would look as fine as the places around it before long because flowers seemed to thrive in Atlanta's weather. Fortune halted the buggy as four men unloaded their belongings and carried them inside.

"Can I go in?" Michael asked and Fortune laughed.

"Go!"

Michael jumped out of the buggy, landing on both feet and running for the house. Fortune came around as Claire started to climb out of the buggy. He caught her in his arms, scooping her up to carry her.

"Fortune! Great heavens, what will the neighbor's say!"

"They'll say the newlyweds are moving in."

"We have a seven-year-old son!"

Fortune grinned, an infectious smile with a flash of white teeth, and she realized he was as excited as Michael. She wound her arm around his neck as he strode up the front steps and yanked open the front door to carry her inside. Men moved around them, setting down boxes of their belongings. She gazed at the hallways, glimpsing off to her left the small receiving room where callers could leave their cards. To her right was the elegant front parlor with new furniture and rugs already in place.

Fortune set her on her feet and took her hand to lead her into the front parlor, its entryway framed by fretwork. For the past two weeks, while the furniture was being delivered, he had stopped taking her to see the house because he said he wanted to surprise her. She stood in the doorway, stunned at the blue satin drapes, blue damask-upholstered chairs, marble-topped tables, and rosewood furniture, a rosewood piano. The bay in the living room had two sets of French doors opening onto the veranda. The house was as elegant as a palace, and she couldn't believe it was her home. Hers and Michael's and Fortune's. She thought of the tiny, threadbare rooms she had shared with Michael. Suddenly her eyes filled with tears, and she wiped them quickly.

Fortune's hand closed on her arm, and he turned her to face him, his brows coming together. "Claire?"

"It's so beautiful! Oh, Fortune, thank you. I shouldn't have kept him from you all those years—"

"Shh, Claire," he said quietly, pulling her to him. He held her close, stroking her head. "You did the best you could, and Michael is a wonderful child."

"This is just so grand." Feeling foolish, she wiped her eyes and moved away from him. "Fortune, it's magnificent."

He smiled and held out his hand. "Come here, Claire." He crossed the parlor and opened the double doors, and she drew in her breath as she looked at a ballroom that ran the length of the house. Sunlight poured through long windows, and French doors could be opened to the outside. Mirrors lined the walls between the windows, and at one end of the room was a small dais.

"Fortune, this is magnificent!"

Fortune turned to face her and held out his arms. "Come here, Claire. We'll dance our first dance in our new home."

Shyly she moved forward to place her hand in his. He put his hand on her waist, and she reciprocated. "I don't know what to do."

"Watch my feet. Just go in a square. One, two, three . . ." He began to hum a waltz, and she followed his lead, watching his feet and then looking up at him. He was watching her, his blue eyes sparkling with happiness. She followed him as he hummed and she hummed with him, their voices mingling as he spun her around the room.

She felt dizzy, happy, amazed at her life with him. And she wanted to ask him now for a baby. Tonight would be the time.

Finally he stopped, looking down at her. "You know how to dance now as well as anyone. We'll practice again before the ball."

He took her hand and closed the tall double doors. "I've already told Michael he's not to play in the ballroom."

As they moved into the hall, she heard running feet overhead. "Fortune, Michael's running—"

"Let him run. He'll calm down. For all the elegance, this house still is a comfortable home and it's his."

"Papa! Mama!" Michael cried. She looked up at the wide, curving staircase with rosettes in the newel post. At the top of the stairs he swung his leg over the banister and slid down. "Yeeee—"

"Michael—"

Laughing, Fortune moved to the foot of the staircase and caught Michael. "Do you like your house?"

"It's grand, Papa! I want to tell William I'm here," he said, wiggling, and Fortune set him down.

"Michael," she called to him, and he turned to look at her. "Stay in our yard. Ask William over here."

"Yes, ma'am."

"Badru is trailing after him. He'll keep him in sight." Fortune took her hand to lead her down the hall.

"Fortune, I can't believe I'm part of this."

"It's your's Claire, just as much as it's mine," he said. His blue eyes were dancing with eagerness, and she wondered if she could ever stir such excitement in him. "Let's look at the rest of it." In the hall, a small woman was picking up boxes to put them away.

"Afternoon, Mrs. O'Brien, Mr. O'Brien," she said, smiling.

"Afternoon, Robena," Fortune said easily. "That box goes into Michael's bedroom."

"Yes, sir."

Claire watched her carry the box upstairs, amazed at the help Fortune had hired: Penthea as a nanny for Michael, Della to cook, Robena to clean, and Badru as butler, driver, and guard. Yet she knew with the large house, she was going to need help to keep it running smoothly.

The back parlor was filled with more rosewood furniture, a leather settee, and a carved desk, where she knew Fortune planned to work.

They moved from room to room, and she was dazed as she entered an octagonal dining room with leaded glass windows and a crystal chandelier above a long, hand-carved English oak Louis XV table that gleamed with polish. The fourteen chairs around it were covered in Aubusson tapestry. A punkah hung over the table to fan the room.

The kitchen was at the back of the house, and it had a new stove and piped-in water. A short dark-skinned woman was working on dinner, and she turned to smile at them. "Mr. O'Brien, Mrs. O'Brien," she said in greeting.

"Hello, Della," Claire said, having met her shortly after Fortune hired her.

"I'm glad you folks are finally here. Mistah Michael has already been in here and had a bit of melon."

"I'll tell him to stay out of your way."

"Oh, no, ma'am. He's so quiet and polite."

At the back of the house off the kitchen were two servants' bedrooms, rooms now occupied by Della and Penthea.

They went upstairs and inspected Michael's room, which was furnished in deep wine colors and rosewood furniture with the oak floor gleaming with polish.

Walking with her hand in Fortune's, they went through the upstairs sitting room, her sewing room, the extra bedroom with high, carved rosewood beds. And finally they entered their bedroom, which ran the length of the front of the house. She looked at the fancy carved walnut bed, walnut tables topped with rose marble, the rose damask drapes and lace curtains, the fireplace and empty mantel. A large bathroom adjoined their room, and she felt as if she had never seen anything as luxurious in her life.

"This is as elegant as your brother's house."

"I'm glad you think so," Fortune said, grinning. He crossed the room to her and placed his hands on her shoulders. "I hope it's good for us here, Claire."

"How could it be anything else in such a beautiful place?"

"That doesn't stop trouble from coming. Alaric will be over tonight to look at the house and celebrate."

"How nice!"

Fortune gave her a pleasant smile, leaning forward to kiss her lightly. He no longer shared the bed with her at the hotel, coming in late, sometimes sleeping on the sofa, sometimes in a chair, and she wondered what he would do here.

"You take this room. I'll take the one next to it."

Studying him, she started to ask him about a baby, but he turned away.

"We better start telling them where to put the boxes," he said briskly, and she felt the moment had slipped away. She would wait until that night, when things had quieted and the servants were gone.

They were busy the rest of the afternoon. Finally that night she bathed in the new bathroom, marveling at everything in it. Feeling an undercurrent of excitement, rehearsing what she would say to Fortune and then rejecting each speech in turn, she dressed with care for dinner, finally selecting a deep blue silk with lace and rosebuds trimming the skirt and bodice, and a rose sash. She fastened her hair on the sides of her head and let it hang down in back, staring at her reflection, her gaze going to the bed.

She went downstairs, her skirts rustling. She stopped in the kitchen to check on the cooking and then headed toward the front parlor. Both men turned toward her when she entered. Dressed in a new gray coat and black trousers, his shirt front frothy with ruffles, Fortune stood with his elbow against the mantel while Alaric stood in the center of the room.

"Claire," Alaric said warmly, setting down his drink and coming forward to take her hand, his eyes filled with pleasure, a broad smile on his face. For a moment she wished it were Fortune greeting her with such enthusiasm as Alaric brushed her cheek with a kiss. "It isn't fair that he has this marvelous house and the most beautiful wife in Atlanta."

"If you keep talking like that, you'll find yourself flying out the door with a swift shove," Fortune said good-naturedly.

"Thank you, Alaric. The house is beautiful."

"Indeed it is."

"Alaric brought a bottle of champagne to celebrate, and there is a present for both of us—or for the house actually. I was waiting for you to open it. First the champagne," Fortune said, turning to pop the cork.

She watched her handsome husband pour champagne into glasses, his dark head bent over as pale liquid splashed and bubbled. Fortune passed out the crystal flutes, his fingers brushing hers, his compelling gaze holding hers. "You look beautiful," he said softly. Before she could answer, he turned as Alaric raised his glass.

"Here's to many long, wonderful years in this house," Alaric said cheerfully, watching her.

They drank solemnly and she looked over the rim of her glass into Fortune's gaze.

"Now you can open his present."

She sat down to undo a large box tied in a green satin bow. She untied it and gasped as she lifted out matching silver candelabra.

"Alaric, how magnificent!" Fortune exclaimed.

"They're beautiful. Thank you, Alaric."

"You're very welcome. Where's Michael?"

"He's eating in the kitchen now, and he'll be in to say hello if he can calm down long enough to talk to you. He is so excited about the house."

"I can't blame him."

"I'm trying to get Alaric to get out of the army and go to work for me at the mill," Fortune said. "I could use him."

She looked at Alaric questioningly, and he shrugged. "I'm giving it consideration. Now, it's time to show me the house."

Fortune smiled and placed his arm across Claire's shoulders to lead the way, opening the doors to the ballroom. Light still shone through the windows.

"Ah, a gorgeous room," Alaric said. He took Claire's hand, turning her to face him. "Claire, I must have one dance. C'mon. We'll get Fortune to sing."

"The hell you will," he said.

"Then I'll sing and you'll wish you had," Alaric said, sweeping her into his arms and beginning to sing in German.

She laughed, following him, looking at his feet for a few steps and then feeling comfortable without looking down. "I just learned to dance with Fortune. And I didn't know you knew German."

"I'm incredibly versatile." He swept her around the room, and when she glanced back to Fortune, he was watching her solemnly.

She drew a deep breath, looking up at Alaric, who squeezed her waist. "Let the devil wonder," he said under his breath, singing the words softly, and she smiled up at him, shaking her head.

As he came back around, Fortune stepped forward. "Shall we continue the tour and you give me back my wife?"

"Of course. If you could sing, you could dance with her."

Fortune grinned and placed his arm across her shoulders again. He not only led her to the back parlor, but she was conscious that he stayed by her side the whole time they showed Alaric through the house. As they descended the stairs to the parlor again, Alaric glanced at Fortune. "You'll win over all of Atlanta."

"Who knows? As long as Michael is accepted—"

Alaric laughed. "Don't be absurd. Michael could get accepted on his own. With you and this house, he'll have no problem."

She glance at Alaric, thinking he was right. Michael didn't need all of his father's social prowess. Michael was a bright, friendly child, and would be accepted for himself.

When Badru announced dinner was ready, Alaric took her arm. Through a dinner of roasted quail, potatoes, steaming yellow squash, she barely tasted anything. A running current of excitement disturbed her while she sat at one end of the table and faced Fortune.

All evening she tried to keep her mind on the conversation, to relax, but words of her speeches kept running through her mind. She couldn't help wondering if she would lose her courage. And what if he objected to fathering a child?

After dinner she left them to let them smoke and drink brandy, and as she sat in the front parlor, Michael appeared. "I have to go to bed soon, but I wanted to see Uncle Alaric."

"He's with your father in the dining room. I'm sure they'll be happy to see you."

Michael left and in minutes all three of them returned with Alaric telling Michael a story about the army.

In another half hour Fortune stood up and placed his hand on Michael's shoulder. "Time to tell them good night."

"Night, Uncle Alaric."

"Good night, Michael. I like your new home."

"So do I!" He ran to Claire to hug her and kiss her cheek, and she gave him a squeeze. As she did, she glanced at Fortune. "I can go upstairs with him."

"And deprive me of your company? No," Alaric said, smiling at her. Fortune grinned and left with Michael.

"The home is beautiful, Claire, and I'm thankful you have it."

"I don't know when I'll get accustomed to it. I feel as if I'm intruding and should leave."

He rose from the settee and crossed the room to sit in a wing chair closer to her. "It's yours and it's magnificent, and I hope you're happy. He's so damned blind to everything. If I were Fortune, I—"

"You're not," she said gently, wanting to stop him from whatever he was about to say.

"He doesn't deserve you, not when he is so damned cold and indifferent."

"Alaric, let's talk about something else. Next time you come, you'll have to bring Priscilla. It was wonderful to meet her. I'll invite her over soon and tell her to bring Edwin."

Alaric watched her, his blue eyes steady. "He's my friend, and I would risk my life for him because he's risked his for me, but he doesn't deserve you, Claire."

She smiled and moved away. "You're nice, Alaric, and you're his best friend. And I'm happy with the arrangement I have." She sat down on the settee. "Now tell me about this ball we're attending. I need to start trying to learn names."

Fortune strode through the door, glancing at Alaric and then at her. She looked into his eyes and longed to be alone with him, wondering if her courage would fail her when she was. He sat in a wing chair and stretched out his legs, and she wished he had sat on the settee beside her. As she gazed at him, he seemed remote, shut away behind invisible walls where she couldn't reach him.

Finally Alaric told them good night, pausing at the door to kiss her cheek. As they closed the door and turned back into the hall, Fortune looked down at her. "He likes you damned well."

"Your friend is very nice."

"Yes, he is. And intelligent in spite of the way he acts sometimes. I wish he would go to work with me. I need him."

"He sounds as if he's considering it."

They walked up the stairs, and at the top Fortune started ahead. "I'll look at Michael."

"Fortune, after you look at Michael, may I see you? I want to talk to you."

"Yes. I'll be there in just a minute." He marched down the hall, shedding his coat as he went, opening the door noiselessly to Michael's room.

She went to the darkened master bedroom that Fortune said would be hers. She left the lamps off, wanting the room dark when she talked to Fortune because she knew she would blush. Nervous, she locked her fingers together and moved toward the window to wait for him.

The door opened and he entered. "Claire?"

"I'm in here," she answered as he closed the door. He had left his coat in Michael's room and had shed his cravat.

"Did you want to talk to me?" he asked, and she could hear the curiosity in his voice. He came closer to the window and moonlight spilled across him.

Her heart drummed and she kept her fingers locked together. All her courage seemed to leave her, yet she wanted him and she wanted a baby.

"Is something wrong?" he finally asked as the silence stretched between them.

"No, nothing is wrong. It's a little difficult to talk to you because we haven't been together as much lately," she said, looking down, trying for a moment to avoid his probing gaze. Another gap of silence stretched between them. He moved closer, placing his hands on her shoulders gently.

She looked up at him and took a deep breath. "Fortune, when you proposed to me, you offered several things." Her hands began to tremble. "I love Michael so terribly much." There was a moment's silence, and she realized he was waiting and giving her time. She wondered if he could hear her heart thudding. "You said we could have the physical side of marriage if I want," she said, the words rushing out in a whisper. "I would like a baby."

Chapter 17

Fortune studied her, moving closer to her to tilt her chin up and gaze down at her.

"You said you would be willing if I wanted a physical relationship—" she repeated, her cheeks flushed a deep pink. Her large, luminous eyes were wide with uncertainty.

"I still love Marilee," he said quietly.

"I know you do, but you're a wonderful father to Michael. I'm strong and healthy, and I would like another child."

Just then Fortune's pulse jumped at the thought of bedding her. He knew she had given thought to her decision before she asked him, and he knew that she was certain what she wanted.

"Claire, I like and respect you. I wish I could change how I feel, but I can't and there will be times you'll know it."

"I understand that, but I want more than we have now. And I want another baby badly. We have so much love to give a baby, Fortune. I watch you with Michael, and you're patient with him. He's blossomed since we've been with you."

He thought over what she was saying. She was a virgin and completely innocent about men. She deserved some kind of courtship before being carried off to bed.

He drew her to him, sliding his arms carefully around her waist as he bent his head to kiss her. "If that's what you want, I told you I was willing. Lord knows, Claire, I've wanted you in my arms for a long time."

She slid her arms around his neck, standing on tiptoe while he kissed her. The words weren't declarations of love, but she was happy with what he had said. And maybe someday Fortune would come to love her too.

His hands ran along her sides and her heart beat wildly. She had wanted him to kiss her for so long now, wanted to be held in his arms.

"Fortune," she said, pulling away to look at him. It was on the tip of her tongue to admit to him that she loved him, but as he looked at her, she thought she would hold back that one last little part of herself. Now it would only stir guilt in him. She pulled his head back down until his lips covered hers and he kissed her.

His hands slid over her back, twisting free buttons to push away the silk dress. It fell in a rustle and she felt cool air on her shoulders. Her heart drummed with ecstasy; if this was all she ever had of him, she would learn to accept it, but maybe she could melt the ice around his heart and reach him and let him get over his grieving.

"Claire, you deserve more than this," he whispered roughly.

"I understand, Fortune, I understand . . ." Her voice trailed away as he kissed her throat. His hands rubbed lightly across her breasts, the nipples swelling against his touch.

Watching her with a hungry, smoldering look that made her tremble with eagerness, he stepped back. His hands moved with deliberation, stroking her, grasping the thin chemise and sliding it slowly over her head while his gaze drifted down to her breasts. Fortune cupped them in his big hands, squeezing lightly, bending his head to take a nipple in his mouth and flick his tongue over it. The silky wet touch made her gasp, and she slid her hands across his shoulders, tugging at his shirt, wanting him to take it off.

"Fortune—" she whispered, wondering if he thought she was brazen for pulling at his shirt. "Fortune, I don't know what you want and what you don't want me to do," she whispered.

He raised his head, looking at her with lowered lids, a gaze so heated her heart seemed to thump against her rib cage. "Thank the Lord you don't know. And whatever you do will please me, Claire." He leaned forward to kiss the corner of her mouth, then kiss her ear, his voice husky and his breath warm. "You can do anything that pleases you. I'll like anything."

"I don't even know what to do."

"You will, love," he whispered, trailing kisses from her throat down over her breasts as he fondled her.

She gasped and clung to him, his words as stunning as his touches. ". . . *love* . . ." She knew he had meant it only in the most casual manner, but how she yearned for him to say that to her!

He straightened and pulled away his shirt. Her gaze went over his chest and she touched him, letting her fingers move across the mat of curls, touching a flat nipple.

"Oh, Fortune—"

With a groan his arms banded her and he bent over her, pulling her up against him as he kissed her passionately. She felt his hard erection press against her. She clung to him, lost to sensation, filled with hot desire and wanting him, her hips moving against him.

With another groan he released her and stepped away, picking up his shirt. "For the next few nights I should sleep down the hall."

She stared at him, suddenly feeling cold. "You've changed your mind?"

He paused, turning back to her and moving close again to slide his arm around her waist. Her breasts pressed against him. "Claire," he said, his voice warm and husky, "I haven't changed my mind. You deserve to be made love to long and slowly," he said, kissing her throat. He looked down at her, his eyes filled with desire. "You didn't have a courtship, and you deserve more than my carrying you off to bed tonight. You know I'm ready and want you, but I want you to be as ready and want me as badly."

She looked up at him, thinking he was being far more considerate than she had expected. She pulled his head down to kiss him, and he tightened his arms around her.

He finally stepped away, his breathing ragged as he looked down at her bare breasts. "I'll leave now, Claire. Otherwise I won't be able to stop."

He turned and left the room, closing the door quietly. She stared after him, her emotions churning, her body primed and clamoring for more from him. Nights of exquisite torment? Nights of his kisses and caresses? Hours to spend with him again? The last filled her with joy—and then the thought of a baby, another beautiful child like Michael.

She held her arms wide and swirled about, dazed, joyous, in love with Fortune. Slowly she lowered her arms and gazed at her reflection. Would it always be enough to have this much of him? Would it be enough without his love?

Sunday he stayed home most of the day, going to the mill only in the middle of the afternoon. He brought papers home to sit at his desk in the back parlor and pore over them that night while she sewed and Michael read.

When Michael had been tucked into bed and she came back downstairs, Fortune closed the door to the parlor and turned out one of the lamps, leaving only the one on his desk burning. He caught her wrist and sat on the sofa before pulling her onto his lap. Her muslin skirt and silk petticoat and crinoline rustled and billowed over his legs as her arm wound around his neck. She caught a soapy smell and the faint whiff of tobacco on his breath. One hand held her against him, and the other stroked her shoulder and arm, sending tingles spiraling from the slight touches.

"Tomorrow evening I'll take you to the Bell-Johnson Opera House to see *Mrs. Jarley's Wax Works.*"

"You don't need to work?"

"It can wait."

"I've never been to the theater," she said, pleased. "Fortune, I had another letter from Papa. It's a long letter if you want to read it, but he said they came through the war with his land and money, because he went to England to stay with a cousin during the last two years of the conflict. The house was burned and now he lives in my brother's house. They still own the land, and my brother has rebuilt and has planted cotton again. I thought you'd be pleased to claim another Confederate in your family to weigh against your having fought with that terrible Sherman. My brother was a lieutenant in the Confederate Army."

"You can tell that to the ladies around here. Write and ask for a picture of him in his uniform. I'll have one soon of Cal."

"That's shameless!"

He grinned and her heart turned over. She touched the corner of his mouth lightly. "You're a very handsome man, and I love it when you smile. I would do anything for one of your smiles."

He chuckled, tightening his arm around her and burying his face against her throat to nuzzle her. "That's not so, Claire. I know better. You're a damned independent woman, and you'll do exactly what you think is best."

She closed her eyes, conversation lost as his tongue flicked over her ear. During the day whenever he had passed her or been with her, he had touched her often, tiny brushes that he seemed to be unaware of doing, yet stirring a fiery longing in her.

She turned her head and his mouth slanted over hers. His tongue thrust inside her mouth as he leaned her back on the sofa, and his hand went beneath her skirt and slid up her leg. In minutes he had the underdrawers peeled away, his hand going to the soft folds between her legs

Claire shifted, feeling his arousal, wanting him to love her. His thumb pressed against her feminine bud. She gasped, clinging to him, her eyes closed tightly as her hips moved.

"You like that, Claire," he whispered, kissing her throat and ear, his hand increasing the pressure. She felt lost in a dizzying spiral, no longer able to think. Holding him tightly, she moved in a frenzy until he took her to a brink and over. She gasped and cried out, and he caught her up, his kiss hard and demanding, his hands fondling her breasts.

Finally he set her on her feet and got up to pour a glass of brandy. "I have to go to bed," he said roughly and tossed down the brandy. Striding from the room quickly, he left her, and she knew that he was about to lose his iron control.

She wanted him in a manner she wouldn't have dreamed possible only a month earlier. She wondered how long he would wait to possess her, because tonight he hadn't acted as though he was going to be able to wait much longer at all.

They went to the opera the next night and to a play the following night. He took her for a buggy ride around Atlanta in the evening, and as he nodded to people he knew, she wondered if his work was suffering from all the time and attention he was giving her. With a surge of love and gratitude she placed her hand on his knee.

He turned his head to look down at her, and she drew a deep breath because there was no mistaking that he wanted her. Again that night when they were alone in her bedroom, he pulled her into his arms to love her, to take her to a brink that made her ache for him to complete his loving. And he shook with repressed desire as he released her, leaving her abruptly, his voice a husky rasp.

She knew his control was wearing thin, and she was no longer able to sleep, her body in sweet torment while she lay awake long hours through the night.

Friday morning she had promised Michael she would take him to town, so they left in the buggy with Badru driving. At the opera house and the theater, Fortune had introduced her to several people, and she nodded at familiar faces of ladies she met in passing as Badru drove along. He stopped first in front of the narrow two-story building with a sign over the door, M RICH'S DRY GOODS, and Badru and Michael waited while she went inside to select some material.

While Badru waited with the buggy, she took Michael to the confectioner. After their purchase they stepped outside into the hot sunshine. "I have to go to the milliner," she said, pointing at a shop across the street. Badru was only yards away, the buggy in front of the large general store. "Would you like to meet me in the general store?"

"Yes, ma'am!" He was gone in a flash, running to the store and opening the door. She glanced at Badru, who was watching Michael. Crossing the wide street, she headed for the milliner, looking at more new buildings going up, wagons pulled by oxen hauling loads of bricks.

She stepped into the small shop, a bell tinkling over the door. It was cooler inside. Samples of hats were displayed, and Claire walked over to a pretty green silk hat trimmed in ostrich feathers and silk ribbons. This is where she had thought she would be the rest of her life, running a millinery shop. She looked at the tall gray-haired woman coming toward her. Except for Fortune, this is what she would have been doing. Or singing in a saloon still.

She purchased the green silk and left an order for a blue velvet. As she started back across the street, Badru saw her with the hat box and came to take it from her.

"Mr. Michael is still in the store."

"Thank you, Badru. If you want to get out of the sun, I'm sure we're all right. Go find yourself a cool drink."

"Yes, ma'am. Thank you."

A bell tinkled when she entered the store, which had rows of shelves, goods hanging on the walls and from hooks overhead.

"Good morning, Mrs. O'Brien," Edwin Northrop called cheerfully.

She glanced at the tall auburn-haired man who owned the store. "Good morning."

"If I can be of help, let me know." She nodded, moving down a long aisle, knowing Michael was at the back corner of the store where there were books for sale.

"Good morning," came a lilting voice, and she looked up to see Nellie Hollingsworth, a woman she had met at the opera house.

"Good morning, Mrs. Hollingsworth."

"Call me Nellie. I know we're going to be friends. And your Michael must meet my Josh. They're the same age. Didn't you say he's six?"

"Yes, he is."

"I saw your husband and he said you'll be having a party when his brother, Major O'Brien, comes to town. He told me how the major was wounded at Shiloh."

"That's right. We expect Caleb and Sophia in several weeks."

"He's told us how the major's wife stabbed a Yankee officer and had to flee Memphis for her life."

"Yes. You'll meet them soon."

"We'll see you Friday night at the Meadows'."

"See you then," Claire said, amused that Fortune had not mentioned that he had been present for the burning of Atlanta. Claire purchased two new pans and a half-dozen utensils that she felt were badly needed in the kitchen. Fortune had furnished the house well, but he was lacking in knowledge about what was necessary in the kitchen.

She listened as Mr. Northrop checked off her list and

added up her bill. "If you'll keep all these things, I'll pick them up as I leave."

"Certainly, Mrs. O'Brien. Michael is buried in the books, eh?"

"Yes, he is."

"Let him look. Not many youngsters are that interested. I'll put all this on your bill."

"Thank you," she said, turning away, still feeling amazed that she could buy whatever she wanted and put it on a bill to be sent to Fortune. Her new rose silk dress, made from the material he had bought for her in Baton Rouge, was ready, but she hadn't worn it, waiting for a special occasion.

She walked back to the far corner of the store, where Michael was engrossed in a book. One small corner held four shelves of books, and it was Michael's favorite spot. She moved around looking at material, pans, and ointments, finally wandering back toward Michael.

"A few more minutes," he said, glancing at her and then returning to a book in his lap as he sat cross-legged on the floor. She nodded, walking along the aisle to look at thimbles. In her peripheral vision she saw another customer, and she glanced up as a man filled the aisle. Handsome with a wide jaw and gray streaking his brown hair, he stood gazing past her, his dark eyes on Michael. She knew she was facing Trevor Wenger.

Chapter 18

His gaze shifted, and his dark eyes bored into her. For a moment she was frozen with fear as she remembered all the years she had run from men sent by Wenger to find her. She had a compelling urge to grasp Michael's hand and rush to the buggy and to Badru's protection.

"You're Mr. Wenger, aren't you?"

"Yes. And you're Claire O'Brien. I'm surprised he married you," Wenger said softly.

She shrugged. "We both love Michael."

He looked beyond her at Michael, and she remembered Fortune's angry words, making her promise she would keep Michael from even speaking to Trevor Wenger. She studied the man before her as he looked at his grandson, seeing a look in his eyes that was unmistakably longing. The man was Michael's grandfather, as much as a blood relative as Fortune. She debated whether to go or not. They were safe in the store, and Badru would come if she called. What harm would there be in letting grandfather and grandson at least meet?

She stood in indecision only a moment longer. "Would you like to meet Michael?"

"Yes, of course. I'd be grateful to you," he answered politely, his gaze returning to Michael.

She turned. "Michael, please come here."

"He looks like his father, not like his mother at all."

"He must have his mother's and your dark eyes."

"Yes, he does," Wenger said wistfully, his voice changing. Her fear of him began to lessen, seeing that he was entranced with Michael. "He's a handsome lad."

Michael strolled toward them in a crisp linen shirt and black pants. He was a beautiful child, and she could understand Trevor Wenger's longing to meet him.

"Michael," she said, placing her hand on his shoulder, "this is your grandfather, Mr. Wenger."

Michael blinked, gazing up solemnly while Trevor Wenger held out his hand.

"Michael, I've waited such a long time to see you."

"Yes, sir," Michael replied obediently, shaking Wenger's hand.

"You're a fine lad. I want you to call me Grandfather."

"Yes, sir."

"No, none of that," he said firmly. "I want to hear you say Grandfather."

"Yes, Grandfather," Michael said in a subdued voice, glancing with uncertainty at Claire.

"You're six years old now, aren't you?"

"Yes, sir. Grandfather."

"And you like books. It would please me to get you a book, Michael. Pick out the book you want, and I'll see that it's yours."

"Thank you," Michael said politely and turned to go back and get a book. Wenger's gaze followed him a moment, and then shifted to Claire.

"Thank you for allowing me to talk to him. Would you ever bring him to visit me? I promise to let him go home with you."

Staring at the man who was blood kin to Michael, who had a right to see his grandson, and who was acting like a normal grandfather, Claire was caught between wanting to say yes and remembering her promise to Fortune.

"I'll have to give it thought," she said quietly. "You almost cost us our lives."

"Never Michael's. And now I regret that I had so little regard for the woman who was a mother to him in place of Marilee. I was wild to get my grandson back, and after all, you did run away with him and take him from me. But that's all past now. I ask your forgiveness. I want to see my grandson. I would never hurt him."

"You know his father doesn't want you to see him."

Dark eyes regarded her in a steady, impassive gaze, and she couldn't tell what he was thinking. "There's bad blood between the two of us, and I doubt that will ever change. He took my daughter from me, and he feels I took his wife from him. But that has little to do with my feelings for my grandchild or my feelings toward you. He's my only grandson, my blood kin. Please may I see him?"

"I'll have to give it some thought."

"Are you in this store often?"

She shrugged. "Michael likes to look at the books, so we come maybe every week or two weeks."

"Then perhaps I can see him here again. But please consider allowing him to come to my house. You can bring that guard who rides with you. I won't take Michael from you. I just want to get to know him. He's the only family I have left."

"I cannot promise anything," she said. She had promised Fortune and she wanted to abide by his wishes even though she felt they were misguided.

"If your husband would stop to think about the boy's welfare, he would see that I can introduce Michael into families that will never associate with a Yankee otherwise. I'm old Atlanta society. He shouldn't hurt Michael because of our animosity."

Michael reappeared with a book, and Trevor Wenger held out his hand for it. He squeezed Michael's shoulder. "I want you to come visit me sometime. I want to know you, Michael."

"Yes, Grandfather."

"That pleases me more than you can ever imagine.

You're a good boy, Michael. I'll be going." He looked at Claire. "Thank you for giving me this much opportunity."

He turned and left, a tall man striding toward the front of the store, looking as self-assured as Fortune.

"Would you like to go see him, Michael?"

When he didn't answer, she looked down and he shrugged.

"He's your mother's father."

He leaned forward suddenly, placing his arms around her waist. "You're my mother!" he said, muffled against her. Feeling both a surge of love and a pang that she wasn't his blood mother, she stroked his head.

"We told you, Michael, you've had two mothers. Marilee and me. She loved you and I love you."

He pulled away, a frown on his brow and his lips clamped shut, and she was struck with the close resemblance to Fortune even in anger. "Papa doesn't want me to talk to Mr. Wenger."

"I know he doesn't, because he took your mother away from Papa."

"And that's when she died."

"Yes. But that wasn't what your grandfather intended to have happen, because she was his child and he loved her. On this one thing, Michael, your father may be letting anger stand in his way of doing what is right."

Michael nodded, but she wasn't certain he understood. "Am I going to see him?"

"I don't know. I'll have to think about it. I know your papa doesn't want you to, but Mr. Wenger is your grandfather. You're his blood relative and you're very important to him. Maybe if you saw him first and then we told Papa, he would relent and see that your grandfather is not a bad man."

Michael looked down the long aisle, and she glanced around as Trevor Wenger looked back once more at Michael and then left the store.

"Michael, let me think about this. Let's not tell Papa

that your grandfather bought the book for you until I've had time to think over what we should do and talk to Papa about it."

"Yes, ma'am."

She saw Badru enter the store and look for her, spotting her and approaching.

"Mrs. O'Brien, are you all right?"

"Yes, of course."

"I saw Mr. Wenger come out of the store."

"I know you did, but he left us alone."

"Yes, ma'am."

"Michael, go tell Mr. Northrop that we're ready for our packages."

"Yes, ma'am," Michael said, hurrying toward the front. As soon as he was gone, she turned to Badru.

"I want to think over what to do. I'd rather not disturb my husband about this encounter right now because he's working night and day. Mr. Wenger didn't cause any kind of trouble, so will you please say nothing about this to Mr. O'Brien?"

"Yes, ma'am, if that's what you want, but he told me to tell him if Mr. Wenger ever tried to talk to Michael."

"I don't want my husband in a duel. The man didn't do anything more than meet his grandson. Do you have children?"

"Yes, ma'am," he said, a pained expression coming to his face. "My wife was killed by soldiers in the war, and her folks moved away with my two little boys."

"Oh, Badru," Claire said, reaching out to squeeze his arm impulsively. "I'm so sorry!"

"Thank you," he said, looking beyond her. "They've taken them up north and sometimes they let me keep them, but I know they need their grandmother."

"Then you must know how Mr. Wenger felt seeing his grandson for the first time."

"Yes, ma'am. I can understand, but Mr. O'Brien is paying me to keep Mr. Wenger away and to tell him when Mr. Wenger's been around."

"Just this once, please, Badru. We don't need bloodshed over a man saying hello for the first time to his grandson."

Badru stared at her a moment and then nodded. "Yes, ma'am, but I've never gone back on my word before in my life."

"This is for a good reason. It's for Mr. O'Brien's good as well. And if he asks you directly, then go ahead and tell him. I don't want you to lie to him."

"Yes, ma'am. But it's about the same not to tell him."

That night after dinner, Fortune took Michael out to look at a new horse he had purchased, and when they returned he read to Michael. When she finally tucked Michael in to bed and returned to the parlor, Fortune was working on some ledgers. She gazed at the back of his head, torn between telling him what had happened and waiting. It was a hot night, the windows wide open. Fortune had shed his shirt, and his black hair curled damply on his neck. When she spotted the scars lacing his back, she clamped her lips, deciding to think about it more before telling Fortune about Trevor Wenger.

After quietly sewing, she finally stood up. "Fortune, I'm going to bed."

He tossed down the pen and stretched, standing up and crossing the room to her. "I have some figuring I need to get done before tomorrow," he said, placing his hands on her upper arms. He had a fine sheen of perspiration on his shoulders and brow. "I'll be upstairs in just a little while," he said, his voice becoming deeper as he leaned down to give her a lingering kiss. "I'll be upstairs soon," he repeated when he raised his head. She longed to stand on tiptoe, wind her arms around his neck, and pull his head down to kiss him. Instead she nodded and turned away to go upstairs.

Feeling restless, she had started to pull on her cotton

nightgown when on impulse she changed to the sheer batiste that she had just finished making. She brushed out her hair and climbed into bed, expectantly staring into the darkness. Time passed and she became drowsy, trying to wait until he appeared.

When his silhouette finally darkened the doorway, she rose slightly on her elbows. "You worked late."

"There are some changes on the plans for the mill. I needed to go over the accounts before I make more purchases." He crossed the room silently in bare feet and stretched out on the bed beside her.

"How's the mill progressing?"

"We're about ready to begin business and I'm hiring men. So much of my day is taken up talking to men," he said. His deep voice was a pleasant sound in the darkness so close to her. She turned on her side to face him, propping her head on her elbow. He turned his head to look at her.

"How many men have you hired now?"

"I have almost twenty, and they all have experience. Every day lost before we open, I feel like we're missing business we could have. Atlanta is getting northern money, and it's going to grow and prosper."

"You still think you'll be accepted by Georgians even though you fought for the Union?"

"Yes. At the ball this weekend we'll meet a lot of people who've lived in Atlanta all their lives. And there will be new people as well."

As her gaze ran over his chest and flat stomach, sliding lower, she licked her lips. Turning on his side, he watched her while he touched a lock of her hair, his hand drifting across her nape. The slight tug on her scalp and caress across her neck made her feel faint, and she realized how responsive she was becoming to him. She tried to ignore his hands moving on her shoulder, sliding to the neck of her gown.

"Fortune, I want you to think some more about allowing Michael to at least talk to his grandfather."

"You have on a new nightgown," Fortune said in a husky voice. His hand drifted lightly onto her throat, tugging free ribbons tied in a bow.

"Yes, I do. Did you hear me?" she asked, struggling to concentrate. "I think Michael should meet his grandfather."

Fortune leaned down to kiss her throat lightly, pushing open her gown. "Never," he whispered, kissing her flesh, unbuttoning the neck more and shoving aside the gown to touch her nipple with his tongue.

She gasped, her hands going to his shoulders as she turned to face him. All thoughts of Trevor Wenger were banished. Fortune's body stretched out beside hers, his leg thrown over hers while he kissed her. Pressed close against him, she felt his hard arousal. He shifted her, his hand moving between her legs, and she moaned softly with pleasure.

Her body burned with a desperate need for him. She wanted to reach for his trousers, to unbutton them and touch him, but she held back, feeling it would be too forward, trying to follow his lead.

Finally he groaned and rolled out of bed, moving away from her. "Go to sleep, Claire," he said, leaving the room swiftly.

She ached, her body ready for love, wanting him. She sat up and tugged off her nightgown, her heated flesh damp. She balled up the gown and fanned herself with it, certain she wouldn't see Fortune the rest of the night. She knew he was trying to get her ready for seduction, and she wondered if he had any idea how well he had succeeded. How long would he continue this sweet torment that left her hot and aching and wanting him, that made her think about him all day to the point of distraction?

She wiped her damp brow, shook out the gown, and pulled it on again. Only when she was hovering on the edge of sleep did she remember she had gotten nowhere with her question about Michael and Trevor Wenger.

Friday came, and she felt an expectancy that she knew had been brought on by Fortune's attention all week. He had brought her to a quivering peak where the slightest caress made her gasp with awareness. The prospect of going with him to a ball tonight, of being in his arms and dancing all evening, made her giddy with eagerness.

She undressed and bathed, drying and sitting down in a wrapper to do her hair. She couldn't fasten it up as well as Sophia and Chantal had, but finally she had it parted in the center, and pulled high on the back of her head to fall in curls down over her back. A half-dozen small white gardenias were pinned in her hair, their fragrance faint and sweet.

She crossed the room to the bed, where her dress was laid out in readiness. With awe she ran her fingertips over the deep blue silk dress that Fortune had had made for her. It was an exquisite dress that must have cost dearly, the most beautiful dress she had ever owned, other than the satin wedding dress.

She donned silken underdrawers, her corset, a crinoline, a sheer batiste chemise. Finally she lifted the dress over her head and carefully lowered it. As it slid over her skin, the silk was a cool caress. She smoothed it and looked at her reflection in the mirror, studying her appearance.

Satisfied, she left the room, finding Michael in his room, where Penthea was reading a story to him. He sat beside her, turning pages with his small hands, and when Claire crossed the room, he looked up.

"You look pretty, Mama. And you smell pretty."

"Thank you, Michael."

"You do look pretty, Mrs. O'Brien," Penthea said. "I'll see Michael gets to bed on time."

"Fine. Do you know where Papa is?"

"He's downstairs. He told me good night," Michael answered, tapping his finger on the book. "Can we keep reading?"

Claire brushed his cheek with a kiss. "Good night. Be a good boy. Good night, Penthea."

She left them, her anticipation mounting as she descended the stairs. Her skirt and crinoline rustled with faint swishes. She went down the hall to the back parlor and found Fortune bent over the desk, looking at papers.

"I'm ready," she said quietly, wondering if he wished he could stay home and work.

His gaze started at her toes and lifted slowly upward. His obvious approval and pleasure made her pulse race almost as much as the sight of him in a ruffled white silk shirt, a black cravat, and black coat and trousers. When he was dressed up, his eyes seemed more blue and distinct than ever.

With a scrape of the chair he stood and crossed the room to her. "You look beautiful, Claire. I feel fortunate."

"No more than I do."

Solemnly he trailed his fingers along her cheek, and she saw the moment he thought of Marilee and moved away. He crossed the room to a table to pick up a box. "Turn around. I bought something for you."

She turned and felt the warmth of his body as he moved close behind her. He trailed a kiss across her nape, and she closed her eyes. His arms rose and as she felt them brush against her shoulders lightly, she realized how sensitized she had come to him, until the slightest brush or contact made her tingle with awareness.

She looked down as he lifted a necklace over her head and placed it against her bare skin while he fastened it behind her head. He brushed another kiss across her neck in a feathery touch that lingered. "This is for you," he said.

Stunned, she looked down at a magnificent setting of diamonds sparkling in brilliant contrast against the deep blue of sapphires. "Fortune, what did this cost!" She spun around, and saw the amusement in his gaze.

He placed his hands on her shoulders. "Lord, Claire, I think the only thing that would make you gasp with pleasure is for me to tell you I've put a deposit into your savings account," he said dryly.

"No, that isn't what would make me gasp with pleasure," she answered in a breathless, throaty voice. His brows drew together as he studied her, his expression becoming solemn.

"You know what does," she said more shyly.

"Yes, I do. But beyond that—most women would be pleased over this bauble. Instead you're concerned about the cost."

"It's so expensive! And it's beautiful!"

"I want my wife to be dressed as well as any other woman at this party," he said, picking up a box with a velvet lining and holding it out. "I'll let you put these on."

She looked at sapphire and diamond matching earbobs, touching the plain gold hoops she had worn for uncounted years. "Fortune, these are magnificent!" Impulsively she stood on tiptoe to kiss him lightly.

Instantly his arm wrapped around her, holding her close as his lips pressed against hers, opening hers. His tongue entered her mouth, making her forget all about the necklace or the ball. She slid her hand onto his shoulders. He kissed her until her heart was pounding, and when he released her he looked down at her with a hungry gaze that made her tremble as much as his kiss had. "You'll be the most beautiful woman there."

She smiled at him and touched his jaw. "No, I won't, but I'll remember all night that you told me so."

He released her and returned to the desk to close his ledgers. Stepping in front of an oval mirror, she removed her old earbobs and replaced them with the new ones. The diamonds sparkled in the light, accented by the deep blue of the sapphires. Amazed that he would buy her such a lavish gift, she glanced in the mirror at him. As if she had spoken, he turned around. "Ready to go?"

"Yes," she answered, looking at the necklace a last time and turning to take his proffered arm. "Fortune, you must dance with me a few times at first to make certain I don't do something awkward. And Alaric has promised to dance with me."

Fortune laughed. "It is certain Alaric will dance with you. He'd like to take you away from me!"

"That's not so," she protested as they left the house. "He's just a very good friend."

"Oh, yes, he's a good friend, but he would take you to bed if he could."

"Fortune!" She gasped with shock, wondering if he was teasing.

As his hands closed around her waist, he remarked, "You're as light as Michael."

"Hardly. But I'm lighter than the iron you lift at work."

He chuckled. "I'm not lifting any iron." He swung her into the buggy and went around to climb up beside her and take the reins. As they moved down the drive, she touched the necklace. He glanced at her. "Alaric is half in love with you."

She laughed. "I think he is half in love with most of the women in Atlanta."

"Atlanta has beautiful women and yes, you're right. Alaric has never really been deeply in love. I hope I'm around to see that happen."

"You have that tone you use when you talk of revenge. Fortune, you have a streak in you—" She clamped her mouth shut.

"Go ahead and say it," he said lightly, turning the corner.

"Not tonight. This is my very first dance, my first adult party. I won't spoil it with any words that aren't joyful."

Fortune reached over to take her hand and give it a

squeeze. He spread her fingers on his thigh. "Your first dance and first party. We'll have to make it special."

"It's very special already."

"I'll see what I can do," he said, placing his hand over hers.

At length he slowed the horses and stopped in front of a three-story Victorian mansion painted a pale blue. Lights blazed from the open windows and doors, and she could hear musicians playing a waltz. A burst of panic swept over her.

"Oh, Fortune, suppose I step on people's toes and do things I shouldn't? I don't know anything about society."

"Don't be ridiculous! Not you, Claire. I didn't see you show this much fear the first night I caught up with you and Michael."

"That's different. Then Michael was involved. Besides, I could fight you. I can't fight these people, I have to be accepted by them."

"You will be, I promise you." He tugged on the reins as a groomsman came forward. Fortune climbed down and came around the buggy to get her.

He linked her arm through his, and they walked up broad steps across a wide veranda. Claire took a deep breath, glancing up at her husband, praying that she would please him tonight.

Chapter 19

Garlands of sweet-scented flowers and massive bouquets of roses decorated the rooms. A white-coated butler came forward to greet them and take Fortune's beaver hat. The house was filled with people, men in black or gray evening coats, women in a rainbow of elegant silk and satin dresses. Claire felt out of place, uncertain what to do, yet Fortune looked as at ease as he did stretched on the floor reading to Michael. A stocky man with a thick black beard and curly black hair came toward them. He smiled at her and offered his hand to Fortune.

"Fortune, I'm so glad you could come."

"Elwood, this is my wife, Claire. Claire, this is Elwood Meadows."

"Happy to meet you," he said, smiling broadly. He stroked his beard as he looked around. "Let me take you around. I have to warn you, Fortune, one of your competitors is here, Clarence Hoagland, who works at Wenger Ironworks. So no brawling, do you hear?"

Fortune chuckled and cast Claire an ironic look she couldn't decipher.

"Lenore, come meet Fortune O'Brien and his wife," he said to a short blond woman who gazed up with sparkling brown eyes as introductions were made. Soon Lenore took Claire to meet other women guests, and she was separated from Fortune for the next half hour. Standing in a cluster of women in an elegant parlor, Claire attempted to memorize their names. A tall blonde named Penelope

Gillman stood next to her, and Claire listened while Penelope told everyone abut a new shipment of grosgrain and moiré that had arrived in an Atlanta store. The room was filled with guests, music coming from the ballroom, the buzz of conversation mixing with the sounds of violins.

"There you are," came a deep voice behind her. Claire turned to see Alaric approaching. His blond hair was neatly combed, and he wore a gray coat and black trousers, a ruffled white silk shirt and white cravat. In short, he looked almost as dashing as Fortune. She smiled at him, seeing him give her a swift appraisal. "Penelope," he said in greeting, brushing the blonde's cheek with a quick kiss.

"Excuse us," he said, drawing Claire out of the circle.

She laughed. "Alaric, you shouldn't take me away from them. You'll start gossip."

"Nonsense. Everyone who knows me or Fortune knows that we're the closest of friends. Besides, I've been waiting for hours. May I have this dance?"

"Yes, you may," she answered, smiling up at him, "but I'll warn you, it's my first real dance. You're kind to dance with me."

"Kind? Don't be ridiculous," he said as he led her through the crowd into the ballroom. "If it weren't for Michael, I'd take you away from Fortune. You're wasting yourself on him."

"No, I'm not. He's very good to me."

"Claire, as he has told me time and again, you've never been in love, so you have no idea what ecstasy you're missing!"

"Yes, I do have an idea," she said, suddenly solemn as she looked across the ballroom at her handsome husband. He was easy to spot, his dark head looming over the crowd. He stood in a circle of men and one woman. He laughed at something she said, and she touched his arm lightly. It gave Claire a peculiar sensation to see the woman place her hand on Fortune.

"Lord, you're in love with him!"

She swung her gaze back to Alaric, who was frowning at her. "Heaven help you, you've fallen in love with a man who has a block of granite for a heart," he said, sounding annoyed.

"He's very good to me and to Michael, Alaric. I can't believe all that he's given me."

"You deserve a man who adores you," Alaric answered gravely. "I jest so much of the time, Claire, I don't think anyone, maybe even me included, knows when I'm in earnest, but if it weren't for Michael, I would try to take you from him."

Shaken, she gazed up at Alaric. "Then don't ever forget Michael, because I would never leave him. I'd never do anything to jeopardize what Fortune has given me. And he said if I ever fall in love he would let me go, but he keeps Michael."

"So if I whirl you out onto the balcony, you won't let me kiss you," he said lightly, and she saw the sparkle back in his eyes, knowing he was once again teasing her.

"No, I won't! And you won't do that to your best friend either. Or to the child who already calls you Uncle Alaric."

"Ah, Claire, you do spoil things. I shall have to find someone to kiss tonight who is willing, single, and more impressed with me."

"Indeed, you will!" she exclaimed with a smile. "I imagine there is a roomful of women here who are longing for you to do just that."

He grinned as they waltzed. "You've been practicing your dancing."

"Yes, I've been practicing with Michael."

He sighed again. "See there. If I were your husband—"

"But you're not."

"And I see he's given you something very lovely. The necklace looks beautiful on you."

"Thank you."

"Well, even if you won't let me whirl you onto the balcony, you can let me make you laugh and hold you a little closer, and give our man of stone something to think about." Alaric twirled her about and she had to laugh.

"That's better. And I shall tell you about the time during the war that Fortune and I stole corsets from a family fleeing Atlanta."

"Corsets?" she asked, amused.

"Yes. I thought it was a box of ears of corn. You see, we had ridden for a whole day without anything to eat, and we saw a entourage of three wagons and two buggies. We robbed them, taking a jug of water, a bottle of brandy, and a large crate they had with the other food. I thought I saw corn husks sticking out of the crate, so we rode off with it. But when we stopped to eat and drink and I pried open the crate, there were three moldy ears of corn and a dozen ladies' corsets!" He glanced toward Fortune. "I'm amazed you haven't heard about it. For a solid month he called me Captain Corset."

She laughed brightly as the music came to an end. Even before they had dropped their arms, Fortune appeared behind Alaric.

"And now, friend, I'm taking my wife from you before you try to dance her out onto the balcony."

"It would serve you right. In fact, I already tried and she wouldn't allow it. But I won't stop trying."

Their voices were bantering, but she could see the hard edge in Fortune's expression. Did he care because of any scandal hurting Michael? Or did he care for her?

Fortune turned to take her into his arms as the music commenced a Viennese waltz. "I'll have to watch him. He won't stop trying to take you from me."

"Don't be ridiculous. He's being polite and attentive and we're friends. And even if he really did mean what he says, which he doesn't, you know I wouldn't do a thing to wreck what you've given me or to lose Michael."

Fortune looked down at her. "I know that, but I also know Alaric and he's half in love with you. He doesn't understand grief because he's never experienced it." Fortune's gaze lowered to the necklace and then lower, where the lace edge of her dress covered her full curves. "You're very beautiful."

"Thank you, Fortune. The necklace is magnificent."

"I was talking about you, Claire, not the damned necklace," he said.

"I know that."

"Alaric can make you laugh."

"He told me about the crate of stolen corsets."

Then Fortune truly did relax. Laughing outright, he said, "Alaric can get into more impossible situations. He thought he had a crate of corn. My mouth was watering and the women in that family were shrieking and crying when we rode away with that damned crate. We had all their corsets. And there was the time he found us a cave. I'd been shot in the leg—"

"I didn't know that!"

"It was slight, only a scratch, but I had my leg wrapped and I was exhausted and it was raining. He found a cave and I crawled inside—to a nest of snakes. Alaric finds disaster the way a dog sniffs out a coon."

She smiled at Fortune and he smiled back at her. "That's the way I like you, Claire. When you're smiling. Or in moments of passion." He pulled her closer to him, bending so his warm breath was on her ear. "And when we get home, I shall take those white flowers out of your hair, one by one."

She felt tingles from his breath on her. Looking up, she saw that desire had darkened his eyes. She became lost in his gaze as they swept down the length of the room.

"I wish," he said, his voice deeper than usual, "that I

could take you home right now. But we need to meet people here and to be seen."

"Did you meet the man who works at Wenger Ironworks?"

"Yes, I did. He knows I'm just starting out, and he paid little attention to me. I don't think he expects any real competition."

"Then he's a foolish man," she said, looking at the crowd, knowing Atlanta would always be a special city to her because she would associate it with Fortune and her marriage. "This is a marvelous city. I've been in so many, but this is different."

"When Cal and Sophia get here, I want to have our first party. Before that, though, I have to get my mill running."

"And I'm sure you have shamelessly talked about your Confederate major relative."

He grinned. "Of course, I have. But it depends upon the company I'm in. There are Union soldiers here as well. Atlanta is a thriving industrial city."

"It won't matter to the women whether you were a Yankee or a Reb."

He grinned. "Southern women don't forget. It will matter, but time will help."

"I don't mind that you were a Yankee."

"That's because you ran away from the South, and you weren't here during the war. And thank heavens you did. If I had thought Michael was in a southern town, suffering from that damned war . . ." His voice trailed away, and he looked down at her. "You're dancing well, Claire."

"I've been practicing."

"Damnation, Alaric—"

She laughed. "No! Michael and I have been dancing."

"You and Michael?" Fortune asked, his brows arching. "You should have told me. I would have practiced with you."

"You're so busy and you've been giving a lot of your time to me this past week when I know you need to work."

"Not many women would view it that way."

"You don't know many women who have had to support a child on their own."

"No, but I could have taken the time to practice with you." He tilted his head and smiled, and she felt a flutter, wishing he weren't solemn so much of the time. "Then Michael will be a marvel on the dance floor by the time he'd old enough to attend parties."

"He'll probably forget. He was a mighty reluctant partner."

Fortune laughed, giving her waist a squeeze. "You probably haven't noticed, but I'm getting looks of envy from just about every man in this room."

"That's absurd, Fortune, but it's nice of you to say so."

He merely shook his head. Pulling her slightly closer, they continued to dance, their steps matching as if they had danced together for years. Her hand rested lightly on his broad shoulder, and she nudged it higher until her fingertips touched the nape of his neck. His eyes narrowed, and she wondered if he felt the same stir of desire that she did. She felt light and giddy, as if she were skipping on air instead of over a ballroom floor.

Later in the evening, while Fortune was engrossed in conversation with two men who owned textile mills, Alaric appeared at her side.

"May I have this dance?" he asked, tugging on her arm. She glanced up at Fortune, who was talking about his mill, and she nodded to Alaric. They moved to the dance floor, and he turned her into his arms. "At last I can dance with you again!"

"Alaric, you have to stop flirting!"

"Your husband is buried in iron and too busy to notice what I do, so let me have my fun, Claire. Besides, someday—"

"No!" she exclaimed lightly, smiling at him. "No somedays. Now stop flirting or we stop dancing."

"That's absolutely impossible for me!" he answered with a grin, and she had to laugh. "When my feet move and I hold a beautiful woman in my arms, I flirt. It's like stretching when you wake up in the morning—natural and necessary."

She laughed and glanced around. "I know you know all the gossip. I've met so many people, and I can't remember anybody's names. Even their faces are a blur."

"Very well. To your right is Egidius Fechter, one of the owners of the City Brewery. That's certainly a fellow to remember. Next to him is Letitia Barnard, who knows everyone in town. Then you have your carpetbaggers, like Rufus Bullock, a Radical Republican. He's thick with General John Pope, who runs this military district—you do realize Georgia is under military rule." She nodded, and he went on, "Bullock has a friend, Hannibal Kimball, who's just constructed the opera house that the military wants to requisition for the state capital. . . ."

When the music ended, a man approached them. "Alaric, I haven't been introduced to my competitor's wife," he said in a deep voice.

"We can remedy that. Claire, this is Clarence Hoagland. Clarence, this is Mrs. Fortune O'Brien."

"I'm happy to meet you," he said as she looked up at a tall brown-haired man with dark brown eyes. "May I have a dance?" he asked, glancing at Alaric.

"Yes, you may," she answered. "Thank you, Alaric."

He smiled. "I claim the next dance, though."

As Clarence Hoagland took her hand, she felt a faint touch of repulsion, wondering at her reaction because he seemed polite and he was an attractive man. She realized her years of avoiding men had made her wary of any that she didn't feel comfortable around.

The music began and she gazed at the crowd, at a loss for conversation.

"Your husband is going into competition with his former father-in-law."

"I'm surprised that people know of the relationship."

"They know. Trevor Wenger wants his grandchild, and he's not happy with the man who is keeping them separated. I hope your husband is ready for a battle in business because he's going to get one." Hoagland smiled at her. "This concerns you little, though, and I didn't ask you to dance to discuss iron. I've worked for Trevor for a long time now, and he talks to me. I know what the situation is between you and your husband."

Surprised, she tilted her head to study him, wondering how much gossip was going around town about Fortune and her. "What situation?"

He smiled. "Anyone who knows Trevor Wenger very well knows that his daughter met a Yankee when Marilee was visiting Trevor's sister in Baltimore. And they know that Marilee married the Yankee against her father's wishes. It's common knowledge that a young woman took his grandchild when Marilee died and that he's been searching for the grandchild for all these years. He was shocked to learn that Colonel O'Brien married you. I'm shocked that you married him."

"Why would that shock you?" she asked, disliking Clarence Hoagland more by the minute. "You don't even know me."

"Because he obviously doesn't love you, although he's putting up a good front tonight. He did it to keep you as a mother to his son, to get a stronger hold on Michael so Trevor can't take him. But you're a beautiful woman," he said, his voice lowering as his arm tightened around her. "You could have waited for a man who loved you."

She bit back an angry retort, forcing a smile as she gazed up at him. "Sir, you might be badly mistaken about what my husband and I feel for each other."

His brows drew together in a slight frown as he studied

her. He shrugged. "Maybe I misjudged, but he doesn't act like a man in the first months of being married."

"And you think I don't act like a woman in the first months of being married?" she countered, smiling at him.

He laughed. "Perhaps I'm wrong. Of course, the man is incredibly well fixed with Trevor's sister's money, so I can see why you would be attracted to him."

She laughed, hoping her annoyance with him didn't show. Wishing the waltz were over, she happened to see Alaric standing on the sidelines watching her. He winked at her and she smiled at him.

"That's the man who acts as if he's in love with you."

"I think if you watch Alaric more closely, you'll find he's that way with every female in the room."

"Only the beautiful ones, I'm sure. And I don't care about him because I have a beautiful woman in my arms."

She was thankful when the music ended. Alaric appeared at once to claim her.

"Thank you," she said perfunctorily to Clarence.

"It was my pleasure, Mrs. O'Brien."

He turned away, and Alaric took her hand, moving with her as the music commenced again.

"All of Atlanta knows about Fortune and Michael and me," she said. "I hadn't realized—"

"Don't be ridiculous. The only people who know anything are the ones close to Fortune or close to Wenger. What did Hoagland say to you?"

"He said he knows we didn't marry for love. He said he could see why I would want Fortune because he's quite wealthy."

"Damn the man!"

As they whirled about the room, Claire spotted Fortune in conversation, his head tilted as he listened to a short, portly man. But he was looking straight at her, and she wished it was Fortune who had caught her attention and winked at her instead of Alaric. Fortune nodded his head and said something to the man, but his gaze remained steadily on her.

"Stop looking at him as if you can't wait for him to come dance. Do me the grace to smile, or half the women in here will think I'm losing my charm."

Claire laughed, looking up at him. "I wouldn't want to cause you any loss of esteem!"

He smiled in return. "That's much better. I shall have to think of something else to make you laugh. Let's see, there aren't many funny tales about your husband. About the only thing amusing me is that he is persisting in wanting me to work at the mill."

"Why is that amusing?"

"I don't feel cut out for that type of life. My father is a merchant, and he wants me to come back home to Philadelphia and learn the business."

"Fortune wouldn't make you an offer if he didn't feel he needed you. You know it isn't out of friendship."

"No, I know that. Working with steel is exactly where a fellow like Fortune belongs—but I won't get into that again," he said with a sigh. His features became serious. "Claire, if you ever need a friend, I'll always be there. You can ask for my help any time. You're married to a man who can be harsh and unyielding when he makes up his mind about something. You haven't crossed him since you exchanged vows, but if you ever do, you may need a friend. Don't hesitate."

"Thank you, Alaric," she answered. "I've never had a good friend."

"Dammit, you've never had anyone you could turn to. If you'd just give me a chance—"

"Alaric, I have Fortune and I have Michael. I would never give up Michael. Never!" she stated emphatically, knowing it was not only true, but it was an explanation Alaric couldn't argue against.

"My charm is failing me like petunias beneath a blazing August sun. Ah, Claire, what you do to a man's pride!"

"You started this," she answered, smiling at him. "And I know your pride will revive like petunias in a rain shower—"

"I'm claiming my wife, you scoundrel" came Fortune's voice, and they turned to face him. He smiled and took her hand from Alaric, pulling her toward him. "Go away, Alaric," he said kindly.

Alaric flashed a brilliant smile. "This may ruin my reputation with the ladies completely."

"Check and see if it has," Fortune said negligently. He steered her away into the middle of the floor. "I got lost in mill talk."

"That's all right."

"It was something I needed to do. I saw Hoagland dancing with you."

"He knows all about me from Trevor Wenger. They're going to give you competition."

With a grim set to his jaw, Fortune looked over her head. "And I intend to give them competition very soon. And what do you mean, he knows all about you?"

She thought about what Hoagland had said and shivered, unaware she had done so until she realized Fortune was watching her closely. "Did he do something he shouldn't have?" he asked in that tone of voice that brought a chill to her.

"No. I just didn't like the man and don't want him around me or touching me. I'm that way about most men. A woman traveling alone with a baby is vulnerable, and I developed this intense repugnance to men I don't want around me."

"I'm glad," Fortune said wryly. "I'd hate to think you liked their touching you." Suddenly he perked up with an idea. "We're newlyweds, so that should give us an excuse to leave early."

"Or start all kinds of wild speculation with people who know the truth."

"Let them wonder. You can watch Alaric's eyebrows touch his hairline."

She smiled up at Fortune, who grinned in return. "It's been a wonderful party, Fortune."

"I'm glad. Let's go home, Claire."

How she wished he meant it with all his heart! Yet she knew he would kiss her when they reached home, and the prospect speeded her eagerness to go. They moved through the crowd to thank the Meadows, and it took Fortune another half hour to tell people good-bye.

The night had cooled, and the air was refreshing as the team of matched blacks moved along briskly. Claire rode beside him, nestled against his side. The closer they came to their home, the more her awareness of him grew.

When they went upstairs, he took her hand to walk to their large bedroom, where he closed the door. One small lamp burned and her new sheer batiste gown was laid out on the turned-down bed.

Fortune slipped off his coat and tossed it aside. Her pulse began to drum as she watched him unfasten his cravat and drop it. His eyes pinned hers, sending her pulse jumping another notch. That smoldering look left no doubt he wanted her. He stretched out his long arms to draw her to him.

"I told you that I would take those flowers out of your hair," he said, reaching up to pull one out. Lightly he trailed it over her cheek, the satiny soft petals tickling her, the sweet gardenia scent noticeable. He drew it down across the fullness of her breasts along her neckline.

She couldn't look away from his compelling gaze, feeling the touch of the flower run across her skin, wanting his hands there, wanting his kisses.

"Fortune," she whispered.

He pulled out another flower and another, tossing them

down, until her hair tumbled over her shoulders and back in a thick cascade.

He pulled his shirt out of his trousers and over his head. Tossing it aside, he reached out to turn her around so he could unbutton her dress. His fingers brushed the back of her earlobes and he leaned down to kiss her neck.

She closed her eyes as his kisses trailed to the neck of her dress, and she felt his fingers tug at the buttons. She longed to turn around and tell him she loved him, but she still held back. She felt cool air on her back as he parted her dress. With a whispery rush it fell to the floor.

"We'll get rid," Fortune whispered, his fingers at her waist, "of this damned crinoline and then that corset that is a sin on you, Claire."

Her pulse jumped, because he had never removed her corset.

She turned around and he gazed at her with hungry longing. He reached up to run his hands through her hair, and she caught the glint of the gold bracelet on his wrist that reminded her that his love was locked away from her, chained with memories.

He framed her face with his hands as he stepped closer. "If Alaric ever tries to take you from me—"

He bit off his words to kiss her, and her heart felt as if it had stopped beating. Fortune no longer sounded like a man who would willingly let her fall in love with another. Was there a chance he was falling in love with her?

She ran her hands over Fortune's bare chest, tangling her fingers in the thick curls. Feeling brazen, yet wanting him so badly, loving him terribly, she let her fingers slide lower.

"Fortune," she whispered in uncertainty, her hands pausing at his belt. She looked up at him, his eyes heavy-lidded, his breathing as ragged as hers. She slid her hands lower, and he moaned as she felt the hard bulge of his erection. He pulled her tightly against him to kiss her passionately, his tongue playing deep in her mouth while his hands moved at her back at the laces of her corset.

She felt dizzy with sensation, wanting him to never stop, expecting at any moment that he would turn and walk away as he had every night during the week.

He stepped back, and flung aside the corset. Swiftly peeling away her underdrawers, he knelt to roll down her stockings, his hands caressing her long legs.

"Oh, Fortune!" she gasped, her hands braced on his wide shoulders while she ached for him.

He leaned forward, his tongue like flame over the inside of her thighs. Standing again, he watched her as he unfastened his trousers.

Her pulse roared, drowning out all other sounds as she looked at his powerful naked body, aroused, so strong and virile before her. She wanted to touch him and discover what he felt like. She wanted to kiss him, to try to make him feel some of what she did.

He drew her to him to cup her breasts and gently flick her nipples. She gasped as warmth shot through her. The ache low in her body increased. She closed her eyes, her hands reaching down to touch his hips, sliding over his firm flesh, her hand closing around his manhood.

She heard his gasp as she ran her fingers over the velvet tip. As she slid her hand along his shaft, she wondered how she could ever mate with him because he was so large, so hard.

And then the thought was gone as he slid his hand between her legs, finding the bud that he rubbed sensuously. She moaned softly, and his lips covered hers, his mouth taking her cry as her hips thrust against him.

He picked her up, carrying her to the edge of the bed to set her down as he knelt between her legs and pushed her back, spreading her legs. He kissed the inside of her thigh, moving higher, his lips moving where his hand had been, his tongue playing over the most intimate parts of her body.

She gasped, arching and winding her fingers in his hair. "Fortune, please, you have to love me tonight . . ."

"I want you ready, Claire," he whispered, his tongue making her writhe with passion.

"Fortune, please," she gasped, starting to sit up. He pushed her back, shifting her legs as he watched her. Her heartbeat thundered as she closed her eyes and let him kiss her, taking her to the brink.

He shifted his body and moved between her thighs. She looked up at him, his manhood dark and erect, his gaze intent. He lowered himself, kissing her breast as he came down, moving over her.

She felt the hot tip of his shaft press against her, and her hips arched to meet him. She grasped his hips, tugging him. "Oh, yes, Fortune! Yes!"

"Put your legs around me," he said in a rasp. She opened her eyes to see his strong shoulders over her, his half-closed eyes on her.

Fortune fought to hold back, to move slowly, to make her want him. He felt the obstruction of the tight maidenhead, knew he would hurt her, yet he knew Claire wanted him and she wouldn't fight him.

And he wanted her with a depth he hadn't thought possible. He thrust into her softness, hearing her gasp and then cry out. He covered her mouth with his, fighting for control, moving slowly and withdrawing, feeling her hips arch up against him, her hands tugging his buttocks to pull him back.

He thrust into her again, slowly, trembling with the effort to keep control, sweat beading his body and running on his forehead. Her hips moved wildly and he felt the tight maidenhead yield, his shaft going deep, trying to drive her to a frenzy, wanting her and knowing that he couldn't hold back much longer.

She gasped and cried out. "Fortune! Please—" Her even white teeth bit her lower lip, and her eyes were tightly closed as she ran her hands down his back and over his buttocks.

And then his control was gone. "Claire." He ground out the word roughly, moving fast, unable to hold back, all thought gone.

Her long legs held him tightly while she clung to him and rocked with him. He climaxed hard and fast, his hot seed spilling into her.

When they had become still, he let his weight down on her softness, knowing she was a wonderful woman and a beautiful woman who deserved better than what he was giving her. He kissed her shoulder and throat, turning on his side and keeping her with him.

"Oh, Fortune," she gasped, burying her face against him. As she clung to him, he wondered if she was crying, if she had regrets. He stroked her long hair away from her face.

"Claire, love, next time will be better for you."

"Fortune," she said, holding him tightly, speaking with her face pressed against his chest. "You're perfect."

He realized what she had said, and he shifted to look down at her, tilting her face up to his. This was her first taste of love, and he knew she was wrapped in the euphoria of it. He was thankful that he had at least given her that much. He kissed her temple.

"You're a wonderful woman." He pulled her close in his arms, realizing that he could spend his nights this way now, marveling that she had wanted him and wanted another baby. Her first baby from her womb. From the time Marilee had told him she was expecting their child, he had been focused on Michael and never once thought about having another child. He hadn't even given it much thought when Claire asked, but now it came to him fully. The thought filled him with eagerness because Michael was such a marvel.

Fortune stroked her hair from her face while she ran

her fingertips over his jaw. "Fortune, I want you with me at night like this."

He pulled her close to hug her. "Claire, you deserve more than this."

Her fingers covered his mouth and she shifted, looking at him and then pulling his head down to kiss him.

Claire clung to him, marveling in his body that was so different, burning with embarrassment when she thought about what he had just done. "Fortune," she whispered, again on the verge of declaring her love to him but stopping short. "I don't have any experience at pleasing you," she said.

He grinned at her, gently tugging a long lock of hair. "Thank goodness," he said. "Experience is not what a man wants in a wife."

"Yes, but loving a virgin can't be as exciting."

"It was good, I promise you," he said, kissing her, amused by her worries. "Claire, a sporting girl has experience but not much else."

"She would be more exciting for you."

"No, she definitely would not. You saw what you did to me. And you saw how soon you caused me to lose control."

"That is the first time, Fortune O'Brien, I've caused you to lose control!"

He remembered some of his bouts of temper with her and was glad those moments escaped her memory right now. He kissed her shoulder, trailed kisses to her full lips, and he felt himself becoming aroused again. He drew a deep breath, his broad chest expanding, wondering if she would be too sore to love again.

"Claire," he whispered, bending his head to take her breast in his mouth, hearing her moan as her hips shifted against him.

His pulse jumped, his erection coming hard as he realized she wasn't going to stop him. This time he could go slow for her, take his time, try to bring her ecstasy instead of pain. He rolled her onto her stomach and leaned over to kiss the small of her back while his hands played over her thighs and her buttocks.

When he finally turned her over and lowered himself, entering her, he went slowly, able to hold back until she bucked wildly beneath him.

Claire cried out, wild with need as she climaxed. Still he held back, his shaft deep and hard in her, moving slowly, withdrawing until only the tip touched her moist warmth. She tugged at him, still wanting him as she reached another climax.

His pulse roared in his ears while her head thrashed about and her legs tightened around him. Passionate and eager, she was responsive to his slightest caress.

Finally he couldn't hold back and moved with her, their hips thrusting until he groaned, his head coming down as he kissed her and thrust his tongue deep into her mouth.

They grew quiet and he kissed her lightly, from her throat down her arm to the back of her hand.

She clung to him, holding him tightly. "I need you, Fortune. We can make our marriage good if we try. I know we can."

"Yes, Claire," he said, stroking her head, letting his hand slide down over her damp, smooth skin, down to the enticing curve of her buttocks. "It'll be good," he repeated, holding her. She turned against him, playing her hands over his chest.

"Perhaps tonight we started a baby."

"Maybe, but usually it isn't that easy."

"So we'll have to keep trying."

He laughed softly, a deep sound in the stillness. "From now on, I'm sleeping in here, Claire." Then he fell silent, knowing she might not feel the same about anything in the light of day, knowing tonight he had the advantage in overcoming any of her objections to anything they had done.

She fell asleep in his arms. He held her close, stroking

her hair, thinking about Marilee, feeling as if memories and his love for her were slipping away from him. For the first time the hurt that plagued him with every thought of Marilee was not as sharp. He looked down at Claire, realizing that perhaps he would get over his grief. Perhaps he could open his heart to love Claire.

He felt a small jolt of shock as he realized for the first time that he might fall in love with his new wife. When he had been traveling with her, still filled with anger, it had seemed an impossibility. Now after growing closer to her in so many ways, he realized he was capable of love again.

He raised his arm to look at the gold chain around his wrist. Marilee was gone. He had part of her in Michael, a part of her in his heart that would never change, but he had to go on with life. He turned his wrist, momentarily calling up a clear image of Marilee, and then carefully he slipped his arm out from beneath Claire and sat up.

He looked at her sleek, healthy body, feeling his manhood harden again. He gazed at Claire's full breasts, her long legs, and then he lifted a lock of hair off her shoulder. His feelings went deeper than wanting her body. That alone would have never stirred him to what he felt now.

He lifted his arm to unfasten the gold links that had bound his heart to Marilee. "I love you, Marilee," he whispered softly. "But I love Claire too, and she's been so good to Michael. You gave Michael to her and brought her into our lives."

He slid off the bed carefully and placed the bracelet on the night table. As moonlight spilled over the small golden links, he knew he was free from mourning at last.

He slipped back to the bed and eased himself next to Claire. He kissed her forehead and pulled her close in his arms. He let his fingers drift down over the tip of her breast, rubbing the velvety nub with his palm, his erection throbbing.

She moaned and he felt the bud swell against his palm.

He bent his head to take Claire's mouth, to kiss her awake again, suddenly feeling a need for her that made him shake. It was as if in shedding the bracelet he had become a void without love. Almost desperately his kiss deepened as he wrapped her in her arms, holding her against him, pressing her hard against his chest.

Her eyes flew open. "Fortune?"

"God, I need you, Claire," he murmured roughly, his mouth coming down to cover hers again.

The warmth of his words wrapped around her like a warm cloak, giving her far more of a thrill than the diamond and sapphire necklace he had given her earlier. He was crushing the breath from her lungs, but she didn't care. She clung to him, wanting to love him, to discover his body that was such a marvel to her.

He kissed her as if he needed to devour her. Suddenly it struck her that something was different about him from when he had loved her before. Was it because earlier had been the first? But he hadn't been this way the second time they had loved. He seemed desperate for her. And then the thought fled as he moved over her.

"I can't wait, Claire. I have to have you now."

His words set her on fire. She clung to him as he moved between her legs. She expected an invasion of her body as wild as his kisses had been, but he moved slowly, making her arch against him and hold him tightly. All thought vanished and she felt as if she was drowning in sensation.

When she felt his body shudder with release, he gasped. "Claire, love, I need you!"

As she felt his hot seed spill into her, his words made her heart race with joy.

When he finally rolled off her, he held her close in his arms, stroking her hair back from her face. Soon he was breathing evenly, and she knew he had fallen asleep. In seconds she felt sleep overwhelm her as well.

When Claire woke, she stared at the ceiling a moment,

then became aware of the arm wrapped around her. She shifted and turned to look at Fortune, who was sprawled next to her, holding her close to his side. He was naked, a sheet across his body below his waist. She felt her breath catch when she looked at him and thought about the night before. She ran her hand across her stomach, wondering how long it would take before she would be carrying his child. Her breath came faster at the thought of nights of love with Fortune.

As she ran her fingertips lightly across his chest, his arm tightened around her. He turned his head, his eyes coming open.

"My word, you wake up easily!"

"That's from soldiering. If you don't, you're dead," he mumbled, pulling her over him to kiss her. His hands began running over her, and in no time they were making love again.

Over an hour later, as she finished trailing her fingertips over the stubble on his cheeks, she sat up slightly. "Fortune, we should get out of bed. Michael will be up and everyone will be working."

He grinned, tickling his fingers across her breasts.

"Fortune!" She slid out of bed and picked up the discarded chemise to wrap it around herself.

"All right, Claire." She gathered her clothes to go into the bathroom. When she came out, Fortune went in to wash.

She glanced at the bed, her cheeks becoming hot as she remembered the night, yet she felt an eagerness for his arms and kisses that seemed stronger than ever. Astounded, she looked at herself in the mirror, wondering if she was a wanton. After all their lovemaking last night and again this morning, she wanted him all over again.

Shaking her head, she moved away to dress in a blue and white dimity with tiny puff sleeves and a blue sash. The bathroom door opened, and Fortune appeared in his black pants.

She looked up to see a faint smile lifting the corners of his mouth. He crossed the room and slid an arm around her waist. "I want you again."

"We should go downstairs, but I want you too," she whispered as he leaned down to kiss her.

She closed her eyes, their tongues touching. He wrapped both arms around her, holding her tightly while he kissed her long and hard.

At last she pushed away. "Fortune! I shall be a mass of wrinkles," she said, trying to smooth the dimity. She was walking toward the mirror when the sunlight spilling through the window glittered on something on the table.

Walking to the table, she frowned. A pile of gold links gleamed in the early morning sunlight. Claire's heart began to drum. She picked up the bracelet, questions bombarding her as she turned to find him watching her. "Fortune, why did you take off your bracelet?"

Chapter 20

Fortune crossed the room to take the bracelet from her and placed his hands on her shoulders. "Claire, I don't know how much I can change," he said quietly. She felt as if she couldn't get her breath. "But I want to give us every chance. My grief is fading away, thanks to you—"

"Oh, Fortune!" She stood on tiptoe and flung her arms around his neck. "Fortune, it could be so good, I just know! I love you," she said, kissing his ear and cheek and mouth wildly.

"Right now, Claire, you're excited from our lovemaking. As the day passes, you may not feel as warmly toward me."

She paused, looking up at him, her eyes filled with tears. He wiped them away. "I know what I feel, Fortune," she said. "And maybe you can love again if you'll let go of your memories."

"I have let go," he said, pulling her against his chest. "I'm beginning to feel like I'm coming back to life. All those years I've lived in memories, looking back and longing for what I lost."

She clung to him and kissed his chest. "Fortune, I'm so happy." Her hand drifted over his chest, down toward his waist. "Now, I want to stay here and make love to you, but we have to go downstairs."

He caught her hand up, smiling at her. "We'll never get downstairs if you touch me like that. Go on. I'll be down in a few minutes."

She smiled at him and brushed his lips lightly with a kiss. As she left the room and closed the door behind her, her smiled broadened into true radiance. The bracelet linking him to his past was gone. There was a chance for love between them.

Sunday morning they took Michael to church, and during the afternoon Fortune went over landscaping plans for their yard with her. He continually touched her, and she relished his attention, wishing it never had to end. He had come home from work earlier yesterday, and today he had spent the entire day at home. When she thought of Saturday night and this morning and how long they had stayed in bed and made love, she felt a fluttery sensation.

Alaric appeared at dinner, and then Alaric and Michael and Fortune all went out to build a house in a tree for Michael.

As they worked nailing boards, Michael ran to climb the tree. Alaric motioned to Fortune. "Hand me the nails."

Fortune was bent over the board he was sawing, working until it was cut through.

"Fortune!"

He looked up to see Alaric staring at him. Alaric's eyes narrowed.

"You didn't answer me. I asked for the nails. Maybe you have the same thing wrong with your hearing that's wrong with Claire's."

"What the devil are you talking about?"

Alaric put his hands on his hips. "I should have known you wouldn't lead a celibate life forever, but God, I hope you don't hurt her."

"Dammit, Alaric, leave my wife alone! You're too concerned about Claire."

"Well, well, what's this? Temper over Claire, over a woman who's actually still alive, Fortune?"

Fortune ran his fingers through his hair and looked at

the house, forgetting Alaric as he thought about Claire. "She's a fine person and I respect her and we'll have a decent enough marriage if you don't meddle in it." He turned to look at Alaric. "She's innocent where men are concerned. You start your sweet-talking charm, and you could turn her head. She's vulnerable. She has a husband who doesn't love her wildly and she knows it. She went into this marriage knowing it."

"You're a man of stone, but maybe Claire is melting the stone. I think I'll place my bets with Claire, although God knows why she would want a man who doesn't appreciate her—"

"Dammit, if you don't stop, you're going to be on your back. I do appreciate her, I just don't love her."

Suddenly Alaric grinned. "Well, well. I do place my bets with Claire. You're not made of granite after all."

As Fortune took a step toward him, Alaric scooped up boards and strode out of the carriage house. Then he stepped back inside. "I hope she makes you pay for all the misery you dealt her!"

"Dammit!"

Alaric's deep laughter carried in the air while he sprinted toward Michael and the tree.

Alaric stayed through the evening, and when Michael went to bed, Fortune wanted to get Claire to himself. He would carry her upstairs to their bedroom and shut the door to the world and love her as he had before. To his irritation, Alaric continued to lounge in a chair, talking about every subject he knew with Claire, making her laugh. The hour grew later and the tall clock in the hall chimed with the passage of time.

"Why don't we have a game of poker?" Alaric finally said. "We don't have to wager. Fortune told me he taught you to play."

"I don't think—" Fortune began.

"That would be fine, Alaric," Claire said politely, and

Fortune stared at her, realizing she was trying to be courteous to Alaric.

"Alaric, it's late," he said flatly.

"Oh, only a hand or two. Where are the cards, Claire?"

She moved to a table and opened a drawer.

"Get the ones from the library, Claire, and the chips that are in there," Fortune snapped.

Startled, she glanced at him questioningly, but then she nodded and left the room. He leaned forward. "Alaric, we've been friends a long time. Will you get the hell out of here so I can be alone with my wife?"

Alaric's eyes grew round, and Fortune saw the deviltment dancing in them. Clenching his fists, he fought an urge to plant his fist squarely on Alaric's jaw.

When Claire returned, Alaric stood up and crossed the parlor to link his arm through hers. "Claire, I remembered I have to be up at dawn tomorrow morning. Forgive me for suggesting a game and then canceling it all in the same breath, but I feel an urgent need to go home."

"Fine, Alaric. Maybe tomorrow night. Come join us for dinner."

"Thank you. We can work some more on the house for Michael."

They walked outside, where the air was cooler, and Fortune moved forward to place his arm around Claire's shoulders and pull her against his side. "Good night, Alaric."

"Night to both of you," he said, smiling. He kissed Claire's cheek. "You're a lucky man," he said to Fortune, and turned to mosey away.

Claire went inside, heading for the back parlor, where she picked up the cards. Fortune took them from her hands and set them down, putting out lamps. His pulse drummed with eagerness, and the moment the room was dark, he drew her into his arms, picking her up to carry her upstairs.

* * *

A week later, Claire was in the Northrop store when she saw Trevor Wenger approaching. She turned to face him, glancing toward the back corner of the room, where Michael was reading a book.

"Mrs. O'Brien. I've been hoping I would find you in here again. May I say hello to Michael?"

"Yes, of course."

"Don't call him. I'll go back there in a moment. Have you thought it over about allowing him to come to my house?"

It was the question she dreaded, yet she knew that sometime she would have to make a decision about it.

"I want you both to come if you'd like."

"My husband feels strongly about keeping him from you, so if I allow him to visit, it'll be against Fortune's wishes," she said, knowing she had given Trevor Wenger hope with her answer.

"I don't imagine your husband's feeling toward me will ever change. Does he have to know?"

She looked away, still mulling it over, torn between what she felt was right and what Fortune wanted. "If I let you see Michael, you must promise me that you'll never hurt any of us again, not Michael or me or Fortune."

Dark eyes gazed back at her steadily as he arched a brow. "I can promise that I won't initiate anything. But if your husband draws on me, I'll defend myself."

"No more beatings."

"No, but he deserved one for taking Marilee and burning Belle Tache. You have my word I won't hurt any of you unless it's in self-defense."

She stared at him, feeling qualms, yet always when she thought of refusing him, she felt it was wrong to keep Michael from knowing his grandfather. He was a pillar of Atlanta society, after all. She could tell Fortune afterward, and perhaps he would relent. She believed Trevor Wenger would never hurt Michael. The look of longing in his eyes and voice was painfully clear.

Yet she couldn't deceive Fortune, and she didn't want to risk the tenuous bond they had forged. She bit her lip in indecision, wishing she didn't have to make this choice.

Feeling fluttery, because she knew Fortune was unyielding on some issues, as ruthless as Trevor Wenger when he was provoked, she looked up at Wenger. "Yes, I'll bring him to visit."

"Thank you, Mrs. O'Brien. I'll be good to him. He's all I have now. When can we do this?"

Glancing through the front window at Badru, she tried to think of the best time. "Tomorrow morning at half past ten would be good. I usually stay home, and Badru will be going with my husband to help with some work."

"Work at his mill. He wants to give me competition," he said with dry amusement in his voice.

"Yes, he does. There's no changing him on that."

"I don't mind. Competition works two ways," he said blandly. "Can you stay until noon to eat with me?"

"No. We need to be back home then."

"I know you're going against your husband's wishes, and it worries you. I want to thank you again. This means everything to me, and I shall repay your kindness. I promise you, you'll never regret this. Now I'd like to speak to Michael."

She nodded and stepped aside, glancing outside at Badru, who stood beside the buggy, waiting for their return.

Finally Trevor Wenger came back up the aisle to pass her. "Thank you, Mrs. O'Brien. I appreciate your kindness. I'll look for you both in the morning."

She watched him walk down the aisle and wondered if she could trust him. Had she done the right thing? Would she ever be able to convince Fortune that it was right for Michael to know his grandfather?

That night as she ate a late dinner with Fortune and Alaric, she stared at Fortune, wanting to mention that she had talked to Trevor Wenger, but she couldn't when Alaric was present, and after he had gone, she tried to think how to begin as Fortune drew her into the back parlor.

Closing the door, he turned to lean against it and pulled her into his arms to kiss her. His hand ran down her back, over her buttocks, and pulled her up against him. Her hips thrust against him while they kissed, and she had only a momentary flicker of worry that in a little over twelve hours, she would be going against his wishes.

Chapter 21

As she drove the buggy, Michael sat beside her gazing around. He wore his new black coat and pants and had on a white linen shirt.

"Mama, what will Papa say when you tell him we've been to see Grandfather?"

"I don't know, Michael. He's your grandfather and he said you're all the family he has left. I'll try to talk your father into understanding that I feel you should get to know your grandfather."

"They hate each other, don't they?"

She looked at Michael, sometimes surprised by what he noticed. "Yes, they do. Your father feels your grandfather took your mother and you from him. Your grandfather feels your father took her from him. But they may get over their hatred, and that's what I pray happens because both of them love you and both of them are related to you."

"I don't want to make Papa angry with me."

"He won't be angry with you," she answered firmly, knowing she was the one on whom Fortune's wrath would fall.

They turned on Grubb Street and she glanced back over her shoulder, suddenly feeling as if Fortune's cold blue eyes were on her. She thought about their lovemaking the night before and felt a twinge of both guilt and fear. She didn't like going against his wishes, and she didn't want to lose the warmth building between them.

For an instant she slowed, pulling on the reins, and Michael looked up at her expectantly. She gazed down into his dark eyes, part of his heritage from Marilee and Trevor Wenger. And she knew she couldn't keep Michael from his grandfather.

She flicked the reins, praying she could make Fortune understand. Just this once she would take Michael to see Trevor Wenger, and then after that she wouldn't go again until Fortune agreed to it.

In another two blocks she slowed and turned up the drive. She looked at an elegant Greek Revival house with six massive Doric columns and a wide fan transom over the door. She wondered if Trevor Wenger had tried to rebuild a house that looked like his burned Belle Tache.

"It's a big house," Michael said. "Look, Mama, he has peacocks."

She glanced at the colorful birds strutting through a bed of purple periwinkles and blue delphinium, and she realized that only a month ago, Michael would have been awed by the mansion. Fortune was making them accustomed to luxury. She thought about her savings, which Fortune seemed to have no interest in. She had written letters, and finally the money had been transferred to the Atlanta National Bank, and she felt better. Since Fortune regularly gave her money that he said was her own to do with as she wanted, almost half of it was going into her savings. Someday it would there for Michael, but right now she still felt better to know there was money that was hers and if she had to use it, she could.

As she slowed in front of the house, a servant came out the front door and Trevor Wenger followed. He was a handsome man, his face creased in a wide smile. His face was narrower than Fortune's, his nose as straight, his lips thin, giving him an imperious air. Yet when he smiled at Michael, he looked friendly.

"Come in, both of you. This is one of the happiest moments in my life. I want to show both of you the house, and I want to show Michael the room I have for him if his father ever permits him to come stay."

He stepped back to allow her to enter ahead of him while a white-coated butler held open the door.

She looked at the vestibule, filled with marble statuary, oil paintings, and gilt furniture. As they walked through the house, larger than their own, she looked at fine porcelain figurines, bronze figures, enameled snuff boxes, and realized he must have collected treasures from all over Europe.

And Michael's eyes sparkled when Trevor showed him a room filled with toys, a wooden rocking horse and wooden hoop, wind-up toys, a bear with cymbals, a set of wooden soldiers.

"We'll go back downstairs to the parlor, Michael, and let you stay to look at your toys," Trevor Wenger said.

"Yes, Grandfather."

She walked beside Wenger as they descended the stairs. "You have beautiful things."

"I collected some during the war years when I lived abroad. Thank heaven they weren't at Belle Tache! Oh, I have something for you, Mrs. O'Brien."

She looked at him questioningly as he motioned toward the front parlor. She entered a room filled with treasures fit for a museum. He fetched a small box made of gold with diamonds, sapphires, and rubies encrusted in the top and handed it to her.

"I can't accept a gift like this!"

"Of course you can. Open it."

She opened it and listened to a Strauss waltz. Instantly she remembered dancing with Fortune the last time she had heard it played. "It's beautiful, but this isn't necessary."

As she reached out to hand it back to him, he touched her hand lightly. "Keep it. It is a mere bauble, a token of my appreciation for your bringing Michael. It means nothing to me, and I can afford to give it to you."

"Thank you," she said, feeling uneasy, knowing she would have to place it somewhere out of Fortune's sight.

"Sit down, please." He went to the bell pull and in minutes a maid served tea and small biscuits and jam.

Claire's uneasiness faded slightly as she listened to him talk about his travels in Europe. "I wish someday I could take Michael, but I know that's probably too much to hope for. If not, I hope your husband plans to take him."

"He does, as a matter of fact."

"Good. Michael seems a very bright child to be reading the books he does. I've talked to Edwin Northrop."

"Michael is bright."

"You're the one who found Marilee while she was still alive?" he asked, abruptly shifting the direction of their conversation.

"Yes. She asked me to care for Michael."

"Those years are over now. I apologize again for the men I sent to find him. I'm thankful now he was with you. And you're a very bright young woman to manage to elude Pinkerton's and the men I hired. Evidently Harwood found you too late. Enough of that. Are you enjoying your new home?"

"Very much."

"It's a fine house, and it should be good for Michael. I'll give you the name of two tutors who are excellent and the agency you can contact to hire them."

"Thank you. I've just started asking around, but I don't know too many people here yet."

"I think you'll find both of these would be excellent."

She spent the rest of the hour talking to Trevor Wenger and realizing he could be charming when he wanted. Finally he stood up. "May I take Michael for a short walk in the garden?"

She hesitated only a moment. "Yes, if you'd like."

"Thank you. Don't worry. I'll come back," he said, smiling at her. "If you enjoy reading, I have a library across the hall. Help yourself."

"Thank you."

Once he had left the room, she stood and moved to the window to look out. In minutes she heard Michael's voice raised in excitement and Trevor Wenger's deeper voice. Their footsteps and voices faded, and she strolled into the hall. She walked to the end of the hall to look through the beveled glass door. Man and boy walked along a path between beds of flowers, and for a moment she felt a ripple of fear. If Trevor Wenger took Michael now, it would take an hour to get back, tell Fortune, and start after them.

She looked over her shoulder. If he did something to her, he could have more than a day's start because Fortune worked late most nights. Uneasy, she stayed in the hall watching for them for the next half hour until finally she saw them wind back along the path.

Feeling foolish for her worries, she returned to the front parlor to sit down until the two of them came inside.

"Mama, you have to come see one of the toys. It's a train and runs along a track."

"Take her upstairs and show her, Michael," Trevor Wenger said.

Michael grasped her hand, and she went with him, climbing a wide staircase carpeted in a forest green. In the room of toys, Michael ran to plop down on the floor beside an oval track. She looked at the metal train, a colorful replica, and she watched Michael's small fingers wind the spring. Then the train moved around a track while Michael sat on the floor to watch it. Her gaze drifted over the toys to the four-poster bed.

"Michael, next time you come, I'll have a different train to go on that track," Trevor Wenger said, and she glanced up at him. She didn't know how long it would be before she could talk Fortune into letting them return.

"Can you bring him back again this week?"

"No. I feel I—"

"Mama, please," Michael said, tugging on her hand. "Just a little while."

She looked into his wide, dark eyes and was torn. Trevor Wenger had won Michael over, but Fortune would be a different matter.

"We can't come back this week."

"Then please let me see him next week," Trevor Wenger said.

Michael tugged on her hand but kept quiet, waiting expectantly, and she didn't want to explain in front of him that Fortune was adamant abut Michael never seeing his grandfather.

"Just a short visit. This doesn't hurt anyone."

"All right. Next Tuesday morning. But if something happens and we can't come, I can't send word."

"I'll understand."

"We should go now."

"So soon?" Michael said.

"Yes."

"I'll see you next week, Michael. You may pick something small that you can carry easily to take home with you."

"Thank you!" He moved to the bookcase to open the glass front and remove a book. As they started out the door, Michael lingered, wanting to wind the train one more time.

"Michael," she said gently.

"Just once more and then I'll come."

Trevor Wenger smiled at him. As they reached the head of the stairs, he turned to face Claire. "Thank you more than you'll ever be able to imagine for bringing him."

She looked up as Michael appeared, and they all turned to go outside to the buggy. When they started to climb in, Trevor Wenger stepped forward and picked Michael up, suddenly hugging him and then setting him in the buggy. His gaze shifted to her. "He's a fine boy, isn't he?" he said in a husky voice.

"Yes," she said, wishing Fortune would relent. Trevor Wenger should be able to see Michael.

"Thank you again. I'll look forward to next week."

She flicked the reins and rode down the horseshoe-shaped drive beneath curving branches of live oaks.

"Mama, will Papa ever stop hating Grandfather?"

"I hope so, Michael," she said, pained that Michael was caught between two men who were such enemies. She wished both of them would stop a moment and think what it might do to Michael.

"I can't tell him I've been to see Grandfather, can I?"

"I'll tell him, Michael, before we go next week, but let me talk to him first. As soon as I have, I'll tell you."

"Yes, ma'am."

She rode home, worrying about how to tell Fortune they had been to see Trevor Wenger. She dreaded an argument with him, particularly because they were becoming so close. Last night he had held her in his arms, stroking her, talking for hours into the night. Rolling on his side, he had propped his head on his elbow to study her.

"I think I'm falling in love with my wife."

She ran her fingers along his jaw. "I hope so."

The memory filled her with joy, and she didn't want to do anything to wreck the fragile beginnings of love. She sighed and turned up their drive. Climbing out of the carriage, while Michael went running to the back and Badru came out to take the buggy and unhitch the team, she walked in a back door, entering the wide hallway. The house was quiet, sunlight pouring through the windows. She removed her tiny silk hat and placed it on a table.

She was about to put down the box that Trevor Wenger had given her when Fortune stepped out of the door of the back parlor.

"Fortune! What are you doing—" The words died on her lips as she looked into his blue eyes that blazed with rage. His expression was as fiery as that first night.

He reached out to take her arm and pulled her into the parlor and slammed the door.

Chapter 22

"Where's Michael?"

"He's in the back. Badru is out there with him." She could barely speak, she was so frightened. "Fortune, let me explain—" His fingers bit into her arms; his voice was quiet and laced with rage.

"I told you, Claire, you were never to let him talk to Trevor Wenger! Dammit to hell, I had your promise. I trusted you!" He looked down and took the gold box from her hand.

"Fortune—"

"So he paid you," he said with such contempt she flinched.

She took a deep breath and raised her chin. "He's Michael's grandfather and he loves Michael—"

"The hell he does! I know how he treated his daughter, and I'm not going to argue about it. He'll try to take Michael, don't you understand? You promised me!" He turned and threw the box against the hearth.

She felt as if something were breaking inside her. "Fortune, he loves Michael, and I was going to tell you—"

"Claire, I've talked to Penthea and Badru. One or the other of them is to be with Michael all the time. You're not going to be alone with my son again!"

"Fortune! You can't—"

"Yes, I can," he said in a tight voice. "I can't trust you. Michael isn't going to see Trevor Wenger ever again. Not as long as I have breath in my body!"

"Fortune, please listen to me," she said frantically.

"I know the man. You don't." Fortune strode past her, yanking open the door and then slamming it behind him. She stared at it, tears forming in her eyes. She knew she had lost what love Fortune was beginning to feel for her.

She leaned against the door as tears streamed down her cheeks. She prayed when he calmed, he would rethink what he had said. She turned to place her forehead against the door as a sob wracked her.

That night, neither Fortune and Michael appeared for dinner, and she wondered if he would try to separate Michael from her as much as he could. She sat in the parlor, waiting to hear them come home until midnight, wondering where he was with Michael. Finally she went upstairs to put on her nightgown and wrapper, sitting by the open window to watch the drive.

It was two in the morning when she heard the buggy and looked down to see Fortune carry Michael into the house. She listened to him as he went down the hall to Michael's room and heard his footsteps come back toward her door.

She held her breath, remembering last night and the hours they had talked, the lovemaking. His footsteps went past her room, and she heard the door close to the bedroom he had used before he had moved into hers.

She quickly went to his door and knocked. He swung it open, his hair an unruly tangle, a stubble of new beard showing on his jaw, his shirt already tossed aside. Without asking, she brushed past him and stepped inside, closing the door and facing him. Only one lamp burned, and it threw long shadows across the room.

"Where's Michael been? You can tell me when you're going to be gone like that," she said, aching to reach out and grasp his hand and plead with him to forget the morning.

"I've had him with me. He slept on a sofa in my office, and I've been taking care of him," he said with clipped words, and she could see that his rage was as strong as earlier. He didn't want her in his room.

She pursed her lips. "Fortune, you're being unreasonable—"

"He's tried to kill me," he answered in a cold voice. "And he did kill Marilee. He's incapable of love. He wants Michael for his own selfish purposes, and he'll try to take him sooner or later. I'm not going to argue with you, Claire." They faced each other; he stood with his feet spread apart, his fists on his hips, his blue eyes blazing, and she realized she had lost his regard completely. She felt the sting of tears but forced herself not to cry, not when he looked as if he was on the verge of asking her to leave.

She blindly reached for the door and hurried into the hall, hearing him slam the door behind her. She rushed to her room, closed her door, and threw herself across the bed to cry, hoping it muffled the sounds.

Three days later, Claire asked Badru to take a note to Trevor Wenger.

"Ma'am, I don't think I should do that."

"Mr. O'Brien hasn't asked you not to see him or talk to him, has he?"

"No, ma'am."

"I need to let Mr. Wenger know that he won't be seeing Michael again."

"Yes, ma'am."

"Thank you, Badru."

She watched him go, wondering if Trevor Wenger would fly into a rage that matched Fortune's or if he would accept what Fortune decreed. Or would he try now to take Michael from them?

She rubbed her forehead. She had a headache. She had slept little, feeling isolated. Fortune had taken Michael with him and avoided her. They hadn't eaten a meal together for the past three days, and she wondered if they ever would again.

Two weeks later in the warm days of September, her relationship with Fortune had not improved, and she was aware that Michael was constantly trailed by Badru, or if he wasn't present, occasionally Penthea sat quietly in the room with him. Michael was more solemn, and she was angry with Fortune for being so blind to what he was doing to his child.

The next week came without any change. She spent her mornings tutoring Michael, having lost all interest in making new friends in Atlanta.

One afternoon as she was coming out of the dry-goods store, Alaric approached. He was in civilian clothing, wearing a gray coat and pants, and he looked dashing with his wide-brimmed hat set squarely on his head and shading his eyes. He stopped in front of her, and the moment she looked up at him, she knew that he had talked to Fortune.

"Claire, I've wanted to see you." He glanced around at her buggy. "Let me drive you. I know a place where we can talk."

She knew it might start gossip, but she no longer cared. She couldn't do any deeper damage to her relationship with Fortune. She nodded, and when Alaric held out his hand to help her into the buggy, she placed her hand in his, smoothing her blue and white dimity skirt. He climbed up beside her to drive, leaving town and turning to her as the team moved steadily along.

"I've talked to Fortune, and he's in a rage over your taking Michael to Wenger's."

She looked away, fighting tears, afraid sympathy would completely wreck her control.

"Claire, I don't know if you can undo what's done, but he's right about Wenger. I was the one who found Fortune when Wenger gave him that lashing. He meant to kill him slowly and painfully, beating him half to death and leaving him tied in the woods to die of exposure and starvation. That's a hell of a way to treat your daughter's husband and the father of your grandson."

She wiped her eyes, and he slipped his arm around her shoulders. As soon as he did, she glanced at him. "Alaric, don't make it worse by starting rumors," she said, shrugging away his arm.

"All right, dammit, I'm going to drive out of town where we can be alone and talk."

They rode in silence until they reached the rolling hills covered with trees. She saw remains of the defenses for war, wondering if the entire South was as torn up as Atlanta. New Orleans and Natchez hadn't been, but she had heard that Vicksburg had had a terrible siege. Her thoughts shifted back to Fortune, for they were never long on anything else. Alaric halted beneath the shade of an oak and turned to her, pulling her into his arms.

Her self-control vanished and she began to cry, sitting stiffly with her hands balled in her lap. "I love him terribly, Alaric. And Michael and his grandfather seemed to like each other. Trevor Wenger was as considerate as possible to Michael. They're blood kin." She wrung her hands together, trying to get control of her emotions, hurting so badly.

"Claire, if I were Fortune, I wouldn't want Michael with him. It took a monster to do what he did to Fortune. And I'm sure Marilee suffered when he forced her to go home with him."

Wiping her eyes with a damp handkerchief, Claire shifted out of his arms and looked up at him, realizing that Alaric had none of Fortune's volatile disposition or his unrelenting will and toughness. Yet if Alaric said he would keep Michael from Trevor Wenger, then both Alaric and Fortune had seen a side to the man that she hadn't.

"You would keep a child from even talking to his grandfather?"

"If it were Wenger and he had treated me the way he's treated Fortune, yes, I would."

"He seemed to love Michael. If you feel that way, how much more Fortune must . . ." Her words trailed away. Tears came again and she cried quietly. Finally getting control of her emotions, she edged away to wipe her eyes. "Sorry. It's done now and it can't ever be undone."

"Yes, it can. Tell him you were wrong and you're sorry. It may take time, but other than Wenger, he's reasonable. You won him over once when he was even angrier. You can get him back again."

"I don't think so," she said, staring at leaves blowing slightly in the breeze. "He's too angry. He said he would never trust me again."

"He'll change. He loves you."

"No, he doesn't. He was beginning to, I think, but that's over."

"I don't think it's over," Alaric said quietly, and she glanced at him. He reached up to wipe tears off her cheeks. "Ah, Claire, I wish you weren't so in love with him. I would take you from him."

She smiled and patted his hand. "You're so kind, Alaric."

"Oh, Lordy. No woman has ever told me I'm so kind."

She gave him another slight smile, knowing he was trying to cheer her. "He takes Michael, and I can't even see him. Michael is withdrawing into a shell."

"Michael will adjust. Fortune will calm down and see what he's doing when his anger cools. In the meantime tell him you're sorry. Tell him you love him."

"I don't think that will mean anything to him."

"Claire, don't ever take Michael to see Wenger again."

She looked into Alaric's blue eyes and wondered if she had run a terrible risk with Michael. "It seems impossible that his own grandfather could be a monster," she said softly.

"He is. You know I view the world more lightly than Fortune, but on this issue he's right."

She shivered, feeling her loss, aching for Fortune to be sitting talking to her. "I better go home."

He nodded, stroking her cheek. "I'm doing what I can with Fortune. He'll calm down."

She didn't think he would. She knew how implacable Fortune could be. She rode without seeing her surroundings, barely aware when Alaric stopped at her drive. As he jumped down and handed her the reins, she realized where they were.

"You were in front of the store," she said. "I'll take you back there—"

"Nonsense. Only a few minutes' walk. Now give me a smile and tell Fortune you did the wrong thing."

She smiled and nodded. "Thank you, Alaric."

"Remember, you can have my help or my brilliant company at any time, day or night."

"Thanks. I'll remember." She turned up the drive, looking at the house that now seemed so big and so empty.

Four days later, she realized she was very late having her monthly. Every day she watched the calendar, not daring to hope or plan or think, yet down deep knowing she wanted Fortune's baby whether he forgave her or not.

She waited, letting the week pass, hoping she was carrying his child.

Fortune came into the office from the mill. He missed having Michael with him, and he glanced at the empty sofa where Michael sat curled up with a book much of the time. He lit the lamps and sat at his desk to go over his books. Cal and Sophia had had to postpone their trip to Atlanta, and now Fortune was glad because he didn't feel like entertaining even his brother.

Anger smoldered in him over Clair taking Michael to Wenger's house. It astounded Fortune that Wenger had allowed her to leave with him. He could have easily taken

Michael, prevented Claire from going home, and Fortune wouldn't have known for hours.

He realized his jaw was clamped so tightly it was aching. He leaned back in the chair, combing his hair away from his forehead with his fingers. His blue chambray shirtsleeves were turned back, and he saw a smudge of ink on his arm.

"You're working late again," came a cheerful voice, and Fortune looked up as Alaric entered.

"Yes. If you would come to work with me, I wouldn't have to do this."

"You'd do it anyway." Alaric sauntered into the room and sank down on a chair, draping his leg over the arm. "Spare me the lecture."

"No. You look miserable, Claire is miserable—"

Fortune raised his head, anger rising. "So you've been by to console her."

"Don't start on me," Alaric said. "She didn't even know I was alive. She can barely carry on a coherent conversation."

Fortune tossed down his pen and stared at the lamp. "Alaric, let's not go over this again."

"I told her to talk to you."

"I don't want to talk to her about it."

"She's sorry. Remember, you married a courageous, independent woman who is accustomed to making her own decisions and acting on them. You know she wouldn't risk Michael for anything. She made a mistake. Haven't you ever made one?"

Anger shot through Fortune. "Alaric, you're straining my patience. It's a wonder Wenger didn't take Michael and leave for Europe that morning. And if something happens to me, you know he'll take Michael from her immediately."

"Then you shouldn't be working out here alone late at night."

"I'm armed and I'm careful and I've had Badru with me the past three weeks at night."

"I didn't see him tonight."

"No. I didn't intend to stay this late."

"I can wait with you."

"No, thanks. I'll be safe. I need to get this done."

"All right. I'll go and leave you alone, but take a good look at your son and what you're doing to him. Michael isn't the same happy little boy."

"He'll cheer up."

"Fortune, forget Wenger and look at Claire and Michael and what you're doing to them."

"Dammit—"

Alaric moved quickly. As Fortune pushed back his chair, Alaric sprinted to the door. "I'm going." He vanished, his footsteps sounding hollow in the empty building.

Fortune looked at the darkened windows and then sat down, bending over the books in front of him, seeing Claire's pale face, remembering her arms wound around him, her body pressed against his. As swiftly as the image came, he recalled that dreadful panicky moment when he had thought Wenger might have Michael. He couldn't forgive her what she had done or for breaking her promise to him.

"Dammit," he said, trying to concentrate, finally getting his mind on the figures in front of him.

When Fortune next glanced at the clock, he was startled to see it was midnight. Engrossed in work, he hadn't realized it was so late. "Just a little more," he said, turning a page. Then something clicked in the hall.

He raised his head, listening. His hand inched toward the gun belt with his revolver on his desk. It had been only a tiny click, yet no one was in the building.

He closed the ledger, feeling his skin prickle, knowing he shouldn't have worked so late when he was alone. He could go into the mill and get one of the men to accompany him home.

He extinguished one lamp and wrapped his gun belt around his hips. As he started to buckle it, Trevor Wenger stepped into the doorway and raised a pistol.

The two blasts were loud. A searing pain erupted in his shoulder, then in his side.

Fortune lunged at him. The third blast was deafening in the small space, and Fortune felt as if a knife had cut through his head. Then blackness closed over him.

"Michael—" he gasped as he fell.

Conscious of Penthea quietly sewing in a corner of the room, Claire read to Michael and finally tucked him into bed, thankful to have an evening with him. She tiptoed out, descending to an empty downstairs. Soon she became restless, wondering if Fortune was working late or with another woman or gambling. She suspected he was working. He seemed to fill all his time with work.

She felt caught in an impasse. Neither of them would give up Michael, and now another baby might be on the way. Would he be as fiercely possessive about their child, or would he treat it as coldly as he was treating her?

She pushed aside that worry. Fortune was far too good with Michael to mistreat a tiny baby. Pray the next one also looked like its father. It was too early to really know if she was pregnant, but each day made her more hopeful. Her own baby. And in spite of his anger, she loved Fortune and this would be a part of him that she could have.

She sat on a settee and sewed until she finally looked at the clock and saw that it was two o'clock. Would he stay away all night? The thought hurt because the only reason she could imagine to keep him away from home the entire night was a woman.

She wiped her eyes, wondering how long she would cry over him. She loved him desperately, missed all that had been growing between them. When he had been so angry before, they had been traveling together. Now she never saw him. How would the situation ever change if they were never together?

Tired, she went upstairs to bed, stopping in Michael's room, seeing Penthea dozing on the extra bed. Claire tiptoed across the room to look down at Michael, thinking she would always feel he was her son as much as the baby she was carrying. She pushed Michael's silky curls back from his forehead and picked up a book from the pillow beside him, wondering if he had fallen asleep reading.

With a sigh she leaned down to brush his cheek with a kiss, feeling love well up for him. She tiptoed out and closed the door, going to her room to get ready for bed.

When she slid between the covers, she was overcome with yearning for Fortune.

Suddenly a stair creaked and she turned her head, listening to hear if he had come home. But then all was silent and she realized that it must have been her imagination. There were no sounds of boots on the hall floor. She closed her eyes, knowing she would doze fitfully as she had all the past nights since Fortune had moved from her bed.

She ran her hand over the pillow, aching for him. "Fortune, I love you," she whispered. Finally she slept.

Claire stirred, opening her eyes, running her hand over the empty bed. She raised up to look at the bed, remembering Fortune stretched on it, remembering his wild kisses, his passion. Hurt enveloped her, as suffocating as a blanket thrown over her.

A faint moan came. She frowned and listened and in a minute heard the sound again. She stared at the darkness, feeling a frisson of panic. It wasn't like any night sound she had ever heard before. Frowning, she swung her legs out of bed and yanked on her wrapper. Fumbling to light an oil lamp, she picked it up to carry it with her. In the hall she looked around, with long, eerie shadows thrown against the wall from the lamp, and the hairs on her arms prickled. The house suddenly seemed enormous and empty. Fortune's bedroom door stood open on a darkened room, and her alarm grew. As angry and remote as he had been, he wouldn't have stayed away from home all night.

She looked at Michael's closed door and heard the moan again. Her heart seemed to stop—the noise came from the direction of Michael's room. She rushed down the hall, flinging open the door.

Michael's bed was empty. Light spilled over the bed, the covers thrown back. Claire raised the lamp. Penthea was bound and gagged, tied to a chest and lying on her side on the floor.

Terrified, Claire ran to kneel beside her and yank away the gag. "Michael?"

"They took him," Penthea sobbed. "They grabbed me and tied me up. They picked him up and carried him out."

"I'll cut you loose, Penthea, but let me get Badru first," Claire said, feeling icy, terrified because Wenger had Michael now. "How long ago did they take him?"

Penthea sobbed and Claire suspected she wasn't going to get an accurate answer anyway. Trying to think what to do, she ran downstairs. The back door was open. Across the lawn she raced to Badru's quarters and pounded on his door. How long ago had they taken Michael? How much of a head start would Wenger have? Where was Fortune? If he was working, they could find him, but if he was with a woman or gambling—

"Ma'am?" Badru said, sounding fully awake.

"Come quick! Penthea's tied upstairs and Michael is gone. I'll hitch the buggy. We've got to go to the mill to find my husband. Run cut Penthea free and then come back here."

"Yes, ma'am," he said. "I'll get my boots."

Thankful he didn't ask questions, she rushed to the carriage house. Her hands kept shaking as she tried to hitch the team, terrified for Michael. She dropped the harness, had to bend to pick it up. Finally Badru appeared in front of her. "Ma'am, I'll finish hitching the horses if you want to wait in the house. In fact, I can ride out to look for Mr. O'Brien."

"No, I'll go with you," she said, wondering if Badru was trying to keep her from discovering his whereabouts. "While you do this, I'll change my clothes."

She ran up the stairs, and passed a sobbing Penthea. "Penthea, I have to hurry to get Mr. O'Brien."

"Yes, ma'am."

"Will you be all right alone here until I get back?"

"Yes, ma'am."

"Drink some brandy. It'll help your nerves."

"Yes, ma'am."

Upstairs, Claire yanked on a poplin dress, her underdrawers and her shoes, racing back down. Badru was driving the team toward the door, and he halted so she could get in. She climbed up beside him. "Do you have a gun?"

"Yes, ma'am."

"Hurry."

"You hold on." He cracked the buggy whip and flicked the reins, yelling at the team, and they sprang forward. The buggy rushed down the drive, pebbles flying, wind blowing her hair away from her face. They careened around the turn and clattered over the street, swaying wildly at corners and shaking when they left town and took the rutted road toward the mill.

Smoke rose from the mill stack and spread across the sky. She saw a light burning in Fortune's office. "There, Badru. There's his office."

"Yes, ma'am."

He pulled in front of the door and she started to climb down. "I'll get him. You wait here."

Badru jumped to the ground and pulled the revolver out of his waistband. "I better go with you." He held the door and she ran past him.

"Fortune! Fortune!" she cried as she raced toward his office. Light spilled from the open door into the hallway, and when he didn't answer, she wondered if he was working after all. Once through the doorway, though, she stopped dead. Fortune was sprawled on the floor, a pool of dark blood spread beneath him.

Chapter 23

"Fortune!" She hurried across the room and knelt beside him. As she placed her hand against his throat, her head swam at the sight of all the blood.

"Badru, he's alive!"

"Ma'am, let me pick him up. We have to get him to a doctor."

Dazed, unaware of tears on her cheeks, she stepped back as Badru lifted him easily. She followed him out to the buggy, where he carefully placed Fortune in the back seat.

"Mrs. O'Brien, we need to keep the wounds stanched." He yanked off his shirt and balled it up. "You hold that against his side. It seems the worst. He's been shot twice, but I don't think the shoulder wound is as bad."

She nodded, kneeling on the floor of the buggy beside an unconscious Fortune while Badru climbed in front. "Mrs. O'Brien, I'm going to ride hard unless you tell me to quit."

"Go." She cried softly, praying that Fortune would survive. The return ride was almost as wild as the ride out to the mill, and she had to cling to the buggy and brace her body to keep Fortune from rolling off the seat. She could feel the warm ooze of blood as it soaked Badru's shirt and her panic increased.

Badru stopped in front of a two-story brick house. She climbed down and watched as he picked up Fortune. "Run tell the doctor we're coming."

She raced up the front steps, remembering Fortune bringing Dr. Newsom over one time when Michael's throat hurt. She rapped on the door. As Badru joined her, she knocked again and then a light shone through the beveled glass of the front door.

When the door swung open, Dr. Newsom stood wearing a dressing gown, his brown hair in a tangle. "Bring him in here," he said, sounding alert and calm, as if he received wounded men at any hour of the night. "Down the hall, Mrs. O'Brien."

"He's been shot."

"You sit down here. I'll look at him." He left and she stood in the hall, stunned by the events of the past hour. And the thoughts that had nagged her now came rushing at her, too painfully clear. *Fortune had been right!* Trevor Wenger was a monster, and he could only have taken Michael for his own selfish purposes.

She paced the floor, wanting to go in with them, not knowing what to do to try to get Michael back. She thought of Alaric. He would go with her if she went after Wenger. And then she looked down the hall at the closed door, knowing she couldn't put Alaric at such risk. Would Badru go with her? If Fortune was dreadfully injured, she would have to stay, to try to find Trevor Wenger and Michael later because she couldn't abandon Fortune.

Too nervous to sit down, she made another turn around the hall, looking at the pictures on the walls without really seeing them. The passage of time seemed interminable. She looked down at the blue poplin, spattered with Fortune's blood, and agony enveloped her. He had been right about Wenger. She clutched her hands and bowed her head, praying quietly that Fortune would survive.

Another half hour passed before the door opened and Badru emerged with the doctor behind him. Dr. Newsom motioned to her.

"He's ready for you to take him home. Both shots went clean through him. Nothing vital got hit. He had a nasty slice across his hand. He was shot in the shoulder, and the other shot went through his right side. If we can keep infection from setting in, he should recover nicely. If infection starts, he'll be in trouble."

Overwhelmed by relief, she closed her eyes a moment. "Thank you, Dr. Newsom. He looked so bad." She turned around. "Badru, will you take the buggy and get a wagon to put him in?"

"Here's laudanum," Dr. Newsom said. "Give him enough to stop his pain."

"Thank you," she said, taking the bottle and watching Badru go out the door.

It took another hour before they had Fortune loaded into the wagon and moved to a downstairs bedroom. "Badru, ride out and get Major Hampton. You know where to find him."

"Yes, ma'am," he said.

She looked at Fortune's heavily bandaged shoulder and middle. One hand had a white bandage. He looked pale and still and vulnerable. She had never seen him that way. It brought back fear for him and worry that they wouldn't get Michael back. And if he didn't, he would search the world over for Trevor Wenger.

She moved close to the bed, wondering how long they could keep from him that Wenger had taken Michael. Fortune needed to heal, and the moment he heard what had happened, he would want to go after them.

Hearing voices, she left the room, closing the door and hurrying to the stairs. Badru and Alaric were in the hall. Alaric wore denim pants and a blue chambray shirt, and his hair was tangled as if he had just stepped out of bed and come at once.

"Badru, will you watch him while I talk to Major Hampton?"

"Yes, ma'am. Penthea has gone to her quarters."

Claire nodded as Badru passed them, and she looked up at Alaric.

"Badru said that he'll live."

"Dr. Newsom said if there's no infection he should be fine. Alaric, Trevor Wenger had taken Michael. I don't know how long they've been gone—two hours, three. It can't have been much longer than that."

"Damn," he said, glancing beyond her at the sick man's door. "He'll be wild. He won't wait to heal."

"If I stay here—"

"Dammit, you can't go after Wenger. If he went out to the mill and shot Fortune, he wouldn't hesitate to kill you." He reached out to grip her shoulders, his fingers clutching her tightly. "Promise me you won't go after him."

"I can't!"

He frowned. "Look, Fortune won't live if he gets up and tears up those wounds and gets them infected. You stay here and keep him from knowing what's happened as long as you can. If I start searching and asking questions now, I can have a dozen men looking in the next hour."

"Oh, Alaric, thank God! Please try to find out where they've gone." Tears threatened and she drew a deep breath. "He's such a little boy."

"Wenger won't hurt him, at least not physically. Send Badru down here. I'd like to take him with me. He knows a whole different group of people. Someone is bound to have seen the Wenger carriage with those yellow wheels. Badru will know the servants, and their gossip goes through town quicker than wildfire. And for God's sake, keep Fortune on laudanum. That way you might manage to keep him quiet."

She motioned to Badru. He glanced at the bed and came into the hall. "Will you go with Major Hampton now? I'm going to try to keep Mr. O'Brien from learning that Michael is gone."

"Yes, ma'am. I would too."

Once the two men had left, she returned to Fortune's

side, gazing down at him, wondering how long she could convince him that Michael was in the house and all right.

For hours she kept watch with him, frightened in spite of Dr. Newsom's reassurances because Fortune lay so still and looked so pale. When he began to stir she found the laudanum and got it ready, along with a glass of water for him. But Fortune lapsed back into sleep, and she looked out the window, wondering when Alaric would return. As her gaze dropped to her lap, she realized she was still in her bloodstained dress. She glanced at Fortune, who was sleeping quietly, and she hurried upstairs to wash and to put on something fresh.

When she returned, he was just the same as when she left him. As she sat on a rocker near the bed, Badru appeared in the doorway. Hoping he had some kind of news about Trevor Wenger, she hurried into the hall.

"I can sit with him, ma'am. Major Hampton is in the parlor, he has some information."

"Thank heavens. The laudanum is on the table next to a glass of water."

"Yes, ma'am. Penthea is starting breakfast."

"How is she?"

"She's fine. She's nervous, but that will pass. And she keeps crying over Michael."

"It wasn't her fault. I was home too when it happened."

Claire found Alaric in the parlor. He was seated on a chair, leaning back with his eyes closed, but when she walked into the room, he came to his feet and crossed to her. His boots were dusty, his shirt and pants wrinkled, and she wondered where he had been.

"We've found out which way they headed out of town. He's going to Savannah. I'd guess he'll get on a boat to Europe because Fortune said he has a home in France and he spent most of the war over there."

"You're sure?"

"Yes. Badru found someone who saw the carriage, and

one of my men found someone. I've sent some men along the road toward Savannah. I would guess that he thinks he killed Fortune and that there's little you can do. He may figure he had the whole night's head start."

"So, if I leave—"

"Dammit, you're not going after him. Claire, you have to promise me if you go, you'll tell me and I'll go with you."

"I don't want you to risk—"

"Promise me," he said, staring at her. "I fought all through the damned war. I'll survive going after Wenger."

"All right."

"Besides, you can't go, because the moment you leave, Fortune will get out of bed and try to go. It'll kill him if he does. I talked to Doc Newsom."

She bit her lip. "I have to try to stop Wenger before he sails for Europe."

"I'll go and take some men. We can probably catch up with him."

"No." She faced him, looking at him intently. "If you had to kill him to get Michael back, could you?"

"I wouldn't kill except in self-defense, but in that case I could."

"Alaric, this isn't your battle. Let me think what to do. I can hire men from Pinkerton's just as he did. They'll have agents all over. One could be in Savannah and watching for them when they arrive. What is it, a week by horse and carriage from here to Savannah?"

"I'll go if you want me to."

She smiled at him suddenly, going to stand on her toes and kiss his cheek. "Thank you. Next to Fortune, you're my best friend."

"Well, I'd like to see that hardheaded husband while you decide what you want to do. If you want to send a telegram to Pinkerton's, I'll take you to the telegraph office."

"Thank you. I think that may be the only thing I can

do. Fortune's asleep," she said, turning toward the hall, Alaric falling in step beside her.

"He's been shot before and survived. If you can just keep him from learning the truth about Michael, Doc said he would mend just fine."

They walked down the hall, and she pointed at the bedroom, moving beside him as Alaric walked in and stood over Fortune a moment. When he left, she followed him into the hall.

"You keep him quiet. Every hour that passes will help. Now I'll drive your buggy, and we'll go send the telegram."

She rode quietly beside him, the sun hot on her shoulders because she had forgotten her bonnet and parasol. Alaric was quiet and she wondered if he was exhausted from the night. He waited patiently while she sent a telegram to Pinkerton's and requested an answer.

When she got a reply, she motioned to Alaric. "They said they would take the assignment, and they would have a man in Savannah by tomorrow."

"It's almost three hundred miles from here. Wenger may be going fast or he may be taking his time. He probably thinks Fortune is dead."

"I want to send another telegram and give them a description of Trevor Wenger and Michael."

"I know Wenger's driver and I know one of the servants he may have taken with him. I'll give you those descriptions."

She nodded and they moved back to the counter. In another quarter hour, they left the telegraph office to return home, and she felt slightly better to know someone was going to try to get Michael before Trevor Wenger sailed for Europe with him.

At the end of their drive Alaric jumped down from the buggy and helped her down, and they walked toward his saddled horse, tethered to a hitching post.

Alaric turned to face her. "Send Badru for me anytime

you need my help. If you want me to come sit with him tonight so you can sleep, I will. If you want me to come try to keep him in the house, I will."

"Alaric, thank you for everything. It helps knowing that Pinkerton's will try to get Michael, and thank you for finding out which direction they went. I couldn't have."

"I'll be by later." Gathering the reins, he swung up into the saddle. She stepped back and watched him ride down the drive. Glancing up at the house, Claire hurried inside.

When she got inside, Badru was helping Fortune back to bed.

"He's been up?" she asked, moving across the room in alarm.

"Yes, ma'am, just to tend to his needs. And Penthea is bringing him a bowl of soup."

"Fortune?" she asked, stopping in front of him. He sat on the side of the bed, swathed in bandages, his eyes glazed. He turned his head, and she realized the effects of the laudanum still hadn't worn off.

"Where's Michael?"

"He's fine. Alaric is seeing to Michael."

Fortune nodded, and she realized he was too groggy to think clearly. She picked up the laudanum, wanting to make certain he had some more after he ate. "I don't think Dr. Newsom thought you would be up today."

"Need my strength," he mumbled. Penthea appeared, and Badru lifted a table to bring the soup close to the bed.

"Thank you, Badru, Penthea. I can help him now," Claire said, turning to Fortune. "Let me do that," she said, steadying his hand as he picked up the spoon. He let her feed him, and she realized he must be just barely conscious.

He ate half the soup and drank a cup of hot tea, filled with some concoction that Penthea had mixed up, and Claire wondered if it was some old family remedy. Finally she helped him ease back down on the pillows. As he lifted his legs he groaned.

He murmured something she couldn't understand, and she moved closer. "Michael," he said as she leaned her ear close to his mouth. "Michael. Must get him. Bastard Wenger—"

"Shh, Fortune. Go to sleep," she said softly, smoothing his thick, wavy hair away from his forehead.

She turned to go to the window. It was impossible to sit down; she felt like pacing the room. She longed to be riding after Michael. If only Fortune were well, they would be racing toward Savannah.

The hours seemed interminable, sitting and waiting, watching over Fortune as afternoon became night. In the early evening Dr. Newsom came to check on his patient and change the bandages.

As he moved to the bed, he glanced at her. "Claire, wash up. You might as well learn how to do this. I'll continue as long as there's a great deal of drainage, but then you can take over. Do you faint easily?"

"No. But I've never seen anything like this."

As he opened a black bag and began to work, Fortune's eyes fluttered. He gazed up at the doctor.

"What've you done?" he asked in slurred words.

"I've patched you up. Someone tried to fill you with holes. Didn't you have enough of this on the battlefield?"

"Wenger did it."

"I know. Claire told me." Dr. Newsom worked, motioning to her to hand him a roll of tape, and Claire watched him carefully.

Fortune groaned and clenched his fists, and she winced for him. Still, she followed Dr. Newsom's directions, and when they finished, Fortune went back to sleep.

"He'll be more alert tomorrow. You'll have to cut the laudanum so he can get up and get his strength back. Try to keep him quiet. I'll leave bandages. You should be able to do this tomorrow. Just do the same thing we did tonight. You can get Badru to help. He knows what to do with wounded men."

"Yes, sir. Thank you."

"I'll come tomorrow evening and check on him."

She walked to the door with him and thanked him again as he left. Closing the door behind him, she wondered how far Trevor Wenger and Michael had traveled.

That night Badru helped Fortune up to relieve himself, and then she fed him a light supper, but it was more substantial than the soup. He ate baked chicken and a potato, and she suspected tomorrow she would have a problem keeping him confined.

She sat in the rocker as the house quieted. Penthea and Badru had both gone. Claire was still wearing her pink muslin, and it seemed pointless to change to a nightgown to sit up in a chair all night.

Fortune was propped on the pillows, and already he looked stronger. The changes were subtle, but his skin was a better color, and he moved around more often even if he did groan occasionally. She looked at the laudanum, deciding to give him more the next time he woke.

Long after midnight she awoke from a doze and, sitting up, was momentarily at a loss. She turned to look at Fortune as memory came rushing back. His blue eyes looked clear and alert.

"Where's Michael?" he asked in a cold voice.

Chapter 24

"Where's Michael?" he repeated tersely.

"Fortune, it's the middle of the night." She got up to fuss over him. "Why, you sound more like yourself. Do you feel like telling me what happened?" He struggled to sit up, and she moved to help him. "Wait, and I'll get Badru," she urged. "He's been helping you."

"Go get him, Claire."

She hurried out to Badru's quarters to summon him. She crossed the yard beneath a bright full moon, glancing at the bedroom windows and hoping she could get some laudanum down Fortune. When she returned to the bedroom, Fortune was seated on the side of the bed.

"Badru will be right here."

"Get your things, Claire. You can come with me. I'm going after Michael."

"No! You can't," she cried.

His hand shot out and closed around her wrist. He pulled her near, his eyes boring into hers, blazing with determination. "I'm going and I need you to go with me. Pack some food."

"Dr. Newsom—"

"I don't give a damn what Dr. Newsom said. We're leaving tonight, and if you won't go, I'll get someone else."

"Fortune, you don't even know where to go."

"Yes, I do. They'd go to Savannah and take a ship from there."

Claire tensed at the astuteness of his guess. "Fortune, please," she said, tears brimming. "Please don't do this. Dr. Newsom is worried about infection setting in."

"I am not letting him take my son to France." His tone was rough and unyielding.

"He has almost a twenty-four-hour head start on you. You can't catch him." She caught Fortune's hand. "Please. I sent a telegram to Pinkerton's and they're going to Savannah—"

"How'd you know it was Savannah?" His voice snapped like a whiplash cutting her.

"Because Alaric and Badru tracked down two people who saw them headed along the road to Savannah. Fortune, Pinkerton's will have a man there."

"You eluded Pinkerton's, Claire," he said harshly. "Pack my things, my revolver, my rifle. One revolver is at the mill, but there's another in the bottom drawer of my chest."

"Fortune, please don't do this. You've been wounded badly," she pleased. "You know I love Michael and want him back, but I love you too. You're too injured to do this. Take a few days to heal and then we'll go after him."

Fortune looked at her, and she knew she couldn't stop him.

As she turned away, Badru knocked at the door. "Mr. O'Brien?"

"Come in and help me."

"I'll get my things and then come back and get yours."

"I want you to help me," she heard him say to Badru, "and then I want you to hitch the team to the carriage."

Terrified that he would aggravate his injuries, she moved woodenly, knowing that she couldn't stop him. She thought about getting Alaric but rejected the idea. Alaric couldn't stop him either.

She rushed to pack, changing to her green gingham, taking one silk dress because Fortune might be in a hospital soon, and she wanted to look presentable to see his doctor. Trying to think rationally about what they would need, she felt panicky. She didn't see how Fortune could travel even three hours, much less to Savannah.

Within the hour, they were in the carriage, their things loaded and Badru driving while Fortune sprawled in the backseat, his head on Claire's lap.

"Anytime you want to turn back, you say so. I can keep in touch with Pinkerton's, and I'll let you know if anything develops."

Fortune's head lolled against her. "We're going to Savannah, and we're getting there before they sail."

In minutes he was asleep. She was tempted to tell Badru to turn the carriage around and go back to Atlanta. She looked at Fortune, his dark lashes, his wide mouth, and she knew she couldn't take him back home. Whether he survived the trip or not, it was something he had to do.

Gazing through the open window of the carriage, she looked at the dark branches of trees they were passing, staring into the bright night while the carriage jiggled and swayed. Two extra horses were hitched behind the carriage to enable them to switch teams often, and she knew Fortune had told Badru to push as fast as he could go.

She dozed, waking and shifting, her legs cramping from the narrow space in the carriage. At one point she awoke to find that Fortune still slept and it was night, the sky as dark as before. The next time she stirred it was daylight and they were slowing.

"I have to stop," Fortune said. "Badru will help me."

"Do you want me to get our breakfast?"

"Get something out of the basket, and we'll eat it in the carriage when we're going again."

She looked at him, seeing pain flare in his eyes, the grim set to his mouth, but she bit back her protest, knowing it was useless. Checking his wounds, she saw the bright red stain of fresh blood seeping through the bandages around his middle.

"Fortune, you're bleeding," she said, tears stinging her eyes over what he was doing to himself.

"I'm all right, Claire."

She stood, her legs aching as she climbed down and moved away from the carriage, thankful for a chance to stretch. Yet she couldn't help wondering how far they would get before he passed out or collapsed. Even if they arrived in Savannah in the next hour, he was too weak to confront anyone. Trevor Wenger would just finish what he had started.

Her hand went to the pocket in her green gingham dress. She had found not only Fortune's revolver and rifle and knife, but also a derringer that she had loaded and slipped into her pocket.

Soon they were back on the road, and she struggled with the basket to pass out servings of thin slices of ham and cold biscuits, apples. First she passed up food to Badru and then turned to help Fortune. Finally he lay back against the seat. "I can't eat another bite, Claire."

"Here's some water and take some laudanum. It'll make the ride easier."

He was watching her intently, and she wondered if he was debating whether or not he could trust her not to knock him out. Finally he nodded and drank the water and took the laudanum. In several minutes he was asleep, his head bouncing against the seat.

The hours passed in an endless nightmare as they shook over rough roads stopping to switch teams and feed and water the horses. At one of the stops, she walked over to Badru. "You missed sleeping last night. I'll drive if you can manage to sleep in the narrow space we have."

He blinked, a look of gratitude sweeping over his features. "I'd appreciate that, Miz O'Brien. Just a couple of hours would do me a lot of good."

She climbed up in front, and after she started off down the road, she glanced back to see Badru's head against the side of the carriage, his huge body wedged in the space on the floor. Crammed on the seat, Fortune was asleep with his knees bent and his feet on the cushion.

When night came, Fortune insisted they keep going. Sitting on the seat with his head in her lap, she felt tears sting her eyes because he was growing worse and the bandage was soaked with blood.

As they bounced along and moonlight bathed Fortune's face, she looked at him, knowing that if she told him she was carrying his child, he would still be just as determined to get Michael.

The next morning as she bathed his face, she leaned close to him. "Fortune, we're coming to Macon. Let me stop and send a telegram to Pinkerton's."

"No," he said in a whisper that she had to lean forward to hear.

"Listen to me," she said urgently, and he opened his eyes to look at her. His eyes were bloodshot, and his jaw was covered in dark stubble. His skin had an unhealthy pallor again, and there was a grim set to his mouth that she knew was caused by the constant pain. "Let me telegram Pinkerton's. They could have already found Michael. Or he could have already sailed."

"He hasn't had time to get there."

"Please, Fortune. A telegram won't take long."

He nodded and closed his eyes.

They came into Macon along a road following the Ocmulgee River. As she walked into the train depot, which had a telegraph office, she prayed that Pinkerton's would have some kind of news about Michael. If he had sailed from Savannah, Fortune would have to stop pushing to get there, and they could get a hotel room here and she would find a doctor to come tend him. Earlier when they had stopped for breakfast, she had changed his bandage and both wounds were oozing bright red blood that frightened her.

There was no smell of putrid flesh, though, and she marveled at his strength.

She sent a telegram and waited to receive a message, her fingers laced together while she prayed there was something. The store was filled with tools and harnesses and pans, and through the front window she could see the carriage. Badru had climbed down and gone to get something at the grocer's. Fortune was slumped in the back.

"Here you are, miss." The clerk handed her a telegram and she skimmed it, reading that there was no sign of Michael and Wenger yet.

She lowered the telegram, glancing at the street outside. Fortune might not last until they reached Savannah. If he would just lose consciousness, she could stop. Knowing there was nothing else to do except keep going, she went back outside. She climbed up and eased Fortune's head and shoulders onto her lap. As soon as they were situated, she held a fan over him to shade his face.

His color was ashen and sweat beaded his brow and upper lip. In a few more days he would have a thick beard. She glanced around as Badru climbed up to drive.

"Sorry, ma'am. I refilled our water containers. Here's some if you can get him to drink a little."

"Thank you. There was no word from Pinkerton's, so I guess we keep going."

"Yes, ma'am." They moved through the town, and she felt a growing reluctance with each block to leave behind a doctor and a hotel room. In a short time they were out of town, riding along a wide dirt road. She stared ahead, watching the land dip and rise. Where was Michael? Was he frightened or in pain, wanting to come back home? She couldn't bear to think about the latter and tried to remember all the toys Trevor had purchased for him. What had he told Michael? Did Michael think his parents had agreed he could go with his grandfather?

She looked at Fortune and knew that he had been right all along about Trevor Wenger. She dampened a cloth and wiped Fortune's brow. In a few moments his eyes opened.

"Here's some cold water," she said, holding the bottle

close to his mouth. He drank, water running down his jaw. "Where are we?"

"Out of Macon now."

"Pinkerton's?"

"They haven't seen any sign of them."

"Tell Badru to go faster."

"Fortune, it won't do any good if you kill yourself getting there. I can't take him from them."

"Going faster isn't going to kill me. Badru!"

"Yes, sir."

"Let's speed up."

She stared at him grimly as his blue eyes shifted back to her. "Fortune, I'm sorry I took Michael to visit him without telling you. I should have talked to you about it."

"And I never would have consented."

"I didn't know what kind of man he was. He wasn't that way with Michael. Marilee grew up with him and she turned out all right."

"Yes, she did." He closed his eyes and she didn't know whether he was tired or he merely wanted to end the discussion.

They rode all through the night, and by the next day Fortune was burning with fever.

"Badru, at the next town you stop this carriage, and I'll find a doctor."

"No, you don't" came a raspy voice that was little more than a croak from Fortune. "Keep going."

"You can't. You have to stop."

His eyes focused on her, and his jaw was thrust out in determination.

"We don't stop."

"Fortune, if I have to pull a gun—"

"You couldn't possibly shoot either one of us, so forget it, Claire. If we keep going, we might catch them. They'll be stopping at night and maybe during the day. He won't think I'm after him, and I doubt if he expects you to come after him. He'll think you're home burying me."

"And I'll have to if you keep this up," she said, tears finally brimming over and spilling down her cheeks. She turned her head quickly, wiping at her eyes. "You are so stubborn—"

She bit off her words and took a deep breath. She couldn't stop him, and hopefully, before he killed himself, he would lose consciousness and she could get a doctor.

Fortune was on fire with pain as he saw the tears spill over her cheeks. He knew he was being hard on her, but if she had kept Michael home, this might not have happened. Or the bastard could have been just biding his time all along, and whether Claire and Michael visited him or not wouldn't have made any difference.

Fortune bit back a groan as he watched Claire cry, remembering all of Alaric's lectures. The last weeks had been pure hell. His thoughts shifted to Michael, and he clenched his fist, praying that he could make it to Savannah in time. He looked down at the hand that was bandaged. It was his right hand, the one he used to fire a gun. If he found Trevor Wenger with Michael, he wouldn't be able to use a gun to stop Wenger or to defend himself.

A pain shot through his stomach and he moaned. Claire turned to him.

"Do you want some laudanum? It would make this easier, and you can't get well when you hurt all the time."

"I'm all right."

Claire wiped his forehead and fanned him, trying to keep him cool to get the fever down. Her back hurt from sitting in the cramped space. Every jolt of the buggy sent a new shock up her spine.

By late that evening Fortune was asleep, and Badru looked as if he was on the verge of dozing. "Stop when you find a place to water the horses, Badru, and I'll drive the carriage."

"Yes, ma'am. I think I'm going to have to do that unless these horses can get there without me."

"We'll stop."

The next day, Fortune's fever seemed worse than ever, but he was still alert. "We have to stop in the next town, Badru. Let's get more food and refill the water bottles," Claire said.

"Yes, ma'am. Good thing he has such fine horseflesh. Sorry animals wouldn't be able to keep up this pace."

"I'm not sure we can," she said, glancing at Fortune.

For the next day and night, she was exhausted, torn apart worrying about Fortune as well as Michael. If she was exhausted and aching from travel, what was it doing to Fortune?

She looked at his flushed face. He wouldn't take laudanum, but he slept most of the time and she was tempted to tell Badru to stop, but every time she started to, she knew Fortune would never forgive her if she didn't get him to Savannah.

And when they got there, what could he do? He would be too ill to do anything. She looked at the back of Badru's head and his broad shoulders.

"Badru, when we get to Savannah, we have to get him in bed. Did he tell you what he wanted you to do?"

"Yes, ma'am. I'm to go down to the dock and look for Mr. Michael."

"If you find him, you might risk your life if you try to take him from Mr. Wenger."

He turned, his dark eyes focusing on her. "That's all right. I'm willing to try. Mr. O'Brien gave me money to move my in-laws and my boys to Atlanta. He's given me back my children. I'd risk my life to get his son for him."

"Badru, I don't know if he'll last," she said quietly, tears burning her eyes.

"He'll last, Miz O'Brien."

Badru turned to glance at her, his features impassive, but the conviction in his voice mad her feel better.

She was barely aware when the landscape changed, the rolling hills flattening out as they approached Savannah.

At the sight of live oaks draped with Spanish moss, she remembered working in Savannah so long ago when Michael had been a tiny baby. It had grown dark outside, and she placed her hand against her belly, sure now that she was carrying Fortune's child. She stroked Fortune's burning forehead, trying to stop the nagging voice telling her that he might not survive this journey. He seemed to have lost a bucket of blood, and she'd had to stop and buy more bandages. As soon as they reached Savannah, she would have to replenish her supply again.

The next morning she was dozing when she realized someone was saying something. She opened her eyes and sat up, her back sore, her legs cramped as she tried to move. Fortune lay with his head against her shoulder, his chest rising and falling in quick, shallow breathing.

"Miz O'Brien, we're here."

She rose and saw rooftops ahead. "Thank God! We can get him to bed now."

"Yes, ma'am." She pushed her hair away from her face. It was a tangle and she hadn't combed it since yesterday. She tried to make herself presentable, knowing they should take Fortune to a hospital first.

"Badru, when we get into town, I want to find a hospital."

"Yes, ma'am."

"No." Fortune's voice was raspy and flat, but she heard him clearly. "Help me sit up."

"You have to go to a hospital."

"Badru, ride down to River Street. Take Abercorn or Bay Street."

"You can't go to the docks!"

He looked at her. "I've come all this way to get there. We're going to the docks."

"Are you going to stand on the docks for the next few days and watch for them?"

"You wire Pinkerton's and see what you can learn. And

yes, until I know he's sailed, I'm standing on the damned dock."

She knew any further argument was useless. Through busy streets filled with bright sunshine, then through shady squares that looked inviting and peaceful, they rode until finally they wound down a steep hill to River Street.

Halyards clinked and men yelled as they unloaded a ship. Vendors hawked their wares while wagons rolled along the street. For a moment she forgot her worries about Fortune as her gaze swept the tall ships moored along the wharves. She searched the crowd for a tall man and a small boy, for Michael's curly head. Badru stopped the buggy in the shade of a three-story cotton warehouse built of dark red brick.

"I'll start at one end, Mr. O'Brien."

"Help me down, Badru."

"Fortune, everyone will gape at you and your bandages, and some policeman will cart you away to a hospital."

"Get me a shirt, and Badru, you help me put it on. I won't put my arm in the sleeve."

"Then you can't use a gun," she said, feeling a mounting fear for his safety. He grimaced as Badru helped him from the carriage. As she had feared, men turned to stare at them.

"Claire, if you want to be a help, go to a ticket counter and find out which ships are sailing to France, and if Wenger is booked on any. Get a telegram to Pinkerton's." He swayed and she thought he was going to faint.

"Fortune!"

He placed his good arm against the carriage. "I'm all right."

"What are you going to do? Where can I find you?"

"Right here. I'll just stand here and look until you get back, and then you can help me walk up and down."

She intended to get him back into the carriage and they

would drive up and down, but she saw no point in arguing about it now.

"Mr. O'Brien, do you want your pistol?"

Fortune shook his head. "I couldn't hold it or hit anything if I had it. No. Leave the rifle on the seat where I can reach it."

He leaned against the carriage, and she hurried away to find a place to purchase tickets and send a telegram.

She sent the telegram first, standing in a small shop in one of the tall buildings facing the Savannah River. "I expect a telegram in return," she told the clerk. "I'll be back shortly to get it."

"Yes, ma'am."

She went two doors away to ask about passenger boats to France and learned there was one to northern France, one to southern France, and one to England, all docked now. The one to northern France would sail in three days. The other two weren't leaving until the next week.

Praying Pinkerton's had Michael or at least knew of his whereabouts, she hurried back to get the answer to her telegram. As the clerk handed her the slip of paper, she took a deep breath and turned it to read: "No sign of Wenger and boy. Stop. Agent John Newhall at Savannah Hotel. Stop. Will inform him your presence. Stop. A.P."

Her spirits sank. Fortune had to go to a hospital, not wait and watch for Michael.

She slipped her hand into her pocket to touch the derringer for reassurance. Hurrying back toward the carriage, she walked in the shadow of tall buildings, her gaze scanning the docks. She spotted the *Merry Barnaby,* the schooner that would be bound for England, but she couldn't see *La Liberté* or *L' Irelande.*

Half expecting to find Fortune collapsed on the cobblestones, she found him leaning against the carriage. Marveling again at his vitality and perseverance she walked up and handed him the telegram from Pinkerton's.

"We're in time," he said as he scanned the message and crumpled the paper to toss it into the carriage.

She wasn't as certain about that as Fortune, yet she knew Trevor Wenger would never have driven at the pace they had. "There's no one booked for passage with the name Wenger. There are three possibilities: *La Liberté,* a ship for northern France, *L' Irelande* for southern France, and the *Merry Barnaby* for England."

"Northern France will be the one," Fortune said grimly. His gaze swept the dock. "We'll have to find that ship."

"Fortune, please, get in the carriage and let me drive around to look for the ship."

He inhaled deeply, grimaced, and nodded. She steadied him as he climbed up, and she was shocked how wobbly he was and how difficult it was for him to get into the carriage. He eased down and she went around to drive. They moved slowly into the throng, going at a walk because of the crowded wharf. Shielding her eyes, she passed along the line of ships.

"There it is," she said quietly. She turned to stop again in the shade of another cotton warehouse. "Just stay in the carriage," she urged him. "Sitting here, we have a better view of the wharf and ship. I'll see if I can go on board to look for them."

He caught her wrist, and a faint smile tugged at the corner of his mouth as he shook his head. "You won't be safe going on board alone looking like you do."

She blinked, looking down at her wrinkled green gingham.

"Did you bring a fancy dress?"

"Yes, I did because I thought I might have to stay in a hotel while you're in the hospital."

"Wait to go on board until tomorrow. I don't think they're on board now. They'll arrive tomorrow or the next day."

"Can we get Badru and go to a hotel?"

Fortune eyed the ship speculatively and she waited. Finally he nodded. "Find him."

"I want to take you to a hospital."

"No. Drive to the closest hotel. I'll get our room and an extra one for Michael. I may not be able to travel home for a while. Badru will have to find a place too. They won't allow him to stay where we do."

She nodded and turned the carriage, glancing at Fortune to see him studying the ship. Fairly quickly she spotted Badru, who was as tall as Fortune and as easy to see in a crowd.

She slowed the carriage and Fortune turned to him. "There are three ships here, the *Merry Barnaby* for England, *L' Irelande,* and the *La Liberté*. I think it'll be *La Liberté,* sailing for northern France, and that ship is back behind us. We're going to a hotel now because it doesn't leave for three days."

"I'll stay and look for the other two ships. I'll stay down here tonight."

"Be careful," Fortune cautioned weakly, "and if you find them, Badru, none of those ships is sailing yet. Come get me. We'll be at the closest hotel."

"Yes, sir. I'll watch."

She flicked the reins and they clopped away down River Street. "There's the one bound for the south of France," Fortune said, and she looked at another tall-masted schooner.

They turned to go up the hill past Factor's Walk. The millinery shop was still there, and she remembered that last night so clearly. She wished she had Michael safely in her arms now.

"There's the Savannah Hotel. Stop in front, Claire, and I'll get a room."

"Fortune, I can."

"No, you can't. I'll do it." She stopped and went around to help Fortune down. "Get some money," he said under his breath as a porter came forward.

Fortune motioned to the buggy. "What's your name?"

"William Ellenhofer, sir."

"I'm Caleb Rafferty," he said, and Claire stared at him, wondering if the fever had finally made him delirious. "I'm ill, and we've traveled a long way. After you've carried our things to our room, take this carriage to the livery stable and board my horses."

"First, get a doctor to come look at my husband, because I know he should be in a hospital," Claire said, giving William Ellenhofer her best smile.

"Yes, ma'am. Dr. Roth's office is just down the street. I'll get him and get your things and take your carriage."

Fortune held out a fat roll of greenbacks.

"Thank you, sir! I'll get the doctor, Mr. Rafferty." He bolted away and she picked up her reticule and took Fortune's good arm.

"Don't let the doctor give me anything to put me out."

"Caleb Rafferty?"

"I wouldn't want Wenger to see Fortune O'Brien on the hotel register. Besides, Michael would recognize Caleb Rafferty if he heard it."

"I don't think there's any chance he'll be where he can hear someone say that name. Only the porters and clerks will know it."

They moved to the desk and Fortune slumped against it. "I want to register for a room."

"Sir, pardon me for saying so, but you look as if you need a hospital," the clerk said, his brown eyes wide behind round, rimless spectacles as he looked from Fortune to Claire.

"My husband is ill, and we've just sent for a doctor."

Fortune reached into the waistband of his pants and pulled out a small bag that clinked. He opened it and dropped a gold piece onto the counter. "I want to stay here and not some hospital." He pushed the coin to the man. "Keep that for your trouble."

"Yes, sir. I'll get you a room on this floor so you won't have to climb any stairs."

Fortune didn't answer, and when she looked up at him, his eyes were closed, sweat beading his face. She wondered again if he would faint.

"Sign here, sir." He didn't seem to hear the clerk, and she took the pen.

"I'll sign for him." She wrote Mr. and Mrs. Caleb Rafferty in large, bold letters, knowing the chance of Michael ever hearing the name was almost nonexistent.

The clerk gave her a key, and she took Fortune's arm. As his eyes came open, he straightened up. "I have our key, Fortune. Room twelve." They walked to the room, and the moment she closed the door, she turned to help Fortune to bed, yanking down the yellow counterpane and covers.

He sank down, closing his eyes, his breathing coming shallow and fast. "Claire, get me up tomorrow."

"I will."

In no time he was asleep and she slumped into a chair, exhausted. A knock came and she opened the door to face a short, balding man with a black bag. William Ellenhofer stood beside him with his arms filled with their baggage.

"Miz Rafferty, this is Dr. Roth."

"Please come and look at my husband."

The doctor crossed the room and looked down at Fortune and then up at her as she moved around the bed to stand across from him. "This man isn't sick, he's wounded!"

"Yes. We were robbed on our way here. Or they tried to rob us and they shot my husband. A doctor treated him in Atlanta, and then we left for here."

"Good Lord, he shouldn't have traveled in this condition! From Atlanta?"

Now she wished she had given another town, but she had already said Atlanta. "Yes."

He shook his head and felt Fortune's forehead, picking

up his wrist to take his pulse. She moved away when he started to cut away Fortune's bandages to replace them.

"Doctor?" Fortune said, the word drawled in a raspy voice.

"Your wife told me about your getting robbed and shot. You should have stayed in Atlanta and not kept traveling. Man, you are in no shape to move!" He pulled away the bandage on Fortune's side. "I'm astounded you've survived this well. The wound is clean, but you need to lie still and let this heal."

Fortune gasped and she clenched her jaw, hating to see him in pain and knowing he was hurting terribly all the time now. When the porter came with the last of their things, she ordered a tub and bath water brought to the room.

Finally Dr. Roth closed his bag. "He's asleep. I'll come by in the morning."

"Thank you. What do I owe you?"

"You can wait and pay me when he's up and around. I hope you don't plan on traveling for a time."

"No, we don't."

"He shouldn't get out of bed for a few days."

She nodded, knowing she couldn't possibly keep Fortune from getting up if he was conscious when the morrow came. She closed the door behind the doctor, feeling somewhat better. Fortune was being cared for, and he could finally lie still in a bed.

The tub and water were brought to the room, and soon she was soaking in it, relishing the water, washing her hair. Every few minutes her gaze went back to Fortune, lying so still in the four-poster bed.

The room was comfortable with wide windows that let in a good breeze. Outside, she could see the branches of tall oaks stretching close to the hotel, their leaves giving cool shade.

By the time she had dried her hair and dressed in a blue organdy, she felt too tired to go to the dining room to eat. Easing herself down, she stretched on the bed beside Fortune.

"I love you," she said, stroking his cheek. His chest rose and fell evenly, and she didn't know whether he was in a deep sleep or Dr. Roth had given him something. Ends of his black hair curled damply against his forehead, and his beard was getting thicker now. She trailed her fingertips over the rough, short beard on his jaw. His eyes remained closed.

"I love you, Fortune O'Brien," she whispered. "I love you. You have to get well. You're going to be a father again."

She looked down at her stomach, marveling at the fact that she was carrying their child. And then exhaustion seemed to pull her down and she closed her eyes, drifting to sleep.

In the night, she stirred to hear him groaning. She sat up, dazed for a moment and then remembering. Lighting a lamp, she moved around the bed to look down at him.

"Water . . ." he whispered, his voice trailing away.

She poured a cup and returned to slide her arm beneath the pillow and raise his head. "Here, Fortune. Take a drink."

She helped him drink, feeling heat radiate from his body like a stove in winter, knowing he was on fire with fever. Finally he turned his head away as if he were too exhausted to talk. She lowered him to the bed and bathed his face with cool water for the next hour, placing cold cloths on his chest to try to keep him cool.

It was almost four o'clock by Fortune's gold watch when she went back to bed. Climbing up beside him carefully, she left the light on so she could see him at once if he called for help.

"Claire."

She opened her eyes to discover sunlight spilling into the room. As Fortune stared at her, his fingers closed around her wrist. "Come around here and help me get up and dress. I want to go down to the dock."

"Fortune, Badru said he will watch. Take one day—"

"No. Come help me. I'll do more damage to myself if I have to get up without help."

She moved to his side, trying to avoid holding his injured side and reaching high beneath his arms to try to hold him as he stood. She felt his weight sag on her, almost shoving her down as he swayed and held the bed with one hand, holding her with the other.

"Fortune, you can't leave this room! You can't even stand alone."

"Yes, I can," he said, and she stopped arguing. "Help me across the room so I can wash."

They moved slowly and she expected at any moment he would crash to the floor, but he finally stood in front of the basin and she moved away to give him what privacy she could.

"Take some money, and get a porter at the front desk to go to the livery stable and get our carriage. I want it ready and waiting."

She nodded, knowing it was useless to protest his going.

An hour later, he stood by the door, holding the jamb, both arms in his shirtsleeves, his rifle in hand. "Help me down to the carriage, Claire."

She had dressed in the blue silk she had brought. It was wrinkled and she had tried to smooth the skirt. She wore a tiny blue silk bonnet and the diamond sapphire earbobs Fortune had given her. She paused in front of him. "Do I look presentable enough to go on board today?"

He had a faint smile as he gazed at her. "You look beautiful. Let's go."

"Fortune, I have your derringer."

He raised the rifle, and she knew he would use it on Wenger if he could.

"Fortune, don't kill Trevor Wenger in front of Michael.

Michael may think we gave permission for him to go with his grandfather. He may not know anything is amiss."

"Let's get down there, Claire. We're wasting time."

She went to his side to help him, agonizing as he groaned when he climbed into the waiting carriage. They rode down to the docks, moving in the crowd to stop again near the cotton warehouse across the wharf from *La Liberté*.

"I'll go on board and talk to the captain. Are you all right?"

"I'm fine. Go ahead."

She knew he hurt terribly. His forehead was beaded with perspiration, his face flushed. He had shaved away the beard, and grim lines were etched around his mouth. She noticed he held his rifle with his left hand. She couldn't imagine how he would confront Trevor Wenger and expect to get Michael from him unless Badru or the Pinkerton agent was present.

She moved through the throng, hearing men yelling and talking, vendors calling. Smells of fish and rotting food and water assailed her. Wagon wheels rumbled on the cobbled street, and she constantly searched the crowd for any sign of Trevor Wenger and Michael.

As she approached the ship, brown water lapped its hull. Holding her skirts carefully, she walked up the gangway, raising her chin. When she stepped on board, a man noticed her.

"Where's the captain?"

He turned and she followed his gaze to see a man in a white and blue uniform with a white cap. "Cap'n."

The man turned and the sailor gestured toward her. "Sir, the lady asked to see you."

"I'm Captain Gramercy," he said politely, his gaze sweeping over her. "How may I help you, ma'am?"

"I'm Mrs. Fortune O'Brien. Captain, could we go to your cabin where I can talk to you privately?"

"Yes, ma'am," he said. "Follow me."

She moved along behind him, aware of stares from sailors working on the ship, keeping her gaze on the captain's broad back and black hair. He opened the door and stepped back to allow her to enter.

His cabin was roomy with a desk, table and chairs, and bunk.

When she sat down on a chair, he sat facing her. "How may I help you?" he asked politely, his dark eyes studying her.

"My father and my son are sailing for France." She paused and looked down at her hands a moment and then met his gaze. "This is very difficult. My husband owns a steel mill in Atlanta and is quite successful. Unfortunately, my side of the family is less respectable. My father is a gambler, and my husband disapproves of him. Even though my father has a notorious occupation, he's quite successful and he's taking my son to France for a visit. This is unknown to my husband, who thinks our son has gone to visit my aunt in Savannah, the only member of my family to have his approval."

"Are they on my ship?"

"That's why I'm here. Last week my husband told me he was going to St. Louis to talk to men there about buying their mill. He's going to be gone for more than two weeks, so I came to Savannah to see my father and son before they sail."

"That's fine, but not all our passengers are on board ship yet. We sail tomorrow morning. They may arrive today. I'll get the passenger list and see if they're already on board."

He leaned over his desk and picked up a sheaf of papers.

"This is the problem," she said, smiling at him. "Since I've deceived my husband about where my son is, my father thought it would be wiser to sail under another name. I can't remember the name he told me he would use."

The captain's eyes narrowed and he studied her, his gaze flicking over her again. "What steel mill does your husband own?"

"O'Brien Steel Works. I brought one of his ledgers because I thought you might question if I'm really Mrs. O'Brien." She held out a small ledger she had found in Fortune's belongings.

"This is highly unusual, ma'am."

"My husband thinks gamblers are the lowest form of life on earth. And my father loves his grandchild and I want him to get to know him. My husband will not allow him to even speak to Michael."

"Ma'am, how am I to know that this isn't your husband taking your child from you and you're trying to get him back?"

She laughed. "My father is a very tall man who can shoot quite well. Even if what you said were so, which it isn't, how could I take a child from a man like that?" She gave him a wide smile. "Captain, when you see us together, you'll know I'm telling the truth. You can ask my son, ask his grandfather. I just want to find them and visit with them before they sail."

He studied her and then looked down at the passenger list. His fingers were thick as sausages, grimy beneath the nails with a smudge of oil across the back of one hand as if he had just come from working on machinery.

She watched his index finger move down the page, sliding over scrawled names that she couldn't read from where she sat. His finger paused and he glanced up at her. "What's his real name?"

"Trevor Wenger."

"I have a Charles Ames who is traveling with a six-year-old boy, Horace Benjamin."

"Oh, my! I recognize the names now that you've said them. That's my father and son."

"They haven't boarded yet, and I don't know exactly

when to expect them," he said, flipping the pages closed and tossing the list onto his desk.

She stood up. "I'll come back this afternoon. I imagine they'll be on board by then." He stood and held open the door. She went out ahead of him and on deck at the gangway, she turned to him. "Thank you, Captain. I'll tell my father what a wonderful help you were."

"Yes, ma'am. You come back this afternoon, and I'll tell you whether they've boarded or not. Most people who bring children don't board until the last minute."

She flashed him a broad smile. "Thank you, Captain. You've been so helpful."

"You're welcome, Mrs. O'Brien. I'll tell them you're looking for them."

"Thank you, Captain Gramercy." With another big smile at him, she turned to step onto the wide, scuffed plank, holding her parasol over her head, touching the rope lightly. As she looked over over the dock, she spotted Fortune standing up by the carriage. Surprised he was standing, she paused as he stepped forward taking his rifle in his hand.

She frowned, her gaze sweeping the dock, and she gasped. Moving slowly through the crowd was the Wenger carriage. She looked at the shiny black closed carriage that could easily carry six people plus the driver and servants on the outside. The yellow wheels turned slowly. She looked back to Fortune, but he had disappeared. She felt a rush of panic, searching the crowd wildly before finally spotting his black hat. He was headed toward the ship, angling to his right toward the carriage. Her heart thudded violently because Trevor could look out the carriage window, spot Fortune, and if the crowd parted, shoot him without Fortune being able to fire in return. She knew Fortune would never fire into a carriage carrying Michael.

She rushed toward them as the carriage moved steadily toward the ship.

All three of them were converging from different directions. The driver stopped the Wenger carriage far back from the ship, and she pushed through the crowd, terrified she would be too late to keep the two men from killing each other.

She glimpsed Fortune and felt another shock. He was walking slowly and purposefully as if he weren't wounded. And the rifle was in his right hand.

She pushed against people blocking her way. "Excuse me," she said, feeling desperate. And then the crowd moved out of the way of the carriage. It stopped and Trevor Wenger emerged while Michael remained inside sitting close to the window directly behind Wenger. If Fortune fired at him, he would hit Michael.

Wenger had a coat over his arm, and she saw the tip of the muzzle of a revolver extending beyond the coat, pointed at Fortune.

"Stop where you are," he said coldly, facing Fortune across a few yards.

Chapter 25

"I have a gun pointed at you. If you want to live, you'll turn around and walk away," Trevor said quietly.

"I came to get my son back, and I'm going to."

Claire looked at Michael's white face and round eyes and wondered if Trevor Wenger had threatened him. Then she saw someone move beside Michael, and she realized a servant must be in the carriage. And she wondered if he was holding Michael at gunpoint.

She looked at Fortune, who was acting as though all were normal. Where was Badru? She prayed he would appear. Yet it would do little good if one of Trevor's men held Michael.

"Let my son go," Fortune said in a low voice, and a few people on the dock turned to stare at him.

"No. He stays with me. I'm giving you three seconds to walk away. After that, I'll consider that you've threatened my life, and I had to shoot you to defend myself."

"There are witnesses."

Trevor Wenger shook his head. "I have my own witnesses, and you know I can get off. No one is going to take me to prison for killing you."

"I won't let him go."

"One . . ." he said.

Fortune swayed slightly, then righted himself. She saw his finger move to the trigger of the rifle, but there was no way he could fire without harming Michael and he knew it. He would never shoot.

Knowing Fortune would be killed in the next second, she stepped between the two men and faced Trevor Wenger.

"You can't shoot Michael's father! If you had any love for your grandson, you would never be so cruel to him."

"Stop protecting O'Brien and get out of the way. You're not Michael's mother. You mean nothing to me."

"Move, Claire," Fortune said, shifting out from behind her, and Trevor turned so the revolver was aimed at Fortune.

"You didn't love your daughter. If you had, you would never have lost her," Claire said, stepping between Wenger and Fortune again. "You killed her by taking her away from the husband she loved. He's a good man and the father of your grandson. Mr. Wenger, love is giving, and all you do is take. You took her happiness and her life."

"I didn't kill Marilee!"

"Oh, yes, you did. That night before she died she warned me to beware of you. She said, 'Beware of my father,' " Claire stated firmly, knowing that was what Marilee had intended.

"Never!" he said, his face flushing.

"You killed her, and she never got to see Michael grow up, never got to live with a husband who adored her and would have cared for her forever."

"I loved Marilee!" he yelled, his face flushing.

"No, you didn't. You loved what you thought she ought to be, something for you to groom and display and control like your horses! I know!" Claire cried. "I had a father like you. A father who wanted to marry me to a man I didn't love! You didn't love Marilee! You don't love Michael! I know, and Marilee knew!"

"Mama!" Michael flung himself out of the carriage and threw his arms around her. She looked over his head at Trevor Wenger, whose face was ashen as he gazed down at the boy.

"I loved Marilee, and I love Michael." His voice was filled with agony. She placed her arm across Michael's shoulders, and with one last look into Wenger's eyes, she eased Michael beside her and turned to walk to Fortune, her back to Trevor Wenger.

Fortune came forward. He took two steps, then suddenly his eyes rolled back. He crumpled as though he were filled with sawdust.

"Papa!" Michael ran to him at the same time she did.

Kneeling, she pressed her hand against his warm throat and felt a fluttering pulse. "We have to get him to the hotel," she said, looking around.

"Ma'am" came a deep voice and she looked up to see Badru push his way through the gathering crowd. "I'll get him," he said. "You take Mr. Michael and go on to the carriage."

She glanced back to see Trevor Wenger standing just as he had been, staring at her, a wounded look of shock on his face.

She held Michael's hand and hurried ahead, seeing Badru pick Fortune up as easily as if it had been Michael.

"Will Papa be all right?" Michael asked in a high voice.

"Yes, he will, Michael," she said, praying that she was right.

"What's wrong with him?"

"He got hurt at work," she answered stiffly, wondering if they would ever have to tell Michael that his grandfather had tried to kill his father.

Badru lifted Fortune into the carriage, and she climbed in beside him while Michael rode in front with Badru.

As they pulled away from the dock, she glanced back once more. Trevor Wenger was still frozen in place, staring at them without the power to move a muscle.

Her gaze shifted to Fortune, whose face was ashen, his breathing rapid and noisy. His skin was burning, and she was terrified he had pushed himself too hard.

"Where do we go, ma'am, hospital or hotel?" Badru asked.

She looked down at the unconscious Fortune, knowing if he were able to talk, he wouldn't allow her to take him to a hospital. "Take him to the hotel, Badru. As soon as we get there, you'll have to go for Dr. Roth."

"Yes, ma'am."

The carriage jiggled over the cobblestones, and she smoothed Fortune's hair away from his face, feeling his burning skin. When they climbed to the upper level in front of Factor's Walk and turned a corner, River Street and Trevor Wenger were lost from view.

As soon as she got Fortune in bed in the hotel room, she said, "Wash your hands, Michael. You can help me take care of Papa."

"Yes, ma'am," he said, running across the room to a basin. She poured cold water into a bowl and dipped a cloth into it. "Rub Papa's skin lightly with this, Michael. so we can try to cool him. Be careful you don't bump against him where he's wounded."

"Yes, ma'am."

While Michael did as she told him, she carefully unbuttoned Fortune's shirt and tried to remove it, finally cutting it away so she wouldn't hurt him. A knock came and she hurried to the door.

"Dr. Roth, come in, please. He collapsed when he was down at the wharf."

"He should never have gotten out of bed!" Roth snapped. Michael moved out of his way, and the doctor bent over Fortune. She motioned to the boy, and he backed away toward her. She could see the worry and alarm in his wide eyes and knew he was frightened.

"Michael, why don't you let Badru take you downstairs while Dr. Roth looks at Papa? It'll be better. Take one of your books."

"Yes, ma'am," he said. His innocent eyes looked up at her, his lower lip thrust out. "Will Papa get well?"

"Yes, Michael, he will," she said, unable to answer the child any other way.

He nodded, and she opened the door to motion to Badru. "Would you take Michael downstairs and watch him? The minute I can, I'll come get him."

"Yes, ma'am."

She turned to watch Michael rummage in his satchel and return with a book. He left with Badru, and she closed the door behind them.

She sat in a chair, waiting while Dr. Roth worked over Fortune. Finally the doctor closed the black bag and turned around.

"I can't tell you whether he'll make it through the night. His fever is burning him up. Try to keep him cooled down with cold water. You can order ice from the hotel. The shoulder wound is infected, and I've done what I can for that. Only time will tell."

She nodded, on the brink of tears, unable to think about losing him now. And what a dreadful loss it would be for Michael. "Thank you for coming."

"He's a strong man. He may fight it off." She nodded and went to the door with him. He paused with his hand on the knob. "I'll come by this evening."

"Thank you." She closed the door and crossed the room to the bed, looking down at Fortune. His skin was flushed and he lay still. She wiped tears from her eyes and leaned down to brush his forehead with a light kiss. "Please get well. Michael and I need you. And you have another child now who needs you, Fortune. Get well for us."

She wiped her eyes again and turned to go into the lobby. Michael was curled in a red chair with his legs beneath him, the book propped in his lap, but he glanced up and saw her and closed the book.

She went to the desk to order a block of ice and tub be sent to their room. Then she turned to hurry back to get cold cloths on Fortune.

All three of them worked to get him cool. As Badru bent over him, placing a folded cloth across Fortune's forehead, she looked at him.

"Badru, you don't have to stay. Michael and I can do this."

"No, ma'am. I don't mind staying, and I can help turn him if we need to. I'm all right, ma'am."

When the ice came, Badru chipped chunks of it, and they placed the ice in the washcloths and wet towels. Finally she took Michael's hand. "Badru, we'll be back in a minute."

As he nodded his head, she took Michael to the adjoining room.

She sat down, motioning Michael to come close. He threw his arms around her, hugging her tightly. "Mama, I want Papa to get well."

"He will, love." She stroked Michael's head and tried to get control of her emotions. When she felt she could face him without tears, she took the boy by the shoulders and moved him back to look into his eyes. "Michael, how did your grandfather get you?"

He frowned and blinked, looking worried, and she wondered if he had had a bad fright. "I woke up and I was at his house."

"You slept through someone moving you from our house to his house?" she asked, surprised. Then she remembered how soundly Michael slept and knew someone could have moved him easily.

"Yes, ma'am. He said that he had gone to see you and Papa after I was in bed asleep and that he was sailing to France soon and wanted to take me. He said at first Papa said I couldn't go and was angry about him asking, but he said all of you talked a long time until it was very late at night and finally you talked Papa into letting me go for one month."

"Oh, Michael, I'm sorry, but your grandfather wanted you with him so badly, he didn't tell you the truth."

"I didn't think he did. I told him I wanted to go home."

"What did he say?"

"He told me he would take me home, but first he wanted to show me something he had bought for me. He always had some reason not to go home, and then he said I should spend one more night with him. When I woke up the next morning, we were in another town. I told him I'd run away."

"Oh, Michael!" She pulled him to her, pained that he had had such an experience with his grandfather. Michael wriggled and she released him.

"It's all right, Mama. He wasn't mean, he just wanted me to go with him. He said when we got to Savannah, if I still wanted to go home, he would telegraph you and Papa to come get me. After that we got along fine."

She smiled, rubbing her fingers along his soft cheek, knowing that once they reached Savannah, Trevor would have put Michael on board the boat. "When I saw Papa, I wanted to go to him, but Grandfather said that I couldn't. Clarence was in the carriage with us, and he wouldn't let me go until I kicked him and jumped out."

"Well, you're back with us now."

"Mama, Grandfather was good to me, except the part about letting me go home."

"He is, but Michael, when you love someone, you must think of them and what makes them happy, and your grandfather hasn't learned to do that."

She gazed into Michael's brown eyes while he mulled over this idea. Finally he nodded and she framed his face with her hands. "What counts is you're here with us now."

"Yes, ma'am."

The afternoon passed slowly, with the three of them taking turns at applying fresh cloths. Seeing Badru had matters well in hand, Claire took Michael out to get some pajamas and clothes for the next day. When Dr. Roth returned that evening, he was kind but said that Fortune's condition was unchanged.

Before Michael went to bed, he walked quietly into their bedroom and went to the bed to touch Fortune's hand. She bit back tears as the boy stepped up on the footstool and leaned close to kiss Fortune's cheek. She looked at Badru, who turned away quickly and wiped his eyes.

"I love you, Papa. Get well, please," Michael said, touching Fortune's jaw. Climbing down, he smiled at her, and she smiled in return, her eyes blurring with tears as Michael kissed her good night and went to his room.

"Badru, you don't have to stay. I can do that now."

"Ma'am, I'm staying. He'll need moving in the night."

She began to sponge Fortune off, seeing the bed was soaked from the wet cloths. She sat down beside him, closing her fingers around his hand and placing her head on the bed.

A few minutes later, she stirred and lifted the cloth on his forehead; the material was hot to touch from his burning skin.

"Ma'am, if you want to sleep, I can do this."

"No, I want to stay with him, but thank you."

Hours later, as dawn lightened the sky, Badru extinguished the lamps. "I'll be back in a while, Miz O'Brien, unless you need me. I can take care of Michael then."

"No. Go ahead. Thank you for staying all night."

"Yes, ma'am." He closed the door without a sound, and she looked at Fortune, pushing his tangled hair away from his forehead. She changed the washcloths and sat down again, taking his hand in hers. Growing sleepy, she put her head against the bed and dozed for a few minutes.

She raised her head, disoriented. She found Fortune's eyes were open.

"Michael?" he whispered.

"He's in the next room. Oh, Fortune, you have to get well!" She ran her hand across his forehead, feeling it wet with sweat. She moved away to change cloths, dipping them in the tub of ice water and returning to sponge off his face. Yet as she did, she realized that he was no longer burning hot. His fever had broken.

"You have a fever."

"I want to—"

She pushed on his chest where it wasn't bandaged, leaning over him. "Fortune O'Brien, I let you come to Savannah and nearly kill yourself getting Michael. Now you'll do what I say so you get well. Don't you move! I can help you with whatever you need, but you're not moving!"

He closed his eyes as if he couldn't face an argument, and soon she realized he had dropped back off to sleep. Weary herself, she sat down and ran her fingers over his chest. His fever had broken, so maybe he had a chance.

The next time he stirred, Badru was getting ready to take Michael out, and Fortune saw them. "Michael?"

Michael ran to him. "Papa, are you all right?"

Fortune put his good arm around the child and squeezed him against the bed, closing his eyes. Claire knew Fortune was fighting his emotions and couldn't answer.

"Papa?"

"Yes, I am, Michael."

"Good! Mama said you'd get well and so did Badru."

"Michael, you go with Badru now and let Papa sleep," Claire said gently, pulling Michael from the bed. He flung a grin at Fortune, and then ran to join Badru. She looked at Fortune and suddenly she couldn't keep back the tears of relief.

"Fortune—"

She moved to the chair, hugging him where he wasn't hurt, one hand in his hair, her arm across his belly. "Fortune, you have to get well for all of us."

He stroked her head. "I will, Claire. You'd shoot me if I didn't."

She sobbed, letting go finally.

After a few minutes, she got control and sat up to wipe her eyes. He had gone back to sleep, and she rechecked his forehead. It wasn't as hot as even a few hours before.

She sponged him off and left cold cloths on him, finally sitting in a chair until he stirred again.

The next time he opened his eyes, she stood up and crossed the room to him. "I'm going to order some food for you."

"I don't want anything."

"But you have to eat it so you'll get well." She left and in a short time porters appeared bringing a tray of chicken soup, biscuits, fried chicken. As she fed him, his blue eyes watched her steadily, but he seemed to have strength only to eat and before he had eaten half the food, he closed his eyes and she realized he was asleep.

The afternoon of the next day, she stirred and sat up to find Fortune watching her. "Where's Michael?"

"Out with Badru."

"Help me up, Claire. I've laid in this bed long enough."

"No! You stay still."

"Claire, I've been still. If I don't get up soon, I'll be too weak to recover. Don't worry, I'm not going anywhere out of this room."

She frowned but finally reached down to help him sit up. He groaned as he swung his legs over the side of the bed. Taking her hand, he laced his fingers through hers and smiled at her.

Puzzled, she smiled in return, wondering what was running through his mind. Perhaps he was still delirious. She felt his brow and he seemed cooler than before. After a few painful, stumbling walks around the room, he sat quietly, finally lying down again and dozing.

During the night she sat at his bedside, sending Badru to get some sleep because Dr. Roth had said the crisis had passed. Soon she was dozing with her head down near him. When she stirred and woke, she found she was looking at an empty bed.

Panic seized her and she whirled about. Fortune stood across the room, clinging to a chest, his face pale.

"Fortune O'Brien!" She stood up and crossed the room to him, taking him by the arm. "You weren't supposed to get up."

He slipped an arm around her waist. "Claire, you're a very special woman," he said softly. He tilted her chin up toward him. "Thank you for taking care of me."

"Let me get you back to bed and we'll talk. I don't want you to faint on me again. Badru isn't here."

Fortune draped his arm around her shoulders. As she started to turn toward the bed, he swung her around and leaned down to kiss her.

She closed her eyes for a few seconds and then pushed away, looking up at him. "Fortune O'Brien, you get back in your bed!"

"Yes, ma'am," he said, laughing.

Her heart was gladdened, because he had to be feeling a great deal better. "Claire, as soon as the hotel kitchen opens, order something for me. Suddenly I'm hungry enough to eat my pillow."

Three hours later, after he had eaten biscuits and molasses and flapjacks and sausage, Dr. Roth snapped shut his black bag. "I don't think you'll be needing me. I'll come by tomorrow just to make certain you're on the mend. Mr. O'Brien, you're one of the toughest patients I've ever had. I thought we'd lost you one night there."

"Thanks for all you've done."

Dr. Roth nodded and headed toward the door.

"Doctor, when can I leave for Atlanta?"

"Are you going to heed my answer, son?"

"Yes, sir."

"I'd wait a week or so until you feel good and those wounds are healed. You'll know."

Claire paid his bill and walked him into the hall. "Thank you, Doctor, for taking care of my husband."

"I didn't know whether he'd make it or not, but I think he's out of danger now. Take care going home and watch out for robbers."

"Yes, sir, and thank you again."

She closed the door and turned back to find Fortune sitting on the side of the bed. "Come here, Claire."

She crossed the room, stopping a few feet from him. He reached out to take her upper arm and drew her to him. "Come closer," he said in a deep voice, spreading his legs apart and pulling her between his thighs.

Suddenly she realized she had sat up with him all night and hadn't combed her hair since the afternoon before. Her green muslin dress was wrinkled, and she reached down to smooth her collar, feeling self-conscious. He needed a shave, his hair was a tangle, but his color was good again. "You've sat up with me every night, haven't you?"

"Yes. Did you think I'd go off and leave you?"

"No," he said, smiling. "Doc Roth said you could change my bandages from now on."

"He's changed them today, and they don't need changing again. Since you've stopped doing things you shouldn't, you're healing."

His expression sobered. "Claire, did you talk to Michael about Wenger? Did Wenger frighten him?"

She told him what Michael had told her, knowing Fortune needed to hear exactly what Michael had said. Finally she finished and Fortune shook his head.

"That damned bastard. Do you think Michael's afraid?"

"No. I think he was far more afraid about you, and now that that worry is gone, he's enjoying himself with Badru. I must say, he's making a big effort to keep Michael entertained. They've been down to the dock and on board a ship. Badru even took him fishing on a flatboat. Michael is doing fine."

Fortune rubbed her arms. "What'll I do with you? Don't you ever again step in front of a man who is pointing a loaded gun at me."

"I didn't stop to think," she said quietly. "Michael looked so panicked and Trevor Wenger looked as if he would shoot you right in front of Michael at any moment. I just couldn't bear it." She touched his face. "I love you, Fortune, and I don't mind that you don't love me in return."

Fortune braced his hand on her shoulder and stood up. His good arm went around her and he hold her, but he didn't pull her close. "I can't hug you or I would."

She touched his cheek. "I was so afraid Michael and I would lose you."

"Claire, I love you too," he said.

Her breath caught, and she looked into his blue eyes. "Fortune—"

"When you stepped in front of that revolver, I can't tell you what I felt," Fortune said. His voice lowered, an intensity coming to it that made her heart pound. "I was so damned frightened that I was going to lose you to him, just as I had lost Marilee. Honey, I loved Marilee with all my heart, but that's over. And my grieving is over. Life goes on. There's room in the heart for another love. You showed me that."

"Fortune," she said, overcome with joy at his declaration. "Do you forgive me for taking Michael to see his grandfather?"

"Yes, I do. I know you did what you thought was best, and you didn't know the man like I did. On the other hand, maybe what you said to him back there on the dock made him stop and realize what he had done. He still could have kept us from leaving with Michael. He had the drop on me." Fortune's voice softened, and he stroked a lock of hair from her face. "I would prefer an obedient wife, but I know that's hopeless to expect."

She saw the amusement in his gaze, but she was still

thinking about what he had told her before. She stared at him, wondering if he really had thought it over.

His gaze sobered and he framed her face with his hands. "Claire O'Brien, I love you. I'd like to show you what I feel, but I can't hug you yet."

"Fortune, oh—" She felt tears of joy well up and she stood on tiptoe, bringing his head down to kiss him, her tongue touching his. His arm banded her waist, and he held her tightly while he leaned over her and kissed her hungrily.

"I want you," he whispered, raising his head, his voice husky. "When will Michael and Badru be back?"

"Fortune, you can't—"

"When will they be back?" he demanded.

"They've gone fishing, Fortune," she said breathlessly as he leaned down to kiss her throat. She caught his chin and his good arm, trying to get his attention. "I won't be the cause of your having a relapse—"

"I'm going to have worse than a relapse if I don't get to kiss you," he said, turning his head to kiss her palm. She drew a deep breath, her nipples tightening as he looked down at her, his blue eyes darkening with desire. "Oh, Claire, I feel alive again. All those years I was only half alive until you came along. Thank God you took Michael because now I have you both!"

"I love you," she whispered, standing on tiptoe again to slide her arm around his neck and pull his head down to her. "I don't want to hurt you," she said, kissing him, then tracing his lower lip with her tongue. He groaned and pulled her against his good side. His hand slid to her buttons and fumbled with them. "Help me," he said gruffly.

She stepped back out of his reach, watching him as she reached up to untwist the top button and open her dress. Languidly she moved from button to button, unfastening the front of her bodice while he inhaled deeply and watched her. She could see his arousal, the hard bulge in his trousers as he reached down to unfasten his pants. She stopped what she was doing and caught his hand.

"Let me do that." She unfastened his pants: he wore nothing beneath them. Her breath caught as she freed his member. It was thick and ready, dark against his belly. She stroked him and he groaned, reaching for her buttons.

"Claire, get this damned dress off before I rip it off."

She unfastened another button and wriggled, slipping it down over her hips. Standing in front of him, watching his reactions, she pulled off her chemise. She wasn't wearing a corset, and she pushed away her underdrawers and her stockings, moving close to him.

"Fortune, you can't make love—"

His arm slid around her waist, and he pulled her up hard against his side, his hand cupping her breast. It had been so long since he had made love to her, and she moaned softly, wanting him, her body straining toward him. Her breasts tingled, a hard bud pressing against his hand as he rubbed it with his palm. She clung to his neck, kissing him passionately, wanting his tongue deep in her mouth, wanting his hardness inside her, aching for him and knowing they would have to stop soon because of his injuries.

And beneath it all ran a current of excitement, the secret that she could now share with him. And she wanted to wait until the moment was right, until his passion had cooled.

He held her and moved with her, sitting on a chair and pulling her down on his lap, his legs going between hers and spreading hers.

"Fortune," she gasped, starting to protest because he could get hurt. Then she was lost as the velvety tip of his manhood touched her feminine folds. She gasped, closing her eyes, leaning forward to kiss him as he pulled her down, his hard member penetrating with a tantalizing slowness that set her afire and made her move her hips.

"Fortune!" she cried again, clinging to him, lost to passion, feeling his thrusts as she moved wildly. His hand slid between her legs to rub the bud of her womanhood while she rose to a frenzied brink, and he leaned forward to take her breast in his mouth, his tongue flicking over her nipple.

She was wild from sensations that rocked her, in ecstasy over his declaration of love, wanting to be one with him completely, heart and soul, to be bound in every way to him and have him bound in all ways to her.

"Now, Fortune!" she cried, feeling his hips arch, his hands pushing her down on his hard shaft as he cried out.

"Claire, love. My love!" He kissed her wildly as he bucked beneath her and she moved with him, feeling his body spill his hot seed. She fell against his good shoulder as they quieted, both bodies damp with perspiration, her arm wound around his neck.

"I love you, Fortune O'Brien," she whispered, turning to kiss his ear, her tongue flicking against it.

He turned his head, his face so close to hers while he pushed long strands of her brown hair away from her face. "And I love you with all my heart, Claire. You're a very special woman, and I intend to try to do everything I can to make you happy."

She stood up. "Fortune, this is shameless. If you've started bleeding again . . ."

Grinning, he pulled her down on his lap. "Sometimes you worry about me too much. I noticed from the first that you were overprotective of Michael, and now I'm in for years of that."

"You'll ignore it completely, as you just did," she said, facing him. Their bodies were damp, a faint odor of love-making noticeable, and they were naked, yet as she looked into his eyes, all she could feel was joy and love and a feeling of completeness with him.

"I have something to tell you. You would have known sooner, but you were so angry—" she said.

"And I'm sorry that I was so angry, but I knew Wenger."

"Fortune, you're going to be a father again."

He stared at her, his brows arching as his blue eyes seemed to pierce through her and his fingers tightened on her arm. "Claire! Oh, love—" He pulled her against his side and she heard him grunt, guessing the contact had hurt him. "My love, that's grand. Oh, Claire, another baby! Our baby!" As he turned his head to kiss her, she saw tears in his eyes.

Before she could say anything, he kissed her long and hard, a kiss of love and promise. He held her away from him. His brows came together in a frown, and she could see the fierceness in his expression.

"You made that damned grueling ride and risked our baby, Claire. Dammit, don't you ever again—"

"You risked your life. I couldn't have survived if something had happened to you or Michael," she said, placing her fingers on his mouth and interrupting him. "I'll not listen to lectures from you, Fortune O'Brien, when you didn't take care of yourself either!"

"We'll talk about that some more when I'm well and have both hands free and can cope with you better," he said. "How far along are you? How long have you known this?"

She smiled at him, drawing her finger through the hair on his chest. "I've missed two monthlies now."

"Seven months from now."

"We'll have to decide when we will tell Michael."

"I think he'll be happy."

"I know he will," Fortune said. "He's already asked me about a little brother."

"Michael? He hasn't asked me," she said in surprise.

"Maybe he felt I would do more about it," Fortune said, grinning. He pulled her to him and hugged her. "Oh, love, I'm so happy. The happiest I've been in my life!"

She knew that wasn't necessarily so, but she loved

hearing him say it. She turned her head to kiss him, finally standing up.

"Now I'm going to wash and then I'll bathe you—"

"That sounds enticing," he said, grinning and reaching for a cheroot. He placed it between his white teeth and picked up a match to light it. "Claire, where's my brandy?"

"I suppose in your satchel."

"Get it, because I want to celebrate."

"Will you please remember you're trying to recuperate?" she said, looking at him striding across the room as casually as if he were fully dressed. His body was mending, his muscles flexing as he walked. "Claire, this is grand!"

She smiled, overwhelmed by joy, still glorying in his declaration of love.

"Fortune, we have a tub of water from the melted ice I ordered to try to cool you. I'm going to bathe," she said. Stepping into it, she relished the coolness that was no longer icy, but room temperature. She sank down and he came back with two glasses and the bottle of brandy.

Handing her a glass, he held his out. "Here's to a woman with a mind of her own, my love and my wife."

"Oh, Fortune," she said, reaching out to touch his thigh.

He looked down at her. "I want to get in with you."

"No!" She stood up at once, splashing water on both of them and the floor. "No, you can't. You might infect your wounds. You have to wait."

He caught her around her waist and took the cheroot from his mouth to kiss her hard, leaning back finally to smile at her. "It'll be a wonderful marriage, Claire. I promise you, I'll do everything I can to make you happy."

"You already have made me happier than I ever dreamed possible."

"I'm going home and offer Alaric so damned much money to come to work at the mill that he'll have to tell the army good-bye. He's a damned good manager, and if he'll come to work, I can spend more time with you."

"I'd like that. Maybe I can talk him into it."

"No, you don't. He's in love with you. You leave long talks with Alaric to me."

"Yes, sir, Colonel O'Brien!"

"When our baby is old enough for christening, we'll have all the family to the christening celebration. And then I'll prevail upon one of my loving sister-in-law and brothers to take Michael and the babe while we have the wedding trip you never had."

"I don't need that, Fortune. We'll be together."

"We'll make it short, love, because I know you won't want to leave a new baby long, but I want you to have a few days all to ourselves that you missed having after our wedding. Missed due to my blindness and stubbornness."

She laughed and kissed him gently. "I'll agree about stubborn!" She wound her arm around his neck, feeling blissful.

Chapter 26

A year later at the altar of the church, Claire stood with Fortune as he handed their five-month-old infant to the minister. All the family stood beside them and Michael was between them. She noticed Fortune placing his hand on Michael's shoulder, and she glanced at her handsome husband. He turned his head to wink at her.

The minister sprinkled the baby's head with water. "I christen thee Kieran Rafferty O'Brien," he said in a deep voice. She looked at the tiny baby, who was sleeping through the ceremony, his dark lashes above his cheeks, black ringlets covering his head, and she smiled. They would have another son who resembled his father.

The ceremony was soon over and they left for home to celebrate.

As they poured into the house, Fortune rounded them up to go to the library for portraits by a photographer he had hired. She smoothed her pink moiré dress, a new diamond ring sparkling on her finger, a gift from Fortune. He looked dashing in his black coat and black cravat, a silk shirt with ruffles down the front. Michael was dressed like his father, and his gaze went constantly to his small brother.

The minute the pictures finished, Michael stood in front of her. "May I hold him now?"

She handed the sleeping baby to Michael. "Be very careful."

"Yes, ma'am." He moved to a chair to sit down while

Chantal and Sophia and the children crowded around them. Sophia's eyes sparkled as she looked up at Claire.

"You and Chantal will have to tell me everything I need to do. I don't know anything about babies."

"You will soon," Caleb said, moving to her side to give her a squeeze.

She smiled up at him, a lock of golden hair falling over her shoulder as she twisted around. Caleb brushed her lips with a kiss, and Claire remembered the first time she had been with Fortune's family, and how she had yearned to have the same kind of loving marriage that his brothers and in-laws had. She looked across the room at him. He stood with a glass of brandy in hand while he talked to Rafferty and Alaric. He winked at her, and she felt a rush of warmth. Now she did have the same kind of marriage. She thought back over the past year and the attention Fortune had showered on her. Her days of living in small rooms, always fearful of men taking Michael from her, were becoming dim memories.

Her gaze ran down the length of her husband, and she felt a longing to be in his arms. For the past week the house had been filled with his family, the brothers enjoying being together for the first time since her marriage to Fortune. She hadn't had a chance to be alone with him, and there had been no loving nights because she had gone to bed long before he had.

Fortune glanced at Claire again, his pulse jumping. She had blossomed in the past year, becoming even more beautiful. Her shiny brown hair was turned under across her shoulders and caught up with tiny combs on each side of her head. She wore a new diamond necklace and ring he had given her, and she laughed easily and often now, her joy giving him pleasure. Her dress was made from the rose silk material he had given her so long ago, and he knew she had waited for a special occasion to wear it. He wanted to be alone with her. He had spent the week with his family, but now he was looking forward to the week with Claire, the wedding trip that they'd never had.

"She's very beautiful. You're a very lucky man," Alaric said.

Fortune turned to look at him. "Sorry?"

Alaric and Rafferty laughed. "The man is in love with his wife," Alaric said lightly. "I don't think you're part of our conversation, so you might as well go over and join her."

Fortune grinned, glancing at Rafe. "You were right so long ago."

"You're a stubborn man, but I thought she might win you over."

"Thank God she did. I better find Cal and check with him."

"Don't worry about Cal," Rafe said. "He and Sophia and Darcy can't wait to take care of Michael and Kieran."

"I hope I can pry Claire loose. She's still uncertain about leaving Kieran for a week."

"He'll be in good hands," Rafe said.

"Fortune, what have you heard about Trevor Wenger?" Alaric asked.

"He went on to Europe and has put his foundry up for sale."

"That's what I was told. It doesn't look as if he'll return to Atlanta. I've heard his house will go up for sale soon."

Fortune shrugged. "I'm going to find Cal, if you two will excuse me. And, Alaric, if there are problems at the mill, you know where to find me. But don't disturb me unless the mill threatens to go under," he added, grinning.

"I wouldn't think of it, but I envy you. You know I've always been in love with her."

"There are other beautiful women—"

"But not any like the O'Brien women," he said with a sigh, and Fortune laughed along with Rafe.

He found Caleb talking to Darcy and placed his hand

on his brother's shoulder. "Cal, I'm going to get Claire and go."

"We'll take good care of Michael and Kieran. Sophia can't wait to have Kieran for a week. Darcy and I will entertain Michael."

"I'm sure you will. You know where to find us if any problems arise."

"Don't worry. We'll keep things running smoothly."

"Thanks. I'll come do the same for you if you want."

Caleb laughed. "We had a wedding trip, but I might take you up on your offer someday."

"Take care, Darcy," Fortune said, clapping his youngest brother on the back. "You better stop growing or you'll have to duck to get through the doors."

Darcy grinned. "Michael is learning to carve in wood. I told him we'd have all week to work on something."

"Thank you both." He glanced around, seeing Claire laughing at something Chantal said. He left his brothers, going to Claire's side. "It's time we get out of here." She turned to him, her dark eyes sparkling as she nodded. "I want to talk to Michael."

He nodded and took her hand as they walked down the hall. "He was holding Kieran, but he left." They stepped outside and found him playing with Daniella and Jared in the backyard.

"Michael!" Claire called, watching him run toward them.

"He's getting taller," Fortune observed. "He may be like Darcy and dwarf us all."

He ran up to them. "Michael, we're leaving now."

"Daniella and I are looking for gold."

"I don't think you're going to find any in our yard."

"We might," he said cheerfully.

Claire leaned down. "Kiss me good-bye." He hugged her neck and kissed her cheek and she held him, smelling the clean, soapy scent on his skin, holding his slender body tightly. She released him and Fortune picked him up to hug him.

"Be a good boy and take care of your little brother."

"Yes, sir."

"Michael!" Daniella called, running across the yard.

Fortune set him down. "We'll be back in a week, Michael."

"Yes, sir!" he called over his shoulder as he ran down the steps and jumped over the last four. "Good-bye!"

"I don't think we're going to be missed," Claire said dryly.

"No. Now we'll tell the others good-bye."

They said farewells to the brothers and then moved to Chantal and Sophia, who were hovering over Kieran. His dark eyes were open and he waved his fists in the air as Claire picked him up for one last hug. She felt a pang, hating to leave him but knowing that Sophia would take good care of him. In a week she would be back home with him.

"Don't worry. Chantal will be here for one more day, and then I'll take very good care of him," Sophia said.

"I know you will," Claire answered, glancing at her beautiful blond in-laws. She looked down at the precious baby in her arms, and love filled her. She kissed his soft cheek, talking to him. Fortune took him from her and held him, and she saw the look of love in his expression, hoping they had a little girl someday because Fortune was a wonderful father.

Finally he turned to give Kieran to Sophia. "Now we're going."

"Don't worry. Everything will be all right. Caleb has promised me he'll be right here. And Darcy will be with us," Sophia reassured them, leaning forward to kiss Fortune's cheek and then to hug Claire.

Chantal hugged Claire and turned to brush Fortune's cheek with a kiss. "I'm so happy for you and your beautiful family," she said, smiling, her hand on Claire's arm and a hand on Fortune's. "Now go enjoy each other and don't worry. We will take very good care of your house and your children."

"Thank you," Claire said as Fortune took her arm. They went out through the side door. With Badru driving, they headed for the Chattahoochee River to take a boat south to the Gulf and Mobile.

She glanced back at the house, and Fortune placed his arm around her shoulders. "Stop worrying. Sophia will fuss over him constantly. And I suspect Chantal and Rafe will stay another two or three days with them before they head back to New Orleans."

She turned to look at Fortune and he smiled at her, sliding his arm around her waist. "Now I have you all to myself for a week."

They drove through downtown Atlanta, past city hall. At the river a steamboat was waiting at the landing when they arrived, and Fortune helped her from the carriage. She watched while he told Badru good-bye and the carriage turned for home.

Fortune took her arm to board the boat, and a tall, bearded man stood at the head of the plank.

"Welcome aboard, Colonel O'Brien, Mrs. O'Brien. I'm Captain Duncan."

Fortune shook hands with him while she greeted him. He motioned to them as stewards carried their trunks on board. "This way, sir, and I'll show you your quarters. We'll be underway in the next few minutes."

They followed him up a ladder, and he opened a door to a large cabin. "Here's where you'll be. Your brother's sent champagne and flowers," he said. "Is there anything you'll be needing?"

"I don't think so," Fortune replied while she walked across the cabin. It was spacious, holding a large built-in bed, a table and chairs, a desk, a copper tub in one corner. Two vases with large bouquets of roses and mixed flowers were on the table and desk. A bottle of champagne was cooling in a bucket.

She turned as the door closed behind the captain and Fortune slid a bolt across it, locking it. "Now you're all mine and no one will disturb us," he said, shedding his coat and draping it over a chair. He crossed the cabin to open the champagne, the cork popping loudly. He poured them glasses and returned with hers.

"Here's to you, Claire," he said quietly, raising his glass.

"To us, Fortune," she said, touching his glass lightly before she sipped the bubbling dry champagne.

He took her glass from her hand and set them both down. His gaze darkened, becoming more intense. He removed her tiny rose silk hat and tossed it on a chair. Then he began to unfasten her buttons.

"Claire, why do you always have dresses that have hundreds of buttons?" he asked softly, bending his head to kiss her throat. He twisted another button free and another. "I know how it'll disturb you if I rip this dress off you, but I don't want to wait."

She helped him, and he removed her sheer silk chemise, her corset, her silk underdrawers and finally her silk stockings, bending down, his fingers drifting over her long legs, and she trembled with eagerness for him.

"Fortune," she whispered, unbuttoning his shirt and pulling it over his head, reaching down to unfasten his black trousers that bulged with his arousal.

He stood naked before her, and she ran her hands across his chest and down over his belly and thighs, sliding her fingers across his hard, muscular body.

He caught her to him, his arm banding her waist tightly as he looked down at her. "I want you, Claire," Fortune said. "Thank God I found you and Michael."

Joyous, she clung to him, gazing up at him and feeling love well up inside her. She ran her fingers through his dark hair and pulled his head down so she could kiss him.

He held her tightly while she clung to him, moaning softly, knowing this was the man for her. Fortune had her heart forever. She tightened her arms around him, so thankful that she and Michael both had him, and now they all had Kieran.

She leaned back to look up at him. "I love you, Fortune O'Brien."

"It's the luck of the Irish, love," he said softly. "Such wonderful luck to find you," he added.

She clung to him, her heart beating with joy. They were beginning a life together filled with love and children's laughter.